VULNERABLE

Dear Reader:

Bonita Thompson treats readers with a journey of love and obsession in her second novel, *Vulnerable*.

She spins the tale with an in-depth cast of characters who are entangled in a web of lust, deception and ultimately murder. The author delivers in poetic fashion and descriptive writing against the Seattle backdrop in the coffee capital where cafés and bookstores are a major setting. Rawn, a schoolteacher at an elite private school, teams up with a model, D'Becca, and once the sparks start to fly, there is no stopping the intense romance. Sicily, his friend and colleague, and Tamara, a stunning boutique owner and mistress to NBA star Henderson Payne, soon become entrapped in their world and relationships prove that anyone is capable of being vulnerable.

This page-turner will keep one speculating on the next chain of events to unfold in the scenic Pacific Northwest. The pace is quick and readers will hang on to every word in this romantic suspense novel.

If you haven't read *The New Middle*, check out Bonita's debut novel centered on those in the middle age spectrum who experience the ups and downs in the aging process.

As always, thanks for supporting myself and the Strebor Books family. We strive to bring you the most cutting-edge, out-of-the-box material on the market. You can find me on Facebook @AuthorZane or you can email me at zane@eroticanoir.com.

Blessings,

Zane

Publisher
Strebor Books
www.simonandschuster.com

ALSO BY BONITA THOMPSON
The New Middle

ZANE PRESENTS

VULNERABLE

A NOVEL

BONITA THOMPSON

SBI

STREBOR BOOKS

NEW YORK LONDON TORONTO SYDNEY

Strebor Books
P.O. Box 6505
Largo, MD 20792
www.simonandschuster.com

ISBN 978-1-59309-624-3
ISBN 978-1-4767-8323-9 (ebook)
LCCN 2015957694

First Strebor Books trade paperback edition May 2016

Cover design: www.mariondesigns.com
Cover photograph: © Keith Saunders/Keith Saunders Photos

10 ... 6 ... 2 1

Manufactured in the United States of America

For information regarding special discounts for bulk purchases,
please contact Simon & Schuster Special Sales at 1-866-506-1949

The Simon & Schuster Speakers Bureau can bring authors to your live event.
For more information or to book an event, contact the Simon & Schuster Speakers
Bureau at 1-866-248-3049 or visit our website at www.simonspeakers.com.

ACKNOWLEDGMENTS

The New Middle

I love bookstores. So in a time when traditional bookstores have become progressively dinosaur, I am especially grateful to the independent bookstores in the U.S., Canada, and England for carrying *The New Middle*. Including the American Book Center (@wwwabcnl) the Hague, Netherlands, Shakespeare & Co. (@Shakespeare_Co), Paris, France, Chevalier Books (@ChevaliersBooks) Larchmont Village, Los Angeles, and Elliott Bay Book Company (@Elliott BayBooks) Capitol Hill, Seattle.

A very, very special thank you to Skylight Books (@skylightbooks), Los Feliz, Los Angeles. The opportunity to launch *The New Middle* at their outrageously amazing bookstore was such an honor!

It is a compliment when a book club chooses to read your book. Shout-outs to book clubs for supporting *The New Middle*.

The year, 2015, was a madly, deeply, crazy year. My family and friends had my back when I faced every anticipated and every unimaginable obstacle. Much love and huge hugs!

Vulnerable

Vulnerable is a novel that has taken numerous forms. In reaching the version that Strebor accepted in 2013, several readers offered kind-hearted feedback to help me shape it to its natural fruition. I want to acknowledge their time and gifts: Karen Roth, Ahmad Wright (the screenplay version), Tanisha Jackson, and Omar Caleb. Their collective thoughts were the ultimate game-changer.

a neighborhood bookstore-café, and she said something about liking his "new look," followed by a wink. By chance was she referring to stubble that shadowed his cheeks and jawline? Rubbing his face with his hands, he wondered was she throwing off an innocent flirtation or was she in effect hitting on him. Rawn could not recall exactly when he last noticed that a woman was flirting. He himself stopped flirting some time ago.

He was in and out of the shower in less than ten minutes. He was wrapping a towel around his lean waist when he heard the telephone ringing in the background, but he chose to ignore it. These days Rawn screened every single call; he made no exception. He was fed up with producers from popular television talk shows calling him every other day. Even though the preoccupation with him had tamed to a degree over the past several months, he chose to buy a cellular because, despite it being unlisted, his landline was now public knowledge. In less than thirty minutes he was dressed in a casual Perry Ellis suit that hung tastefully on his tall and lean physique. He stood at the front door, his worn-leather satchel slung across his chest. He bowed slightly as if he were saying a silent prayer. On his front porch he bent over and reached for *The New York Times*.

Fifteen minutes later Rawn entered Café Neuf and it was typically crowded. The bakery-café was rich with the smell of strongly brewed coffee and scrumptious French baked pastry. He stood at the entrance and studied the room. Straightaway he caught the local dot-com millionaires, Rowena and Sean, at their regular table wearing their trademark all-black. The café became their temporary office while their rambling waterfront home was being renovated. Cellulars rang incessantly, and top-of-the-line laptops congested the birch and poplar wood table. Jean-Pierre, the owner of the well-liked Café Neuf, always accommodated his regulars and knew

PROLOGUE

I n a deep sleep Rawn kept hearing this faraway voice—*It's between you and me*—and the tone was eerily familiar. His eyes popped open. The syncopation of his day hinged almost entirely on how much sleep he had. If he could manage a good night's sleep, all the minutiae, which defined his day, would not be so exasperating. But like a sequence of mornings lately, he woke up having experienced another fatiguing night and he was bone-tired. Rawn adjusted his deep cognac-colored eyes to the essence of premature autumn sunlight. He wished like hell he could stay in bed and let the day that was about to unfold do whatever it was going to do without him contributing to the collective consciousness. Annoyed, he tossed the bedding to the empty side of the queen-sized mattress. Finally, he was getting used to sleeping alone.

Absent-mindedly, he came to his feet. The room felt cool against his naked skin. Soft signs of early dawn trickled in from exposed roof windows which defined the neatly squared room. Rubbing sleep from his eyes, he became conscious of the fact that he was not sweating, nor had he been disturbed by a dream he could never quite remember. Immediately this struck Rawn cold; he had come to depend on trying to make sense of his dreams. Still not fully awake, he strolled to the bathroom.

He always let the shower run until the room was so steamy he could barely see a foot in front of him. Rawn observed his tired face in the bathroom mirror. Not long ago a young woman he knew only by sight approached him at his table. He was sitting at each one by name. Of course he was well-acquainted with Rawn because he was a frequent customer, not to mention he spoke French. Likewise, Jean-Pierre, like so many on Crescent Island, knew all the good, the bad, and the ugly details of Rawn's once private life. For months he was relentless Crescent Island gossip. What had happened last year forever changed the young man who dropped by Café Neuf most mornings for an espresso and rich buttery croissant. Jean-Pierre had a soft spot for Rawn. He gestured for the young man.

"Hey, good morning, Jean-Pierre," he greeted the Frenchman.

"I open terrace. Let you sit in back. It be not so stressful, *peut-être?*" Jean-Pierre shrugged.

Rawn looked over his shoulder at the animated room. "I can wait until a table's free. It's cool, Jean-Pierre." He tried to pull off a nonchalant tone.

In his thick French accent, Jean-Pierre said, *"D'accord!* Take the table when it come, *oui-oui?"*

"Merci," Rawn said. His intonation was virtually flawless.

He stood by a couple waiting for a table. It was impossible to not take notice that they were in the middle of a rather intense conversation. Politely Rawn nodded to a young woman seated alone nearby, primarily because he felt her eyes trace his every move from the moment he entered Café Neuf. She slid a laptop inside a high-end brand-named backpack, and as she headed for the door, folded an issue of the *Weekly* under her armpit. She offered Rawn a subtle nod when she passed. Rawn's eyes traveled to her excellently shaped legs concealed by a pair of black opaque nylons.

Taking a deep breath, he flipped the newspaper to below-the-fold. More and more, he lost interest in what he read about in the newspaper or heard on the news. What was happening out in the world had no direct influence on him personally, not right now. It was rather apparent there was a moral crisis in America. Still, Rawn could not seem to focus on teens with handguns, the political and intellectual climate, foreign crisis, the Middle East, the president and his conflicting approval ratings as a result of a scandal, and the *soi-disant* thriving economy. Although he was naturally curious and typically engaged, the way the new worldview was rapidly transforming humanity—eco-friendly, technology, globalization—did not pique his interest.

When he turned to the sports page, Jean-Pierre approached him and said in a low voice, "A table, it come. Take it, *rapidement, mon ami.*"

Rawn looked to the couple a few feet away. They were caught up in a heated exchange and couldn't care less that a table had become available. Because seating was first come, first serve, customers generally dashed for a free table. The couple's conversation began to get increasingly passionate and Rawn caught "You have colossal nerve!" and "Go to hell!" through clenched teeth. The woman gave the man a finger and stormed out of Café Neuf. Rawn thanked Jean-Pierre and walked to the empty table. When he sat at the table-for-two, he could see beyond the French doors that the once tender blue sky had turned heavy, low, and gray.

"*Ça va!*" The familiar waitress greeted Rawn in good spirits. Her sultry mouth accentuated her strikingly attractive face.

He thought she might have quit or he missed her whenever he came into Café Neuf, because Rawn had not seen the waitress in—certainly before everything went down last year.

"*Ça va!*" he replied.

"What would you like this morning?"

Rawn was not up to meeting her warm, kind eyes; instead he looked beyond her slender shoulder, concentrating on copper-colored photographs of Paris *arrondissements* which classily lined the mauve-painted wall. "A café au lait and chocolate croissant."

"Would you prefer non-fat, low fat, soy…?"

"Good old-fashioned milk," he spoke in a tone verging on sarcastic.

"*Oh*-kay! French or American roast?" She knew his preference. Yet she was making every effort to engage him; throwing some loving-kindness his way which did not accompany an ulterior motive.

He dropped his eyes to the newspaper and said, "French."

"The bowl or a cup?" The waitress shrugged subtly, her mind playing with the idea that he was different now; aloof.

"Bowl." He purposely avoided eye contact. He stated, "*C'est tout.*" Rawn preferred that she not hover.

With a tight smile, the waitress departed swiftly, and her very gentle scent—jasmine or lavender, Rawn did not really know— caressed the air. When he first laid eyes on her, he decided that a man had to ease into the waitress. She was unapproachable, and not because she was cold or standoffish. There was something about her. The standard line—whatever a man generally used to get the attention of a very attractive woman—would not work on this one. She was classy, and more importantly, comfortable in her skin. She was complicated—if not mysterious—because she was not average.

Minutes later she carefully placed his French roast café au lait on the table, and Jean-Pierre's to-die-for chocolate croissant. "Here you go," she said. "Anything else?" She pressed her plump lips together as if doing so kept her thoughts buried deep inside her head.

"I'm good." Rawn sensed the waitress wanted to say something to him. He had learned the look, the demeanor. He assumed she was like most people who struggled to be appropriate. But what exactly was *appropriate*?

When the waitress left his table, she was so poised, so graceful. She stopped at the table next to Rawn's, and in a sincere voice inquired if the customers enjoyed their croque monsieur and whether they were ready for their check. Once, a little more than a year ago, Rawn ran into the waitress at PCC. Comfortably dressed in well-fitted jeans, her cropped lime-colored chenille sweater exposed a small butterfly tattoo slightly left of her navel. Before approaching her, Rawn observed the waitress leisurely walking through the aisles of the market. A subtle detail made her eye-catching; a *je ne sais quoi*-ness. When he finally managed enough nerve to approach her, they held a casual conversation for a while, talking and laughing so effortlessly in a way that happened when two people naturally clicked. No pretense, no façade, no status-dropping nonsense like where-did-you-go-to-school and what-do-you-do? When he inquired about her to Jean-Pierre, the French-man offered nothing more than the waitress lived in Seattle, and her name was Imani.

Rawn was attracted to Imani the very first time he laid eyes on her. On at least one occasion he sensed the attraction was mutual, and then out of the blue, she disappeared. A good year had come and gone since he last saw Imani, and it only struck him that particular morning. He had been suspended between the present and what used to be.

Without thinking, he reached for the small silver spoon and scooped up a sand-colored, miniature rock-shaped sugar cube in the porcelain container on the table. He dropped it into the bowl of steamy warm milk and black, strong coffee Jean-Pierre had imported from France and brewed in a French press. It was a bold aroma. Rawn sipped his café au lait mindlessly, slowly, and occasionally picked at his croissant. He studied Imani working the vibrant room with natural ease, and handled the demands of the dot-com entrepreneurs, Rowena and Sean, with such ingrained finesse. It was her spirit that resided over the room, and Imani brought class to the place. By no means was Café Neuf a hole in the wall. The bakery-café had a unique ambience: thick planked dark wooded tables, and Patrick Bruel music that did not interfere with the energetic conversations that most often took place at the intimately situated tables. Part of its charm was that Jean-Pierre, and any help that worked for him, greeted and took orders for customers in French. While Rawn observed Imani closely, it became apparent to him that there was very little about her he did not find engaging. Standing, and taking one last sip of his café au lait, he considered, for one split-second, what his fate might have been had he been courageous enough to ask her out at least once. He was hoping to slip out of Café Neuf unseen.

It started to rain when he crawled into his Jeep Wrangler, tossing the *Times* and his satchel to the passenger's seat. Turning over the engine, it occurred to Rawn that he forgot to grab his umbrella before leaving the apartment. A year ago he walked to work, and it was something he only recognized recently—not so long ago he cherished the beauty of the day as it took shape: the rhythm of business owners washing down sidewalks and opening up; runners putting in their time before the demands of life took over; city centre residents walking their dogs; and morning dew on the grass. It was the first touch of a new day; still innocent, still filled with expectation. Eventually he decided to drive to work because when he took the ferry people stared; rarely was he fully present and aware of how the day evolved. Instead he spent more time mentally negotiating between this and that.

Over the past month he developed a routine: Rawn composed himself and went through the mental exercise to deal with the students he taught in South Seattle that persuaded him on day-one

that they were absolutely indifferent to learning. He turned up
Dante Godreau playing on his CD player. It took several rings
before he recognized that his cellular demanded his attention. Rawn
was still not used to having a cellular. "Hello?" Grinning, he said,
"Khalil! Hey, man. Yeah, I'm about to cross the floating bridge."
Rawn listened thoughtfully to his best friend while concentrating
on the traffic leading into the overcast, silver-colored city. "Hell
yeah, it's raining," he joked. "My flight leaves at ten. Well, check
your e-mail, bro. I sent my itinerary to you last night. Cool." Unexpectedly, he began to feel a burst of excitement about heading
to L.A. for the weekend. "See you then. Definitely. Later, man."

Rawn had not quite come to terms with teaching in the hood.
Be that as it may, when the opportunity was presented to him, he
had not received offers which corresponded favorably with his
qualifications; thus could not bring himself to turn down the one
teaching position offered to him. Nothing from his teaching past
prepared him for hallways flooded with boisterous, loud, and ill-
mannered students. His perception of urban youth was swiftly
revised. Hearing "nigga" casually fall off the tongues of not only
black but Asian and Latino students troubled Rawn deeply. He
was accustomed to being around born-and-bred-for-success kids.

The first day he taught at his new school, he asked his bored
and tattooed eighth-graders if anyone wished to open the discussion
of "separate but equal." Each student looked pokerfaced, bored.
Girls admired their nails polished with dramatic colors like fuchsia
and citron green, while the boys talked to each other or perused
Vibe and *Spin*, fantasizing about their own images gracing the
publications someday. Lamentably, becoming a hip-hop artist was
the only dream they trusted. Rawn's pressing goal was to get each
student to recognize their potential. As an educator he wanted
every student who entered his classroom to realize their individu-

ality, and the potential they had to influence history based solely on their unique participation. There was a point when Rawn learned that his responsibility was to take raw talent and give it energy, spirit, *life*. Every student whom he taught should have entered the classroom already aware she or he was a rising star no matter their background. Without that principle he feared he would fail his students, because he had yet to acquire the skills to pilot a young person who lacked at least a scintilla of hope. A dim spark was sufficient to work with; still, Rawn needed the student to have a little faith in the process.

It did not take a week for him to finally get it: these students did not relate to his ideas. And when he submitted his reading list the first week of school, reluctantly it was approved. But true to form, the students were unmotivated as ever when he announced to his literature class that they would read Richard Wright's *Native Son* the first half of the semester. Furthermore, in three weeks there would be a class discussion on Part I of the novel, along with a typed, 300-word essay each student was expected to hand in by the end of the class hour. Moans and groans erupted throughout the classroom. After only a week at his new school, Rawn had a good sense about the type of young minds he was there to penetrate, and they were not even close to being ready to read the classics. *Romeo and Who?* they would ask. In truth, Shakespeare was way too deep.

Rawn had not discovered the reward that came with teaching overactive and combative eighth-graders. And the students were not used to a black schoolteacher who dressed all *GQ;* his parlance did not harmonize with theirs, and he told them like a broken record that they could not listen to music on their headphones while in class. Moreover, they were not comfortable with being challenged with philosophy and whatnot. While they knew every track by heart on popular music CDs, they never even heard of J. Edgar Hoover.

Something changed a week ago.

"Twisted? Tiananmen Square. Can you open up the discussion?"

"Tannum what?"

"*Tiananmen* Square." Rawn studied the student closely.

Twisted slumped deeper into the seat. He lowered his eyes to the empty desk.

"Luis? *Roe v. Wade.*"

Luis grinned, his head shaking side-to-side. "Don't know, dawg."

"Remove that hoodie, please." Rawn waited, but Luis simply grinned. "Luis!"

The look he gave Rawn suggested he needed to think about it. Eventually, although with exaggerated bravado, Luis removed his hoodie which exposed a shaved head.

"Okay, listen! *Listen!* This will be the last time I say it: Everyone in this classroom knows that *Mr.* Poussaint is more appropriate. Hey, look, I can accept Poussaint. But *dawg?* Leave it outside *this* classroom. Luis?"

"Yeah, whatever."

"I want you to get this: drop the 'whatever.' So I take it you know nothing about *Roe v. Wade.*"

Luis shrugged; and he was perturbed that the man was all up in his face, making him look bad in front of his classmates.

"How about *Brown v. the Board of Education?*"

With his arms crossed stiffly over his chest, Luis slumped deeper in his seat.

Rawn's eyes lingered on Luis before he stated, "Kurtis? Neil Armstrong."

"Neil…come again, bruh?"

"Like dawg, drop the *bruh!* Who is Neil Armstrong?"

"I...I..."

"If you have no idea who Neil Armstrong is, own it."

"Look, man. Dang. Why you gotta be all over a brother like 'at?"

Rawn met the gaze of several students in the classroom. Calmly, he walked to his worn leather satchel on the desk and pulled out a Toni Braxton CD. He held it up and said, "The first person who can tell me where you can find 'give me your tired, your poor, your huddled masses yearning to breathe free' can claim this CD."

All the students were immediately attentive; some leaning forward to get a better look at the CD Rawn held in his hand.

"*Toni?*" asked Jamaal, his always-ten-minutes-late student with one excuse after another—the bus, the rain.

"I already heard that CD!" another student said.

"Regardless...Who wants the CD?" Rawn interrupted.

"I do; I want it!" several students said in unison.

"I'm not asking you to recite the poem. I'm not asking you to name the title of the poem. I'm not even asking you to tell me what it means. It's on a plaque on one of our country's most famous statues. Come on, think about it. First person to name that statue walks out of this classroom with the CD." Rawn, remarkably patient, waited.

Disappointed, Kurtis slumped in his seat. "Why you be like that? What huddle masses mean anyway, dude?"

Twisted threw his hands out at Rawn in frustration. Some students remarked beneath their breath, while the attention span of others swiftly waned.

Rawn had hoped the experience would demonstrate the hindrance of lacking knowledge. Instead he acquired valuable details from his own experimentation. The students had not been giving him a hard time since the first day of school because they did not like him. They failed to answer the questions not because it was cooler *not* to, but because they had never learned about the subjects Rawn inquired about. And if they had learned any of it, the information did not stick. This had never really occurred to him before. With a slow sigh, he gazed over the classroom with a new set of eyes. For weeks Rawn went through the motions; prior to the CD exchange, he had never been that engaged with these students.

"Lakeisha, can you tell us something about Malcolm X?"

Like every other student in the classroom, with her arms crossed inflexibly over her chest, her bottom lip poked out, her body language all but stating *I have better things to do with my time!*, Lakeisha said, "Denzel played him in a movie." She made a large bubble with her bubblegum, followed by a perceptible pop.

"Come on, Lakeisha. Surely there's more you can share. Malcolm X is a man who influenced the Civil Rights Movement in ways you may never fully appreciate, even while *you* have reaped benefits. Yes, 'Denzel played him in a movie'"…Rawn made air-quotes. "But seriously…"

"I guess you don't hear good, cuz I tolju what I know!"

"Now if I know somethin' 'bout X, you gotta know, Keisha!" said Twisted.

She looked over her shoulder at Twisted seated directly behind her and rolled her eyes. With an accent straight out of Brooklyn, she said, "Whu-*ever!*"

Momentarily Rawn kept his eyes on Lakeisha. He took a few steps toward her seat and looked directly into her coffee brown, almond-shaped eyes and asked, "Who is Monica Lewinsky?"

"Now you're tryna insult me. Who don't know who Monica is!"

"Who is *Monica?*"

"Monica!" Her head moved in a circular motion to give emphasis to her meaning.

"But *who* is Monica?"

"Girlfriend went down on the president."

For a split-second the classroom went completely silent. A student in the back of the classroom, with nothing to lose, blurted out a surprisingly calm, "Wow!"

The comment got a rise out of the students. They all broke out in effusive giggles. One student, whom Rawn vaguely recognized as a student even enrolled in his class, yelled out, "The president up in the House gettin' blow jobs…" A series of high-fives followed. In terms of classroom discussion, it was the most feedback Rawn had ever gotten from this class of would-be underachievers. The reaction produced a wide grin from Rawn. Unconsciously pleased, he stood in the front of the classroom observing their strange elation, and he sensed a level of renewed hope. There was a palette of potential sitting before him. With his arms crossed, new ideas began to take root.

A young girl raised her hand and exclaimed, "And Monica got her own lipstick. I mean, it ain't *her* lipstick, but she made it celebrity. I mean, like, Club Monaco sold out 'cause she wo' it in a interview. She got some game."

With a nod Rawn said, "Okay, okay." While his eyes rested on Lakeisha, he was speaking to the entire class when he said, "Since you seem to know something about Monica Lewinsky, let's discuss Monica Lewinsky and the president. But let's look at it from more than the salacious perspective."

"What salacious mean?" Jamaal asked no one in particular.

"Duh!" Twisted said. "Like sexy, man. *Yo!*"

"Come on, like ain't that what the whole thing was about? Sex and some damn dress with yuk stains on it?" said a female student seated in the rear of the classroom.

"That's actually a practical question. Your name again?"

The student, wearing braces on her teeth, grinned. "Shanequa."

"Yes, Shanequa. But no, there's much more to Monica Lewinsky and the president than a dress and lipstick and all that other sensational—'sexy'—stuff. I want us to look at the multifaceted issues—the subtext—surrounding Monica Lewinsky and the president..."

"Like *whu?*" The student shrugged flippantly.

Rawn sat at the edge of his desk, captivated. "Like politics."

CHAPTER ONE

Fourteen Months Earlier

I t was a slow and quiet Saturday and steady rainwater fell over Crescent Island. Rawn waited in Café Neuf hoping that it would lead to light drizzle—spit, they called it in the Pacific Northwest. He nursed the end of an iced coffee while he caught up on some reading he had put off during the school year. A sensuous, striking woman entered Café Neuf. She had take-notice features and was model tall, although not too tall, slender, with a delicate yet visible cleft in her chin, and seductive olive-colored eyes. She wore a silk pimento-colored all-weather coat cut less than an inch above the knee, and her shoulder-length hair was damp and limp.

Perturbed, she said loud enough for Rawn to hear, "Dammit!"

Jean-Pierre rushed up to greet the woman making a miniature puddle at the entrance of his popular bakery-café. *"Bonjour, bonjour. Vous désirez quelque chose? Une table, oui?"* Jean-Pierre was a handsome, stunted man with dabs of gray in his thick coal-colored hair. Next to the woman, she towered over him. Rawn guessed she was a regular because typically Jean-Pierre slipped in and out of French to those he knew, either by face or by name.

"It started pouring!"

"Oui-oui, the weather…" the baker said, and he shrugged. "You take-away?"

"No, Jean-Pierre. I don't have an umbrella. And I didn't mean to snap. I could afford to relax. *Oui, une table.*" Her pouty mouth shaped into a quiet smile.

"*Après moi, mademoiselle.*"

He pulled out a chair at a table next to Rawn's.

The tables at Café Neuf were intimately positioned, and having a private conversation was next to impossible without someone eavesdropping. It was the bakery-café's most noted appeal. Rawn had overheard his share of Crescent Island gossip.

The wet woman flopped in the chair and exhaled her breath like she was fed up and plain disgusted.

"*Un* café au lait?"

"No, Jean-Pierre. Something forbidden. Something—I'll have a brevé-latte. Oh, and Jean-Pierre, sprinkle a mixture of nutmeg and cinnamon, *un peu, s'il vous plaît*. And make it a double, and dry."

"*Certainement, mademoiselle.* I know how you like your *forbiddu*." Jean-Pierre's grin revealed a pair of crooked, tobacco-stained teeth.

"By the way, Jean-Pierre, how's Imani?"

"*Bon*, good!"

Jean-Pierre left hurriedly. The woman, whose entrance shifted the energy in the room, could sense Rawn's eyes judging her.

"What?" she stated. A quizzical brow lifted.

The corners of his mouth curved a bit. He reached for his iced coffee and took a sip. The sound of the last drop of liquid oozing through a straw broke their stare, and he returned to his book.

"You think it's funny?"

Rawn knew the remark was directed at him, but he was not necessarily in the right state of mind to deal with this uptight white woman in a bad mood.

"It's not funny!" she declared.

He let a few seconds slip by before he turned to look at her. "Have we started a conversation?"

"Excuse me? *No!*" She frowned.

"So...exactly who are you talking to?" Unbeknownst to him, intrigue began to play out between him and the wound-too-tight woman. Rawn looked closer at her. He was amused by the fact that she behaved liked a spoiled child unable to get her way.

In a casual demeanor she looked over her shoulder at the un- usually empty bakery-café, seeking out a patron or two. "I spent three hours in Gene Juarez." She combed her fingers through her moist hair to stress her point. "And these are two-hundred dollar shoes! Look, now they're ruined." When she inhaled deeply, her small nostrils flared.

Rawn took a fleeting glimpse at the scarlet suede mules, but his eyes lingered on the woman's long, bronze-colored legs. Although casually dressed, she was classy, even if she acquired it somewhere along the way. Her style was more East Coast; definitely not Pacific Northwest.

"*Voilà, mademoiselle.* You like something more?" asked Jean-Pierre.

Rawn observed Jean-Pierre closely. The baker was obsequious toward the woman; his authentic French charm was overkill. Granted, the customer was striking and mysterious, but her body language alone insinuated she was like many beautiful women— insecure.

"No, *merci,*" she said.

She did not bother to meet Jean-Pierre's kind gray-blue eyes. She dismissed him by sipping her brevé-latte with her back to him. The café owner glanced over to Rawn, shrugged with that audible turndown mouth so characteristic of the French, and with a wink, left their tables. The woman took off her rain-soaked coat and reached for a cellular in the pocket. She dialed a number, waited while she drummed her French manicured nails against the stun- ning wood table, and it was obvious she received no answer. Exasperated, she exhaled deeply and made another call. Because she was not getting an answer, her frustration was all the more demonstrative. The whole scene—her behavior—was dramatic, like her entrance, and Rawn sensed the mysterious lady was putting on a show for his benefit.

When he closed his book, he watched her while she examined her reflection in a compact mirror. Her deep cinnamon-colored hair with wheat and straw highlights, thick and bluntly cut to meet her broad shoulders, started to turn into wiry curls. While a white woman was not his type, there was no doubt Rawn was curious who she was. Did she live on Crescent Island or was she passing through? He had seen some fine white women, to be sure. But Rawn was naturally drawn—and soulfully connected—to women of color.

Coincidentally, he had a conversation about that very thing a few days ago. He and his good friend and colleague, Sicily, were roaming through shops at Bellevue Square Mall. Let Sicily tell it, every other couple in the mall was mixed. In general, she would get worked up when she saw a black man with a white woman, and Rawn told her: "You're overreacting, Sicily."

"It's not like a black man can't find a black woman. Come on, everywhere I go in Seattle I *see* black women. You'd think there was some kind of shortage. I've met plenty of black women here. It's raining single black women in Seattle. But what can they do? There are sisters that will always be alone in this town."

"Come on, Sicily. Aren't you being a bit dramatic...parochial?"

"Statistics don't lie. Besides, you're a man. It doesn't affect you."

"Why should you care? I mean, you don't want those men anyway."

"Thank Goddess you aren't into white women."

He finished what was left of his cold espresso. Standing, Rawn said to the woman in a sullen mood, "Take care." He headed for the French doors leading out of the café.

With a slight turn of her head, the mysterious woman stated in a quiet voice, "You, too." Through her compact mirror, her soothing olive-colored eyes traced his exit. She attempted to be discreet yet wanting to get a closer look.

From the time he left Café Neuf until he reached his front door, Rawn thought about the woman in a bitchy mood, with her ruined two-hundred-dollar shoes and stylish pimento-colored, all-weather jacket—her long legs and silky, thick hair. Rawn, unconsciously, thought about her for days.

CHAPTER TWO

S icily was tired. The day was way too long. Not to mention she was still feeling a sense of betrayal by her always-reliable empathy. She had a knack for contemplation. She was not the melodramatic type. An hour ago, while sitting in end-of-day traffic, Sicily reflected back on the afternoon. She could imagine what she might have looked like, not to mention how she may well have sounded, to the other members of the board. She came *this close* to speaking her mind at the monthly board of directors meeting. By now she knew full well her ideas—which were brilliant—and suggestions were going to be pooh-poohed. She did not personalize it, though. According to the board's president, her contribution was "very valuable" and "very creative," *but*, Sicily, *where will we get the funds?* always followed. Not only did Sicily bring her *name* to the board, she was headmistress of a top predominately all-white private school. But even with a Ph.D., she knew deep down that was not enough. There were two black male professionals—a computer game designer and a software entrepreneur—but she was the only black female on the board. For that very reason she tried to maintain a reasonably composed demeanor, because if she was not mindful, her homegirl façade could slip, easily.

Whenever the high-profile *brothers* leaned forward and offered any "input," rarely were their ideas "tabled." It might come as a surprise should she have shared this tidbit with any one of her friends, seeing as how the common thinking was that black women had it easier in the business world more so than black men. *Was that some urban myth?* So when Sicily recommended something she considered vital, and the board president said yet again, "Where will we get the funds?," Sicily sighed, pushed her seat away from the desk and stormed out of the meeting. She was sick and tired of hearing *Where will we get the funds?* The hierarchy of the board earned serious six figures. They certainly took home a good chunk of change more than Sicily. Half the members rubbed elbows with wealthy people who had their names on buildings or donors with hospital wards named after them. Sicily had no lifeline. In more ways than one, she was in a lonely place.

She tossed her silk pashmina to the plump polyester sofa. With her arms crossed over her chest, she bowed her head, unable to shake her anxiety. Sicily looked out at the close of another day—cool, breezy, and a trickle of late-day sunshine. There were three, sometimes four days before she saw even a hint of sunbeams, and at times the bleakness of the days made her nearly lose her mind. Yet Seattle had finally started to feel like home. More than Philadelphia. More than Manhattan. She made some discoveries about herself and she liked what she uncovered in this—what her brother called "way up in the Boondocks town!" It took a minute, but meditation really helped her to be *still*. Besides, she could not go back to Philly. Not now. And New York? That's what drove her to relocate to the Pacific Northwest in the first place. Taking a deep breath, she flopped in the sage-colored armchair. Her living room and dining room faced Elliott Bay; her bedroom and spacious bathroom looked out over Pioneer Square. That kind of view did not come cheap. No, she worked too bloody hard. Seattle was home now.

She loved the Pacific Northwest backdrop this time of year; especially Seattle: in between a gentle summer and the traces of a serene autumn. "But I'm lonely." Her eyes bulged. The sound of her own voice ricocheted off her ears. Sicily was taken aback. *Did I say that aloud?* She certainly did not mean to. Verbally putting it out there meant that she was consciously aware that she was indeed lonely. If it stayed in her head, it was only a thought, not necessarily a reality. When was the last time she did not have a serious conversation with a woman who was not lonely? Her life could be busy as all get-out, but she knew. *She knew.* When Sicily passed women on the street, in their faces she witnessed the loneliness, the sorrow, the regret, the lack of something unnamable in her life. These were women from a myriad of socio-economic backgrounds. When women wept from an empty place, color, class and education had little to do with it.

Sicily decided a drink would relax her. She reached for a Ste. Michelle bottle in the wrought-iron wine rack. It was a refined red she bought last time she and Rawn went to Chateau Ste. Michelle. She had not planned to open it this soon, but she was antsy. After pouring a glass, she went back to her armchair and stared out at the day while it began to fade softly into a dramatic dusk. In that moment it became obvious to her that summer was almost over— the hues of the day vanished earlier in recent days.

Throughout the board meeting she had to keep pushing away the intrusive thoughts about the date she had a few nights ago. It took experience, wisdom, or both to figure it out: If someone did not return her call within a day and a half, she could scratch that one off the list. It became her thirty-six-hour rule. There was little reason to even put them in contacts. As a rule, Sicily was honest. She let the date know that the chemistry was not there. Yet more people than Sicily cared to think about were immature, narcissistic, and anxious when it came to being honest. It stroked their ego to play games with people's sentiments. Likewise, they operated under the belief that they needed drama and chaos so as to feel relevant. It was such a pathetic cliché, but it did not mean it was any less true: *You have to kiss a few idiots...* She was halfway finished with her glass of Cabernet Sauvignon when she finally became aware of the sound of her new ringtone. Her cellular was in her mailbag across the room.

Sicily dashed for the mailbag she bought at Everything Dayna—and a few too many women were carrying the same bag and in the same color around Seattle. Eagerly she rummaged through the stylish, junky handbag, saying beneath her breath, "Where is that thing?" She reached deep into the bottom. "Why do I carry all this crap?... Yes, hello! Rawn." Not conscious of it, but the intensity of her body naturally relaxed. Sicily reacted like his voice was a prescribed drug that did the trick. "I was thinking about you. Did you get my message?" She sat in the armchair and curled up; the self-pity that only moments ago started to kick in began to ease up. "So you're up for going to Kingfish tomorrow? And you'll be here by...I can drive. No, really, I don't mind. Okay. See you then. 'Bye."

When she released the call, Sicily stared out at the stunning sunset; vivid colors perched over the calm bay. She sighed. *Goddess, I want a lover.*

Kingfish Café, with its storefront façade, was an unassuming restaurant in a residential street where closely quartered houses and ancient trees dotted the Capitol Hill neighborhood of Seattle. Amid an intimate setting, Rawn and Sicily leaned against a wall sipping wine, expecting a table to become available any minute. A number of people sat or stood nearby having drinks and indulging in conversation. A small queue trailed out onto 19th Avenue into the Seattle air that was characteristically cool and damp.

"Are you going to resign from the board?" Rawn asked.

Sicily pondered momentarily, her mind seemingly elsewhere despite the fact she had looked forward to seeing Rawn all week. "No. I like the contribution they make to the community. AIDS has taken too many friends away from me. Between the Academy's trustees and the A Blanket for My Friend board…I didn't become a member of that board to deal with a lot of B.S. AIDS isn't a game, and politics has no place with something this important."

"You're serious? Politics has its hands in everything. And life… hey, there's always going to be some B.S. in life."

Sicily looked into her wineglass, contemplating. She stared at the dark plum-colored wine. "Rawn, really. Do you always have to go deep?"

He grinned to himself, casually looking at the queue on the sidewalk that never seemed to move, not even a foot.

"I thought I met someone," she said, to change the subject.

"What happened? No, let me guess. Not your *type?* As much as you get on my case about…"

"You're right—not my type. But that wasn't the problem."

"So what happened?"

"I'm not sure. Maybe it's that first sign of flighty. Besides, the date was too young."

"How young?"

Sicily nursed her wine while scrutinizing the people whose faces she could scarcely make out from the warm glow of the room. *"Young."*

"Young as in cradle-robbing—what?"

It was rare Sicily did not feel some level of contentment whenever she was in Rawn's company. Giggling, she remarked, "Close enough. Nineteen."

"Nineteen! Where did you two meet?"

"U-Dub. A student."

"What were you doing with a student at UW?"

"I had a committee meeting over there. Our paths...crossed. We hung out. It was fun. I knew it couldn't be anything else."

"Nineteen. I guess not. I saw someone."

"*Saw*—what, like a celebrity? What are you talking about?"

"I have to say, this one did get my attention."

"Well, did you say anything?"

Rawn ruminated. "I wasn't sure it would lead anywhere. Besides... I—I didn't bother."

"It's not like you're looking for someone to marry. Where did you see her?"

"Café Neuf."

"Why didn't you say something? Do you think a *sister* on, of all places, Crescent Island, would turn down your extra fine...?"

"She was white."

"Like Caucasian white?"

"Like Caucasian white."

"*What?*" Sicily frowned. "That's why you didn't say anything. That's more Khalil's thing." They each drank their wine choices, and Rawn gazed at the mix of people lingering nearby. "How's Khalil, by the way?"

"He's in London."

"You know, I don't see you with a white woman."

"You have trouble seeing me with any woman. You didn't like Jas. You thought she was using me. Using me for what?"

"Then she moved to L.A. and slept with your best friend. I mean, look, Khalil is who he is and I love that he makes no apologies. But Jas? Even Khalil deserves better. She was with Khalil because she thought he could help her get a record deal. I mean, he's a sports agent with connections, I'm sure. But... Sisters without credibility...she makes us—the credible ones—look bad."

"And DiDi. You loathed her..."

"Oh, please—her!" Sicily butted in. "She has three snotty-nosed kids, or is it two kids?—I forget. That's the last woman you needed. Besides, she was only twenty-six, goodness gracious! She wanted a daddy figure because the daddies to those snotty-nosed kids weren't responsible and hadn't paid child support in who knows when. Who, in their right mind, has three kids by three men...?"

"Two!" Rawn interjected.

"Sorry, *two* different men, and before she even turns thirty? I'm thirty-five and I've never even been proposed to. And I have far more to offer than a woman who spreads her legs... Who doesn't discriminate."

Rawn chuckled. His eyes followed the svelte waitress passing by. It was hard to disagree with Sicily because, while she was opinionated, there were few flaws in her argument.

"What about that Café Neuf waitress? The one with a name like—something Kwanzaa—Unity, no...See, now she's fine. Without all that drama. She has credibility!"

"How do you know? You never even talked to Imani."

"Oh, trust me, she's *credible*."

A waitress interrupted Sicily. "Your table's ready. Follow me."

Rawn and Sicily tagged behind the poised waitress to their table in a softly lit spot of the dining area. Over her shoulder, Sicily said, "Now she's what I'm talking about."

Rawn lowered his voice. "Sicily, give it a rest!"

Every tangible detail about Tamara suggested anonymity. Her beauty was natural. Most men—and women, too—would pause and give her stunning look a prolonged appraisal. Shy of six feet tall, she was seductively built. Tamara stepped out of the black sports car in a pair of skin-tight black slacks, and a next-to-nothing halter top that revealed her full cleavage, slender abdomen, and a small but visible tattoo. The line of people waiting to enter the café could not help but witness her awkward misstep. She reached for her date, Henderson Payne, who managed to catch her before she slipped and fell. The crowd looked on at the couple inquisitively, as their appearance created a buzz. Both were accustomed to attention, but for totally isolated reasons.

Tamara slipped off her open-toed shoe. "Oh, no, my heel. It's loose."

"Tamara, baby, I'm sorry. We don't have to eat out tonight. We can order from my suite. It's more private than this restaurant. Even better, I know the owners; they'd have something delivered for me."

Tamara attempted a makeshift repair and slipped the sandal back on her foot, using Henderson's multimillion-dollar right arm to maintain her balance. "No," she said. "I want to *dine* at Kingfish, that's why we came. I'll manage."

"Woman, you're six feet tall barefooted. Why do you wear stiletto heels anyway?"

"Let me ask you something, Henderson." She leaned into his chest.

"Oh, no. Here we go." Henderson placed his hands into the pockets of his trousers and, without intending to, posed like a male model.

"Come on, I'm curious. Where does your wife think you are right now?"

"She thinks I'm in Seattle taking care of business. Why?"

"Does she know you're having dinner with me? Your ex-lover? The one you were sleeping with while she was carrying your third child? The one that nearly…"

"Hold up, now. You need not go back in time and dredge up…"

"I'm just saying…"

"Do you mind?…" Henderson held out his hand which suggested *after you.*

Tamara reached up and kissed Henderson's cheek, leaving a deep berry-colored imprint on his skin in the shape of luscious lips. "I promise to be a good girl, I promise. I won't embarrass you."

He moistened his mouth with his tongue, considering how good she looked under the glow of the streetlight. Henderson draped her arm into his, and they strolled past the crowd of people still waiting to get inside the café. Henderson opened the door for Tamara, and people inside waiting for tables promptly fell all over themselves to shake Henderson's hand, and a string of hellos and how-are-yous and shoulder bumps traveled with them while they made their way to the crowded bar.

Rawn often spent a good amount of time deciding what he was in the mood for. He was a picky eater. Sicily had already decided and asked their waitress to bring an order of catfish cakes to get her started. She twirled a lock of hair with her finger and nursed her wine, checking out the clientele. She thought, the pseudo-sophisticated crowd, and her line of thinking helped to amuse herself. Rawn was still mulling over the menu when she looked over at him. Sicily looked away and her eyes—accentuated by hazel-colored contacts—wandered to the bar. They fell straight on Henderson Payne dressed in his traditional urban black. *He is one fine man. Who is he with?* Sicily's back went ironing board-straight. Henderson towered over a woman sitting on a stool striking a pose, basking in the attention they were receiving. Henderson was definitely with her—they were too familiar, too *cozy. That man is so brazen!* His date was naturally striking; clearly ersatz. Henderson liked them tall and unanimously attractive. Sicily checked out the outfit the companion was wearing. Smirking, she took notice of others dining nearby to see if anyone else had recognized Henderson. Nearly everyone was looking his way, but were they looking more at Henderson or the woman who accompanied him? Even if she was not in a well-known Seattle restaurant and openly flirting with one of the highest-paid players in the NBA, her presence would command one to do a double-take. *She can't possibly live in Seattle. Our paths would have crossed long before now.*

Tamara needed to get out of the townhouse, and when Henderson rang her up and asked if she wanted to "hook up" because he was in town "for a minute," she was dressed and waiting for him in twenty. The type of girl that did not require too much makeup to camouflage small imperfections, all Tamara needed to do was to decide on what she would look good in. Since she was bloated—that time of the month, and unfortunately for Henderson—she needed to wear black! Before he called, she was starting to feel sorry for herself. Calling friends in Amsterdam and Istanbul and back home in D.C., and family in the Caribbean; not one unreliable soul was answering their phones! Now, feeling more herself, she looked around the room with its Pacific Northwest energy while combing her long fingers through her cropped hairdo that emphasized her exotic features. She placed her hand on Henderson's chest like it was the most natural thing she ever did, and she could hear the chatter, but like years ago, Tamara was unfazed.

While Henderson made polite small talk with a "fan," she searched the dining room for any familiar faces—clients, for one—and detected this woman sitting at a table with a man across the romantically lit room, staring at her. *What is she gawking at?* Henderson leaned toward her and said into her ear he needed to take a call. Tamara nodded with understanding. She smiled broadly to the woman who was very interested in what was going on between her and the married ballplayer. When the woman across the room clumsily reached for her menu putting on like she was not remotely intrigued, Tamara laughed. But curiosity could leave one spellbound: the woman who sat across the room could not keep her eyes away from the bar. For a split-second, Tamara wondered if she had some Henderson Payne history. But then she thought better of it because the woman, while attractive, was not his type. Tamara bent forward—her naturally full breasts nearly exposed from the skimpy halter top—and blew the nosy woman a deliberately seductive kiss.

"Oh, my Goddess," Sicily reacted.

Nonchalant, Rawn glanced Sicily's way. "What?"

"I...nothing." She looked down at the menu and pretended to be looking at it because Sicily needed something to distract her. "Haven't you decided? I'm starved."

"The catfish cakes should be here soon," said Rawn.

Yet Sicily could not stop looking over at the bar.

Rawn grew curious. Sicily was preoccupied by whatever was taking place behind him, so he looked over his shoulder. Searching the room, he caught sight of Henderson Payne at the bar. No sooner, Rawn's eyes fell on the beautiful and seductive woman seated beside him.

CHAPTER THREE

I
t was a crisp summer morning when Rawn strolled along Street One and spotted the white woman he saw at Café Neuf a few days ago. Her vivid eyes were concealed by fashion-statement sunglasses. Despite her being dressed casually in a pair of faded red Converse sneakers, capri-style leggings, and a sleeveless sweater in bright watermelon that clung to her lithe silhouette, it did not play down the polished look that caught his eye at the bakery-café. She walked hurriedly, and only a few feet in front of Rawn. Because the island was secluded and attracted high-profile types, the mysterious woman from Café Neuf could easily be mistaken for a celebrity on holiday attempting to be incognito.

She turned on Heather Avenue, and Rawn, unbeknownst to his own curiosity, turned onto to that street too. It was that very day his life took a detour, and dramatically adjusted the direction of his fate. He lost her in the crowd of tourists and locals. His interest intensifying, Rawn poked his head through a few of the shops nearest to the corners of Heather and Street One, but the intriguing woman from Café Neuf had vanished like a solitary cloud. He walked into Starbucks, but the coffee bar was oddly empty with the exception of customers at the counter and at the pick-up order bar. Several doors down was Barney's, a sports bar which was crowded and very loud on any given night. Rawn did not antici-pate her being in the bar. When he walked in and headed toward the back by the pool tables with the pretense he was going to use one of the public telephones, he caught sight of her sitting in a booth. The woman sat with a tanned man with good looks and wearing workout clothing.

Rawn feigned using one of the pay telephones for several minutes, listening to a phantom on the other end. He had an excellent view of their table. The couple ordered another round of imported beer. Rawn liked how the woman from Café Neuf handled her beer and drank it from the bottle rather than from a glass. It took nothing away from her charismatic femininity. From his point-of-view the couple's conversation bordered on passionate. More like two people with strong opinions on the topic of say, politics. At last, Rawn saw two men leave a table on the opposite side of the room. Eagerly he claimed it, and told the waitress when she came to clean it off, he would take a Corona. Not long after he sat and was served his beer, the couple finished their drinks. The man with good looks and a dark tan left loose bills on the table and they laughed with a rush of excitement while leaving the bar. Rawn nursed his Corona for ten minutes, paid his check and left Barney's.

It had turned very cloudy, and the intensity of the sky made the island look dark and somber while he sat in the sports bar. On his way home he stopped at G Street Wok for Chinese, a noisy, disorganized and always busy take-away. It was the third time that week he had stopped off for something to eat. Earlier, he was thinking how ridiculous his routine had become: dateless nights, going to bed alone, and eating take-away meals from a carton or that he pulled from a paper or plastic bag. Sometimes leftovers he heated up in the microwave.

Not long after the school year ended, he found himself signing on to the Internet and having conversations with strangers in chat rooms, starting to rely on pseudo connections instead of developing companionship he could actually touch. At some point it became obvious to him that he began to depend too much on the Internet. Rawn decided he was turning out to be like too many people who fell into a trap and had become socially isolated. When he was with himself, he was fine with that. He did not feel desperate or lacking during times of solitude. But Rawn stopped going online to *chat;* he no longer wanted to get too involved with, or devote time on, the lives of people he most likely would never meet.

He always missed teaching during summer recess.

Being alone was not his choice. Rawn resented the options that were accessible to him. Every single woman he met was too this or too that. She was not *only* this or *only* that; she was *too* something: too chatty; too insecure; too self-conscious; too soulless to retain his attention. While he might have been, as his mother claimed, "too picky," he was not looking for "the one" necessarily, so he was not as choosy as his mother might have suspected. It did not matter how the relationship, brief or otherwise, evolved; the woman had to hold his attention. Even his friend Khalil, who would lower the bar if he did not want to sleep alone, agreed it was getting more problematical to find a woman who could maintain a man's attention for any length of time. It could have been the lack of ambiguity, he was not sure. The last time Rawn was in L.A., Khalil told his best friend: "Man, there are some fine women in L.A. Milk *chocolat*, dark *chocolat*, nutmeg, cinnamon, cappuccino, vanilla, caffé con leche…But once I get laid, look, I'm done…" Except in Rawn's mind the single lifestyle was a scary, shot-in-the-dark place to be these days. For Rawn, meeting someone in a bar or club and taking her home for a night of casual sex had become—complicated.

Trying to find a single woman without children who was likewise smart was a challenge for a single man, especially for a black man. And a woman who was engaging and thought-provoking was equally tricky. A good example of the woman he enjoyed spending time with was Sicily, who was his closest friend in Seattle. Her organic looks alone could pique the average man's interest. Likewise, Sicily was intelligent, creative, and captivating. Perpetually, Rawn met women who came across confused, or had an androgynous nature: she was curious about being with other women or she was not sure how she felt about men. With a Ph.D. in psychology, Sicily once told him there was something in his attitude—something in his psyche—that drew those types of women into his life. The few blind dates that had been set up by informal friends, by the end of the second date, any appeal that was there had worn off and Rawn did not feel the need to see her again.

He learned that in one split-second life could be like a strand of yarn that came loose from the sleeve of a sweater. It was the morning he received a call from his mother that forced him to evaluate all the stuff he tried to avoid over the past two years. He was sitting in his office grading papers, and when her voice greeted him, Mrs. Poussaint chose not to beat around the bush. Rawn was always asking his mother about Janelle, the woman he had planned to marry after graduate school. Mrs. Poussaint sensed her son's conflict with Janelle because he cared deeply for her, but his love for her was not the same as her love for him. When he broke things off, Janelle was beside herself.

"I read it in the *Post* over the weekend, Janelle's getting married."

"Married?" Rawn was on his feet before he was aware he was even standing. "To.... Who is she marrying, Mama? It's not someone that I know?"

"I think he's a Johnson."

Not that his being a "Johnson" meant anything to Rawn.

"William graduated from Penn. He's a specialist, but I can't recall what kind. Your father knows him."

He's a doctor? Was he older than Janelle?

He was not altogether certain if his mother was trying to make him feel jealous or angry, or was this her way of nudging him to finally get over the fact that he ended things with Janelle and broke her kind heart. The truth of the matter—Rawn did not know what to say. He never saw it coming. And even if there were warning signs, he had no idea his reaction would be so—well, visceral.

"I guess she went on with her life. After all, it's been…what, nearly two years?"

More accurately, one year and eight months. Was that long enough to have met and fallen in love with another man? They were once best friends—they were lovers—for four years. They had been publicly engaged. *She found—met—someone and fell in love that quickly?* Then he was never the right man for Janelle.

"When is Janelle getting married, Mama?"

"In May. I suspect you'll get an invitation. After all, you two have managed to remain friends."

"That would be great," he purposely exaggerated. The news— the blow—was horribly physical. Rawn tried to steady his thoughts. He believed in Janelle; he *cared* about her. Except the word *care*, in comparison to love, was small. His leaving Denver, his home-town, and moving on without her was likewise releasing her so that she could explore and grow and experience a sense of indi-viduality. And perhaps some time down the road they could find each other again. Destiny, fate, that sort of thing. They were young, and they had no idea what it was truly like to know themselves or experience the many possibilities that were out there—in the world. Janelle felt more safe than right. Rawn craved a kind of raw love, or was it lust? It was not that he was being insensitive; he had absolutely no idea how it would affect her, but he admitted to Janelle what he wanted and needed. Rawn would never forget the look on her face when he ended it.

"I suppose she'd invite you to the wedding," his mother said, but he could read between the lines since Rawn knew all too well how his mother thought. It sounded more like, *Do you think you can actually* sit *through her wedding?*

"I'm happy for Janelle. She must have found what she needed. Janelle wouldn't marry if it wasn't right."

So the Doctor—a "Johnson"—from *Penn* would take her to Africa. She would finally see the Ivory Coast, Liberia, Uganda, Niger— and there was Mozambique, where Janelle was dying to go, and where she could speak French. Although Rawn grew up speaking French with his Haitian grandparents and with his Creole family in Louisiana, Janelle had an ear for languages and she spoke French as well as, if not better than, he. They had planned all kinds of trips to places like Paris and Cairo and Budapest right after Janelle was established as an attorney and when Rawn finished grad school. But somewhere along the way, things changed. Forthrightly, Rawn's feelings changed.

"Are you sure you're okay, Rawn?"

That motherly tone yanked him back into the here and now.

Rawn felt the wailing in his throat; a knot caught at the base, and when he swallowed, it seemed only to make the knot grow, like a tumor developing into an incurable cancer. He wanted to scream at his mother: *Hell, no! I am not* okay! *Why did you call me and tell me this?* On the other hand, Rawn understood that his mother was only giving him information that he would eventually become privy to on his own.

"Mama, I need to go. Tell Daddy and Tera hello. I'll talk to you later."

"'Bye-bye, Rawn, dear. Take care of yourself. We love you." He couldn't bear to remain on the line and listen to his mother's often-times long-winded farewell.

His concentration had been destroyed, his nerves shattered. He was wounded by the news of Janelle's pending wedding. He had no idea she was seriously involved with another man. As much as he tried to deny it to himself—and in the months leading up to his mother's call, he had entertained the thought—a part of him had wanted Janelle back.

CHAPTER FOUR

The temperamental Pacific Northwest sun that tranquilly blended in with steel gray hue defined the sophisticated suite at the Four Seasons. Tamara's eyes popped opened and she was immediately aware that Henderson was already up. He sat in a chair on the other side of the suite looking over papers. While his back was to her, his body language warned her that Henderson was in a solemn mood. It was not like they did anything, so he had nothing to feel guilty about. She was over Henderson, and Tamara was not fully aware of it until she slept next to him and felt absolutely no urge. While Henderson was over Tamara as much as she thought she was over him, he did not have the same willpower.

Tamara decided some time ago, hands off—no married men! *How many failed marriages did I have a hand in?* She pressed her eyes shut, trying *not* to think about how she most certainly had a hand in nearly ruining Henderson's marriage. Of course there had been other women besides her, but it was Tamara's relationship with him that did the most damage. It did not cost him financially, but it took everything he had emotionally to save his high-profile marriage. Henderson fought hard and fought dirty. If Daphne were to leave him, she would need to be very vigilant and maintain a steady look over her slender shoulder because he was a payback kind of guy.

Like Tamara, Daphne went by one name. She was the ex-super-model, and the woman Henderson loved beyond any other. The one he chased from one continent to another until he persuasively romanced her away from a British rock star. Daphne stayed in their shattered marriage. But not for the sake of their children; she certainly did not stay for Henderson. Rumor had it she remained in their marriage because she abandoned her own identity to be his wife. Dutifully, she sat at home games and looked breathtaking; looked stunningly gorgeous through three pregnancies despite having gained over thirty pounds with each—the third and last finally producing a son. Ten years ago Daphne was huge! Her earnings provided her with an apartment that offered views of Manhattan's skyline and the East River, a condo on Wilshire Boulevard, west of Beverly Hills, and an apartment overlooking the Seine. She had not only a career; Daphne was equal to Henderson and all but as controversial. One could only imagine the bitterness she must have felt being placed in the position of being gossiped about because of her husband's notorious infidelities; the fact that she had to compete with his stable of one-, two- and three-night stands. She was now *Mrs.* Henderson Payne, and the attention was less on her, something Daphne struggled with, because the public interest was almost always on him. Tamara could only imagine that she resented being her husband's public appendage. Daphne could not go back to the visibility she had as an in-demand runway model. Not only was she ten years older, likewise she was no longer waif, or what she was referred to back in the day—heroin chic.

Tamara played with the idea in her head: *Why can't I be attracted to people who are emotionally and psychologically available? Why can't I like—or fall for—people who liked—or fell for—me?* Henderson's theory still stuck in her head four years later: *Daddy issues.*

"Hey, baby," Tamara said.

Henderson looked over his shoulder, and instantly his grimace turned into his trademark grin—a set of naturally white and even teeth—was all she even noticed. *He is so damn fine. Why are the fine ones always complicated, married, tragic, vain and emotionally bankrupt?*

"Hey," he said back. Offhandedly, he reached for his classy watch on the table and looked at it fleetingly. "I can't miss my flight. Are you hungry?"

"Tea sounds delightful!"

"Do you mind taking me to Sea-Tac? You know what to do with my ride."

Henderson was bare-chested and in a pair of silk pajama bottoms. As a rule, he slept in the nude, even on the road. Actually, hours ago, he took Tamara by surprise when he slipped on the PJ bottoms before he crawled under the fine bedding that draped over the king-sized bed. When he rose from the chair, Henderson reached for paperwork that he had been studying soberly when she disturbed him, and said, "Order me something, okay? I'm in the shower."

"Okay," Tamara said in a subdued voice. "Bacon or sausage?"

"Surprise me," he said with a wink.

Tamara waited until she heard the shower water running before she pulled herself up with her elbows. She squinted at the slice of calm sunshine trickling into the large suite; the bank of ominous clouds that attempted to take over the sky disappeared, at least for the meantime. Tamara noted the time on Henderson's cellular.

Hastily, her feet met the soft carpeted floor. Clad in a black lace thong and bra, she slipped into her outfit from the previous evening. She checked herself out in the mirror and finger-combed her cropped hairdo. She looked closer at her image in the mirror. "Oh, God. I'm starting to look…my age. How much longer can I hold the attention of a man like Henderson?" *Is he still attracted to me or am I nothing more than* familiar? *I've been hearing lately that thirty is the new forty?*

While walking across the suite to her heels at the foot of the bed, she used her fingertips to remove any sleep in the corners of her eyes. She wet the tip of her pinky and wiped mascara that smeared beneath her almond-shaped eyes. Tamara tucked the heels under her armpit and reached for a pen and scribbled a note to Henderson on the hotel stationery: *I'm running late. I need to meet a client. Bisous-bisous.*

Outside his hotel suite, she slipped on her sandals and eagerly trotted to the elevator. Waiting in front of the elevator doors, she thought better of leaving the way that she had. She told herself if, at the count of five, the doors did not open, she would go back. At three the elevator arrived. When the doors closed, in an explicit voice, Tamara prayed: "God, I need you to help me out. I can't get caught up in drama anymore. Don't put me in the same place and at the same time with men like Henderson again. Send me a man who's available—not only physically, but emotionally." Just when the doors opened, she finished her prayer with a frantic, *"Please!"*

CHAPTER FIVE

The day was as clear as crystal, and the sky a stunning cobalt blue. Heading eastbound on the twin bridges, the tranquil color of forest green and spots of clouds in the distant horizon blended exotically into one. Imani was hitting about 57 miles per hour when she had to brake fast to keep from slamming into the Land Rover ahead of her. Instantly, the early day traffic began to swerve right and left like there was an earthquake rattling the floating bridge; automobile after automobile came to an abrupt, screeching halt. Imani feared the possibility of the Armageddon at some point in the New Millennium, so she freaked! Catching her breath, she studied the road ahead, trying to ascertain what had happened. She had not heard anything on the radio that would indicate there was a pileup, not even a fender-bender. Through her rearview mirror, she witnessed dozens of cars lined up behind her, and in the accompanying lane. She was running late. *I need to break down and buy a cell phone.* She switched off the "smooth jazz" station—the music was a distraction. Trouble started barking at a kid making faces at him in the car next to hers. "Shush!" Imani snapped at Trouble. "Stop it!" Trouble ceased barking for a few seconds before he began barking again. "Trouble!" Imani was getting testy and annoyed. She knew she should have left Seattle sooner, but that was not the real issue. From the time she got out of bed she was feeling strange. The elusive sensation reminded her of the day her mother collapsed and Imani called 9-1-1. Within minutes of reaching the ER, her mother's life—her life story— ended.

It was simply not avoidable; Imani had to look at the time. *I should have taken the ferry.* She stretched her torso to get a better look, but cars spread beyond what her eyes could perceive. It was not like she could just pull off at the next exit. Over 6,000 feet above Lake Washington, the closest exit was a good mile, and she could barely see the exit sign from her vantage point. Trouble barked again. Imani turned and snapped, "Trouble! I mean it, stop barking." Her warm brown eyes darted to a little boy sitting in the passenger seat in the SUV next to hers, sticking his tongue out at the Afghan hound. When Imani caught the little boy's eye, she gave him a long stare and held up her hand which implied *stop!* The kid, reacting like a child whose hand was caught in a cookie jar, snapped his neck in a new direction. Imani exhaled deeply, leaning her head against her fist. The sailboats dotting the aqua-blue body of water caught her eye. Wetting her lips, she cut her eyes away from the sailboats and tried to stay calm. "Come on! What's going on up there?" Only moments later did she hear a helicopter overhead which made her say to Trouble, "It's serious. Trouble, and we're so late!"

Ninety minutes later she dashed into her Pilates studio, and the receptionist stopped her with, "I take it you didn't get my message?"

"Trouble!" The Afghan hound sat obediently. "What message? No," Imani said. "Take care of Trouble for me. Did Patsi take my one o'clock?" Imani dropped her tote to the floor.

"No, I mean yes. But...Imani, you got a call. Something's happened." The receptionist reached down to smooth Trouble's soft coat of sable-colored fur.

"Okay, but...How about my twelve o'clock? Who took over the class?"

The receptionist reached for Trouble's collar. Her look was a mixture of dismay and empathy. "I wish you'd gotten my message."

Still annoyed for having to sit on the floating bridge for nearly two hours, Imani snapped, "What message?"

"You need to call your sister."

"My sister? You mean Kenya?" Imani barely spoke to Kenya, and knew that her calling the studio meant something was up. Divorce? No, her marriage was solid. Besides, she probably would not bother to call Imani with that news. *Pregnant?* That might warrant an e-mail, but a call, and to the studio? Their father, Dante Godreau, the celebrated jazz pianist, was on both of his daughters about grandchildren. Imani was not feeling that; Kenya would tell Dante and Dante would tell Imani. She refused to go to any number of dark places. Imani reached for her tote and draped it over her forearm. "What did she want?"

"Imani, you *need* to call your sister!"

The pitch of Patsi's voice gave Imani pause. The receptionist was so unyielding.

"Call Kenya," said the receptionist, in a no-nonsense tone.

When Imani opened her studio, no one on Crescent Island had even heard of Pilates. After a serious Vespa accident while vacationing in Montenegro five years back, she had to end her career as a professional dancer. Roughly ten years ago, a colleague introduced Imani to Pilates, and following her accident it helped to put her body back into alignment. Something Imani lacked was concentration, and Pilates worked wonders for her awareness of the breath; likewise, her balance.

She traveled for a year until she met someone, and she fell deep; so much so she lost all sense of her *self.* When they broke up, it was both devastating and heartrending. Imani was not sure she could trust herself again. While visiting a close friend, Jean-Pierre's wife, Carmen, on Crescent Island, her spirit felt renewed and whole and she decided to move to Washington. The Pilates studio was

Carmen's idea. Imani, who customarily waited until she stopped overanalyzing the pros and cons of a decision, enrolled in a Pilates teaching course in Vancouver, B.C. two days later. She dared not ask her father, Dante, for one red cent. As an alternative—and it was potentially risky—Imani took every dime she saved while dancing and opened the first Pilates studio on Crescent Island, and purchased a fixer-upper in Seattle.

"It's not like you to be impulsive," her father said.

"This one, Dante. *Feels* very right."

"And it has nothing to do with Blaine?" her father, Dante, asked.

"Of course not," Imani snapped. *Blaine had everything to do with it.*

"Kenya?"

"Where have you been, Im?"

"Well, hello to you, too."

"I don't have time for this. You need to get to New York. Papa's in the hospital."

"Why? What?…"

"You need to get to New York as soon as humanly possible. I'm leaving Toronto in two hours!"

"Kenya, you're scaring me."

"Have you watched the news? I know you don't have cable, but you do listen to the radio. It's all over the news, Im."

Imani reached for her chair and pulled it close, then sat. "Kenya, you have to tell me what's happened to Dante."

"Im," Kenya sighed. "It's serious…he—he may not make it."

"What the hell are you talking about?" she yelled into the receiver. Mechanically, she stood and planted a hand on her hip.

"Get your ass on a plane!"

Stunned, Imani looked at the receiver. "No she didn't hang up on me."

CHAPTER SIX

Kickboxing never let D'Becca down. When she put in a workout she felt such freedom, and any angst was released. Whatever stress claimed her spirit, kickboxing took care of it. Troy, her dear friend and personal trainer, could detect her aggression with each kick and punch. When the fifty-pound heavy bag scarcely missed his groin, he said, "Whoa, hey!"

"Sorry!"

"Look," Troy said, "let's call it a day, all right?"

D'Becca, hyped and sweaty, felt better at that moment than in weeks. "I needed that, thanks." She tried to control her breathing.

Troy helped her take off her striking pads. "You want to talk about it?"

Wiping sweat from her forehead with the back of her hand, D'Becca said, "What do you mean?"

"Come on, it's me, Becca."

She reached over and gently caressed Troy's cheek with her lips. "I'm fine, really."

His eyes lingered on her face for a brief moment. "Tonight?"

"Tonight."

"You know I leave for South Beach first thing, and I won't be back before the New Year."

"I hate that you're opening up a gym in South Beach. Not only am I losing my trainer, I'm losing one of my dearest friends."

"Come to Miami. Hang out. My place is more than big enough for the both of us." Troy studied his friend, trying to decide where her head was. "The climate's about to change here. Soon it'll be raining every single day. You'll get really moody—that winter blues thing you go through every year since I've known you. You love South Beach."

"I used to love South Beach. I'm not in that frame of mind anymore."

"But a hiatus will do you good."

"You know I can't do that. Don't even tempt me," she warned him, fanning her damp and flushed face with her hands.

Troy took her into his arms and they shared an affectionate, lingering embrace. He released her and said, "Go! Tonight. Seven?" His left brow placed an emphasis on *seven*.

"Seven! Cheers!"

D'Becca started walking toward the showers, and Troy slapped her buttocks with a towel. "And I mean seven, Becca!"

"Seven. I cross my heart and hope to die." D'Becca sketched a cross against her chest with her index finger.

Although he said it in a voice that was not intended for her ears, D'Becca heard Troy say, "You need to learn to choose your words carefully."

Twenty minutes later, she was towel-drying her hair while reciting a mantra: "I will be on time." In a pair of boyshorts and a demi bra, D'Becca reached for her ringing cellular nearby. "Hello. Hey." After listening to the caller momentarily, her shoulders drooped in apparent disappointment. "What now? So when?" And with an edge to her voice, she said, "Fine." D'Becca rolled her eyes. Not exactly sure when, but she had finally reached a breaking point with the lame excuses and hollow apologies. "Okay, sure. *Sure.* 'Bye." She stared at the cellular before tossing it to a gym bag nearby. The workout with Troy must have mentally prepared her for this moment. Even while she was quite let down, oddly, D'Becca did not pity herself as she had done numerous times in the past. *Maybe—Am I immune to being treated this way?*

When D'Becca entered Street Two Books and Café, the first person to catch her eye was the black guy she saw in Café Neuf a week before. If the concept that nothing happened randomly was a sure thing, then to presuppose that they both being at the same place at precisely the same time could only mean that it was incontrovertible fate. But that was purely based on whether one believed in that sort of thing. She could ignore the fact that she saw him—because so what that she did—and chalk it up to no more than a coincidence. A fluke was something she trusted far more than metaphysical ideas about nothing in life happened by chance. Still, running into the same person twice—and in the same neighborhood?—was not something that happened to D'Becca. Surprises, serendipity, that kind of stuff—it was not her brand of karma.

Leisurely, she browsed through the café-bookstore, her sullen mood not yet lifted. She could easily go for some Chunky Monkey right about now and not even feel a pang of guilt. Yet she was not so low that she did not have the willpower to talk herself down. When D'Becca felt lack—of love, of attention, of compassion—food or shopping was her cure. Standing in the center of the classy bookstore owned by Troy's ex-lover, she tried to recall exactly why she came. The magazine section was to her left, and she could grab *W*, *Elle*, *Vogue* and *George* since she was there. Along the wall, lined with magazines on every subject imaginable, two men were flipping through tech and sports magazines. When she passed them, D'Becca felt their eyes travel the length of her; and while she was in no way fazed by the attention she received, it felt kind of good that she managed to maintain some level of effect on men.

She reached for *Seattle* and stared at the cover. Sebastian Michaels, the fifth richest man in Washington State, was on the cover. He had a year-round tan—not too dark, but darker than his natural skin tone. His salt-and-pepper hair made him look distinguished, and the suit he wore was most likely designed by his personal tailor in Italy. The cost of Michaels's yearly wardrobe could put, at the very least, a dent in India's rising poverty. D'Becca flipped through the magazine until she came to the article on the high-profile entrepreneur. Before she could start to peruse it, the bolder one of the two young men sharing the magazine section with her said, "Hello!" He held a race car magazine and an iced espresso drink, and wore a silly, immature grin. Right off, she detected that he was the type who took chances when it came to women solely because he had nothing to lose.

D'Becca took her time meeting his startling green eyes. "Hello," she said, but barely looked up from the magazine.

He was *young*. Maybe twenty-six, if that. *I don't want to hurt his feelings, but I really am seriously not in the mood. The attention* he's *giving me doesn't make me feel any better about myself.* D'Becca replaced *Seattle* on the shelf and she could see the guy's lips start to form words—some corny, inexperienced, sad and pathetic line he used on every woman he tried too hard to pick up. She interrupted his generic introduction she had heard far too many times with, "Excuse me," and walked around him.

Why am I in here? Visibly bored, she started looking at titles displayed on a small table. She reached for a book and glanced over to the black guy from Café Neuf. He was toward the rear of the store at a picnic-style table stacked with "employee recommendations." Curious, she watched him. Every time he picked up a book he read the blurbs on the back cover. She began to mimic his actions by picking up a book, pretending to be interested in the cover or the flap, and then replaced it and repeated the action several times. When she looked back over to where Rawn was standing he was still there, taking a serious interest in the employee recommendations.

On impulse, she approached him holding several magazines in her arms like she did schoolbooks when she was a child. "It's you!"

"Excuse me." Rawn frowned.

"You were mean to me. Remember? At Café Neuf?"

"Mean?" Rawn chuckled. He pretended to be vague about having seen her at Café Neuf a week or so back and replaced the book on the table. "So, you live around here?"

"Yes. Do you?"

"I do."

"Are you into poetry?" D'Becca retrieved the book Rawn replaced on the table moments before.

"Actually, I've been trying to ease thirteen-year-olds into it. It's good to start early as possible with poetry. Besides, the Internet— if it's going in the direction I think that it is—it's only a matter of time before it will eventually change the way young people learn. The influence, and well…Poetry won't stand a chance if the Web changes the way we process information."

"You're an idealist, I see. Poetry's a hard sell."

Amused, Rawn replied, "It can be." He watched her looking over a poem from a book by Browning. "Listen, I was about to go and have a coffee. You want to join me?"

"You aren't…Are you picking me up?"

He chuckled, and her insinuation made Rawn feel awkward. "I asked if you'd like to join me for coffee."

"I came here to get a book for a friend. Why don't I join you afterwards?"

"Okay, sure," his tone casual.

D'Becca walked around him, flipping her hair off her slender

neck, throwing him that same attitude she exhibited at Café Neuf—
uppity and insecure.

Rawn sat at one of the tables in the bookstore's small attic café.
He looked around to see if he could seek out D'Becca in the bookstore below, but he was unable to spot her. *Did she leave?* Thought-
lessly, he glanced at his watch, and his waiting for D'Becca felt
much longer than it naturally was. Out of the blue, she appeared
at the table, and came across in a way that suggested to Rawn she
had looked all over to find him.

"There you are," she said in a cavalier voice.

She sat in the accompanying seat and placed a bookstore bag on
the table and her oversized bag on the striking maple hardwood
floor.

"What did you buy?"

"An Oprah book. A friend in Deauville is into books she chooses
for her book club, and I send her the ones she isn't able to get her
hands on. It's amazing!"

"What's that?"

"The Oprah Winfrey phenomenon. She can share her 'favorite
things' and the Zeitgeist trusts her judgment and they go out in
droves and buy a favorite *thing*. How do we ever really know if we
sincerely like something, or if we're swayed by an invisible force
to go along with it?" D'Becca sighed. "I don't know your name."

"Rawn."

"D'Becca."

"That's different."

"What's different?"

"Your name."

D'Becca avoided Rawn's warm and sensual eyes, making every
effort not to display even a nominal degree of intrigue.

"What did you want?" And he added, "I'm buying," out of respect.

"I'm taking a risk. Surprise me."

When Rawn left the table, D'Becca could not resist checking him out. *This guy is dangerous. I'm not in a good place. This is trouble.* She tried to distract herself by looking at her watch even though she made note of the time while climbing the wide-planked stairs that led to the café. Occasionally she looked over at Rawn at the bar talking to the barista preparing the beverage. D'Becca admired her French-manicured nails so as to prevent from looking over to Rawn being cordial, if not reverential, to the teen-something barista. D'Becca smiled secretly; some part of her was reacting to how attentive and friendly he was to the young café worker while she flirted in that not-really-experienced sort of way.

He returned with the tea served in a small porcelain teacup and sat with a private look on his face. Apparently the barista said something to him and he was embarrassed for her, or amused.

D'Becca took her first sip of the tea. "If we could taste paradise, this could be it. Good choice." Her full mouth spread subtly.

"I'm sure you've heard it before, but you have a—your smile pops!"

"Pops?" She chuckled, looking directly into her cup of tea. Her voice blasé-like, she said, "Thank you."

"You don't look like someone who lives on Crescent Island."

"How is someone supposed to look who does live on Crescent Island?"

"Do you own a pair of Birkenstocks?"

With a hearty laugh, she exclaimed, "Hell no!"

"Enough said!"

"Well, do you own a pair? Because it's not like you—your energy doesn't *feel* like someone who's from the Pacific Northwest."

"That's not because I'm black, right?"

"Of course not. You're...you have a look, a feel. Classic comes to mind." D'Becca scanned the six-table café. "You see that guy?" she said. "Over there," she directed with her chin. Rawn followed D'Becca's gesture. "He *feels* like he belongs in the Pacific Northwest. And he has that nerdiness, L.L. Bean thing going on."

"Yeah…"

The young man, with an early thirties look about him, sat across the small attic-style room and Rawn could only see his tight dirty-blond curls; his upper body was hidden behind a laptop. His table was cluttered with a coffee mug, an already-read *Wall Street Journal*, an empty plate, and several books on a variety of subjects that he had not yet purchased piled in a chair.

"He probably made his first million at Microsoft, retired and is trying to decide exactly what he wants to do now."

"I know someone who retired from Microsoft last year. He's thirty-five. He's in Dubai right now, and he's—he has private jet money. So," she said, and took a small sip of her vanilla mint tea. "What should I be looking like?"

"There are no women to compare you to."

She glanced over at the order counter. "Not the barista?"

Rawn checked out the barista reading *The Stranger*, her elbows resting on the counter. "She's got that Capitol Hill look about her—tatts and piercings."

"Why are you here?"

"You mean on Crescent Island? Teaching brought me here."

"Ah, there's the connection: Easing thirteen-year-olds into poetry."

"When I visited Gumble-Wesley Academy–it's where I teach… I liked it and decided to get a place on the island instead of in Seattle." Rawn leaned his forearms on the edge of the table. "What about you?"

"That's a long story. It's complicated. It's crowded. It's sad. But I'm trying to learn not to be so hard on myself."

"You make it sound like your life is like a Jane Austen novel. Everyone has a story that has a range of things we didn't expect."

"True." She looked into his magnetic eyes and could not bear to hold them for long. "Sages and mystics—they claim but for the complicated and the sad, one cannot have a life worth talking about. It makes sense, but in theory. In the real world…"

"What exactly has happened in your life? What, are you like a walking wounded?"

"No, I'm not a *walking wounded*, but each of us has *some*…regret?"

"Regret? Sure," said Rawn, his eyes resting on his cup on the table. "But I suppose I haven't lived long enough to know what it's like to hold on to it."

"Well, perhaps not. It's coming. What are you, twenty-nine?"

"Thirty-three," he corrected her. "And with a birthday on the way. You don't look like you've lived long enough to have that much regret."

"How old do you think I am?" she asked.

"Oh no, I miscalculated once. Never again."

D'Becca was the type who never felt the need to lie about her age. Over the years, she met a number of women whom she believed were self-conscious about aging, which meant they struggled with the woman they had become. She never got that, and she always hoped that as she aged she would feel even better about herself. Although desperate to live this beautiful life she had long imagined as a child, even back when she was naïve and insanely insecure, D'Becca not once fibbed about her age. "Thirty-seven, and with a birthday on the way."

"Thirty-seven?"

"Thirty-seven and some change, yes."

"And when's your birthday?"

"December."

"Okay, I know my mother would think this is rude…"

"No, no Botox or facelifts or Restylane. But…yes, my lips. Collagen. And I confess it's because so many other women in my line of work, and actresses, do it. It's the one thing I felt I had to give in to." She was forthright.

His eyes fell onto her hands, wrapped around the small teacup. "You look…nice," he felt obliged to tell her.

Solemn, she thanked him. D'Becca lowered her eyes since his rested on hers longer than she felt at ease with. "This is really good tea, by the way."

"I think you said that already."

"Oh, I did, didn't I." D'Becca was on the verge of feeling—this guy was a little too…He was starting to make her feel much too self-conscious, something D'Becca had not felt in a long while.

"Are you through here?"

"You mean in the bookstore?"

"Yeah."

"Well, yeah, I guess. Why?"

They walked through city centre where a variety of shops dominated the quaint streets near the pier and landed a stone's throw from, what the locals loosely referred to it as, "the centre." The streets leading into Rawn's neighborhood, between the pier and the centre, were wide-laned and tree-lined. The homes, built close to one another, were modest but charming, unlike the homes in D'Becca's neighborhood, Crescent Hills, on the opposite side of the centre. The real estate was pricy, and pseudo-baroque with meticulously manicured lawns that were so perfectly green they looked synthetic. Where D'Becca resided, each address in the rolling neighborhood had luxury vehicles parked behind gated driveways. Conversely, street parking was the norm in Rawn's neighborhood, because many of the dwellings had no off-street parking.

"I've always liked this side of Crescent Island. It's attractive," D'Becca said.

"What? As opposed to Crescent Hills?"

"The real charm is west of the centre. Expensive real estate doesn't necessarily mean charm."

"Why are you living on Crescent Island? Why not live in the city? Seattle has some really great neighborhoods."

"When I was working in Paris and Milan, I dreamed of coming home—back to the States—and living in a place that was unspoiled. A well-kept secret. I couldn't believe it when my dream came true. I mean it was here all this time and I didn't even know it. I'd heard about Crescent Island—the forgotten island—but never came over here. A few years back I had this large, really great apartment on Queen Anne Hill. I loved it, and not because it was also rent-controlled. It had one of those not-so-easy-to-come-by Seattle views—Lake Union from one window, and the Needle from another. Yet I wanted to be tucked away. Like so away from anything remotely urban."

"Do you like what you do—modeling?"

"Sometimes."

"I'm not familiar with your work, and I don't mean to…Isn't modeling a short-lived career?"

"Is that your way of saying I'm too old to be modeling?"

"No…" Rawn chuckled.

"I like that about you already."

"What's that?"

"You're earnest." D'Becca had a faraway look in her eyes. "I think about it often. Not being prepared. When I lived in Paris, there were days when I'd walk through each *arrondissement*. I was very much alone. When I wanted to remind myself of why I was there, I'd walk through the Jardin du Luxembourg, or I'd sit in the church in Saint-Germaine-des-Prés for hours. It was something about that church. I didn't have a franc to my name. Yet I was so happy. I didn't know it back then, but I was. Happy."

"I can see you in Paris broke, and happy. You would make the most of it, I can tell."

"I came to Seattle without anything except a small, cheap bag I bought at—it was a store like Kmart. It was stuffed with Tees and denim, which I lived in back then. I was this skinny girl, sixteen, if you can believe that. I wanted to go to L.A., but Seattle was as close as my three-hundred dollars could take me, and far enough from my small North Dakota hometown that could smother you to death."

"Things appear to have worked out." D'Becca did not deliver one of her spirited comebacks. Rawn looked over to her. "So have you got any other plans?"

"I need a back-up plan for my back-up plan since the first back-up plan failed." She chuckled, attempting to camouflage what she genuinely felt. "Unlike you, I don't have fancy degrees. I self-educated myself when I came to Seattle. I spent every moment in the library when it was open learning about everything. I remember trying to get through the *Bhagavad Gita* one summer, but I wasn't ready for that. My first year in Paris, I even tried to read *Dangerous Liaisons* in French. I'd read most of the book on the Métro, but I spent just as much time referring to my French dictionary. It's how I began to understand French. Anyway, I read some of the great poets, like Rumi and Gibran. I read Gandhi books and I must have read and studied every speech I could get my hands on by the Kennedy brothers and King. I learned Spanish completely on my own, and I can speak it pretty well. I was a glutton for all kinds of knowledge, and with only a GED."

"Did you eventually learn French when you worked in Paris?"

"I never really learned the language. I can have short conversations in French, and there are words I can say with a really sexy accent," she joked. "But I hung around mostly American and British models. Other models I often worked with…their first language was Dutch or French or German, and they wanted to improve their English…I picked up the language here and there. I actually speak *fran-glais*. Can you speak French?"

"My family's Haitian. They speak French and Creole."

"But not *fran-glais?*" she teased.

"Not *fran-glais*."

She looked over at him. Through her travels and throughout her life after leaving North Dakota, D'Becca had befriended black men. She never saw a black man in the way she *saw* Rawn.

"You have discipline, that's good," Rawn said. It brought D'Becca out of her wandering thoughts. "Have you thought about going back to school?"

"I was all about becoming *somebody*. I wanted to be relevant, and I also needed to survive. Besides, I eventually managed a really great life back then. When you're in the middle of loving your life, you don't think about the future that much. And, besides, I was into a lot. Drugs—mostly E, but it was like the thing everyone did so… And I slept around. But I'm not particularly proud of that part of my story. I see it so clearly now, and that makes life so fascinating."

"What's that?"

"How we learn in hindsight instead of learning in the process." Her mind wandered. "I grew up too fast. But because I did self-educate myself—that's the part of my story I'm most proud of."

"Story? That's interesting."

"What about you? What part of your story would you frame?"

Rawn was attracted to the fact that D'Becca was so quick-witted. She was clever.

Before he could respond, and out of the blue, a hard rain descended from the mysteriously dark sky, mixed with mothball-size frozen raindrops. Instinctively, Rawn reached for D'Becca's hand and said, "Come on, let's go to my place. I'm a block away."

Hand-in-hand, they jogged through the hail and rain—the overlapping cherry blossoms, which speckled some of the streets in the neighborhood, offered them a degree of shelter.

The apartment was dark when Rawn unlocked the door and they went inside, catching their breath. In quick strides he walked across the room to illuminate the space. D'Becca stood by the opened door, the clearly audible sound of heavy rain striking against the asphalt. She wanted—needed—to leave. She did not trust herself to stay, even for a little while. Her afternoon with Rawn was intrinsically pleasurable. It should end now while she felt strong enough, and the nascent of their connection was casual; there was very little depth. Her eyes lingered on the shiny black piano taking up a corner, and the books that were arranged all over the room.

"I like your place. How many books do you think you have?"

"Half of them are back-home. But here, probably one-hundred."

"There must be another room where you store them."

"The kitchen, my bedroom." Rawn shrugged.

D'Becca could not shake it: Rawn touched her intensely, and it was a new feeling; deeper than anything else she could recall being struck by before. "Amazing!" She swallowed hard.

"Let me grab a towel so you can dry yourself off."

Rawn left her in the living room and D'Becca shut the front door. She began walking around the generous room, taking in how personal and unpretentious it was. She decided Rawn had an artsy nature. She loved the black-painted hardwood flooring and generous windows. She started flipping through his albums and was surprised someone his age even bothered with LPs anymore. From the corner of her eye, she could see a photograph atop a set of books, and D'Becca was moved to reach for it because Rawn was posed with a young woman. It had to be his sister, Tera—the resemblance between them was striking. If their smiles were sincere, in that moment they were quite happy and the world owed them nothing. She returned the photograph to its place and walked to a chess set made of granite which was set on a small, round table. Gingerly she touched one of the pieces. D'Becca was not schooled in chess, although she was familiar with the pieces. Studying the arrangement of the pieces, she could tell Rawn was in the middle of something because a king, a bishop and a pawn were not in the initial position. Above the chess set, she was arrested by a stunning piece of artwork in an expensive-looking frame. The painting stood out in the otherwise unassuming room.

Rawn returned holding a towel. "Here you go."

She reached for the thick chocolate-colored towel and started to dry herself off. "Thank you. I was admiring your painting."

Rawn glanced over at the hanging artwork. "It was my grand-father's. He was an artist. When he passed away, he left some of his work to me. Perhaps you can see the New Orleans theme in his work."

"Yes, I do. I love New Orleans." She draped the towel around her neck. "Can I take off my jacket? It's soaking wet."

"Yeah, sure."

Rawn helped D'Becca take off her jean jacket.

"You must be a big fan of Dante Godreau. You have all of his albums."

With his head bowed slightly, Rawn replied, "He's...*was* a genius."

"It was so tragic, his sudden death. It reminds me how swiftly life can be taken away. There you are, standing in a bodega to purchase a pack of smokes..."

"I've always been a fan of Godreau's music," Rawn butted in. "He changed—his influence on a generation was incredible. It wasn't that widely commercial influence. But he managed to leave his flair on the culture, and he stayed relevant. You know?"

"I saw him once. In Rio de Janeiro. Did you know that one of his daughters lives in Seattle?"

"Really? I didn't know that."

She wanted to shift the mood. D'Becca sensed that Rawn was still moved by the musician's violent, recent death. "So... Can I see the rest of your apartment?"

A year from now, Rawn would not be able to recall how it got so far so fast, and why he invited D'Becca to his apartment. But a force would sculpture the outcome of that choice. His decision was not necessarily reckless but no doubt impulsive. And in that moment Rawn concentrated more on how unsure of himself he was feeling more so than the impetuosity of the situation; it was not how he generally handled situations with a woman. He always made sure he had an *out*. "Sure. Come on."

They entered the large kitchen where books were piled in various areas of the room. Bottles of wine were in a simple wine rack and majority of them with Chateau Ste. Michelle labels. A cookbook was set on the counter like it had been looked through that morning; and there was an espresso machine and French press. At one end Rawn made a corner into office space, and a computer and dozens of books assembled the farmhouse console table and the sandstone floor.

D'Becca liked what she saw and in her mind tried to think of a way out—she was too attracted to Rawn, and she was at risk of losing herself.

"You make life seem so simple."

It was the first time Rawn detected some level of vulnerability.

Not just in her voice, but in her body language, in her eyes. D'Becca let her guard down.

"What do you mean?" Rawn asked.

"I don't know. In talking to you. Being around you. You make it seem so easy." She looked thoughtful and curiously apprehensive.

"Not always, but yes, I think life's pretty straightforward."

"God, I wish I could think like that."

"Come with me."

They walked a hallway ten feet long give or take, and Rawn stopped to point out another painting hanging on the wall.

"This one is quiet. Gentle. Not as extravagant as the other one."

"You have a good eye," he said. "I agree with you."

"You have a Steinway. Do you play?"

He wiggled his hand facetiously. "A little."

Rawn and D'Becca held each other's eyes. She moved into him and as natural as she took in the air she breathed, her tongue traced over his moist, full lips—it was as though she had been dying to do it all day. There was little, if any, resistance, but a part of Rawn was unwilling to take it to such an extreme level. He wanted this woman; there was no ambiguity whatsoever. When D'Becca kissed him, he was powerless to defend himself.

She unbuttoned Rawn's rain-drenched shirt which clung stubbornly to his deep cocoa skin. He slipped her soft-fabric tee over her head. They kissed long and hard; their passion was raw. With the tip of her tongue, D'Becca outlined a tattoo the shape of a music symbol an inch above Rawn's left breast.

"I'm out of condoms." While his voice was low, there was nothing vague about his words.

"It's okay." She continued to kiss his saline skin, dark and smooth as rich, velvety chocolate.

"No, really." Rawn intended to sound convincing.

With a whispery reply, D'Becca said, "It's okay."

"Let me double-check."

"I'm safe. Aren't you?"

When his nipple was in D'Becca's mouth, Rawn could not bring himself to suspend the rhythm. She pressed her collagen-injected lips against his chest like she had been trained. She unbuckled his leather belt and unfastened his in-style jeans.

"Where's the bedroom?"

In the dim room, with streams of the shadowy sky trickling in through the roof windows, D'Becca methodically removed every stitch of Rawn's clothing. Calm and seductive, she was confident, taunting him with a lick on his skin here, a sultry kiss there. She got excited in watching Rawn try to contain himself. When she caressed his full and hungry manhood, it aroused her. Since she was seventeen, D'Becca had not been with a man her own age, and certainly not one younger than she. Every lover—and even a number of what she called hit-and-runs—was at least ten years her senior, and taught her a number of ways to give men pleasure. Each man taught her something new, and there were some who taught her how to please herself. In retrospect, D'Becca could not recall every lover she had in some faraway land where she had spent nights and days and afternoons getting closer and closer to becoming the woman that would blow Rawn's mind. Likewise for D'Becca, she felt a violent tremor when he released himself inside her and it never felt like that before; and what she felt was so intense and urgent.

The quiet night was calm and extraordinarily serene. D'Becca, her breathing gentle, nestled into Rawn, her full breasts against his chest while she slept soundly. He was feeling the exquisite mixture of fear and elation. Later, when Rawn could look at the moment with clear, objective eyes, he would consider his lust for this woman—it was fierce and determined, and so much so he was willing to play Russian roulette with his life because Rawn always, always used a condom. In that impassioned moment, the chemical that created a severe pleasure sensation, a rush—epinephrine—kicked in. One afternoon, months from now, he would be sitting somewhere dazing blindly at whatever was in front of him, and he would ask himself *why?*

CHAPTER SEVEN

A humming sound interrupted Rawn's peaceful slumber. Somewhat disoriented, he raised his torso and searched the immediate area to see where the sound was coming from. When the humming sound ceased, he rested comfortably against the fluffy pillow and closed his eyes. No sooner than Rawn began to slip into a peaceful sleep, the humming started up again. Confused, annoyed, he rose from the bed and began tossing the covers around, knowing that the sound was very close by. Naked, he jumped from the foot of the bed and looked around, growing impatient and frustrated. D'Becca was gone. The light sleeper that he was, he should have heard—at least felt—her slip away into the cool, pale rays of dawn. The humming noise finally abated. Rawn collapsed on the bed and yawned. Once more, the humming started up again, and because it seemed closer to him than before, he got on all fours and began seeking out the bothersome distraction. When he looked beneath the bed, he located D'Becca's cellular hidden behind his shoe. Rawn reached for the silver-coated mobile and permanently silenced the ringtone.

She's got to come back to retrieve her cellular.

When he stepped out of the shower, water glistening against his satin skin, Rawn reached for a towel and fixed it around his waist. The telephone rang. He expected it to be D'Becca. After all, she left her cellular and he knew she would eventually want to get it back.

"Oh good, I caught you," Sicily greeted Rawn when he answered the telephone.

"Hey, what's going on?"

"I'm procrastinating doing laundry so I'm on my way to the mall on CI. I can drop by and pick you up. You want to come? We can grab something to eat."

Rawn entered the kitchen and opened his fridge and saw nothing he had an appetite for. "Nah, I'll pass." He grabbed an apple in the fruit bowl on the kitchen table. He cleaned it with his towel and walked through the apartment.

"*Rawn!* What exactly do you have to do today? Are you playing at the Alley tonight?"

Rawn sat at the piano and placed the apple on top of it. His shoulder balancing the receiver, he began to caress a few keys. "No."

Sicily sensed Rawn was not telling her something.

Before she started making subtle inquiries, he stated, "I might be hooking up with someone later."

Straightaway, Sicily was intrigued. "Hooking up? You mean like as in a *date?*"

In serene spirits, Rawn laughed. "Not a *date*, per se. But I might be…I could be spending time with someone later."

Sicily sat, legs folded in the lotus position, on the sofa holding a water tumbler. "So what does it depend on? You or her?"

"Neither, actually." Pecking at the piano keys gingerly, Rawn cradled the cordless with his shoulder.

"So did you finally get up the nerve to ask the waitress at Café Neuf on a date?"

"Come to think of it, I haven't seen her in a couple of weeks. Maybe she quit. But, no, it's not Imani."

Silence played through the telephone wire. Rawn continued to peck delicately at the piano keys.

"Okay, I get the hint. When it's share-worthy, you'll share. But if you change your mind, you can reach me on my cell."

Walking to the kitchen, Rawn took one last bite of his fruit and tossed the apple core to the trash like he would if he were shooting a ball into a hoop. He washed his hands and while drying them leaned against the counter. His mind traveled back on the night before, the day before, and the intoxication and anticipation that defined the entire day he spent with D'Becca. He recognized the verve that infiltrated his soul. He felt this feeling before—the rush that came with learning someone new and getting caught up in the start of something fresh, unfamiliar. When learning someone new came with a rush, a tease, everything else paled in comparison. But *this* thing—whatever it was—had a different feel. It was far more tangible than anything he explored in the past. He could not help but wonder was the whole experience no more than a spontaneous evening of memorable sex.

Sicily decided against going to the mall on Crescent Island since Rawn chose not to go with her. Besides, she had not been to a yoga class in over a week. On her way to class, with the yoga mat slung across her chest, she strolled leisurely through the neighborhood that she often thought she shared with every tourist that made its way to Seattle. It was a blissful smell—late summer; and yet her heart ached. Sicily never recalled feeling lonely and had no clue when the loneliness kicked in. For years her life was shaped by education, career aspirations and career demands, and a host of friends and family that sustained her. While in graduate school, as a thesis, she wrote a play and it impressed her thesis advisor. Sicily had no way of knowing how writing down her own self-discovery in a thesis would dramatically hijack her life. Before she could catch her breath, the play she wrote was being produced off and then *on* Broadway, and went on to receive several Tony Awards.

Her life was moving so fast back then, and people she trusted and loved were dropping out of her life and people she would come to learn were not to be trusted were becoming the center of her life. All kinds of invites came at her left and right: art gallery openings, network morning talk shows, *Charlie Rose*, *Nightline*, speaking appearances, and stays at five-star hotels at the expense of anyone but her. She spent much of that time numbed by the exposure that accompanied her public success, and she was emotionally unprepared for the dark side of high-profile achievement. So caught up in the rapture of the lifestyle, she forgot what sincerely mattered. Sicily, for a short period, was riding so fast and so high her attainment blurred personal boundaries: the values she had always lived by, and her spiritual ideology. The expectations that came with her height of success rocked the foundation of her worldview and she struggled between two worlds.

When she was approached by one of the most elite private schools on the West Coast, Gumble-Wesley Academy, to consider the position of headmistress, Sicily jumped at the chance. In doing so, she managed to recapture a lifestyle she was most comfortable with prior to her public persona and the social pressure that came with it. The first few years were calm and her life unfolded so simply in Seattle. And now—and it appeared to come from nowhere—Sicily deeply wanted to be with someone. She felt this desperate need to share her body, her mind, her *soul*.

When she relocated to the Emerald City, she felt terribly isolated. With an East Coast background, and having been raised and educated in the Northeast, the first few months in Seattle, Sicily was dreadfully out of her depth. The Pacific Northwest was vastly different; with its gloominess and dampness and intense overachievers. Quickly, she crammed her days with long hours at work. Time she had to spare went to charity, although she admitted to Rawn her altruistic nature was not altogether sincere; Sicily did it principally as a means to network. At some point, though, the time she gave to the community began to touch her spirit and it then no longer mattered what it could do for her social and career connections.

The overcast days that blended one after another began to take its toll. She would take weekend trips to visit friends in the naturally cool but sun-drenched climate of San Francisco, which balanced things out for Sicily. And not long ago, after five years on the West Coast, she began to notice a shift—first subtle, but gradually overt. She was at ease in Seattle and carved a wonderful life for herself; still, something not quite definable was missing, even while her life was uniquely harmonious. It was not until recently Sicily managed to figure out exactly what that vague lack was. Like many women her age that were childless and unmarried, her life was a balance of career, people she loved spending time with, and activities that filled up the empty spaces. She put herself out there time and time again and went on dates as often as she could make it happen, but of late she was becoming more and more pessimistic. Besides, it had been difficult to meet professional and single people in Seattle. Even though it attracted talent of all types from anywhere and everywhere because high-profile cultural icons—Amazon, Boeing, Microsoft and Starbucks—were locally headquartered, Seattle was, even though culturally adept, nothing more than a bedroom community.

Sicily browsed through shops along Rainier Square, her mind preoccupied. School would soon start and thus would rearrange her schedule. This was the time of year she longed for—a new season, and the striking hues of fall. It was this time of year Sicily truly loved. Her heart opened and felt light, and she grew increasingly curious at what might be coming around the corner.

There was a sense of anticipation. Every Pacific Northwest autumn brought her something special, something random.

Z Gallerie was one of her favorite stores in Rainier Square. She could stay all day. When she purchased her Pioneer Square loft, Sicily dropped in Z Gallerie expecting to get decorating ideas but ended up staying for nearly two hours, and she overspent. Afterward, and despite feeling a tad guilty, she stopped at Torrefazione Italia and overindulged in a decadent pastry and a blissful double-shot latte. Now, while browsing through the surprisingly empty store, she was less excited, more disheartened. In spite of that, she was determined to buoyant her spirits. She caressed chic, comforting pillows and admired exotic colors that gave her a hint on how she might redecorate the dining room. A splash of different hues would redefine its look. Perhaps a new piece—say a vase—in the corner of the room would jazz it up just-so. When Sicily turned to walk toward the vases nearby, a tall woman looking at shower curtains caught her eye. Although her back was to Sicily, it was without question she was the same woman Sicily saw at Kingfish Café in the company of Henderson Payne. *What the hell did she mean by blowing me that ridiculous kiss?*

Engaged, Sicily studied her closely. She was some number, that one. Her black Lycra pant clung to her toned curves, and the sleeveless black V-neck sweater exposed a tattoo. *Self-centered, obviously.* Of course it was blatantly apparent at Kingfish she demanded to be looked at, noticed. The woman turned so that her face was revealed to Sicily. When the vain woman looked in her direction, Sicily turned her back to her, dreading the idea that she might have spotted her. On impulse, she ducked behind a shelf of cookery and watched the tall woman reaching for her ringing cellular. Sicily was too far away to eavesdrop on the conversation, but the tall woman did not appear to be disappointed in hearing from the caller. She began to walk toward Sicily—either toward vases or candles. Not aware that she was even reacting viscerally to the total stranger, Sicily dashed toward the rear of the store and out into the seating area of Torrefazione Italia to steer clear of having a face-to-face with Henderson Payne's Kingfish Café companion.

"I didn't think you'd notice I even left, Henderson," Tamara said, reaching for a tall scented candle. She sniffed the candle to get a whiff of its bold fragrance. "I had back-to-back appointments with clients. I had to go home, shower, change clothes—I needed to look respectable. Remember, I hadn't been home in two days. And look, one of those clients is Sebastian Michaels's wife. I'm not name-dropping! No, look, my clients—and yes, Sebastian Michaels's wife is a client—they trust me because I present a certain..." Her laugh was free and girlish. The weak spot she still had for Henderson surprised her, but a year ago Tamara accepted the truth: Henderson would not leave Daphne, not even for her. "Well, I'm glad you made it home safely. Okay, baby. Love you, too." She released the call and pressed her lips together. For a few moments she stared at the cellular before replacing the lavender-scented candle.

Tamara was good at sensing when she was about to make an emotional purchase. Exactly why was she feeling so *unloved* all of a sudden? Could it have anything to do with spending time with Henderson for the first time in nearly a year? Did he open up places she thought she had closed? If she could get someone trustworthy to babysit the boutique, she might visit friends in Seville. She loathed Seattle when it began to segue into fall. Not only was it too wet and too colorless, it was equally so-so dull. She made her way toward the Fourth Avenue exit, and her mind started

awfulizing. *Why am I still in this dismal town? It's time to find some-*
thing new, and challenging. This place no longer serves me. It's only
been three years and I am already sick of this place. Why do I keep doing
this? What Henderson said to me the other night—was it true? Am I
always running away? And if he's right, what am I running away from?

She headed toward her leased townhouse near her "by appointment only" boutique, and Tamara could feel her heart grow heavy.
Usually she could pinpoint exactly what she was craving, but she
was losing her edge. She had absolutely no clue what she was in
the middle of. Every now and then she felt something lacking in
her life, and when the feelings barged in, they were concentrated
and she began to get this gnawing hunger. Tamara would jump up
and pack a bag and get out of her familiar surroundings, like she
had been on the run and authorities were closing in on her. She
was the type to circumnavigate her way in life; she never chose to
go through whatever she needed to go through. Especially intense
feelings. When she regrouped, her mood inevitably subsided and
she became homesick.

By chance, having been around Henderson, she was beginning
to feel the need to find some *thing* or some *one* to contribute to
her life in a much deeper way. By chance she needed to stop being
so caught up in herself and consider having a child. A child would
have to come before her own neediness; it would redefine and
reshape her life, but was that what she wanted? Seeing as how she
would turn forty in a few weeks, was time running out? Did she
want to raise a child simply because she momentarily felt that in
doing so it would add something to her otherwise empty life?
Tamara never felt the least bit maternal.

For years she convinced herself that Henderson would leave his
wife. In the beginning, when they first started seeing each other,
Tamara was merely attracted to him, and for all the superficial

reasons: his sex appeal, bad-boy façade, financial worth, who he knew and the fact that he could afford her companionship. In time, she came to know a deeper side of the man behind the controversial image and she fell in love with him. She dared not share it with another living soul, but Tamara waited for him like a desperate woman; like a first-class fool.

She used the keycard to unlock the entry to her building. When she reached into the metal mailbox to retrieve her mail, her cellular chimed. Not in the greatest of spirits, Tamara waited for the number to appear and debated whether she was really in the mood to talk to Pricilla, who was currently on a book tour. She wrote a self-help book about something having to do with *self* healing. *Can I deal with this fraud right now?*

"Hi, girl," Tamara greeted her friend. "Yes, it's good to hear your voice, too. Earlier I was thinking about you. Oh, really? So how's the book doing?" Entering the elevator, Tamara rolled her eyes, only half-listening to Pricilla, who stopped short of bragging about the fact that her second book had already outsold the first. Swiftly, Tamara checked her stack of mail. "Oh, fantastic! When will you be in Seattle?…"

With dry-cleaning in one hand and an iced coffee in the other, Rawn was in a serene mood. He strolled up his walkway, and the last person he expected to greet him at his doorstep was D'Becca. She sat on the edge of his small curve-cornered porch. "Hey!"

"Hey," D'Becca said back.

The silence between them played out for a few measured moments. Both stood stock-still, and they were feeling suspicious of the other. One waited for the other to speak; to broach a subject that would end the awkwardness of the moment. Whatever they talked about needed to progress past the night before, which, in the face of a new day, now seemed careless. For a hushed few seconds, they shared a gentle stare. They began to speak at the same time—

"My cell…"

"You left your cell…"

In unison they laughed.

"Aren't you going to invite me in?"

He chuckled while taking in the full essence of her.

Rawn had never known a woman like D'Becca. Granted, his repertoire was limited to women not as sophisticated, and he was only intimately familiar with black women. At the very least, there was a cultural distinction. D'Becca was enigmatic, and that darkness she was cloaked in turned him on in a huge way. There was no way for Rawn to see what was coming.

"Come on," Rawn said, inviting her in.

They made love, and on the most intimate of terms, all through the afternoon and into the early evening. When they were not stimulating each other, they lay breathless and held each other with tender closeness. Their conversations were neutral—topics that were not superficial, merely safe. And what they were sharing in those moments had nothing absolutely to do with yesterday and would have no bearing on tomorrow. When D'Becca, reluctant, stepped out of his bed and slipped on her boyshorts at close to two in the morning, Rawn urged her to stay over. But she said, "I have to go." She could not stay overnight. "Why?" he wondered aloud, although he wished he could take it back; he had no intention of speaking the thoughts that were cluttering his head. She had a booking out of town.

"I'll take you to the airport," he offered.

"No, I'm fine." She smiled warmly. "Good-night, Rawn. And

stay in bed—don't move." She kissed him with sincere affection, leaving a hint of her feminine scent and the very essence of herself in his moonlit room.

Once he knew she was out of the apartment, Rawn lay in bed thinking about the past day or two. Whatever he was feeling was amazingly sharp. He began to doze, but his mind kept him from falling into a deep sleep. Ideas played inside his head about D'Becca. Rawn had not considered such questions about women from his past, but specific inquiries started bouncing around his psyche: Was he coming from the heart or was this strictly hormonal? Did he have any real interest in D'Becca as a *woman?* If he never saw her again, would it matter? Finally, and most significantly, did he respect the woman that slipped from his arms like a thief into the dark, crescent moonlit night?

CHAPTER EIGHT

W hen D'Becca returned to Crescent Island, calling Rawn was at the top of her agenda. Their week was spent Rollerblading along city centre square, and the trails along the scenic park. They sat on the candlelit terrace at Café Neuf and talked and laughed with such rhythm and abandon; and walked the sometimes lively, sometimes deserted pier at night holding hands like lovers who had not known each other very long—that innocence, unfamiliarity, lack of intimate facts that was so transparent in two people with very little history. When a mild autumn took over the ending of an unusually dry summer, the days grew cooler. Still, a generous burst of prolonged sunshine draped over the island.

Since running into her at the bookstore-café, the amount of time Rawn spent with D'Becca surprised even him. In any given moment that he was with her, he decided then and there whatever they were experiencing had reached its plateau. Lo and behold, she would call him and ask if he wanted to do anything, and even though Rawn had plans, he cancelled them and acted in accordance with her invitation. It never mattered to him where the relationship was headed. At the time it was seemingly inconsequential. And even when he sensed something secretive about her, or that she could sometimes be elusive, Rawn did not ask questions in large part because it was not about knowing all the details of D'Becca's life. It was quite simple: he was *into* this woman, and picayune details were plain trivial.

The days and nights they spent together blended swiftly into weeks and any free time they had to spare they spent together, sharing most of it at Rawn's. Upon returning from a spur-of-the-moment trip to Victoria with D'Becca, Rawn was greeted with four messages from Sicily, two messages from his best friend, Khalil, and one from a musician friend inviting him to play at Moody's Jazz Alley the following evening.

"Where are you?" Rawn asked Sicily when she answered her cellular.

Waiting for a red-eye near the pick-up bar, Sicily replied with, "And where have you been?" The way in which she spoke came across possessive. "I've left…"

"I know, Sicily. I'm home."

"But where have you *been?* I thought something might have happened to you." When he chuckled, Sicily was not amused. "Rawn! You always return my calls. What was I to think?"

"I was out of town."

"Out of town? Did you go to visit Khalil in L.A.? You didn't mention you were going down to SoCal." Sicily reached for her order and pantomimed "thank you" to the barista. Making her way to the door, she continued, "You're being awful evasive."

"Listen…"

"You know, you really need to get a cell phone. It's 1999 for goodness' sake."

"You and Khalil are always on my back about…"

"The landline is so passé. That's as old-school as basic cable. You'll be lucky if you can find a payphone in a few years. So where did you go?" She stepped into her SUV.

"Come to the Alley tomorrow night."

"The *Alley?* You know I don't like that place." Sicily adjusted her drink in the beverage holder. She switched the mobile from one ear to the other. Turning over the engine, she said, "I assume you're playing."

"So I'll see you tomorrow night?"

She pulled out of the Third Avenue parking space and reached for the omnipresent paper cup. Ever the multi-tasker, Sicily held the drink while managing to balance the cellular against her ear, and turned effortlessly off Third onto Seneca, halting for a pedestrian in the process. "Yes, I guess. What, about eight, nine?"

"Nine sounds good."

Plein Soleil was playing at a theatre in the University District. Years before, Rawn read the novel, *The Talented Mr. Ripley*, on which the film, *Plein Soleil*, was loosely based. When he read that the 1960s dark and suspenseful thriller was playing for one week and its run would end in two days, he invited D'Becca. After the film, and while walking to the car in the parking lot adjacent to the U-District theatre, D'Becca suggested they go to Palomino for dinner.

On the drive to the restaurant they talked spiritedly over each other while discussing the film. Determined to make Rawn jealous, D'Becca went on and on about the sociopath played by Alain Delon—"he's *so* sexy"—and she was sucked in by the stunningly photographed Tyrrhenian Sea. Rawn, on the other hand, saw the film from a strictly artistic perspective. He was impressed with the Hitchcockian plot and progressively perplexing schemes, the melodrama—a slow and methodical build-up—which he believed was severely lacking in popular blockbusters of the late-twentieth century.

Generally energetic and a good place to be seen, it was a slow night at the restaurant. Prior to being served after-dinner coffee, the ambiance at their table changed within moments solely because of the sound of D'Becca's ringtone. She took her cellular everywhere—when she sat on the toilet, in the shower, even when she jogged. Finally, Rawn asked her what was the need for having her mobile phone at her fingertips 24/7, and she offered him a justification he would later consider lame and having something to do with her work. It was progressively turning into a way of life, using mobiles in public places. She was terribly presumptuous, assuming Rawn was not put off by her talking on her cellular to Troy and Beth Ann and Savannah and someone whose name she never dropped while in his presence. He went along with it as much as his temperament could tolerate, but he tactfully pointed out to her a few times that she lacked basic manners by taking a call while she was in his company. Sitting across from her at the table, he said, "How important can it be? It's almost ten o'clock, and we're on the West Coast. For once, don't answer."

D'Becca detected an edge in his tone. Not once had Rawn been testy or provoked by anything she said or did prior to that evening. Accordingly, she chose not to answer and slipped the mobile in her clutch bag, but the discord put a damper on the entire evening—a good film, a nice meal, and agreeable company. It was not until they ran through a heavy rain—and they laughed generously about having to run through rain yet again—did D'Becca laugh from the heart. Her charming, girlish laugh captivated Rawn in some way, and her inexplicable spirit. He was not certain, but he sensed he had fallen entirely in lust with this woman.

When they were in the car, he said, "Let's go to your place tonight. It's been a month since we hooked up at Street Two Books, and I've never been to your place."

She turned over the engine, and while pulling out of the parking space, asked, "Why are you suddenly so interested in going to my place?"

They were at the street signal at Second and Union. Rawn had been distracted by the fashionably dressed mannequins in a men's clothing store window. He turned to meet her profile and mindlessly studied her staring out into the night beyond the windshield wipers tossing the steady rain to and fro. He replied soberly, "I've never been to your place. That's all."

A few years after Crescent Island was established in the early 1900s, a Scandinavian immigrant purchased commercial property on the east side of Crescent Lane, a quiet, tightly constructed street tucked out of the way. Directly beyond the pier, Crescent Lane could easily go missed. The street was small but retained some of the most exclusive commercial property on Crescent Island, precisely because of its stunning views. In the early sixties, a black man by the name of Jesse Moody, who was the first person of color to purchase property on the island, approached the Scandinavian immigrant about opening a restaurant on upscale Crescent Lane. He was turned down flat and numerous other times subsequent to his initial approach. The Scandinavian immigrant's son was of a different generation and with a liberal mind-set, so following the death of his father and when he ran into Moody, the Scandinavian immigrant's son inquired if he was interested in space he had available. Not only a good businessman, the immigrant's son understood that the tone and texture of the ethos had evolved; consequently, Crescent Island—it was only a matter of time—would become diverse.

Many years had come and gone since Moody wanted to open his restaurant. He had been plotting the idea of a jazz club when he ran into the Scandinavian-American on the golf course. He explained his ideas. Because of the late-night noise, the immigrant's son suggested that Moody use space that had been sitting for quite some time in the basement of an art gallery with an alleyway entrance. Hence, the night-spot took on the name Moody's Jazz Alley. Since its opening in the early 1980s, it became legendary. Quite a few famous musicians strolled in unannounced to play sets with the regulars. Moody's did not only put Crescent Island on the map; the once very private island became one of the state's primary tourist traps with romantic bed-and-breakfasts and tranquil parks and hiking trails. Despite the Washington State invasion as a result of advanced technology and the invasive dot-com phenomenon, the island maintained a rare quaintness with extraordinary scenery from every direction.

More commonly referred to as the Alley, Moody's was a popular jazz club that attracted an eclectic crowd. Saturday was the Alley's busiest night, and to negotiate parking was always a challenge since there were no parking lots within walking distance. D'Becca lucked out when a couple was getting into their car no sooner than she pulled into the crammed and narrow street two blocks from the popular night-spot. She made her way toward the club through the cobblestone alleyway and heard the familiar and sensuous sound of George Michael's voice singing "Father Figure." To her surprise, there was a queue wrapped around the building. Rawn had not warned her that she might encounter problems getting into the club. D'Becca bypassed the crowd of laughter and high-pitched conversation and walked up to the bouncer. He was a large man with a shaved head and nicely trimmed goatee; cubic zirconia studs sparkled from his ears, and his eyes were veiled behind sunglasses the Blues Brothers made fashionable back in the day.

With a few musicians in her past, D'Becca knew how to work the situation. "Good evening," she said, throwing the bouncer adequate charm. "I'm a guest of Rawn Poussaint."

The bouncer, who did not change his demeanor, looked D'Becca up and down. He fingered the doorman. When he approached, the bouncer leaned into the doorman and spoke a few words low enough so that D'Becca could not overhear. The man nodded and looked straight into D'Becca's eyes. "Come with me," the doorman said.

When the bouncer removed the black velvet rope to let her enter, D'Becca heard a few derogatory and irate outcries by those still hoping to get in, and the protests followed her straight into the noisy club.

Moody's was packed. D'Becca was told by the doorman that she would most likely have to stand since there were no seats at the tables or at the bar. She pulled out her cellular and leaned against a wall. "Hey," she said. "I know it's late. Are you alone?" D'Becca waved to a passing waitress. "How's South Beach?"

"Yes?" the waitress greeted D'Becca.

"An apple martini, please."

Wordless, the waitress made note of D'Becca's request in her head, and before she could walk away was stopped by another club guest wanting to order a drink.

"I'm at Moody's Jazz Alley. Have you ever been?" D'Becca looked around the crowded room and did not see Rawn anywhere. She suspected no one in the club would recognize her. "Rawn's playing, that's why. No, he plays piano. He played 'Moonlit Sonata' for me and I was floored. He's really pianistic, Troy. No, at the Alley he plays jazz. Well, what can I say, he loves jazz. He's crazy about Godreau. Yeah, the jazz pianist killed last month. Look, it's not what you think. I like him. He's complex but still easy to be with. And yes, I know what I'm doing. Troy, I miss you. Maybe that *is* why I started a friendship with Rawn, I can't really be sure." D'Becca listened for a while, and ended her call with a solemn, "Sure, okay. Love you."

Ten minutes later the cocktail waitress returned with her martini, and D'Becca gave her a twenty and told her to keep the change. She squeezed through the crowd attempting to make her way to the bar to find somewhere to sit. A gentleman always gave up his seat for a lady. By the time she reached the bar, Rawn and four other musicians were walking to a corner of the room and stepping up on the elevated platform. The area closest to the platform was set up like a cozy living room with intimately arranged velvet chairs, sofas and ottomans of deep charcoal and vermilion, and lava lamps that glowed in psychedelic colors against the dim backdrop of the club. The area was roped off, and beyond the rope were conventional nightclub tables which surrounded the platform. On nights when a band did not play, the platform was made into a dance floor.

The musicians began to play a breezy number, and when it ended, they eased into another song. In this number the primary instrument was the piano, and for most of the performance Rawn played solo. D'Becca never saw him so loose, so secure within himself. It struck her how much time she had spent with him but had not noticed the lights and shadows of his persona; and she realized how intimate they had been without really getting to know each other. In her head she saw him as a mysterious yet sensitive schoolteacher, not someone who sat in a dim club, traces of alcohol mixed with body odor and perfume and cologne suspended in the air, playing jazz. But he was fully in the moment, and played like it was his life's calling—a divine purpose. When the song ended, the crowd clapped and whistled. A loud, masculine voice bellowed, "*Bravo!*" from the rear of the club, and cheery voices, slurred by alcohol, echoed praise. The energy in the room was electric.

While she leaned against a wall, Sicily could see clearly that Rawn was in a good place. In fact, she had never seen him so free-spirited. While he was a confident personality, there were times when she felt Rawn overanalyzed life and he could be quite deliberate. An old soul, it was his gift and his curse. Rawn once told Sicily that he felt an unexplainable connection to his Haitian grandfather. He was a solitary man, contemplative, but he was likewise engaging and quite amusing. Sicily thought Rawn was describing himself. Despite her swearing that she would never set foot in the Alley again, something in Rawn's voice persuaded Sicily to cross the floating bridge. After two years of knowing him, Sicily had not yet figured out how he managed to talk her into things.

The musicians had ended their set when a man holding a penny-colored drink in his hand stepped up to Sicily. "Howyoudoin'?" he asked ever so nonchalantly.

This man and everything outwardly about him was the very reason Sicily loathed the Alley: she had to switch up. To be polite, she replied, "Good, thank you."

"You like da band?"

Sicily took a small sip of her burgundy wine. "Yes."

"Can I refill that forya?"

To get a better read on the man standing in front of her, Sicily met his dark and narrow eyes. She put on her public façade and said, "No, I'm good." She hoped that her voice came across neutral. "I have to drive back to Seattle. One's my limit. Two if I drink it an hour before I get behind the wheel."

"Oh, baby." The man grinned. "Ain't chew responsible." He eased in closer because he wanted to make sure she could hear him over the noise—the chatter and laughter and a duet by Babyface and Stevie Wonder playing. He pressed his free hand against the wall, moving even closer to Sicily to the point she felt trapped.

Sicily smelled his musk, which might have indicated he had not bathed or showered prior to dressing up in his trying-too-hard suit and coming to the club. He attempted to mask that fact by putting on strong cologne. *Or is that Aramis I smell?* Sicily was rather embarrassed for the man. Besides his less-than-impressive style, the shirt sealed the deal for Sicily. A polyester blend, it was unbuttoned to expose several gold chains tangled into a large gold medallion. *It's so Mr. T!*

"Are *you* a man who's responsible?"

"Oh, yeah, baby. I takes responsibility."

I takes responsibility?

She dropped her eyes in her drink. "There's a woman out there who'd be lucky to meet you." She stood off the wall the color of Sangria, and to put the chitchat to bed, said, "I need to find my friend."

"Hey, listen, I'm Rodney. What's yo name?"

"Sicily."

"Sicily? Wow!" He never stopped grinning. Perhaps his most redeeming physical trait was his teeth. They were amazingly white. "That's like Cicely Tyson, right? That's one fine woman!"

Sicily extended her hand. "It was nice chatting with you, Rodney."

Rodney held Sicily's hand momentarily before he reached down and kissed it, and flabbergasted, Sicily's eyes almost popped out their sockets. When he looked into her eyes, he said, "Whoever said eyes was windas to the soul, they musta' been talkin' 'bout you, lady. Are them your real color? I mean, you know, are they contacts? Don't matter; I feel somethin' in yo eyes."

The Alley gained a reputation as a need-to-be-seen-there place. While its status leaned more on the musicians who played there, both renowned and local, the crowd it attracted made it *the* place to hang out. Hence, the clientele expanded, mostly because of word-of-mouth. Moody hired a bouncer from New York to weed out the riffraff. Apparently, the bouncer's judgment was question-able. For a few quiet moments, Sicily held Rodney's shifty eyes. She retrieved her hand, and with an insincere smile, turned to leave, saying over her shoulder, "Take care, Rodney." He tried to keep the conversation going with something about exchanging e-mails, but Sicily could not bear another minute in his presence.

Rawn stepped up to the bar behind D'Becca, who was having a conversation with a woman seated next to her. The bartender, Derric, leaned against the bar engaged in their exchange. Rawn walked up behind D'Becca and playfully placed his hands over her eyes. She let out a girlish snicker while removing his hands. When she looked up to him, her face softened. D'Becca took his face into her hands, and they kissed each other on the lips. The woman seated next to D'Becca said, "Bejesus! The pianist. You were absolutely fabulous. You should be opening up at Carnegie Hall, or somewhere." Her small teeth shaped her especially jovial face.

Rawn acknowledged Derric behind the bar with a nod. "Thank you," he said to the sociable woman.

"No, really. You're good. How long have you been playing?" The chummy woman picked up her rainbow-colored drink with an umbrella tilting to the side and sipped through the straw like she was drinking Kool-Aid.

"I started taking lessons at seven."

"A rum and Coke, Rawn?" Derric yelled over the lively voices at the bar and Brian McKnight's "Anytime" playing.

"Sounds good. Thanks, Derric."

"My treat," the friendly woman said, not directing her comment to anyone in particular.

"Candace was proposed to. She and her fiancé went shopping for rings today."

The friendly woman, Candace, held out her hand to show off her engagement ring. Rawn's left brow lifted subtly at the size of the karat. "Congratulations," he said.

"There you are!" Sicily approached Rawn at the bar. "I was looking high and low for you. I collected two business cards and then there was *Rodney!*" Sicily eyed her good friend. Gingerly, she brushed loose curls away from her face.

"Sicily, I want you to meet D'Becca."

Sicily and D'Becca shook hands.

The friendly woman extended her hand and said, "Candace."

D'Becca leaned toward Sicily and spoke over the music, "Rawn speaks fondly of you."

"Well, thank you, Rawn."

Rawn reached for his rum and Coke on the bar and took a drink.

"Can I get you something, Sicily?" Candace asked.

"I have to drive back to the city."

"Candace is celebrating. Her boyfriend proposed to her this morning, and on bended knee," D'Becca shared with Sicily.

"Mazel tov!"

"Why, thank you. Is this your first time at the Alley?"

"Every now and then Rawn drags me here."

Friendly Candace retrieved a twenty from her bosom and placed it on the bar. "I'm going to the ladies," she said. "D'Becca, can you hold my seat?" She slipped off the stool.

"I'll keep it warm." Sicily propped onto the stool and crossed her ankles.

"Rawn tells me you were a playwright in another life. And your play made it to Broadway. I'm in awe!"

"While I might be a member of the Guild, I never really saw myself as a *playwright*."

"But you did win a Tony?"

"I won a Tony," Sicily confirmed. She discovered by accident just how to downplay the subject of her former life with a particular tone and a few firm and choice words. She could skillfully change the subject if she shifted the attention on to the other person and away from herself. "You look familiar. Have we met before?"

D'Becca reached for her second apple martini. "Not that I recall."

"It'll come to me. You definitely look familiar."

"Let's toast," D'Becca said.

"To what?" said Sicily.

D'Becca was euphoric: "To new friendships!"

Chateau Ste. Michelle sat on over 3,500 acres in Woodinville, approximately twenty miles northeast of Seattle. The French-style château had two state-of-the-art wineries, and Rawn and Sicily, over the two years since acquiring a friendship, had attended several summer concerts; and on two separate occasions when Khalil was in town, brought him to the Chateau for a wine tasting. When Sicily called Rawn early that morning and invited him to go with her to the Chateau and he agreed, he appreciated that the invitation was no more than a ruse. Sicily was dying to know all the details related to his relationship with D'Becca. Rawn was confident it was the only reason for the ride out to Woodinville. By telephone he could control the conversation to a degree, but a thirty-minute drive with only the two of them was another matter altogether.

Rawn and Sicily browsed through the winery. He nursed a Merlot and she a smooth Sauvignon Blanc. When they arrived, a wine tasting was about to start and thus they decided to join the group. Before leaving, they decided to look for wines to buy. Sicily, more spontaneous, chose a sparkling wine for Sunday brunch occasions, while Rawn, more deliberate in his decision-making, was still undecided. She picked up a bottle and read the label, occasionally glancing over at Rawn being so bloody fastidious.

"I seriously never thought I would see the day."

On the drive to Chateau, Sicily had broached the subject of D'Becca. But it was dropped when the disc jockey on the radio mentioning that the station, along with a number of other jazz stations across the country, was going to have one minute of silence to pay homage to Dante Godreau, the famed jazz pianist killed some weeks ago. Afterward, they had talked about Godreau the rest of the drive and Sicily had forgotten all about addressing the D'Becca issue.

"See what day? What are you talking about, Sicily?"

"You. My best friend, my Dream Guy. Sleeping with a white woman!"

Rawn had a temperament that clashed with Sicily's and yet they got along beautifully. Because she had not yet learned how to get him worked up, it pissed Sicily off. He said to her in a composed voice, "Get over it, Sicily."

"I'm only saying...I never took you as a black man who would dip into white chocolate."

"Isn't that old-school thinking?"

"Old-school? No, old-school thinking is not having a cell phone. Look, Rawn, you're an educated man. You come from a family with some paprika. But would your parents be content with their son bringing a white woman home for Thanksgiving?"

"Where did Thanksgiving come from?"

"You said on the drive here that you were going home for Thanksgiving, and didn't you say something about D'Becca wanting to meet your parents? I've never...Well, I did meet your father briefly."

Rawn looked over to Sicily, and the fact that she was jealous of D'Becca took him totally by surprise. It was not because of D'Becca's race; Sicily was green with envy.

"What bothers you about D'Becca? And I mean besides the obvious. She was impressed with you."

"That woman is really into you, Rawn. What is this? I mean taking her to the Alley! You've never taken a woman to the Alley to hear you play. Except Jas, and that's where you two met so that doesn't count."

Rawn's shoulders slumped; he bowed his head.

"Okay, does Khalil know? About D'Becca, I mean?"

"We haven't talked. He's been working in London. Some deal he's making with a soccer player over there."

"I can see Khalil. He loves to mix it up, so he puts it. I have to tell you, I am—I'm too through! You know, you could have prepared me." Sicily replaced the bottle of wine. "I knew she looked familiar. I see her modeling lingerie in the truckload of catalogues I get in the mail. How old is she?"

Rawn did not like the tension that floated back and forth. Subdued, he blindly reached for a bottle. He really preferred that Sicily give it a rest already. He wished that she extended him the same courtesy he gave to her and not judge whom he chose to get involved with. Friendship did not necessarily work that way. It was the strangest thing to Rawn: Sicily did not want him; however, it became apparent that she preferred that other women not be with him either.

"You always attitudinize this issue. Why should you care whom I choose to be with?"

Sicily inspected the immediate area like someone ascertaining whether or not it was safe to steal something. No one was in earshot of them, but she lowered her voice nonetheless. "If you can't meet a black woman on Crescent Island, they are plentiful in Seattle. Fine women. Gorgeous women. Successful, together, brilliant, and alone women! I see—I meet women like this on a regular basis. Why choose a white woman? That's all I'm asking. And look, you really had a strong attraction for the waitress at Café Neuf. I'm curious, did you ever so much as ask for her number? I mean, looks to me like you didn't waste time getting D'Becca into bed. How hard did you work this, Rawn?"

"I can't believe you're standing here suggesting that I consciously *chose* D'Becca over Imani... It's—you surprise me, Sicily."

"You surprise me!" she snapped.

With a sigh, Rawn shook his head. He was more turned off by Sicily's inflated contempt than anything else.

"Answer this: are you going to stand here and look me in my face and tell me color never played any part in your being with D'Becca? Not even a tiny bit?"

Rawn rarely got rattled, but Sicily was doing a good job of making him feel uncomfortable. "I'm not sure; I can't say. But..."

"There are too many black men in this state hooked up with white women. And I don't get it! It's...I'll leave it there."

"So you'll never bring this up again?"

"I can't promise, no. But..." She exhaled a deep breath. "Let's go. My stomach's growling."

Sicily headed for the cashier, and the attitude she left hanging on the air was thick. With a near-empty wineglass in one hand and a bottle of Pinot Gris in another, Rawn was not prepared for Sicily responding so strongly toward his seeing D'Becca. Even while his relationship with D'Becca was not serious, it made him consider how others would feel—his parents, sister?

CHAPTER NINE

When the early traces of September arrived, it assuaged the fervor between Rawn and D'Becca. What they shared in the late-summer days came to pass and they were two people indecisive about what should come next. While she was in and out of town, Rawn had a hectic two weeks with his new school schedule. Subtle ambiguities between him and D'Becca first came to light one Friday afternoon. Rawn had taken the ferry into Seattle to pick up a suit he had fitted at a clothing store on Sixth Avenue. He was walking back to the ferry terminal when he turned onto Second Avenue between the Seattle Art Museum and Benaroya Hall. He spotted D'Becca, who was scheduled to be out of town. Rawn called out to her. It started to drizzle. He took lengthy strides to catch up with her but was held up because of a small group of preschool children roped together, and led by a young woman with a shaved head and oversized hoops dangling from her ears. A messenger on a mountain bike whizzed by and distracted Rawn momentarily. He called out to D'Becca once more, but she vanished into the interior of a midnight-blue BMW. The silver raindrops slipped off the luxury automobile's severe polish. The windows were tinted so Rawn was unable to get a good look at the driver. He stepped up onto the sidewalk, opening his umbrella. Curiously, he watched the midnight-blue sedan merge into steady traffic.

For Rawn, what he and D'Becca were into was quite simple: two people taking care of each other's present needs and wants. There was no commitment; they did not adapt to any standard relationship rules. They were consumed by passion and physical lust. The first month they were eager and fascinated with each other, which preserved their imaginary connection. Their time was spent eating G Street Wok and feeding each other with chopsticks in bed, or they had something delivered and ate by soft-lit lanterns on Rawn's patio. Those were the days when each and every night their bodies tangled into a knot and they had intoxicating sex. Old needs and wants were contented, yet a new set of wants and needs began to solicit attention.

When school resumed for Rawn, more and more their schedules and routines began to conflict; and D'Becca was in and out of town more frequently. Between his teaching at the Academy and her one-, two- and three-day trips out of town working, they shared time by candlelight, embracing, and talking *in* bed. Along the way the passion between them tempered and a mysterious emotional connection developed. But this was the natural maturity of two people spending a great deal of time in each other's company. Even while sex sustained their relationship, it was no longer the reason for their spending time together.

Rawn knew full well that his immediate interest in D'Becca was completely sexual—it was not about *feelings*. When he was with her, he sensed that she had a boundless desire for intimacy and used sex to attain that closeness with another human being. Rawn longed to experience an emotional and sexual connection with a woman—the two blending simultaneously. He cared deeply for his ex-fiancée, Janelle. Their lovemaking was all well and fine, but something—a detail he could never quite put his finger on—was sorely lacking in their relationship. In the long run he began to trust that his love for her—it was not strong enough. Whenever they made love, for Rawn it was as though he was making love to a dear *friend*. Not a lover who was similarly his friend. When he had time to contemplate over his relationship with Janelle, he came to trust that they wandered off into a sexual relationship because they had common interests and enjoyed being in each other's presence. Yet in the end, they were better friends than they were lovers. With Janelle there was pleasure, but not that fire and desire, what Rick James and Teena Marie sang so soulfully about in their passionate duet.

D'Becca, on the other hand, had a dark, dark secretive place and Rawn became obsessed with her enigma. He kept trying to get closer, and closer. The idea that she might have wanted only sex from him and his sex alone rubbed him the wrong way, even if that was his own agenda. His ego, but more importantly his male pride, would not—could not—go there. It seemed the harder he pushed away the idea of her wanting him purely to satisfy her physical urges, the more the notion came at him—doggedly. At the time it was happening, he did not care enough to ask questions or get too caught up in the essence of who D'Becca really was. Much later, when Rawn had the time to analyze the numerous intimate moments spent with D'Becca, he would recollect nearly every single one of them with such amazing clarity.

When brilliant red and marigold leaves of a new autumn surfaced, a discernible nudge piqued Rawn's attention: D'Becca's often abrupt unavailability, the Beamer, and things that did not appear to add up. Still, Rawn was not altogether open to what was directly in front of him. Halloween or thereabouts—when the clocks were set back—was when particulars began to peeve him. Sometime later, he would recall it so lucidly because the elementary students were making costumes for trick-or-treat, and went all over the Academy decorating classrooms, the hallways, and the lunch-room in black and bright orange, with spider webs and ghosts and goblins. It would be clear to him even more so because it was Sicily's favorite time of the year.

One late afternoon Rawn walked the longer route home from the Academy that led him down Lombard Avenue, the street D'Becca lived in. In subtle ways the neighborhood reminded him of the community he grew up in nearby Denver. The breathtaking trees with leaves of burnt umber, and pumpkins propped on porches and stairs at the entryways to swanky high-priced homes. Although he knew she was still in New York and would not be home for another three days, something drew him to D'Becca's street. When he came upon her teal-colored car parked along the vacant curb, it did not register immediately. Rawn had offered to take her to Sea-Tac, but she said she would drive herself and leave the car in the short-term parking lot. "If I don't have a hired car, I park at the airport," D'Becca had explained. Instinctively, he walked up to her townhouse, and a pair of bright red galoshes was left on the ceramic slated porch. He reached for the buzzer on her intercom, but old-fashioned common sense made Rawn freeze. He did not know why, but his mind held him at bay. In what way would fate have been altered if he had chosen otherwise? He went back to the sidewalk and looked up at her townhouse. He stood there for a few minutes before he ultimately chose to leave.

While walking home, he decided not to rush to any conclusions as to why D'Becca was back from her trip but had not telephoned him. The very thought of her not calling him when she was back in town pushed him around, and the idea boxed with the dark side of his psyche. He loathed the thinking about it, the fact that it kept recurring in his mind, over and over. He was angry. Had she lied to him all along? Had she even been to New York? After all, Rawn had no hotel name; no way to contact her in New York. If he called her on her cellular—she could be in Timbuktu!

When he reached his apartment, he felt a strange sensation rip into his heart, dripping residuals of escalating doubt into his rapidly pulsing soul. First it was the discreet man in the Beamer. When Rawn inquired about it, D'Becca said so casually, so convincingly, "Oh, no. That wasn't me," but deep in his core Rawn knew full well that it was her. Now this? Was he blinded by some illusion?

It was a strange night. Rawn drank a Corona, and before starting a second, fell asleep on the leather sofa. The following morning he had what he decided had to be a migraine and reached for ibuprofen in his medicine cabinet and chased four down his throat with a tall glass of orange juice. He called Khalil and left him a message on his home phone: "Call me, man." Showered and dressed, he walked to the Academy. He took the long way; he was going to stop to speak with—no, confront—D'Becca. It was something he had to do. He *needed* to do it, he told himself. He was going to clear this thing—whatever this thing was—up!

D'Becca's Z3 was not parked in front of her townhouse, and when he went to her door and rang the bell, she did not answer. Calm came over him; a gentle sense of ease. Perhaps she let someone borrow her car and they took the liberty of keeping an eye on her place—watering plants, feeding fish, or whatever. While that was certainly plausible, Rawn had never met any of D'Becca's friends. Her closest friend lived in Deauville, and Troy, whom D'Becca spoke to every day, was in South Beach overseeing the opening of a gym. What would Rawn have said to D'Becca if she did answer her door? He had never been invited to her home, and as far as D'Becca was concerned, he had no clue where she lived. However, a few days after seeing her step into the Beamer in Seattle, Rawn wanted to make sure that D'Becca did not live with a man. One night, when she left his place, Rawn followed her home.

For the first time he recognized that he was too accessible to this woman, but that did not work both ways. A sense of betrayal began to gnaw at him. Rawn was a man who could look in the mirror and say to the reflection, *I approve.* But of late he was second-guessing himself. He was not one to be ambivalent. When he reached the Academy, he stopped in his office before heading to his classroom, and he called Khalil and said with unconscious urgency, "If you're in L.A., call me, man."

CHAPTER TEN

Tamara was unable to concentrate on the spreadsheet. She lost track of time a few hours ago. It was shortly after ten and she had not eaten since breakfast—a cup of black tea, and a smoothie made with fresh strawberries, organic bananas, soy milk, one egg yolk, and protein powder. Her intentions were not to skip lunch, especially since it was her biggest meal of the day. But two clients dropped in unexpectedly to be fitted, and because they were wives of men who had high-paying professions, Tamara could not find it in herself to turn either one of them away. They were shopaholics, and they filled their spare time almost entirely on superficiality. Before Tamara knew it, it was dinner-time; yet Tamara was too distracted and so she had no appetite. Emblematic of a small enterprise and self-run business, she wore several hats. Since time presented itself, she decided to go through invoices and approve them for her accountant.

Once she got started, she was on a roll. When she initialed the last invoice with a simple oversized T, Tamara did everything she could—checked her e-mail, updated her contacts, collected receipts for her quarterly taxes, started sketching a design, and opened junk mail—to avoid calling Henderson. She even found herself starting to look forward to seeing Pricilla, her college roommate who was quite the celebrated author since the publishing of her best-selling book a few years back. But of all the people! Tamara could barely tolerate Pricilla on her best day. Not sure how she pulled it off, but Pricilla managed to take advantage of the self-help phenomenon and succeeded. While she could depend on Pricilla, Henderson was the one person she could talk to. When they hung up from their sometimes two-hour phone calls, she felt more like the self she trusted. He knew how to reach her in ways no one else could. She liked his mind. And she was not ashamed to admit it even to Henderson, the deceit that came with maintaining a relationship with him when Daphne demanded that he not, felt good. While they were no longer physical, Tamara still depended on him as a dear, dear friend.

According to the time on her laptop, it was short of eleven o'clock and Tamara was not only wide awake, she was antsy. If she left now and went home, it would be nearly impossible for her to fall asleep when her head hit the pillow. She would toss and turn until dawn. With a small but unhindered view of the city's skyline, and even in the refuge of beautiful things, the severe stillness throughout the condo often made her feel depressed. A year ago she hired a part-time assistant, and occasionally when she took a trip, she trusted the young fashionista to watch over Threads. But the assistant fell in love with an up-and-coming Canadian musician and moved to Vancouver, B.C. to be with him. Tamara had not found anyone she trusted enough; thus, she could not up and leave. The melancholy was asphyxiating her. She turned off the laptop and decided to listen to music and have a glass of wine. Oftentimes, in moments like these, music and wine or half a joint brought her back to herself. But the pills, they did a number on her libido.

With champagne in her hand—the only alcohol she had in the fridge—and Dante Godreau playing soothingly from the speakers, Tamara relaxed on the plush velvet chaise in the rear of the boutique and crossed her ankles. The mellow sounds of Godreau would do the trick, even if it was a Band-Aid covering up a gunshot wound to the neck. Yet she had not been stretched out long enough to let the stress of her day go before she leapt to her feet. Her problem—when Tamara stood still, she felt empty. Whenever she allowed herself to be quiet, to be *still*, she had good sense enough to recognize that there was nothing there. Although she dared never to speak such thoughts aloud, she felt it deep in her soul. Of late, she posed questions to her reflection in the mirror while applying bronzer to give her face a fresh glow: Who the heck are you? What do you stand for? What are your values? Tamara had always been a contradiction. She was fearless and yet terrified. Both kindhearted and self-centered. Loving and equally detached. An only child, she never had to share. Sometimes, particularly when she was in her self-pity stage, she deeply regretted the DNA that genetically linked her to her parents, seeing as they had a hand in shaping her story line. However, Tamara could be remarkably sensible when she was emotionally objective and thus took full credit for the outcome of her life. Even though she was a successful designer and popular musicians wore her designs to the Grammys and American Music Awards, and on-the-rise actresses wore her designs to public events, she felt like a failure. Were it not for her parents, Tamara would not have had the luxury of jet-setting from continent to continent until she could figure herself out. Were it not for Henderson, she would not have her own boutique and design apparel for an affluent clientele.

So often she wished she could go back in time and start all over again and wipe the slate clean. She would not make the same choices twice. Even if it meant she would have to expunge every pleasurable second she experienced with Henderson, Tamara would not hesitate; she would do it in a heartbeat. If it meant that she could be admired, respected, and genuinely *awed*.

Regret was a waste of time, but isolation made her feel lonely.

Standing in the back of the store, a tight fist pressed against her hipbone, and the flute of champagne she held at its rim, she dared herself to cry. *Don't you even!*

The telephone rang and she swirled around as though she heard someone attempting to break in. It was late; no one would think to call her here this time of night.

Tamara rushed to the ringing telephone, placed the flute on the cluttered desk and reached for the receiver. Panicked, anxious, she said, "Hello?"

"There you are," Henderson said.

Tamara tried to clear her throat—the tears that were dying to get out were trapped in her gullet. "Hey, baby. How did you know I'd be here?"

"Okay, what's what?"

"What do you mean?" Tamara reached for the flute and took a gulp of the bubbly.

"We play Portland. Drive down."

"Henderson…"

"It's not about that. Look, I know you, Tamara. Something told me to call you. I—maybe it's the connection we have… If you weren't so stubborn… Woman, I want to see you. You're the one friend who has a lot of my secrets locked up in your head. Come to Portland."

Tamara could feel her anxiety subside, like the stillness of the terrain after a tsunami. She would never confess it to Henderson, but she was not sure where her feelings were going to take her this time. The fact that he called her suggested to Tamara he was worried that she might be struggling. *I should refill my prescription, and to hell with my libido. I'm celibate at the moment anyway.*

When they made history together, she could go to dark places from time to time. Henderson often managed to talk her down, to pull her back from the brink. Since they did not talk as often as they used to, and saw little of each other, he was entirely unaware of how intense and unpredictable her moods were becoming.

It took no more than a moment for her to switch from freezing cold to sizzling hot. In her good-natured voice, Tamara said, "Of course I'll come to Portland."

A nor'easter was moving in, but Imani was hardly fazed by the clusters of heavy winds. She sat on a bench, making every effort to distinguish between her mood swings, trying to make sense of their fleeting nature. How long had she stared at the silver pigeons pecking at breadcrumbs nearby? She was not exactly sure how she found it in herself to break down and call Blaine, and what route she took to get to Washington Square. She could have taken a seat on the bench ten minutes ago; it could have been hours for all she knew. Of late, she lost track of time. One minute she was peeling a banana, the next she was sitting in the middle of the floor of her father's loft, her face buried in her hands, crying and having the hiccups. Imani was forgetting to brush her teeth.

Five weeks ago, when she called her half-sister whom she spoke to a few times a year, Imani had no idea her call would mutate her life forever. The change was so dramatic. Her sister Kenya was six years older than Imani, and Kenya's mother and their father had a one-night-stand while he was touring in Canada thirty-nine years ago. Kenya resented Imani, and Imani always assumed it was because their father was more present in her life growing up, not to mention he married her mother while he had no more than a casual relationship with Kenya's mother. The bitterness was often too intense to bear, so Imani kept her distance. But she did feel love for her sister and managed to be civil through phone calls, and generally during the holidays. Their father's birthday fell on New Year's Eve; they met every year in New York to celebrate. Dante arranged for the same suite at the Marriott every year. They could see the ball drop on Times Square from their window. It had been a ritual since Imani was five years old.

When she had returned Kenya's call, Imani was unsuspecting of what she would hear on the other end of the telephone wire. Following her conversation with Kenya, instinctively, she had taken the ferry back to Seattle. One of her Pilates instructors lent Imani her cellular, and while crossing Lake Washington, she had made calls to the airlines, the pet hotel, and Jean-Pierre. Once she made it back to Seattle, Imani had driven blindly through mild afternoon traffic to her houseboat in Lake Union. Hurriedly, clumsily, she had pulled clothes from hangers and grabbed lingerie from drawers and toiletries from wicker baskets and had rushed to Sea-Tac and sat through a crowded and turbulent red-eye across every other northern state only to wait over an hour for a taxi at LaGuardia. The cabbie had dropped her at the door of her father's loft in TriBeCa, and Imani was so exhausted but too excited to even rest her eyes.

Kenya had greeted her with a constrained, "Finally! But it's too damn late!"

"What do you mean?" Imani had stood in the doorway of Dante's loft holding a designer overnight bag she had had for years. Her tired eyes were hidden behind a pair of sunglasses she bought on L.A.'s Melrose Avenue during one of their rare trips together to do something fun and irresponsible. More importantly, the trips were so that she and Kenya could bond.

"I can't believe you're still wearing those sunglasses, Im."

"What do you mean *it's too damn late?*"

While Kenya called their father Papa, Imani called him by his birth name, Dante. His Lower Manhattan loft overlooked a small and quiet park on a criss cross street. Imani had flopped in a large, thick down-blend sofa. Glimpsing at the mauve-colored building across the way, she had watched a few nannies talking to one another in the park, baby strollers at their heels. When she was an infant, her mother would roam through that very park humming her lullabies. Imani always reflected back on her childhood in black and white, never in color. It was so strange. Removing her sunglasses, she had exhaled audibly, and her face had turned into a painful grimace. Through her tears, she could see Kenya standing a few feet away. Quite thin, Kenya was clad in old Levi's with holes in the knee, and her T-shirt endorsed McGill College in fading letters. Because her vision was blurred, Imani could not be absolutely sure, but she thought she had caught a grin on Kenya's makeup-free face.

With her hands trembling, Imani had wiped the tears from her eyes and along her cheek and chin. The pain she had felt went so deep she thought she might die from it.

Kenya had combed her fingers through her glossy black hair. When she sat on an ottoman, her elbows to her knees, she had asked, "Do you want to see Papa, Im?"

In a barely discernible voice, she had told her sister, "Yes."

"Do you want to get some rest first?"

She had sniffed and wiped snot that rested between her nose and plump upper lip. "No. No, I need to see Dante."

"You have to be tired. You flew all night."

"No," she had said. "I couldn't sleep right now."

"All right. I'll change and we can go."

Weeks after her father's funeral, she sat in the square and it began to empty out. The nor'easter was sweeping up dust and debris along the walkways. Despite feeling the chill in the air, Imani did not move. She never felt so alone.

"Imani?"

Slowly, she raised her head, and by the sight of Blaine's handsome face Imani's heart slowed and right then she knew she would be at the very least, safe. Blaine was a man Imani trusted to be "the one." He was much too good-looking for his own good; yet it was his looks and well-recognized cleft that paid his way through Princeton. Imani trusted that by now she was over the fact that he was one of her not-so-bright judgments. The moment her eyes met his, she realized she missed him more than she ever could have previously conceived. *Love is bountiful.*

He bent down and placed his large hands over hers to ease her nerves. Her eyes looked fatigued and bloodshot. Faint lines gathering along the corners of her eyes were not there when he last saw her, and they gave her beautiful face maturity, character. He figured she must have been crying herself to sleep for weeks, if she slept at all.

"Why haven't you returned my calls?"

"I don't know." Imani bit her lip.

"I'm sorry I couldn't get back to the States in time for Dante's funeral. I feel bad about that." He placed his palm gingerly against her cheek and tried to offer her his seductive grin.

Imani pursed her lips and attempted to say something, but the words were too stubborn.

"Come on," Blaine said. "Let's go to my place." When she did not stand, Blaine took her by the hand and said, "Come on, Imani."

When she came to her feet, her legs were wobbly. She collapsed into Blaine's warm and generous arms.

CHAPTER ELEVEN

Rawn's Jeep climbed the elevation on I-5 leading back into Seattle. The city's skyline—commonly referred to as the Emerald City—gleamed in the distance like Oz. Khalil was talking on his mobile and Rawn, in a good mood, grinned. Khalil had been talking about Moon for a couple of months now. He met her in London at a cocktail thing hosted by someone they both knew. Moon lived in London, and Khalil's job had him travelling between L.A. and London for six months. When their relationship became more than casual, often they had conflicting schedules, but because Khalil had more autonomy, he could do business remotely—in hotels and airports, or on a flight. As long as he had his laptop and BlackBerry, he could accommodate Moon's European schedule, Khalil was trying to talk Moon into going skiing with him during the holidays, but she wanted to visit her family in Indonesia.

From day-one, which was on the first day of school when they were in sixth grade, Rawn and Khalil were best friends. Over the years, they had each other's back without asking why. They showed up no matter what else was going on in their lives. A few years ago, Khalil dated a sitcom actress, and in time he would come to admit he became too fixated with her. It freaked the actress out, mainly because she had been aggressively pursued in the past, and once even stalked. Khalil was arrested when he showed up at her quaint Manhattan Beach house unannounced. He had not received a notification about her filing a restraining order against him.

Rawn was on the next Alaska Airlines flight to L.A. to bail him out. For years they found themselves attracted to the same girl. In ninth-grade they actually fought—punches and kicks, the whole works—over a girl. They arrived at the principal's office with bloody and torn shirts. But when they finally got beyond it—and they never talked about it again—they let nothing or no one get in the way of their friendship. More specifically, a female.

Rawn finally managed to squeeze his Jeep into a parking space on First Avenue.

When they entered New Orleans, the restaurant was bustling. Without reservations, they had to wait for a table. Once they were seated, musicians started playing.

"Call Sicily, man. She lives around here, right?"

Khalil was six feet tall with the physique of a quarterback. With his trademark five o'clock shadow, he had fine features but deliciously full lips, and everything about him made a statement that he was self-important. Apparently others agreed, for he managed to attract people without much effort. Rawn, more exoteric, was the opposite of Khalil.

"Call her."

"Man, damn. What's her number?" Khalil punched in the numbers Rawn recited. "Pretty soon, nobody's going to know numbers by memory." When Sicily answered, Khalil shifted into bait mode: "Hello, baby."

Sicily sat in her overstuffed chair by the wall of windows. An exotic full moon poured into the room. She should have followed her perfectly tuned instinct and not answered the telephone. With a frown on her face, she said, "Excuse me."

"I've been thinking about you. And I'm talking dirty thoughts, too, baby."

Sicily's torso straightened. She had been reading over minutes from the Academy's last board of trustees meeting. In a velvet jogging suit, a glass of wine nearby, Godreau's newly released greatest hits playing soulfully in the background, she finally managed to relax. After a meeting with a student's parent that afternoon, she was still unsettled. She put it on herself, she knew that; but as a matter of course, Sicily felt like she had to tread cautiously with the parents of the students at the Academy. These were parents that knew a trustee or was a friend of a friend to someone on the Academy's board of trustees. Now an obscene call? *What the hell!*

"You have the wrong number," she said into the receiver. She was about to punch release when she heard the caller breathing heavily into the wire. With a smirk, Sicily said, "Please! Get a life."

Khalil and Rawn were laughing. In a low voice, Rawn said, "Tell her we're at New Orleans, man."

"I guess you don't remember me."

I would remember giving a man my number.

"Your memory doesn't seem to be serving you too well..." Khalil kept at it.

Slowly, her lips shaped into a wide, pleasing grin. "Khalil!"

"I punked you good."

"Hell, you were starting to freak me out. Where are you?"

"I stopped in Seattle. I'm only here for a minute, but I want to see you."

Sicily exhaled her breath, gazing over paperwork she was swimming in spread here and there. "I..."

"We're at New Orleans. By the time you get here your order will be ready. Tell me what you want."

Even Sicily had a hard time resisting Khalil. It was the plain truth—he knew how to charm a girl. "All right. Okay! It should take me twenty minutes, thirty tops door-to-door. Order the pan-fried oysters for me."

"Love you, baby."

She made a kissing sound into the receiver and Sicily was thunderstruck by how excited she was, resting in the knowledge that she would see Khalil. "See you soon." Rawn was the man she would have hoped for if things were different, but when she got together with Rawn and Khalil, Sicily flirted on the outside and tingled on the inside—she loved being in the circle of their masculine charm. Khalil was emotionally complicated; the type women were often drawn to because he was a risk. Rawn was elusive, intellectually seductive, and punctilious. The two were an even balance. If they could bottle their respective chemistries and put it on the market, they could come back a few more times and never go broke, irrespective of the Dow.

"She's on her way," Khalil said. "Before she gets here, you want to explain to me why I had to make a detour. What the hell is going on, bro?"

CHAPTER TWELVE

T he sky was heavy while a dense, temperamental sun shifted through thick and dark clouds. From the corner of his eye Rawn could see a squirrel perched on the windowsill. He reached for the Sunday *P-I* and began to flip through it, tossing *Parade, Pacific Northwest* and endless coupons to the floor, and skipped to the sports page. He spent all morning reading and grading eighth-grade essays. Their minds were clever and sharp and he marveled at their wit. Was it the access to so much information, and by merely clicking a mouse, that made them more informed than he was at thirteen?

When they were engaged, Rawn and Janelle agreed to a plan: establish themselves in their respective careers, travel and then purchase a home. Both came from tight-knit families, so for them having children was a done deal. Rawn understood it so plainly now: he was not ready to be married, and certainly not emotionally ready to raise children. How many men met a good woman but at the wrong time?

When the telephone chimed in the distance, he dashed for the ringing cordless on his desk in the kitchen, and anticipated—hoped—that it would be D'Becca.

"Hello!"

"Did I catch you at a bad time?"

His face relaxed. "Hi, Mama. You know your timing's always good."

Rawn cherished talking to his mother. Their conversations were more like two friends and less like mother and son, and Rawn's day was fuller after their talks. Yet it was not his mother's voice he had so wanted to hear.

"I can't believe I caught you. It's been rather difficult to catch you these days."

"Is something wrong?"

"Why should something be wrong? Because you're grown doesn't mean I can't still worry about you. I've gotten no calls…"

Rawn butted in with, "I've had a hectic few weeks, Mama. Since school started, my schedule's been all over the place. With the events committee meetings the first weeks of school, and then… My schedule's all nice and neat now…my calendar's more predictable."

"You don't do so well with predictability."

"Is Tera still in London?"

"She'll be back next week. By the way, she said she had dinner with Khalil."

"Yeah, he breezed through here. He mentioned they hooked up."

"Who is she, Rawn?"

"Excuse me?" Unconsciously, he frowned.

"You're always distracted when you meet someone new."

"Mama, come on. That's not true."

Mrs. Poussaint exhaled. She said to her son, "Ask anyone who knows you. Ask your father! Ask Tera or Khalil. What's your good friend's name there—Sicily? Ask her. You get distracted every time you meet someone, even if it's not serious or doesn't lead anywhere."

Rawn was not going to have this conversation. D'Becca was not someone he needed to discuss with his mother.

"Okay, you're going to do the silent treatment bit with me. I didn't call to dig into your love life, Rawn. I wanted to let you know before your father called so you wouldn't be blindsided."

"Blindsided about?…"

"He's going to be in Seattle."

"Where's Daddy now?"

"He's in Portland on a consultation, but he's speaking at a medical convention in Seattle."

"And when will Daddy be in Seattle?"

"He'll call you. He's probably only going to be there overnight. Although he might stay an extra day if it doesn't rain. He'll want to play golf."

Rawn took a deep breath. "I assume a round of golf won't kill me," he said sarcastically.

When he finished talking to his mother, Rawn flicked the channel to the first of two football games he had planned to watch. Second quarter was just starting. At half-time he dashed to Fred Meyer for groceries. By the day's end he was bored and it was not altogether clear to him at the time, but D'Becca's presence had reshaped his life. When she was not in town, there was a palpable void. When exactly did that happen, he wondered.

Rawn met his father at Pier Eleven on a cool and misty Friday evening. They embraced and Stephen Poussaint eagerly began to discuss the conference in the city, and how he wowed Seattle's elite medical community with his powerful speech. He was a man with a demanding presence. When *Lady Sings the Blues* was a hit film, Dr. Poussaint was often told he was a striking resemblance to Billy Dee Williams. He was tall and large, and Rawn's cognac-colored eyes were identical to his father's, except mellower, kinder. Dr. Poussaint was barely a teen when his parents left Port-au-Prince and made their way to America. They settled in New Orleans.

His father gripped his son's forearms like he so often did with Rawn. It was his way of testing any control he might still have had over his son, even now when he was his own man and chose his own way in life. He said, "Didn't I see you a month or so ago?" With a curious brow, he concluded, "Something has changed."

Laughing, Rawn said, "Come on, Daddy. I made reservations at Rochelle's."

Holding each other with manly affection, they walked the pier toward Rawn's parked Jeep.

Rochelle's was a popular cuisine on Crescent Island. It attracted clientele from Seattle, Bellevue, and even as far south as Tacoma. Nestled at the end of an abandoned cobblestone street, the best way to secure a table was by reservations, but even then it was a hit or miss. Regulars typically did not bother to reserve a table. The restaurant was semi-full, and Rawn and his father talked through their meals and were now waiting for Rawn's dessert, the restaurant's popular soufflé, and Dr. Poussaint's double-shot cappuccino. Rawn knew that his father had avoided the conversation about his continuing to work at Gumble-Wesley Academy. For months he tried to talk his son into taking tenure at university. Preferably Stanford; it was Dr. Poussaint's alma mater. But Rawn preferred guiding young minds along the path of knowledge and fresh wisdom.

"So what's Khalil up to?"

"He was here. Did Tera tell you that when she went over to London they had dinner?"

"She said they went clubbing, too." Dr. Poussaint reached for his glass of sparkling mineral water.

"I take it you missed that article of him in *Savoy?*"

"Your mother mentioned something about that. Something to do with his being one of the top twenty-five sports agents in the country. How many black sports agents are there anyway?"

"I have no idea how he managed it. But he's representing Henderson Payne now."

Dr. Poussaint finished his glass of carbonated water. "I knew he'd land in a spot that would exaggerate his relevance. Khalil has balls but lacks substance. He's so much like his father."

With downcast eyes, Rawn chuckled merely to appease Dr. Poussaint.

"You know, his old man and I bet…it had to be about ten, twelve years ago, which one of you would marry first."

"Surely you didn't bet that I'd marry first."

"Actually, I did. And this was before you and Janelle were engaged. Khalil is…" Dr. Poussaint smirked. "So cocky. You, Rawn, are more… You're like your mother."

"Is that supposed to be a bad thing? Because your tone suggests that it is."

"My tone suggests no such thing. That's your problem, Rawn. You analyze too damn much. Get out of your head every now and then."

Rawn reached for his lemon water and took a long gulp.

"So, who's this young lady you're seeing?"

"What makes you think I'm seeing someone?"

"Your mother, she's the one who believes you're spending time with someone. Of course I told her it was not possible because it wouldn't be like you not to share something like that with me. But the moment I saw you at the pier, I knew."

"You knew what exactly?"

Dr. Poussaint looked over his shoulder like he was looking for someone. "Where's our waiter? I asked for a cappuccino ten minutes ago. Didn't you order dessert?"

"The soufflé's made to order. It takes about twenty minutes. You should have ordered one. It's good."

"So where do you think they had to go to get some espresso, Italy? Anyway, I'll take a forkful of yours if you don't mind."

Only moments later the waiter arrived with Rawn's soufflé and Dr. Poussaint's cappuccino. "Here you go," he said, and placed the dessert and creamy espresso on the table. Attentive, he refilled Dr. Poussaint's glass with mineral water. "Can I get you anything else?"

"We're fine. Thank you."

Dr. Poussaint took a good and slow look around the restaurant.

"Bon appétit!" said the waiter.

When the waiter departed their table, Dr. Poussaint said, "We're the only black people in here." In a condescending tone, he added, "Well, there's a busboy!"

"The last time you were here you liked your meal. I thought… that's why I made reservations to guarantee we got a table."

"What the hell do you see in Crescent Island?"

Crestfallen, Rawn picked up his fork and started to eat the decadent soufflé.

The mist from the previous evening produced a striking turquoise sky the following morning. While the air was brisk, it was a stunning fall day. Rawn took his father out for breakfast at Café Neuf, and even though he played golf only when he went home for visits, he decided he could manage a round with his father who played as often as his hectic schedule permitted. Rawn and Khalil never took to golf like their fathers. For Rawn, after twelve holes, he was ready to end the day. The sport was such a bore.

Growing up, golf was how Rawn and his father bonded. He was barely seven the first time his father took him to a golf course. He was a caddie for his father and his colleagues one summer, but by age ten, Dr. Poussaint had his son on the practice range. Rawn could never quite connect with golf, but intuitively he understood being on the golf course was where he spent the most intimate moments with his father. A neurosurgeon, Dr. Poussaint saw little of his children, Rawn and Tera, while they were growing up. Rarely did Rawn see his father at the dinner table or share breakfast with him. It took years to ascertain that it was common for children not to share breakfast and dinner with their father, although the reasons often varied. Were it not for Rawn's bogus interest in golf, he might have spent less time with his father as a boy.

Before taking Dr. Poussaint to Sea-Tac, he agreed to meet with Sicily and her friend at Union Square Grill for dinner. Rawn, Dr. Poussaint, Sicily, and Sicily's friend Lorraine were seated at a table in the crowded downtown Seattle restaurant waiting for their orders. Dr. Poussaint flirted harmlessly with Lorraine.

"What do you teach at the university?" Dr. Poussaint asked.

"Comparative literature."

"What exactly *is* comparative literature?" Sicily mocked.

"Daddy, did I tell you Sicily wrote *Opposites Don't Attract!?*"

"You mean that Broadway play, back in the—it had to be, what, ten years ago?"

"That one."

"Rawn never mentioned you were a playwright. I thought you were…Was there not some scandal or controversy over the issue of nudity in *Opposites Don't Attract!?*"

"In the beginning I guess it was somewhat controversial."

"It seems I read in *Ebony*, or somewhere… Did you not fall ill?"

"Daddy…"

"No, Dr. Poussaint's correct. I didn't have a nervous breakdown as was erroneously reported in various publications. I was extremely exhausted and needed to…I decided to go back to school. I loved that time in my life, but it was… It was a stressful life. Not to mention, public. You have to be emotionally prepared for that kind of life or it will…let's say, *trick* you."

"I remember it now, yes. In fact, Rawn's mother and I tried to get tickets. Twice when we were in New York, but it was sold out." Somber, Dr. Poussaint leaned forward, the gossip surrounding *Opposites Don't Attract!* coming back to him unmistakably now. "Yes…you were celebrated. I remember reading about you. You were young—in your twenties when you wrote *Opposites Don't Attract!*, were you not?" Dr. Poussaint looked closely at Sicily.

She nodded and reached for her wineglass, diverting her eyes. She met Dr. Poussaint only briefly a year ago. But Sicily understood from conversations with Rawn that his father was censorious, and he sat across from her and gave her that look—like he was critiquing her.

"In your twenties? I didn't realize you were *that* young, Sicily," said Lorraine.

"What? I'm old now? It was ten years ago."

Contentedly, Lorraine laughed and reached for her wineglass. "I actually caught *Opposites Don't Attract!* I haven't been to New York in years. Is it still on Broadway?"

"It ended its run about a year ago. *Rent*'s a hot ticket now."

"So, Rawn, Sicily tells me you're dating a model. Would I know her?" Lorraine said.

"If you get sexy lingerie catalogues in the mail." Sicily chuckled.

"You're involved with a model?" Dr. Poussaint inquired.

Rawn eyed Sicily briefly. After a few seconds slowly passed, he met his father's chestnut eyes.

"Why would you deliberately lie to me?"

Rawn reached for his glass and took a gulp of the liquor.

"You told me last night you weren't involved with anyone," his father said.

"I wouldn't use the word *involved*. I'm seeing her. It's not serious."

"How can you not be *involved* if you're *seeing* her? Your generation… Who is this model?"

"You wouldn't know of her."

"Is she famous?"

"What exactly does that mean?" Rawn said, irritated.

"Is she successful? Like...what's that model's name?"

"Naomi Campbell?" Lorraine asked.

"No, the other one."

"Tyra Banks?" Sicily said.

"Yes, her. That's what I mean by *successful*."

"How can you determine someone's success when you relate it to fame? Fame is not what it used to be, Daddy. Success and fame aren't synonymous."

"You're patronizing me. You know damn well what I'm getting at."

"Actually, I'm not sure that I do."

Sicily and Lorraine were gradually but surely growing uncomfortable.

Sicily, making every effort to be discreet, eyeballed the lively restaurant. Dr. Poussaint was a man of great accomplishment. Only twenty at the time, he marched with Dr. King in '63. Before he was thirty-five, he had performed brain surgery on a few men considered to be among Colorado's business elite. Although naturally classy, his charisma transformed into *street* in one split-second. Not his demeanor necessarily; it was his tone—hostile, belittling. He still had a few scores to settle in life. Sicily analyzed—that type of attitude went way deep.

Her eyes low, Lorraine nursed what was left of her drink. She contemplated on whether she should call for the waiter and order another bottle.

"Is she making a living strictly from modeling? Can she take care of herself? Because if she's unable to take care of herself, she'll eventually depend on you. Women like that...they're shallow and uneducated. They get caught up in drugs and have no self-respect. They're narcissistic."

"Daddy, that's...You don't even know her!"

Dr. Poussaint studied his son. "How old is this model?"

"What difference does that make?"

"How old is she?" Dr. Poussaint snapped.

"Thirty-seven," Rawn said, and he exhaled a deep breath.

"I thought models were over the hill by thirty!"

"I've met D'Becca. She hardly looks over the hill," said Sicily, eager to rotate the tense energy at the table by using a bit of off-handed humor.

"Where does she come from, Rawn? Who are her parents? And why isn't she here with us this evening?"

"She's out of town."

"How convenient!"

Before the meals arrived, Sicily was beginning to feel embarrassed for Rawn.

When their meals did arrive, Lorraine breathed a sigh of relief while Rawn pressed his back against the booth. It was difficult to determine if he was humiliated or merely perturbed.

CHAPTER THIRTEEN

"Who was Narcissus?" Rawn asked.

By the very fact that he did not direct his question at anyone in particular, the students knew their laid-back teacher wanted someone to open the discussion. Rawn spent less time testing his students than he did engaging them with fervent dialogue. He loved a good debate.

"He's like this Greek god or something...and he was very beautiful," a student volunteered.

"Okay," said Rawn. He stood in the front of the classroom dressed casually in Tommy Hilfiger, his arms crossed. "Is that it?"

"He was in love with his sister."

"Really?" Rawn said.

With a shrug, the student said, "Yea-*uh!*"

"Does anyone else agree that Narcissus was in love with his sister?"

"It depends on how you interpret it, right? I mean he *loved* her and maybe his feelings were intense. You know, intense for the love of a sister. But I didn't get it—that he was *in love* with his sister. You know, the whole Narcissus thing is about him being in love with himself. That's crazy, right? Because I don't know anyone who's in love with themselves."

"I was more interested in Ovid's interpretation," said Richard.

"Who's Ovid?" a student blurted out.

Not only Rawn, but every other student looked to Luce, a student on scholarship at the Academy. Although she had great potential, Luce had family problems which led to her extreme distraction at school. Her mother and father were going through a very messy divorce and she bounced between homes. All the teachers gave her the benefit of the doubt, but the Academy was a school that prepared its students for Ivy League universities. By ninth grade, each student at Gumble-Wesley had already read a handful of classics. Luce was not prepared to go to ninth grade. Rawn made every effort to work with her, but there was not enough time and attention from him or any other teacher. Luce was confused, and emotionally scarred with a low attention span.

Peter, who sat next to Luce and often ate with her during lunch recess, spoke up with some reluctance. "Luce! You know, Ovid had his own take on the whole Narcissus myth."

"Oh," Luce said, and went back to chewing on a fingernail.

Rawn winked at Luce and said, "Thanks, Peter." He walked to the aisle where Luce was seated and said, "Luce, tell us about Echo."

It was not Rawn's style to ask a particular student a question. He allowed each student to participate or remain anonymous. For those who chose to sit in silence, he judged them more harshly during tests and mid-terms. Every other student in the class leaned forward. Not so much because they wanted to hear what Luce had to say. No one would disagree: Luce was naturally gifted, which was how she managed to get into Gumble-Wesley. It was because she made the grave mistake of asking a ridiculous question, which led Rawn to believe she had not done her homework.

"Echo. She was in love with that faggot! She was so in love with the *idea*."

Luce's friend, Peter, was amused.

Rawn, standing nearby, nodded. "So, who believes that Narcissus was homosexual?" Rawn was not particularly pleased with Luce's answer because it would open up a subject he was not prepared to discuss.

"Homosexuality" was a hotbed topic for thirteen-year-olds. More often than he cared to, he pulled himself back when he sensed he went too far. Rawn understood the importance of emotional intelligence and taught within that framework. He urged his pupils to be curious about what obstacles try to teach you, and to respect diverse ideas and viewpoints. It was important, he often reminded them, to travel, be curious about the world, and to read lots of books. Generally he was conscientious whenever he insinuated his own ideas on his students.

"It's a Greek thing," a student blurted out. "Every Greek story there's some kinda androgynous stuff going on."

"I want you to write down 'androgynous' on a scrap of paper, and I want you to tell me what you think it means. Hand it to me before you walk out of this classroom," he said to the student.

"The tale is confusing," another student said, picking the topic back up. "I'm not sure I understand it."

"It's a metaphor," a student interjected.

Snickers came from a few students.

"One thing Greek fables teach us, Mr. Poussaint. They sorta reflect where our head is at different places in our culture," offered another student.

"Really?" Rawn walked back to the front of the class. "How's that?"

"Narcissus was awed or whatever...When he looked in the lake and saw his reflection, he was like confused and at the same time so blown away at himself. Think about it. Celebrities are a lot like that. Confused with their fame and popularity. You know, trying to reconcile with the whole *why me?* because of who they really are underneath the façade. I'm sure there's unresolved stuff going on; like self-doubt. You know, they ask themselves: Why am I so special; what have I done to deserve all this attention? But they're also like *awed* by it all at the same time. We're the ones putting them on pedestals. We're as confused and awed as they are. It's crazy. Image. Awe. What does it all mean? That's kinda what I got from Narcissus."

"You're suggesting that we pump famous people up at the expense of ourselves," Rawn suggested. "Okay. But let's not forget the idea of Greek myths," he said. "Narcissus is one of many." Rawn leaned against a wall, his arms crossed. "The story of Narcissus stopping to drink water from a lake and seeing his reflection for the first time and being *awed* by the beauty he sees reflected in the lake— is he spent by his own beauty? Is he the object of his own desire? Is he simply overcome: By an idea, a revelation?" Rawn walked to the center of the classroom. "I want you to really consider the myth of Narcissus in modern popular culture. Craig hinted at it when he brought up the whole concept of image and celebrity, and the subtext that surrounds each. Give me your ideas—knock out three, four pages—of how you see where Greek myth has an influence in modern culture. Choose quotidian influences: the Internet, styles, music. Literature."

Rawn left the faculty doors on the east side of the Academy, and what immediately grabbed his attention was D'Becca's sporty Beamer. She took up two spaces in the visitor's parking lot directly in front of the school. It struck Rawn that she was audacious, if not presumptuous, enough to show up at the Academy. While walking toward her car, he thought it through what he might say to her. Yet as he got closer, he felt a warm sensation flow through him, followed by a sense of raw pleasure.

The hood to the Z3 was down, and a winter-white silk scarf draped over D'Becca's head of pulled-back hair and swung loosely around her neck. She could pull off that Audrey Hepburn influence rather well. Rawn bent down and kissed her feverishly; his mouth had the taste of hunger.

"I'm so glad to see you." The softness of her olive-hued eyes gave Rawn reason to believe she was quite sincere, and she missed him as much as he had *longed* to be with her.

"Are you?"

A quizzical brow elevated, as if she were questioning him questioning her.

"Yes," she replied, her voice soothing and calm.

Rawn pulled up behind D'Becca in front of her townhouse. On the way to her place, he tried to resolve in his mind what exactly made her suddenly decide at this particular time to show him where and how she lived. They did not make it to the front door before Rawn was partially undressing her. D'Becca's anxious fingers fumbled with the keys to get into the townhouse. When the door opened, he eased her to the maple-colored hardwood floor and lifted her long and snug-fitted Lycra skirt above her hips. With the heel of her leather boot, she attempted to close the door, but her concentration was hopelessly distracted.

She was not wearing underwear, which gave him easy access. Every inch of him stimulated D'Becca—he had such rhythm. His thrusts were hard and deep. She bit his chin where a scar—which he received after falling from his skateboard when he was eight years old—left a subtle impression. When his breathing became heavy and his heart rate intensified, she began to feel a thrill, a rush, and her moans were soft and sounded like sad cries of a wounded animal in pain. He moved his mouth to hers.

She ripped opened his shirt. When she caressed his nipple gingerly with her forefinger, although a different size, texture and color, it was as ripe as her own.

He went limp inside her. D'Becca whispered, "I missed you." Her heartbeat was short and swift, and her inhalation and exhalation, long and vigorous. "I missed you."

The first signs of morning sun irradiated the moss green-shaded room and it was flooded with vivid harvest daylight squirting through shuttered windows, each marginally ajar. It was remarkable that the sun was so sharp; winter was only a few weeks away. Rawn awoke to the aroma of strong caffeine and moved his arm limply to touch D'Becca. Her side of the bed was empty. Although he knew that D'Becca jogged five miles several mornings per week, she had a way of disappearing before he woke up. Because he was a light sleeper, Rawn decided when she got out of bed, she purposely tiptoed, and went wherever she went—some secret life she guarded. He never bothered to bring it up, because when she left his place, what she did on her own time had not mattered; not really. He lifted his head and looked around the bright room. After taking a shower, he went downstairs with his usual morning energy, a towel wrapped around his trim waist.

"D'Becca!" he called out, and out popped her cat. Rawn forgot the feline's name. "D'Becca!" he called once more, going from room to room.

The townhouse was roomy with an elevated ceiling. It was a personally decorated place with art D'Becca carefully selected by talented, albeit struggling, artists, and some she herself sketched. When she was a child, she used to draw and thought she might one day go to someplace like Verona, where Romeo and Juliet fell in love, or Florence and be a starving artist. Growing up an only child in a small town, with parents too emotionally damaged to demonstrate their love, the idea sounded exciting. D'Becca could not wait to traverse famous bridges and see up close and personal all the extraordinary landmarks she read about in paperback novels. But like many things, the idea did not stick with D'Becca. Her talent was strictly dilettante, but she had each artwork—landscapes and mountainsides—preserved in oversized frames that took up two walls. Another wall exposed her work as both a print and cat-walk model. In her youth—before her life started getting crowded and out of balance—D'Becca was striking and work was so easy to come by. Back then she had no idea she had taken that time in her life for granted—young, eye-catching, street-wise with a hint of naïveté. Rawn was amused by D'Becca's art. He entered the kitchen to get a cup of whatever he smelled, and the aroma floated throughout the townhouse. After pouring the French pressed coffee into one of D'Becca's European-styled cups, he returned to her bedroom and dressed.

On the drive back to his place, he could feel a gnawing, a sense of frustration he had not been aware of before; although it was too concentrated to not be something that began a while ago. If it had been with him here and there, he was not in the right place to face it until now. D'Becca's presence, slowly and quietly, re-arranged the patterns of his daily routine, and his life adapted to her schedule. While she was out of town, he analyzed the pros and cons of their relationship. But it was not until his father inquired about his intentions as far as D'Becca was concerned that he began to examine it, or them, with any real sense of focus. He had been too obsessed with the desire and the need; the very thought of anything else with D'Becca was beside the point.

It struck Rawn how soon into a relationship one partner or another began to fantasize if the relationship had the potential for marriage. Based on people he had known, he came to understand they did not take the time to learn basic facts that, in the long run, would eventually have an impact. For example, what would you die for? What is your deepest desire? What does money mean to you? Would you consider adoption? Do we share the same values and morals? No matter what, can I—will I—be not only satisfied but faithful to this person forevermore? Have you ever donated sperm to a sperm bank? Let's get *tested?*

More often than not, people rarely dug into such details. Perhaps because one would assume such specifics would be shared without having to be elicited. In his mid-twenties, Rawn began to understand why so many marriages failed, and it was perhaps what scared him when he was engaged to Janelle: the fear of not living up to the man she thought he was. Should their relationship not succeed, Rawn would spend the remainder of his life struggling with that failure.

CHAPTER FOURTEEN

"Yeah, I'm meeting up with an old friend. She's here doing this whole book thing."

"You sound like you don't want to go," Henderson said.

"That's not true." Tamara was unaware of the defensive pitch in her voice.

"What did she write about?"

"A few years back she wrote this book and for whatever reason people bought into whatever the hell she was writing about. I guess this one's on the same subject."

"Which was my question: what's the book about?"

"Hell, Henderson. I didn't read the book."

"You said this was a friend of yours?"

"We were roommates when we were at Barnard."

"But she's a friend, you say?"

Tamara sighed. "Yeah, I guess."

"You guess? Damn, girl, don't you know?"

"Okay, she's a friend. Why are we having this conversation?"

"You can be selfish when you want to be, you know that? Why exactly did you not support your *friend's* book?"

"Now that she's got this whole following, I guess I need to check out what the fuss is all about, huh?" Her laughter was hearty, but exaggerated. Tamara painstakingly spread lipstick on her slender lips.

"It was good spending time with you in Portland. If I didn't do it then, I want to thank you, T."

Tamara had Henderson on speaker. She stopped admiring her reflection in the mirror and her eyes darted to the receiver hanging in its carriage. "What's going on with you?" Tamara pressed her lips together to blend two shades to get the ideal color scheme she wanted: subtle henna. Back when she lived in Amsterdam, she bought a brand of lipstick not available in the States, and the color was called Perfectly Perfectly Berry. Tamara was unable to find it online. On several occasions when she was in New York she stopped in Sephora hoping to find a color as close to Perfectly Perfectly Berry as she could get. It would seem that the shade was apparently no longer popular. That never stopped Tamara.

"What do you mean, what's going on?"

Tamara took a long appraisal of herself in the mirror. She dropped the two tubes of lipstick in the bowl stacked with assorted shades of lip-color. She picked up an eyebrow pencil, and before enhancing her eyebrows, said, "Are you and Daphne having *issues* again?"

"We agreed we weren't discussing Daphne anymore."

"Oh, I'm sorry. But correct me if I'm wrong: you two *are* having some disagreements?"

Henderson heaved. "You must be PMSing. I'd better let you go."

"I must be? There was a time when you *knew*. Where are you, Henderson?"

"What difference does it make where I am?"

"Are you at home?"

"No, I'm driving down Crenshaw."

"I'll talk to you soon. I need to go," she said with a hint of attitude. *"Ciao bella."*

With her hands on her hips, momentarily Tamara stared at the receiver hooked inside its carriage. "He's tripping," she said to herself.

Elliott Bay Books was in bustling Pioneer Square. The bookstore had regular readings and book signings, and authors of every caliber were honored to headline at Elliott Bay. Despite the opening of the mega bookstore Barnes & Noble in Pacific Place, the independent bookstore retained a strong following. When Tamara entered Elliott Bay Books she was taken aback at the swarm of people. The reading was held on the lower level, but the crowd waiting to get downstairs met her at the entrance. *Damn! Are these people here to see Pricilla?*

"Excuse me," Tamara said, making her way to the staircase that led to the bottom floor.

"Where does she think she's going?" one woman said.

"She has nerve!" said another.

"Hey! You have to get in line." A large-framed woman stepped out of the queue and gave Tamara *the look*.

"The author's my best friend," Tamara remarked arrogantly. She was even shocked to hear those words caress her ears as much as the women who heard her speak those words. She never thought of Pricilla as her "best friend," even when she was the only *close* female friend Tamara had. On some level, Henderson must have known that, which could have been why he pressed her about Pricilla in their conversation earlier. When she managed to squeeze her way down to the bottom floor, Tamara's eyes had to be deceiving her. Every chair was taken, and there was barely enough room for standing. *I know I'm not standing.* Tamara heard something about having to turn people away by a passing bookstore employee. She worked her way into the café to order tea. The queue was long. She met Pricilla's picture at the entrance, and her "best-selling" book supported on an easel-like thing. Still, she could not help but interrupt two women waiting on line in the small café to make double sure she had the right bookstore. "Are these people waiting for the author?"

"Yeah," said the woman.

"Uh-huh, girl," said her companion.

"Pricilla Miles?" Tamara tilted back a bit, her body language suggesting *no way!*

"Yeah."

"Are you two waiting for the author?"

"Yeah, but they told us we have to stand. We RSVP'd, too."

RSVP'd?

The luxury of living in Pioneer Square was the idea that everything was convenient. When she first moved to Washington, Sicily looked at several high-rise condos on Crescent Island. The island had some of the most stunning views, but nothing really moved her. Besides, while Crescent Island was extremely attractive, quite picturesque, even, she wanted to be in the midst of urban life. After looking at a number of short-term apartments on First Hill, Sicily's realtor called her with a steal: a loft being sold by someone who capitalized off the tech boom and made a fortune. His startup demanded his time in Silicon Valley full time and he decided to let the loft go. It was an "attractive deal." Sicily was not looking to buy right away. She wanted to get a feel for the Seattle neighborhoods, and decide where exactly her soul felt most serene. But out of curiosity one early Saturday morning, she met the realtor at the loft, and once her eyes touched the stunning, sprawling living room windows, she had to catch her breath. Not to mention the flock of boats sailing along Elliott Bay, and the view—Sicily was in love. Emotional investments were always chancy, and she would have to readjust her cash flow, no doubt. She called her business manager to see if she could make the investment. What attracted her to Pioneer Square was how much it reminded her of Lower Manhattan, in subtle yet striking ways. The baroque buildings, the undeniable charm, the faux European influence. When it did not rain, horse carriages were parked along First, or strolled along the square with sightseers in tow. In spring, the cherry blossoms that lined the square left a hint of its subtle scent on the mild, clean air.

It was a dry night. Having dinner alone at a neighborhood bistro was beginning to be the norm. Sicily did not mind an occasional night alone, but when it was the rule more so than the exception, it cut deep. With six billion people pulsating on the planet, no one—not one person—should be alone. Wandering along Second Avenue, she decided Rawn was right: *I'm pickier than he is.* But was that why she was alone? Was it because of her intense selectivity or was it simply that she had not met someone that made her re-evaluate the way she looked at the world?

"Good evening," a gentleman exclaimed, crossing Sicily's path along the semi-busy sidewalk.

Somberly, she said, "Good evening."

Since Rawn met D'Becca, she could not rely on his companion-ship in the same way she had in the past. Even when he dated other women, it never interfered with the time they shared. But D'Becca was another matter altogether.

The square was energetic, principally because the night was dry and reasonably warm. When the weather turned cooler and it rained at least one part of the day, the square was less saturated. The homeless headed for the nearby overpasses to sleep. On im-pulse, she decided to grab something hot at Seattle's Best Coffee. She talked herself down at the bistro, even when she had a taste for the three-flavor three-layer chocolate cake that along the way became known as the triple shot. Usually Rawn ordered the cake and she would nibble on it; enough to satisfy her desire for some-thing decadent.

Before she stepped off the curb to cross the street, Sicily rubbed shoulders with two women that did not blend in with the usual foot traffic. She made an effort to maneuver between them.

"Excuse…" Sicily began to extend an apology until her eyes met one of the women.

"Well, hello!" Tamara said.

Sicily was annoyed by the very fact that, on two separate occasions when her path crossed with this woman, she became uneasy. "Hello."

"Didn't I see you at Kingfish?" Tamara inquired.

"Oh, right! You have a long memory."

"Hi, Pricilla Miles."

Sicily and Pricilla exchanged casual handshakes.

"The author?" Sicily asked.

"The author, yes."

"I have your new book. Well, I haven't gotten a chance to read it. But I ordered it on Amazon.com a few nights ago."

"Tamara."

"Sicily."

"Hey, we're going to the Library Bistro for drinks. Join us," Pricilla said.

"Oh,…"

"We're meeting a few of my friends. Come on. The more the merrier."

"Yeah, come along," said Tamara. "Pricilla has to do an interview. She promised the *Seattle Times* journalist fifteen minutes. And because she's the type to show gratitude, she's even invited a few diehard fans who are meeting us there. Come hang, it'll be fun."

"Unless you have other plans…" Pricilla said.

"Hey, why not? I can spare some change."

"Fabulous!" Pricilla swung her wool scarf around her neck. "This is what I love about Seattle…"

CHAPTER FIFTEEN

"Did you love her?"

Blaine was sitting at the edge of the antique bed bench, swirling a spoon in a large soup bowl of hot and steamy homemade minestrone. Finally, after weeks of sleeping an hour here, thirty minutes there, Imani was starting to sleep longer through the night. If she slept three hours without waking up, she was doing good. Kenya had called Blaine two weeks ago and said in a frustrated voice, "You have to do something. She's staring her life away. She owns a business, Blaine. She can't stare out the window of the loft like time stopped because our father died. She's got... You have to do something. She'll listen to you. *Please!*"

Blaine, a financial advisor, commuted between Boston and New York. He was in his Boston office at the time Kenya called him. He had said he would try to get back to Manhattan by the weekend, but Kenya had been pushy and persistent. "Look," Blaine had said. "I care about Imani, but there's nothing else I can do. She has to go through—she has to grieve on her terms."

"Did you love her?" Imani asked.

He avoided her question. "You're awake."

"Did you love her?"

"Soup's going to get cold."

"Yes or no?"

"You need to eat."

"Did you love her, Blaine? Why can't you answer the question?"

"That was years ago. Aren't we past this?"

"Did you love…"

"Yes. Yes! But not in the way you think."

Imani turned on to her side and pressed her eyes shut. "I don't want any bloody soup."

"Come on, you love my minestrone."

"I'm not hungry and you don't have to babysit me. I'm a grown woman. To borrow from something you once said to me, things are never what they appear."

"Which means?"

"I'm not some weakling, Blaine."

"What about your life back in Seattle?"

"Everything's under control." She turned on her opposite side, purposely putting her back to Blaine. "You can leave the soup. I'll heat it up later."

Blaine placed the steaming hot soup on the bed bench. He walked over to the side of the bed where Imani rested, and her body stiffened by his closeness. He bent over and touched her. Reluctantly, he began to rub her back with affection.

"Don't do that, please."

"Come on, Im. Don't be like this."

Irritated, she threw the bedding off her lower body and raised her torso and it took Blaine totally by surprise. In a knee-jerk reaction he moved back, like he was dodging an anticipated blow. "Don't call me that. I hate that. You and Kenya…every time you get around her you call me Im? My name's Imani. I-ma-ni!"

"I get it. You're angry because Dante's…"

"Don't presume to know what I think or feel or how I might be…"

"Imani, I'm on your side. Why are you angry with *me?*" Blaine pressed his large palm against his chest.

"I am not angry at you!"

"Really? And you think this attitude is directed at the freakin' wall?"

"Don't be so smug."

"Let's start over."

"Start over from?…" She spread her hands.

"When we were right. When we were *friends*."

"I never knew we stopped being friends." Imani hugged her knees.

"You know what I mean."

"Uhhh, really!"

"Imani," Blaine exhaled. "Come on, work with me here."

"Why did you come back from Boston? Did Kenya call you? The truth!"

Not that he wanted to, but Blaine looked into Imani's stressful but soulful eyes and said, "Yes. I'll admit, I wasn't up for this, but I'm glad I did. We need to get some things straight. I think it's time."

Imani folded herself into a ball and reached for the covers. "I'm not in the mood."

Blaine slipped off his shoes and gingerly lay beside Imani, spooning her. He whispered in her ear, "I'm sorry, baby. But don't you think it's time to forgive me?"

When they first met, Rawn and Sicily hit it off straightaway. She was so impressed with him she made the decision to hire Rawn without his having to meet directly with the board of trustees. It caused a bit of a ruckus, but Rawn's CV and his references from Denver were so exceptional they let her decision stand. Sicily expected Rawn to make a play for her in due course; it happened enough in the past for her to predict that it would most likely happen. But in truth she never actually gave him the opportunity. Their relationship came with one clear understanding: remain low-key while at the Academy. The trustees, and most of the faculty and staff, knew they were friends but had no idea how close they were when they were off campus. Sicily, not necessarily Rawn, wanted to keep it that way.

With raven hair flowing over her shoulders and velvety mocha skin, Sicily came across so poised. The average man would not make a play. It would take someone very comfortable in his own skin, because Sicily threw off a persona that suggested she was not accessible. When *Opposites Don't Attract!* won several Tonys, she was celebrated in New York and in her hometown, Philadelphia. What she did not see coming was that her public life would be the thing to out her. Someone—a so-called friend—leaked it and it was printed in the *Post*'s Page Six. Since she was a sophomore in college, she tried to tell her parents the truth, and even once *Opposites Don't Attract!* made it to Broadway, Sicily still was not ready to come out to family. But when her relationship with one of the actresses in the play became public, Sicily had no choice but to be forthcoming.

Having to face people—she went into a downward spiral, although the talk was that she suffered major depression and had a nervous breakdown. In truth, she abruptly disappeared from her celebrated life without so much as a goodbye and checked into a luxurious spa in Taos for two weeks. While she knew of yoga and meditation, Sicily thought both were a bit Zen for her liking. But the retreat at the spa required one hour of meditation before a hearty breakfast that was strictly organic, and thirty minutes prior to bedtime. An hour of silence nearly killed her, but she loved the one-hour yoga class. Meditation put her in touch with emotions she was not familiar with, or avoided confronting. She worked diligently to become more attuned to her inner compass, and in due course something clicked. She knew going back to school for her Ph.D. was the direction she needed to take.

Leaving behind the life that drained her emotionally, psychologically, spiritually was the best decision she had ever made. Sicily learned six months after moving to Seattle that there had been reports of her attempting suicide, which was erroneously printed in various low-brow publications. While there had been a retraction or two, the information was out in the public domain for several years and thus the untruths morphed into urban legends. The *Post* claimed she went to a spiritual retreat on the West Coast where the rich and famous went when they could not handle life. And according to one publication Sicily was now "Born Again." Despite the gossip, real or imagined, she tried to redefine herself in Seattle and Sicily managed to do quite well. Her life was not in perfect balance—no life was. Yet she had the right dose of emotional and physical well-being to lead a fulfilled life.

It was not uncommon for Sicily and Rawn to have lunch together, but they rarely went off campus, and when they did, it was to Café Neuf because Jean-Pierre always held a table for them. So when Sicily invited Rawn out to lunch and away from the Academy, he knew something was up. He learned on this particular afternoon Sicily had met someone; she had a lover. This was of notable interest to him because it had been a while since he heard Sicily speak of anyone who remotely interested her. When Rawn first learned of her sexuality, he was rooted to the spot. He would never admit it to Sicily; when he first met with her over lunch, and followed by a series of meetings, he was both impressed by and attracted to her. They had sat in a nearly empty restaurant and their conversation led them both to believe they were raised by upper middle-class overachievers, and appreciated many of the same things and the same way of life.

Once he started at the Academy, he tried to work up the nerve to ask her out. A few years his senior, she was the person he reported to at Gumble-Wesley, not to mention she earned double what he earned and Rawn was not exactly sure how Sicily felt about that. But as time progressed, he grew reluctant because while she was friendly and they became fast friends, she did not exhibit the same curiosity in him as he knowingly displayed toward her. The last thing he wanted to do was to create any awkwardness between them; and besides, it would be nearly impossible to shield their intimacy for any length of time. Above and beyond, what if things did not work out? No, Rawn chose not to risk it.

The knowledge of Sicily's sexual orientation was revealed to him one evening about six months after they had met. Sicily had recommended they dine at Kingfish Café. Rawn was reaching for his drink when Sicily had said casually, "I think I should tell you, I'm lesbian."

Rawn missed his bottom lip, and some of the dark beverage dribbled off his chin and onto his heather-taupe cashmere sweater. While the room was filled with animated energy, there was a tense silence at their table. He made an attempt to play down his being stunned. Rawn was too crushed by the disappointment to smoothly collect himself. It had taken him a minute to absorb what he had heard, but it was a bombshell that blew him away.

"Oh!" He had struggled to remain cool.

"That's why I waited so long to tell you."

"I-I-I…didn't…"

"It was the last thing you expected from me, wasn't it?"

"Frankly?" he asked.

She nodded.

"Maybe I should have guessed." It had been his pride that replied.

"I can't tell you how much it pisses me off, people who don't understand the dynamics of loving someone of the same sex, and then pass judgment."

"I'm sorry," Rawn had said.

"You think it's not possible for a woman not to see the same things you see in a woman? I'm confident I react to a woman I find attractive in much the same way you do. Every woman *looks* at other women, but not all of them are attracted to them. They might admire how good they look in a particular style, or how they keep their body fit and toned. Every woman checks out a woman if she looks good in a pair of jeans. If she looks like she's got herself together, some women will unconsciously attempt to emulate her. Women naturally respond to a woman who throws off something…different. But with a woman like me, it's deeper than the superficial. I've felt passion with women I never felt with a man."

"I see." *What a waste*, Rawn had thought.

"I have this reaction from every man I've been honest with."

"Reaction?" Rawn had laughed, and felt himself growing increasingly annoyed. "Have I *reacted?*"

"Rawn! You know you've reacted. Because of the way I look and how I carry myself. Men, they hit on me, they want me. Look where we work for crying out loud. You don't think those uptight white men don't make passes? They have this sneaky flirt thing that they do. Yes, they're subtle, but I think that's only because they don't know how to approach a woman like me."

"Woman like you? Which means…?"

"You know, educated, successful, and I know I look good. You see, they hope you'll take the subtle bait. Last week I was at QFC and this man came right out and asked me on a date. He barely introduced himself. He threw this one at me: 'I have two orchestra seats to *Phantom of the Opera*. Would you be interested in going?' At QFC in bloody produce. Can you stand it?"

"Men are naturally attracted to beautiful women. No man would automatically guess you to be lesbian. And even if he thought…"

Sicily had scarcely even heard Rawn. The words had been spoken more to herself than to him: "You should see the looks I get from their wives, like how dare you try to steal my man, you bitch. If they only knew. Give me a break." She had frowned, and her look came across like she had taken a bite of a dill pickle. "When one makes his move and I don't respond...You get tired of being defensive. Men are way too complicated. I see women do some of the craziest stuff over a man. They lose themselves; they allow a man to hijack their self-esteem. Perfectly intelligent women, smart and clever women, they lose the essence of who they are when they meet a man that...I don't know...that knows how to woo, woo, woo."

"And it's so different with two people of the same sex?"

"Well...I get tired of people always trying to figure out how you *turn* out gay!"

All Rawn had thought about that evening was what a waste.

"Years ago, I went with a group of colleagues to see *New Jack City*. Afterwards, we all went out to dinner. I tell you, I've never heard women talk about a man the way these women talked about Wesley Snipes. *Oh, girrrrrl, he is sooooo fine! Girrrrrl, I'd leave my man for him without thinking twice! Girrrrrl, I'd love somma that!* It was silly, so ridiculous." Sicily had sighed harshly. "Wesley Snipes was no more than an actor playing a part to me." After reaching for her wineglass, she had pressed her back to the seat.

"Attraction is complicated, you know? A few students have a crush on me. I have some influence over them whether I want that responsibility or not. But any attraction some young girl might have is so innocent—it would be foolish to give it any weight. Before I finished high school, I had to have at least ten crushes. A few on my teachers. It takes nothing to confuse feelings..."

"Oh, no. Please don't tell me you're one of those?"

"One of *those?*"

"Allah! Sexuality—like you say about attraction—is too complicated,

and especially when it comes to trying to define it. Why does homosexuality have to be *defined* and heterosexuality *is?* It's not so much about sex, being homosexual. I—maybe this wasn't a good idea."

"Okay, look. Sicily, you're acting as though I'm judging you or something."

"Well, are you?"

Lowering his voice he had leaned into the table, and Rawn stated, "I'm glad you told me; that you trust me enough to share something so private. Being lesbian, Sicily, is actually...It's provocative. Nothing between us changes. Truthfully, it makes sense to me now."

"Really? Why?"

Rawn had dodged the question, but when he went to sleep that evening, he realized he was quite discouraged. For months they had played an intricate game of lust, desire and ambiguous flirtation which naturally transpired in a platonic friendship. For weeks after she had told him about her sexuality, Rawn began to imagine what it would be like to make love to two women, which he had never fantasized about before, at least not knowingly; and more so what it would be like to make love to Sicily and one of her lesbian friends. But time had passed, and he had long since dismissed her as a woman he would ever experience, and her sexuality never came up again. But sitting in Luigi's, a good mile away from any restaurant or café frequented by those who worked at the Academy, Sicily was in one sharing mood. The restaurant smelled of rich garlic, and it was typically crowded and noisy with energetic voices and spirited laughter. Gossip and passionate dialogue could be overheard at every table by the busy, swift waitstaff. Not necessarily attentive, Rawn casually listened to Sicily speak of her new lover.

"This woman is special, Rawn. I don't—I can't afford to mess it up. It's difficult to find a woman like this one. I've never run into someone like her in Seattle. Oh, Rawn. She's one of a kind."

Good-naturedly, he smiled, and broke in with an occasional, "Uh-huh."

Sicily went on and on, nearly out of breath while she spoke of this woman like a young schoolgirl with a silly little schoolgirl crush. He was half-finished with his seafood pasta and Sicily had barely touched her pasta salad.

He reached for an Italian roll in the wicker basket. "When will I meet her?" he asked.

"I'm glad you asked," said Sicily. "I thought Thanksgiving would be nice. That's if you've decided not to go home."

Sicily was so happy; this thing must have happened out of nowhere and they rushed into something. Depending on the people involved, the first few weeks of a new relationship could be intense. It verged on obsession, and it was all one could talk about. Think about. Until the person felt familiar. Rawn would have picked up on this relationship had it started many weeks ago. Listening to her, watching her, Rawn was beginning to feel a tinge of jealousy. For several years they had been everything but lovers. Sicily spoke of her new lover with such passion; she was verging on pure ecstasy talking about this woman. He could not make sense of why he reacted to it in the way that he did. He pondered contentiously the remainder of the day why her bliss made him feel annoyed, when he should have been very pleased she found someone.

After lunch, and later in the day, Rawn replayed what Sicily once said to him, not too long after they met: "I want to be loved, of course. Loved madly, addictively, and to the exclusion of any other." Back then it sounded quite profound to him, but the way she was acting; Rawn never saw her so excited over a girlfriend. In the last year it took everything Sicily had to go on a first date.

When he entered the apartment, Rawn walked to the rich espresso leather ottoman and sat for quite a while, his mind filled with noise.

While it surprised him, he was pleased that D'Becca had not called. He was deeply confused, and needed some time to sort out what was really taking place inside his head. Sitting in the dark trying to quell his inexplicable thoughts, the phone chimed, but he was grateful for his new high-tech answering machine his mother sent him as a birthday gift.

"Poussaint, it's Chap." He could hear the deep-throated voice from the distance. "I'm on my way to the Alley. Hey, drop on by the club if you can. Oh, it's about six forty-five on Tuesday. Later, man."

Rawn rushed to the phone in the pitch-dark kitchen, but when he reached it, there was a dial tone. "Dammit!" he said, annoyed. He gathered his keys and bomber jacket.

The night air smelled of recent rain and a full moon made the evening sky look dramatic, mysterious. He started his Jeep, and Rawn began to concentrate on all sorts of things: fundamentally his relationship with D'Becca. He was clueless where their relationship was headed, or if it was on the verge of ending. And there was Christmas and his plans to go home to see his family and old friends. He and Khalil made tentative plans to go skiing in Vail. He was indecisive on whether he should invite D'Becca, although Khalil had encouraged him to do so since he was bringing his London girlfriend, Moon. Rawn felt a swell of emotion while conjuring up everything, everything but the fact that he had learned earlier in the day that Sicily was in love. He realized no matter how intelligently he reasoned or how passionately he rationalized, he was envious of her new relationship, and more precisely, with a woman.

Moody's Jazz Alley was unusually packed for a Tuesday night. Rawn moved through the crowd like a regular, speaking to familiar faces in passing, and signaled the bartender to send his usual to the piano.

When he sat at the piano, he nodded to the other musicians. A freckled redhead brought Rawn's drink and openly flirted. He took a taste of his rum and Coke and eyeballed the crowd, and with finesse blended in with the band. They began to play a darkly romantic number—a hit that won Dante Godreau his first Grammy. They played their set for well over an hour, dedicating the evening to Godreau, and Rawn felt so loose and free he managed to lose track of his earlier thoughts and the demon they left behind. When he decided to end the evening, it was midnight. Before he headed home, he sat alone at the bar and nursed a beer. The room was especially lively. Rawn's favorite version of "Unchained Melody" played in the background, and for the first time he listened closely to the lyrics.

He felt a presence—someone—standing very close to him at the bar. A woman, probably no more than twenty and dressed provocatively, between ordinary and attractive but trying too hard, grinned, and held a drink. She looked too young and without enough history to be drinking a brandy. Even the way she held it made her look inexperienced. It only added to her insatiable need to be anyone but who she was at that moment. He wanted to tell her: *The older you get the more complicated life becomes. You might want to rethink trying to rush this.*

"I like how you play," she said, easing into a candid flirt.

Rawn felt sorry for her. D'Becca crossed his mind because when they first met, she said to him, "I grew up too fast."

Leaning against the bar, she said, "You good, too. You got this groove going. You got a girlfriend?"

Rawn took a better look at the provocatively dressed young woman. Plump cleavage oozed out of a low-cut sweater. While he was so not in the mood, he did not want to take his present frame of mind out on her. "That's a matter of interpretation."

"What that mean?" she asked.

"What do you consider a girlfriend?"

"You know." She grinned wider, which made her dimples deepen.

"My interpretation might not be the same as yours. So tell me, what makes a woman a man's girlfriend?"

She looked unsure, and her face said: *he's trying to fool with my head or something.* He trusted that she was not a young woman who was used to having thought-provoking conversations with a man. Not even something as simple as the distinction of things: Right versus wrong; good versus bad. Where she came from, it was common knowledge what the differences were. There were no nuances.

"You messin' with me, right?"

"No," Rawn said, sincere.

She glanced down at her chipped nail polish and Rawn realized he might have embarrassed her.

When he stood, he finished his beer. "In answer to your question—yes, I have a girlfriend." He winked, adding, "Take care."

The young woman gazed at Rawn disappearing into the slim crowd standing at the end of the bar. A man slapped him on the back in a friendly way, and then like out of thin air, the young woman lost sight of him.

CHAPTER SIXTEEN

When Rawn called and invited D'Becca to Sicily's for Thanksgiving, she was ecstatic to be sharing a holiday with people she could relate to. While she did not know Sicily all that well, she was impressed with her and liked her attitude. Slipping into a pair of black Lycra slacks, D'Becca had to admit to herself she was really curious about Sicily's new girlfriend.

"I've gained weight since I last wore these? No way!"

Tripping over a pair of black stiletto booties in the middle of the bedroom floor, D'Becca dashed to her wardrobe mirror across the room and looked front, back, sides, and then back to front and then to back. She let out a heavy sigh. After peeling the snug-fitting slacks off her hips, she stepped out of each leg and hurried to her scale in the bathroom wearing only a push-up bra. She tapped the poise weight on the physician's scale more to the left than to the right, because her eyes had to be deceiving her. "One-hundred and twenty-eight? No way!"

D'Becca was professionally 5'11, but in truth she stood 5'9-½ barefooted. At one-hundred and twenty-eight pounds she would hardly be considered overweight. Yet in order for her to keep working she needed to be no more than seven stones—one-hundred and twenty-three pounds give or take, and not an ounce more. Even at that weight she could not do swimsuits and lingerie. While they were not the high-profile designers she used to work for in her early days, several American designers still requested her. The popular sleek cut that was en vogue at the moment hung ideally on someone with her stature.

Once she slipped the fitted sweater over her head and saw how all-black truly did make her look thin—well, *lean*—D'Becca felt pleased. "You look fab!" she complimented her reflection in the mirror. Because she gave Rawn her word that she would not be her established ten-minute late self, she decided against spending fifteen minutes camouflaging her delicate flaws with makeup. Instead she used her thick and fluffy makeup brush and swept mineral powder over her face and topped her look with a flashy watermelon-colored lipstick that made her collagen-injected lips appear even more voluptuous. In quite good spirits, she checked the number on her caller ID from her ringing cellular. Her vulnerable side was desperate to answer, but she chose to let it go into voicemail. D'Becca reached for her leather jacket, scarf and gloves at the foot of the bed and was blowing her horn in front of Rawn's at exactly three sharp.

Since the streets were virtually deserted, they arrived at Sicily's thirty-seven minutes later. She opened her door to receive her holiday guests warmly in an ink-black dress that gingerly traced her petite frame. Her hair was often pulled back or she wore it straight with a nice gloss to it and it bounced when she walked, but today it was a mane of tight curls cascading sensually over her shoulders. Once, Khalil inquired whether or not Sicily wore extensions, but Rawn was not sure either way. Her face was made up carefully, and the scent she wore, delicate and feminine, brushed against his taupe-colored sweater when they embraced and the smell would linger on him throughout the evening. Sicily and D'Becca did the European double-cheek bit and kissing the air routine that Sicily picked up during her Broadway days, and D'Becca picked up during her days when she worked European runways. One evening, when Sicily decided to have an impromptu gathering, Rawn and D'Becca dropped by and D'Becca and Sicily discovered that they had people in common—six, or less, degrees of separation.

Sicily's loft had the familiar smell of burning logs in the fireplace, and steam-cooked vegetables. Smoked turkey blended with all the rich holiday spices. Scent oil burned and left a smell of gentle ginger floating over the extended living area. There was an entrancing view of Elliott Bay from every floor-to-ceiling window that artfully defined the space. Sicily's loft was warmly decorated in nontoxic colors of beige and cream, and blended evenly with strong highlights—olive and cinnamon. Framed by soft ivory brown walls, it had a grand ceiling and oversized artwork, including a portrait of Sicily. Her Tony set alone above the fireplace and over it a framed poster of *Opposites Don't Attract!*

Sicily's latest girlfriend—Rawn remembered her the second he laid eyes on her. It was a while back, but the last time he was at Kingfish Café, he saw her there with Henderson Payne. She came across as being comfortable in her skin and deliberately threw her sexuality around because she knew it would get the attention of men; and more to the point, women would be provoked by the attention she received from the men they were with. Rawn knew enough about Tamara's history with Henderson because his best friend, Khalil, was his agent. *What the hell is she doing with Sicily?* She stood at the opposite end of the room, near the naked paned windows and the exposed-brick wall, holding a glass of white wine. Provocatively, Tamara wore a pair of black skin-tight straight-leg suede jeans. Her white sheer poet's blouse with extended cuffs was see-through and cut low to expose a tattoo that was at the start of her cleavage—the letter H, oversized but in lower case.

At once, D'Becca was captivated with Tamara, and Rawn picked up on it even before she started in on her compliments and strange attentiveness toward her. D'Becca's world—and the world Sicily once knew; the same world Khalil was a part of—lacked boundaries. They were uninhibited people, hugging and kissing and touching. It was not a judgment so much as it was an observation. While the three women seemed to have an enigmatic energy between them, Rawn felt out of his depth. D'Becca, Sicily and Tamara started chatting and laughing and acting like old friends from back in the day. They talked about people they had in common, Paris and Milan and Manhattan. Rawn, feeling somewhat excluded, could not stop looking at Tamara. She must have picked up on his curiosity because occasionally she glanced his way. Subtly, she began to flirt, and the amorous nature of her looks was premeditated. Sicily's new friend began to annoy him. And yet he was unconsciously drawn to her; almost hypnotized by her sex appeal. He wondered if she was still involved with Henderson, and if that were the case, why was she with Sicily? The way she had spoken of Tamara, Sicily was desperately *in* love with her, and what started between them happened on the fly. In the end, Rawn presaged the outcome: It was inevitably that Sicily would get hurt.

Before he could catch himself, Rawn broke up their girl-talk with, "Where did you two meet?" Even he could hear the tightness in his throat.

Sicily flipped her hair off her neck, holding her glass of white wine in her naturally feminine way. When he first noticed that she was drinking Chardonnay, Rawn was unconsciously surprised. It was in large part because she mentioned on their first trip to Chateau Ste. Michelle winery that she did not like white wine; red was her preference. Everything about her—her attitude, body language, the gentleness, the quiet glow that scattered like ashes over a woman's aura when her life was right where she wanted it to be—suggested Sicily fell, and deep. She was different in this setting—with Tamara in the room. The influence over her was remarkable, and Rawn was not sure what to make of it all.

"I should have known you weren't paying attention. I told you where we met," Sicily replied.

Tamara tilted forward, her toned legs crossed while her hard cocoa-brown nipples were visible through the sheer poet's blouse. "I first saw Sicily at Kingfish. She was with you. But we met three weeks ago. A friend and I had left Elliott Bay Books, and we bumped into Sicily. She was alone and we rescued her from whatever she would have done had we not met her that night. My friend invited her to join us. It was all very—what did you call it, Sicily: a contract between souls?"

Rawn had no intention of being sarcastic. "Just like that?" he said.

With a delicate touch, D'Becca placed her hand on his thigh. "Rawn!" And with the look of surprise on her face.

"Just like that," Tamara said straight into Rawn's soothing eyes. She wet her tongue with a nip of wine.

The energy in the room shifted and D'Becca decided to change the mood. "Rawn and I met in a similar way."

"How so?" Tamara asked.

Rawn knew she couldn't care less.

"Well, back during the summer I'd just returned from two weeks in New York. It never got below ninety. It was unbearably sticky and I couldn't wait to get away from the exhausting energy in that city. I mean I wanted to walk out onto the sidewalk and not meet nearly eighty percent humidity. I made an appointment with Gene Juarez first thing. I spent all afternoon…"

"I love that place," Tamara interrupted.

"Do you?" Sicily asked, looking over to Tamara.

"Oh, lady. There's this masseuse…her name escapes me, but… I'll get the name. Try her, luv. Trust me."

Flirtatiously, Sicily said, "I do, and I will."

"D'Becca, you were saying?" Tamara's eyes left D'Becca and for a split-second, she met Rawn's gaze.

"I'm a block from Café Neuf and it starts to pour down rain," D'Becca continued. "All day I spent in Gene Juarez and for…naught!"

Sicily and Tamara were quite amused while Rawn had no clue what was so droll.

Sicily picked up the expression on his face and said, "It's a girl thing, Rawn. You don't know what it's like to spend hours in a salon and then in ten minutes, your hair is a hot mess."

"You see why I wear mine short. I used to have hair down to here," Tamara said, pointing a tad above her elbow. "I finally said to hell with it and chopped it off."

"Rawn was amused by the fact that I'd ruined a perfectly good pair of shoes *and* my hair was ruined. But a few weeks later I ran into him at Street Two and we—we clicked. Maybe we experienced a kinda soul contract, too."

"Hmmm," said Tamara.

"Yeah, our experiences are similar. I never even realized that." In that moment, Sicily was exceptionally happy.

"Who made the first move?" D'Becca asked.

A hush fell over the room for several slow moments.

"It's something you know," Tamara said, picking the subject back up. "Neither one of us actually made a *move*."

"Well, someone had to do something," D'Becca said.

"Who—between you and Rawn—made the first move?" Sicily had never bothered to ask Rawn, but it was not for the lack of curiosity that she failed to inquire.

"D'Becca did." Rawn looked straight at Sicily.

"I did," she admitted. "Rawn can put a spell on a girl. Watch out, Tamara."

"You haven't met Khalil yet, I take it?" Sicily asked D'Becca.

"I know a Khalil." Tamara's voice was so blasé, and because she was one-dimensional, she failed to make the connection.

"Not yet, but we're going skiing in Vail with him and his girlfriend, aren't we?" D'Becca looked over to Rawn, seeking confirmation.

Rawn, his head lowered, said in a quiet voice, "It's a plan." His cognac-colored eyes roamed to Tamara and that's when he decided she was hollow.

From the moment they arrived, a burning question stayed at the tip of his tongue, although Rawn felt it impolite to ask it. But then D'Becca broached the subject without him having to.

"Tamara, I've been dying to ask."

Tamara extended D'Becca a cunning look.

"Weren't…didn't you…you're the one who had a thing with Henderson Payne that was splashed all over the tabloids?"

"I like that. You're direct."

"I know Daphne. We've worked together."

"Well, Henderson and I are very close friends. I love him, of course."

"Wait!" D'Becca placed her wineglass on a decorative coaster in front of her on the perfectly squared table. "Threads! By appointment only. I've been to your boutique. You are *the* Tamara that owns Threads, right?"

"I *knew* you looked familiar! I couldn't place you."

"Well, D'Becca's a model. You probably saw her modeling something in an ad, or in one of those *My Little Secret* catalogues that every woman gets in her mailbox."

"I remember D'Becca from fashion week a few years ago. But yes, you've been to Threads. I believe you're on my mailing list."

"I love your designs. That dress BabyGirl wore to the Grammys was stunning!" She retrieved her wineglass with a happy grin. "Not *pas cher*, but quite chic. A friend of mine modeled one of your originals at Ebony Fashion Fair. And I bid on a dress for an AIDS charity in L.A. Someone else out-bid me, though."

"How much?" Sicily was interested to know.

"I bid two thousand. I'm not sure what the final bid was."

"Goodness, Seattle's too small for my blood," Sicily said, in an exhaustingly good mood.

"Are you bi?" Rawn asked.

"Rawn!" said D'Becca.

"Really, it's okay." Tamara said, "I don't define myself. My mother's Jamaican and my father's Caucasian, from Washington, D.C. They're politicians. And much to my mother's chagrin, I don't identify myself as any one race—black, white or biracial. Straight, gay, bi. It's all labels. Who cares? I play by my own rules."

When Sicily kissed Tamara and their tongues stroked, Rawn, unconsciously, crossed his legs. D'Becca leaned into Rawn and said, "Sicily's like so hot."

A Scandinavian pine table was perfectly set for four. D'Becca loved the elegant centerpiece and candleholder, and the Kenyan dinnerware. With tears in her eyes, she said, "Sicily, maybe you haven't outdone yourself, but this, it's absolutely lovely. I am so touched for being included."

It was an elysian meal. There was no other way to describe it. Rawn and D'Becca stayed long enough for seconds of dessert, which they shared—an espresso sweet potato cheesecake Tamara made from an online recipe that was beyond decadent. While Rawn watched the ending of a football game, D'Becca, Sicily and Tamara washed, dried and put away the dishes and leftovers while they gossiped.

Good-bye felt terribly long to Rawn.

D'Becca could not stop talking about Sicily and Tamara. In the car, speeding across the floating bridge, she went on and on about the two women who were so "majestic" to her, and how much she enjoyed Thanksgiving and how long it had been since she had a night like "this one." "Holidays," she told Rawn, "can be so wonderful when they are shared"; but her words were meaningless to his ears. And he listened intently to D'Becca, hoping to feel a connection to her, and optimistic that she would touch his heartstrings. But nothing, nothing she said meant anything to him. D'Becca could have been any woman he picked up off a street corner who was hitchhiking for a ride home. And for the first time since he had known her, Rawn felt nothing for her; his mind was quite preoccupied. He needed to be alone. Firstly, because making love to her would most likely create more chaos in his head; and secondarily, he was not exactly sure he could even be *with* D'Becca.

"D'Becca, please," he butted in on her rambling conversation. Rawn failed to know what on earth she was talking about. "Take me home," he directed.

"What?" She yielded at the stop sign a block away from her townhouse.

"Turn here; take me home."

D'Becca followed his instructions. Presumably, he wanted them to sleep at his place instead of hers. When she pulled up to the curb and turned off the engine, he said, "Let's pass tonight, D'Becca." Gingerly he caressed her cheek with his warm lips, his breath bitter from alcohol, espresso and the spices that enriched the Thanksgiving dinner. "Good night." A voice in the past always alive and tender was now cold, detached, and tight.

D'Becca was so astounded she felt tears dampen her bare lashes. By the time she was home, she was not sure what route she took to get there. For at least ten minutes she parked in her garage and stared into the darkness. She blinked when she heard her cellular ring. She reached for it in her leather jacket pocket, and once she identified the caller, she spoke softly, "Hi, Troy." Thirty minutes later, after making herself a cup of soothing Ginseng tea and hoping it would relax her, she curled up with her cat, Chai, and Pricilla Miles's best seller which she borrowed from Sicily, it registered: Rawn was jealous of Sicily's relationship because he was very attracted to Tamara. The sexual energy between them was fervent and she could not avoid it if she tried. And if D'Becca did not miss it, certainly Sicily could not either.

CHAPTER SEVENTEEN

He could not sleep, and Rawn knew he was going to battle with the sheets. On impulse he called Khalil because he was a night owl. When he answered his landline, Rawn was relieved. He shared with his best friend in great detail how Thanksgiving at Sicily's unfolded, and it managed to make him feel better. Perchance he needed to voice his confusion.

Khalil lived above Sunset Boulevard in a cottage that hung off a cliff and offered an awesome setting of L.A.'s sprawling panorama. With a bottle of beer in his hand, he leaned against the patio door taking in the sights down below. He could hear, although faintly, music coming from a popular nightclub on the famed boulevard. Rawn said on one of his visits: "Man, I sure hope the 'big one' doesn't come any time soon, because this place will slide right off this hillside and land straight on the Strip." It was a quiet West Hollywood night and Khalil was feeling a little lonely; he would never confess that to Rawn, though. "Man, sounds like to me you're in the middle of a ménage à trois. I'm seriously feeling this, bro."

"What's the deal with Tamara and Henderson?"

"That's outdated. He's back on track," Khalil said. "Hell, I think Tamara's fine and everything, but a little too… She's too demanding. Henderson's head got turned around for a minute, but Tamara's not the kind of woman you lose everything for. Now Daphne? Man, she's the ultimate!"

Rawn bent over and looked inside his refrigerator. He was talking more to himself than to Khalil: "I should have brought some leftovers home. I'm hungry."

"Look, if you're thinking about dipping into Tamara, man, don't drink that Kool-Aid. That chick, she's that can't-get-rid-of trouble. That woman wreaked serious havoc in Henderson's life. In order to put that whole thing to bed, he silent-partnered some boutique she wanted to open in Seattle. That's where he was playing when they met, and she moved there to be near him. She makes Glenn Close look like she had an infatuation for Michael Douglas in *Fatal Attraction*. Man, she knows how to turn a brother sideways, so…"

"It's Sicily I'm worried about."

"Sicily's a big girl who can surely take care of herself. I have to admit, though. I never would've fantasized Tamara and Sicily hooking up. Can you imagine? Whew! That's got to be…I'd love to be in the room when the lights go out, know what I'm saying?"

"Is she still mixed up with Henderson?" Rawn leaned against the kitchen counter in the dark; the full moon streaked the room with an amazing glow.

"They have this weird friendship, that's the most I know." Khalil walked back into the well-lit cottage. He reached for the remote control to turn off the television. "There's something missing with that woman. She uses her sexuality for personal gain. There's always an agenda with her. Sicily has to know that Tamara isn't someone she can get serious with. That woman's dangerous."

The following morning when the telephone brought Rawn out of a deep sleep, he was pretty confident that it was D'Becca. But he turned his back to the whole idea of getting together with her to go shopping and to catch a film. Although they made plans, he was not in the mood, pure and simple.

Less than two miles away, D'Becca slammed the receiver down and voiced angrily, "You bastard!" She was furious, and to distract herself she started on the StairMaster until she was weak from fatigue—over forty-five minutes of a high-impact workout. She stripped the damp unitard off her moist body and took a cool shower. Towels wrapped around her head and her body, with a click of her mouse, she ordered the French *La Femme Nikita* DVD from Kozmo.com. By the time it was delivered and she sat down with a bag of Tim's to relax and enjoy the film, D'Becca was much too antsy.

Hastily, she grabbed her scarf and keys and stepped into her Z3 without knowing where she would end up. She passed by Rawn's and could officially say she had done a drive-by. Food immediately crossed her mind. D'Becca had an eating disorder—food kept her from going mad when she really wanted to go mad; it was her coping mechanism. The craving for comfort was so intense she began to shake. She needed to nourish her empty places. Barely stopping at the stop sign, she turned onto Crescent Island Boulevard and pulled into a market parking lot. Larry's was not crowded. A cashier and a bagger talked casually at the nine-items-or-less checkout lane. A couple in workout clothes strode through the aisle where the smell of freshly grounded Millstone coffee beans permeated the space. D'Becca's first stop was in the gourmet section where she reached for a box of Seattle Chocolates. After yesterday's meal, D'Becca should have a New York cleansing cocktail, but Troy's idea of eating tofu for the next few days—that was definitely not going to do the trick today. She tossed a box of tampons in the cart and headed for the ice cream section, snacking on the blissful chocolate along the way. Momentarily, she contemplated between a Ben & Jerry's fat-free sorbet and Chunky Monkey. She and Rawn got in the habit of eating Chocolate Cherry Garcia. They talked about life while they shared the pint, and it was those simple moments that made her relationship with Rawn *real*.

Once home, anger still claimed every ounce of her. D'Becca felt so bloody angry she could scream at the top of her lungs! She began to pace, growing increasingly uptight, anxious, and this kind of nervous frenzy drew her to do something rash, something desperate. She continued to pace and pace, trying to avoid finishing off the bag of Tim's. She reached for her cellular and started making a call. *No*, she talked herself down. *You can't.*

So not to go to a dark place, she tried to busy herself by cleaning the townhouse from room to room, moving and singing to the sounds of Seal over and over again—"Bring It On," "Dreaming In Metaphors," "Kiss From A Rose"—until she was plain sick of Seal. She reached for another CD from the stack—Taylor Dayne. The sound of her voice singing "Tell It to My Heart" added to the depth of her implacable sorrow. D'Becca needed to push back her misery, her emptiness. The thought of *stuff*. Which emotion was she experiencing, of the four primary emotions characteristic of emotional overeating: fear, anger, tension, shame? She wanted desperately to *be* with her feeling, whatever that feeling was. She began to overthink. Rawn, was he *with* Tamara? Something was going on between them; their body language at Thanksgiving was adequately transparent. Jealousy was not D'Becca's thing. She felt it deep in her core—Rawn wanted Tamara. She walked through every room. With love songs playing—songs about desperation and despair—she let her weakness take over and pulled out the Chunky Monkey. Her willpower could be so unreliable. It was food that knew how to soothe her emotional distress. Unlike people—*men*—food never let her down.

It had all started when she went to Milan—the bingeing, the purging. The powers that be told her she needed to lose at least ten pounds, and D'Becca could not believe it. All the boys who gave her attention back in her small hometown in North Dakota had told her she was *too* skinny. But she did lose ten pounds; in fact she lost fifteen pounds, and she worked throughout the season. She was told she would make it in Paris. But when D'Becca went to Paris, she was told she needed to lose a few inches off her hips. *Lose ten more pounds, ma chère.*

Chai was fed and she cleaned her litter box, but D'Becca found she had nothing else to do. The boredom overwhelmed her. She could very well go to Pacific Place and shop alone, or perhaps make an appointment to get a massage. But D'Becca wanted to spend the day with Rawn, and she had been looking forward to spending time with him. She thought to herself, *I could be like the young woman in the TV commercial: I could study a sunset or discover a color or memorize clouds or be amphibious.*

Fed up, lonely, D'Becca breathed deeply, leafing through her tattered black book with dozens of international numbers. Everyone was far, far away. Spontaneously, she called Sicily, and by chance she would discover that Rawn was with her. She was oddly relieved when Sicily answered on the second ring. When she said she was about to head out to take advantage of Black Friday, D'Becca said, "Is Tamara joining you?"

"Are you kidding? This is a big day for Threads."

"Do you mind if I come along?"

"Sure, it sounds like fun. You want to drop by and park your car, or do you want to meet at the mall?"

"Well…"

"Have you eaten?"

"Chunky Monkey."

"Girl, doesn't that do the trick?" Sicily laughed.

"Every time," D'Becca managed to say in a definite voice.

"Well, look, we can grab something light at Il Fornaio. After last night… Tamara's cheesecake—with espresso *and* sweet potato— was so-so divine…" Sicily laughed even louder.

Is her happiness all about being in love?

Sicily continued. "We couldn't miss each other if we met at the open café. Whoever arrives first grabs a table," she suggested.

The idea of not being alone lifted D'Becca's spirits.

"Say three?"

"Three's good." D'Becca made note of the time on her two-time zone watch. Chai leapt on top of the table and she gently nudged her off.

"Three," Sicily confirmed. "In the terrace, yes?"

Sicily was a lifesaver.

"No, no. Don't worry. It's my pleasure," Tamara said, reaching for a straight pin from the wrist-held pincushion. She inserted a pin on the side of the sleek black dress. The glamour of the dress was the delicate flare directly above the ankle, and the hem ever so subtly brushed against the ground.

"Have you had an exhausting day?"

"It was really a zoo this morning. This small place—I had ten women in here at one point. Imagine the energy. It's the only day of the year I allow clientele to shop without an appointment. I finally managed to sell that mini you liked but dared not wear in public. By one o'clock I had the nerve to feel lonely. I managed to rush over to Briazz and grab a salad. Not two seconds after I returned, you popped in. I'm glad you caught me."

"You need to hire help, Tamara."

"I'm going to call an agency Monday. Good help doesn't come cheap."

The thin, pale woman gazed at her reflection in the mirror, her arms raised while Tamara continued to take in the dress. Her client always had a rather melancholy cloud hovering over her, and she was desperately unhappy. No, the better word would be *miserable*.

Six months ago she designed the black dress for Ingrid Michaels— the one she was now taking in. It was a first for Tamara. No client had ever come to her and requested to have a dress taken in.

A slender, not a minute older than twenty, hip-hop artist was finishing up the West Coast leg of her U.S. tour, and while playing one sold-out night at the Tacoma Dome, dropped in Threads with her entourage. She bought a seductive Tamara Original that Tamara had not been able to sell to any of her regular clientele; perhaps because it was a smidgen too revealing. But the very young artist showed up wearing it at a glitzy red carpet event and dozens of photographs were published capturing the flavor-of-the-month hip-hopper in the Tamara Original. The next day Tamara's telephone would not stop ringing.

Six months ago the elegant black dress fit Ingrid Michaels like a Maserati on the Autobahn. Now, as she stood in front of her, Tamara tried not to state the obvious: *Woman, you are skin and bones.* "So what's the occasion?" she asked to take her mind off other things. Not only for the sake of Ingrid, but likewise herself. Tamara was trying out this staying present idea Sicily talked about, and Pricilla wrote about in her *Times* best seller.

"Our last one…She's soon off to Cambridge. I'm going to miss her."

"She'll love being near London. It's no more than an hour by train."

"It's her seventeenth birthday this Saturday. I can't believe how fast time flies." Her voice was hollow and pathetic.

There was nothing Ingrid Michaels could not acquire if she wanted it. The idea that happiness was not for sale applied in her case. She was the least cheery, least fulfilled woman Tamara had been around, and certainly the most depressing client. The bulk of her clientele were career women in their thirties; some in their

early forties. They wanted the East Coast look, and while some of
the popular department stores—The Bon Marché, Nordstrom—
carried the latest styles, Tamara emulated the East Coast trends
and her designs were never, never duplicated. While a few regulars had seen her dresses worn by a public figure and tried to talk
her into having the design made for them, Tamara was firm. She
had an implied contract with each client: she would never produce
two of the same design. It was precisely why she never agreed to
have her designs sold in major department stores, even when she
had been approached numerous times. Once she used the design,
she handed it over to her accountant, who had each Tamara Original locked in a vault.

But dear Ingrid loved to spend her unfaithful husband's money.
She would have a dress designed because. Tamara did not really
care whether she ever wore them, yet Ingrid did wonders for her
business. Each season she had a well-publicized auction to raise
money for one thing or other, and Tamara's designs were exposed
to women married to some of the wealthiest men in Washington
State. Ingrid was genuinely altruistic, and her business sense was
to be admired. The woman knew how the marketing game worked
because prior to marrying her entrepreneurial genius of a husband
and having back-to-back children, she was VP or some such thing
at a Fortune 500 company marketing their products in New York
and Chicago. Tamara imagined her being like Diane Keaton in
Baby Boom—before Keaton's character inherited a baby.

"Time does have a way of flying by, doesn't it? I remember when
I was living in Amsterdam. That was the very best time of my life.
What was yours, Ingrid?" Tamara slipped the last pin into the
delicate fabric.

"I thought your best time was with Henderson Payne."

"Shock!" Tamara laughed.

Ingrid managed to lift the corners of her small mouth ever so faintly. "The West Village and NYU. I loved New York back then. And I was so pathetically naïve."

"Oh, what it would be like to still be pathetically naïve—to not know what you now know. Anyway, what would we do differently if we could go back and rearrange things, even with the knowledge we now have?" Tamara stood and looked into Ingrid's pale green eyes reflecting back at her. "Velvet will be out of style next season," she warned her client. "Okay. Three inches, that's what I'll need to take in. I'll definitely make sure my seamstress has it ready no later than midmorning on Saturday." She could not miss the watery eyes, and prayed a tear would not fall. She could not deal with some rich woman's issues today. *The downtrodden always managed their tribulations with some dignity.* "Ingrid?" Tamara said.

"Oh, yes." Habitually, she tucked her shoulder-length hair behind her ears which exposed a pair of stunning ruby studs. "Three inches. I like velvet. I love this dress." She looked up into Tamara's reflection in the wardrobe mirror and pantomimed, "Thank you."

Before Tamara could usher Ingrid out of the boutique, the sad—miserable—woman let go. Something about her husband planning to leave her as soon as their daughter was off to Cambridge.

"I admire the fact that he's giving you advance notice. How kind," Tamara said, clearly being sarcastic.

"One thing about Sebastian. He's a middle-aged man who isn't drawn to much younger women."

"Well, how old is this woman he plans to leave you for?"

"If I had to guess… She's probably in her mid-thirties. At least she's not in her twenties. I always knew I'd have to face the day that Sebastian fell out of love with me and fell into the arms of another woman. He's gone more than he's home. Any woman would be foolish to think that their husband—someone like Sebastian, wouldn't stray. I used to despise women like you, Tamara. Having affairs with married men. I always hoped the woman wouldn't be in the same generation as my son. God is benevolent after all."

"But it doesn't feel any less degrading, surely?"

That's when Ingrid Michaels became unglued.

It took another fifteen minutes before she could pull herself together and dash from the boutique into a waiting tinted-windowed Range Rover. After checking e-mail and online orders, Tamara placed the closed sign in the window before another drama queen came rushing in, taking up too much oxygen in the tight space. She could not imagine what hair stylists and bartenders had to go through. *Mon Dieu!*

Once she listened to her voicemail, she was crestfallen that she missed Sicily's call. She would love to have met up with her and D'Becca for drinks. And they were probably gone by now.

"Hey, luv. I'm leaving in ten. I need to change, and I'll try and find you and D'Becca at the mall." Tamara released the call. She began humming while she closed up; feeling carefree at the very idea she had something to do.

Twenty minutes later, she entered the parking lot and eagerly sought a space. *Why didn't I walk?* No sooner than she entered an aisle, two women, one tall and the other not so tall; one black and the other white, caught her attention. It was D'Becca and Sicily walking ahead of her, and it looked like they were going to take the elevator into the mall. They were laughing, their arms linked inside each other's. *Are they drunk?* Before she could toot her horn to get their attention, a car behind Tamara blew at her. In her rear-view mirror, she watched the impatient driver throwing her hands up in the air, in all probability out of frustration. *Go to hell!*

Hastily, Tamara squeezed her SUV into a "compact car only" parking space. She headed toward the crowd at the bank of elevators.

When she made it to the first level of the mall, she could not spot Sicily or D'Becca anywhere. They got lost in the horde of holiday shoppers. But then Tamara thought she spotted D'Becca entering Restoration Hardware. *No, that was someone else.* Tamara eagerly sought them out from one end to the other, yet her patience was being tested, and the clusters of people began to get on her nerves. Eventually, she grew emotionally exhausted. *That damn Ingrid Michaels took everything I had.*

She left Sicily a voicemail message. "Where are you? Look, I got your message late. I'm at the mall. Since I'm here, I'll rummage through the sales. You can reach me on my mobile. If I miss your call, leave me a message where I can find you."

Tamara had anticipated the mall would have turned into a dead zone by now. *I'm not in the mood for this.* When she turned to head back to the parking lot, she bumped straight into Rawn. Strangely, Tamara sensed he had been standing directly behind her while she was calling Sicily. What a miraculous coincidence, thought Tamara.

"Oh, hi," she said.

"Hey!"

"Shopping?"

"I checked out The Store of Knowledge. I wasn't impressed."

His eyes lingered on her for a moment longer than Tamara felt comfortable with. "I was thinking the same thing. Not in the mood. Hope I'm not coming down with anything. I mean, shopping is something I'm always in the mood to do, you know!"

They stood in the center of the crowded floor. Shoppers crashed into them; some made an effort to walk around them, annoyed that their path was blocked.

"I spent the day in the boutique. When I was about to make my escape, a client waltzes in. She's a big one. What could I do?" Tamara shrugged.

She struggled with having to look him in the eyes, and Rawn picked up on the fact that she was noticeably different from the woman he met the evening before at Sicily's. In a pair of faded blue jeans, a white Tee and a distressed black leather jacket and no makeup, she looked astonishingly striking; natural. The evening before, did she flirt and all but come on to him merely to create tension? Or was it to *get* attention? Now that the opportunity presented itself, she was not interested. In fact, her behavior intimated that she was uneasy even being in close proximity to Rawn. *This woman is a trip.*

"Well…" She looked fleetingly at her wristwatch, feigning curiosity about the time.

"Maybe we could grab a bite to eat. I haven't eaten today."

Tamara's face softened. "Guess what. This morning when I woke up, the first thing I thought about was that smoked turkey from last night."

"And I was craving some last night."

In unison they laughed, purging the chill in the air.

"Yeah; let's go grab something." Tamara looked anxiously around the crowded mall.

"Looking for someone?" he asked.

"No," she lied. "Hey, look. Why don't we go by my place? I'm in walking distance. I have some caviar, some aged cognac…"

"I don't do caviar." Rawn's look suggested that he was dead serious.

"Really? Okay, well…" She reached in her soft-leather clutch purse for a set of keys. "I have some leftover Pagliacci. It's West Coast, but good pizza."

"Sure…"

"Come on." Something in her shifted at that moment, and her smile radiated her oval-shaped face. Tamara was friendlier now, more relaxed, which confused Rawn.

He liked Tamara's place. An aesthetically pleasing décor, he would not have imagined it laid out in the way that it was. Although pretentious, it was an oddly warm place. With a pseudo fireplace, it felt homey even while it was swanky with charcoal-sable colored carpet and oversized vases and a throw in faux mink that was neatly folded against a loveseat. Large candles adorned the front room, and several childhood photographs were strategically placed on a table. Surprisingly, a photograph of Tamara, Sicily, and Tamara's writer friend, Pricilla Miles, in what looked to be a bar, was set on a side table. Even while she was full of herself and phony, her place depicted a side of her he saw at the mall: self-conscious, reserved. She sat in a sofa with her legs folded beneath her while Rawn sat in a large and cozy chair with thick rolled arms. It did not take long for them to finish off what was left of the large pie, which Sicily brought by on Thanksgiving Eve. She kept Tamara company while she made the dessert—the very rich espresso sweet potato cheesecake that everyone, despite being stuffed, had seconds of on Thanksgiving Day.

Later, when he needed to recall how things moved so swiftly, Rawn would not recollect who brought up Henderson. He would call to mind that Tamara's version of her relationship with Henderson Payne was in contradiction to what Khalil shared with him. While people saw things from their own perspective, no two stories could be so dissimilar and both accurate.

She had been talking casually about Henderson for a few minutes. Rawn was not necessarily interested, but he guessed she needed to talk about him. "It was after he came back from playing ball in Italy," she said. "We were at a function in L.A. Someone had a private party for their friend at a club in Hollywood. He was alone. I mean he wasn't with Daphne. There was street talk that he was in L.A. to meet with the L.A. franchise. He was tired of Seattle.

He wanted another *ring*. Not that he didn't already have two, but with Henderson...He's incredibly competitive. Of course that's a part of his appeal."

Solemn, Tamara met Rawn's gaze.

"We slept together that night. He was staying at Chateau Marmont—in this romantic bungalow. The ambience... We had a great time. I'm sure he loved Daphne, but I knew once he made love to me, he could never be the same with her again. I fell in love with him that night and I knew that he fell for me. There was no going back, at least not for me."

Rawn tried not to judge.

"I had an abortion," she admitted, and in a rather impassive voice. "He asked—no, begged—me to abort it and I did. I did it for him because I loved him and he asked me to do it *for him*. I know he loves me, but it's complicated because of his children."

Rawn did not know what to say to her. He could not understand why she was sharing all these personal details with him. They barely knew each other, and what was the point of it? Something nudged him to ask her, "Are you in love with Henderson Payne or the athlete?" It did not come out in the way he had intended.

Her smile was sneaky and hard to interpret. She leaned forward; her breasts were perceptible through the vanilla-colored tee. "No, of course not. I'm not impressed with celebrity. My standards are high. I'm never with someone who isn't successful. Men in particular who are successful and/or rich, they have a way of—they have a degree of power, and that's one of the most intoxicating aphrodisiacs a man can have. With Henderson and me, it was intense. It was...we were both probably fixated. No matter what you've heard, Henderson ruined his relationship with Daphne. He wanted me even more than I wanted him. He still does...want me. They were in a lot of trouble before we even met."

"Do you care about other people?"

"I like you. Your honesty is…sexy. Most men are not honest, you know. They are selective when it comes to details. And in answer to your question—there's no incentive to invest in a third party. That's really what you're getting at, *n'est-ce pas?*"

"Something along those lines." He was purposely vague.

"Sicily means a lot to you, doesn't she?"

"She's one of my closest friends."

"I know you wish she weren't gay."

"I was disappointed; I'll cop to that."

"Why are you with D'Becca?"

"What do you mean?" He grimaced.

"Come on, Rawn. Really!"

"Are you saying that D'Becca?…"

"Don't get me wrong. D'Becca's a beautiful woman. I like her. But what are your feelings for her? It's been what—almost four months? That's no longer casual."

"Are you and Sicily *casual?*"

Rawn could not quite pin down Tamara's nature. Her moods were like a kaleidoscope—she switched from this to that, and it could be demanding to distinguish the range of personalities beneath her guile. He decided it was a protective shield Tamara learned how to use. She feared being weak, at a disadvantage, and she did what was necessary so not to get hurt. She was right, he decided: what would be the incentive to invest in a third party? Tamara only cared about herself.

With a smile Rawn considered trivial, Tamara said, "I like Sicily. She's everything I would want a man to be."

"What does that mean?"

"She's socially and emotionally appealing. She's financially stable. She's dedicated, successful, noetic, and *real*. To borrow from Pricilla Miles: authentic. Oh, I am beginning to overuse that word. Anyway…she's willing to compromise all of those attributes—for love."

"Don't forget that Sicily is one of my best friends. So be careful what you choose to share with me."

"I have nothing to hide from Sicily. You being here, she would understand that."

"Really? Because I'm not..."

"Oh, trust me. That woman knows who she's dealing with."

"Really?"

"Really. And you changed the subject."

"How so?"

"D'Becca?"

"D'Becca and I have an understanding."

"Are you sure?"

"I'm sure," he said.

Rawn leaned into the seat and rested his head on the back of the chair. Talking with Tamara, it made him start to entertain whether he should actually take D'Becca to Vail with him for the holiday. Did he really want her to go? He probably would not have considered inviting her but for the fact that Khalil mentioned it in a conversation. Rawn had considered asking Sicily until she told him a week before Thanksgiving that she had met someone—Tamara.

He looked up and Tamara was standing over him. He was not sure what to make of her expression. Not minutes ago she was telling him that Henderson was her soul mate. He still was not sure why she was with Sicily. One minute she was giddy and open, the next sharing sad love stories. What did she want from him? Why had she invited him to her place? Thanksgiving night, she was openly teasing, and he knew Sicily must have noticed it, but did she even care? Obviously, Sicily did not see Rawn as a threat. Rawn was certain D'Becca picked up on Tamara's flirtation. Tamara knelt to the charcoal-sable carpeted floor and eased herself between

Rawn's legs. He was powerless to react. His mind was not advancing quickly enough to the situation that appeared to be unfolding, and his body could not contain his passion.

"Hey, Tamara. Wait. What's going on?"

"Look at me," she said. "Look into my eyes. What do you see?"

"Tamara..."

"I know you want me, Rawn. It's all over your face. I saw the way you looked at me last night. And now..." She placed her hand on his crotch and gently, adeptly massaged him. "Wow! You are *hard*, baby."

He reached for her hand. "Stop it, Tamara," Rawn snapped.

"Come on. It's between you and me. Sicily, and D'Becca for that matter—they never have to know."

She unfastened his jeans, and once her hand was inside his briefs, Rawn gripped her by the wrist and said, "Tamara! What the...are you doing?"

She laughed at him. "Please don't even try to play me." She put her face in his crotch and once the fullness of him was inside her warm mouth there was nothing—not one thing—Rawn could do at that point but to acquiesce.

His head covered by a hoodie, Rawn rested against the stone-hued wall of D'Becca's, waiting for her. The temperature dropped considerably while he was at Tamara's, and Rawn had to keep his hands in his bomber jacket pockets to keep them warm. He tried to think of what—how he was going to handle the turn of events at Tamara's. While his mind moved in and out of competing thoughts, a dark and shiny Beamer pulled up. Rawn noticed it because no one ever got out of the vehicle; it sat idling for a few minutes on the side of the street opposite D'Becca's. Rawn moved away from the light of the crescent moon that replicated the island's semi-circle landscape. He watched the Beamer for a good five minutes before a man stepped out and lit up a cigar. He appeared to be looking Rawn's way, although there was no way the man could make him out from the distance. The man leaned on the vehicle another minute or two before he pulled out what looked to be a cellular. With the cellular to his ear, he stepped back in the BMW. Soon after he pulled away from the curb. Unaware of himself, Rawn's heart slowed, and he exhaled. He could see his breath against the frigid night air.

Shortly thereafter, D'Becca stood at her door trying to open it with her key. She was totally unaware of Rawn standing in the shadowy corner. "Shit," she said. Rawn knew she was inebriated. She wobbled while attempting to hold several shopping bags, and to open the door with her key simultaneously. After several tries, she still had not managed to unlock the door. She bent over to reach for the dropped keys. "Come on," she coached herself. "You can do it."

Rawn walked up behind her and wrapped his arms around her waist. D'Becca gasped. When she turned around, encircled in his loose arms, she was relieved but no less irritated. He could have been any black man coming out of the dark, and the hoodie shielded much of his face.

"Don't ever sneak up on me again!" she stated angrily. "It's dark, Rawn. How did I know it would be you?" She pressed an open palm against his chest and pushed him away.

"Everything all right, D'Becca?"

In unison, Rawn and D'Becca looked to the voice in the invisible night.

"Oh, hi, Charlotte. How was your Thanksgiving?"

"Went to Everett. And yours?"

"Lovely. Thank you."

D'Becca rushed inside the townhouse. In one swift sequence, she tossed her keys into a crystal bowl and dropped her BeBe and Barneys New York shopping bags to the foyer floor. With a harsh sigh, she peeled off her jacket.

"Where have you been?" she shouted. "I called you," she fussed loudly. "Did you forget that we were going to shop and see a film? How inconsiderate, Rawn—damn!" She planted her hands on her hipbones.

"I went to Pacific Place, but I didn't see you."

She stared at him for a few seconds before she started to walk out of the foyer, half-stumbling, saying, *"Please!"* beneath her breath.

"Are you going to walk away while we're having a conversation?"

D'Becca stopped at the arched doorway that led to her grand living room. "Conversation?" She chuckled.

"What's the problem, D'Becca?"

"What's the problem?" She walked into the living room while Rawn remained at the entrance. "You're the problem!" She combed her fingers through her hair; D'Becca could feel that her equilibrium was way off. *I had one too many.* "What are we doing? Huh, Rawn?"

He looked genuinely confused. "What do you mean?"

"Us? What are?…Are we?…Never mind."

Rawn was in doubt as to what he should do. He was still distracted by what went down at Tamara's. There was Sicily. No way could he ever tell her what happened, and for various reasons. But it had not occurred to him that what happened at Tamara's would in any way affect D'Becca. He tried to open his mouth to say something— anything! Still, his words would not budge.

"I care about you, D'Becca."

"You *care?*"

"Yeah." Rawn watched D'Becca wear a similar expression Janelle had worn when he used that very same word—*care*—with his ex-fiancée.

"You never told me you were once engaged."

Rawn managed not to expose his surprise. She must have talked to Sicily.

"What else haven't you told me, Rawn? Since you *care* about me."

"D'Becca…" he exhaled in frustration.

"Am I just some—some curiosity to you?"

Sicily could get a little free with her mouth when she had a few. Obviously, D'Becca and Sicily met up earlier and had some sort of bonding afternoon; a lot of drinking was involved, and at the same time, he and Tamara were—whatever they were doing. What happened at Tamara's today had nothing to do with him and D'Becca. Sicily, if she were to find out, would be wounded. *It's between you and me.* No matter how awkward it would make him feel in Sicily's presence, Rawn was going to have to live with that.

"Are you even listening to me, Rawn?"

"Yeah," he said in a voice that lacked conviction. "I'm listening."

D'Becca, a good four feet away, saw something in his eyes she had not seen before. Something had changed. It showed in the way he was now *treating* her. His face was guarded and cold. While she was out of town, something happened, or it was about the evening they spent at Sicily's. They were not the same. Her feelings were stronger than his; she could see that now.

"Good night, Rawn."

She bypassed him; he reached for her. "D'Becca, wait!"

"Let go of me. Leave!" she argued.

"D'Becca…"

She slapped him good across the face, and Rawn, shocked, reached for his cheek. He was not exactly sure what to do. "What's wrong with you?" he fussed.

"Get out!" she shouted.

"D'Becca, what?…"

"Get the hell out!" She yelled at the top of her lungs, "*Get ouuut!* Damn you, get *out* of my house!"

When he closed the door behind him, he locked eyes with D'Becca's neighbor returning to her townhouse from walking her dog. The Doberman pinscher barked ferociously at Rawn. It took several ongoing loud barks before the neighbor told the dog to "shush."

"Good evening," he said.

She stared at him for several quiet moments—a look of criticism on her face—before she said in a tight voice, "Good evening."

D'Becca sat at the top of the staircase, her face buried in her trembling hands. It was no mistaking, she told herself. Although it happened without her realizing it, she was in love with Rawn. Troy had asked her just the day before: "Where is this going, Becca?" For so long she did not use a title to define the man in her life. She never once thought of Rawn as anything other than a man she felt comfortable being with. When, how did she lose herself to him?

CHAPTER EIGHTEEN

For many years, the tree at Rockefeller Center represented everlasting joy in Imani's mind. Yet while she stood watching the sun breaking through soft clouds, she did not feel the same connection to the Rock's ambiance; not as she did when she was a child. *Am I too jaded?* With such passion, she loved ice skating and spending time with Dante, and to sip hot cocoa while they strolled along the energetic streets, observing tourists shopping at the high-end stores. Although he traveled a great deal and he was always on the road, when Imani was a child, Dante made it a point to be home for the holidays. In every city he played, he sent her a postcard, and Imani would wait with bated breath for each one to arrive in the mailbox. When she was in her first year of college, she met someone that reminded her of Dante. Not physically, but in spirit. Even though things did not work out between them, she searched for the same qualities in that man from her sophomore year in every man she would meet. She could not forget how she trusted him, and he listened to Imani. The thing that touched her deeply was how attentive he was toward her. *Like Dante.*

So it came as a surprise even to Imani that she chose Blaine, and fell so hard for him. With dark and stunning good looks, she met him at a rooftop bar when he was in his last year at Princeton. She was twenty-nine and he was twenty-six. While she admired him working as a model to pay his way through an Ivy League university, something about his marketing briefs did not sit well with Imani. Especially since the advertisement was plastered on every other bus, bus stop, and taxi in the city, not to mention on a billboard in the heart of Times Square. Kenya said she was being judgmental, and perhaps she was biased, although unconsciously. Therefore she put her narrow-mindedness on reserve and began going out with him. Looking back now, she cannot believe how gullible she was, and it made her heart ache years later reminiscing their time together. When they began dating, a woman he had once been romantically involved with lived with Blaine. He told Imani he was helping her out, and that they were "just friends."

Imani thought about those postcards Dante sent her a lot lately. When she purchased her Seattle houseboat, the first thing she did, with a bottle of wine at her side, was to lay out hundreds of postcards on the floor and carefully selected dozens and spent hours making a collage. The next morning she headed for Aaron Brothers and purchased a 36-by-48-sized frame. For weeks it was the only thing she had in her houseboat: a collage of postcards from every corner of the world hanging on her bare wall. After leaving New York and Blaine, she wanted Seattle to be a new beginning. When it came to men, the postcards were like Imani's anchor. They reminded her not to settle for good looks and un-adulterated charm. Nothing good, she knew in the pit of her soul, ever came out of falling for a man when his looks and charm carried a girl away and made her lose all sense of basic logic.

With her eyes pressed shut, Imani breathed the thought: *I miss you so much.* She did her very best to bite back tears. She wanted to be strong; still, she felt the sadness and loss of her father so deeply. Since her mother's death, she had leaned on Dante more than she realized. His death brought that to mind. Naturally, when someone dear passed on, suddenly there was so much to share. Things left unsaid for years were bold and fierce in the mind, and desperate to be expressed. While she and Dante were very close, it was her mother who was there all the days and weeks and sometimes months Dante was not. Something her sister, Kenya, never quite understood—Imani too was an abandoned child.

Blaine advised her to go back to Seattle. He would keep tabs on the investigation of Dante's death, and inform her right away of each and every new lead. He promised. Imani would be *physically* in Seattle, and would make an effort to begin her healing process. Yet her mind, her heart, her spirit would die a slow death in misty, hazy Seattle. The only person she felt closest to was Jean-Pierre, but she missed Trouble something crazy. Still, she needed to stay in New York and be a face for Dante. While she trusted that the NYPD was taking his death quite seriously, her staying in New York and being close to the investigation was something Imani needed to do. The detectives assigned to his case gave them hope; still, Imani and Kenya looked at them with skepticism. While he might have been a popular musician and notable public figure, Dante was likewise controversial. He had been very outspoken about nearly everything that just pissed him off—Vietnam and America's racial injustice throughout the seventies, apartheid in South Africa in the eighties, to only name a few. From their respective television sets, Imani and Kenya, while growing up over four hundred miles apart, watched their father being handcuffed and sent off to jail.

"Hey!"

Imani looked around and found Blaine holding Dean & DeLuca. "No foam." He winked.

She reached for the cup and put effort into something close to resembling a smile, but Blaine, more than any other man except Dante, knew her too well. She sipped through the opening of the cup's lid. "When do you drive back up?"

"I want to get back before dark. So, soon. I'll come down next weekend. In the meantime, try to go through Dante's things. I know it'll be difficult, but it'll also help."

"It's been too emotional to even consider looking at his finances, his will…Kenya's good at this kind of stuff. I'm letting her handle all of Dante's business affairs."

"She went back to Toronto?"

Imani sipped her espresso. "She'll be back Friday."

"Will you be okay all alone in this city that doesn't know how to sleep?" Blaine swallowed, touched by the woe her father's death produced in Imani. He gazed at her taking in the cold morning, and he could tell she did not want to be alone.

"I can continue to go through all the letters and cards and notes we received. It really helps to read the love perfect strangers had for Dante. Kenya and I decided to respond to every single one, no matter how long it takes."

For a little while, silence played between them.

"Blaine?" She squinted to look up at him. While it was a frigid late morning in New York, a glacial sun filled the lively streets.

He looked into her soulful eyes. "What?"

"I forgive you."

Since Dante's death, Blaine had been guarded and wary in Imani's presence. He never knew one minute to the next what Imani would say to him; confusing her grief over Dante with her long-standing anger at him. And if Imani did not know better, she would have thought Blaine was on the verge of producing a tear. Patiently, he waited well over two years to hear her say those words. He knew nothing he said would ever make her understand how sorry he felt, and what a fool he had been. He never told her, but he chalked that time up—the cheating on her—to bad judgment and immaturity. Back then he was a visibly successful male model and he had an assortment of options, and Blaine took advantage of nearly every single one.

"I never meant…"

"It happened. And I know you didn't intend to hurt me. But you did. Had Dante not been killed, I most likely would still be unable to forgive you. But they say, no sooner than God closes a door, he opens a window."

"And you know I hate that Dante's gone, but..."

"I know." She purposely stopped his words.

"Damn. Imani, you smiled."

Her laughter, often irrepressible, made her eyes water. "Yes, I know."

Their embrace was natural. It was emotive and long, like the affectionate hug they shared many weeks ago; when Imani saw Blaine for the first time since she packed and left New York and relocated to Seattle. Through their embrace, they both felt the physicality of their emotions—the genuine love that was real between them.

When she released him, Imani said, "Kenya asked me something interesting before she left for Toronto."

"What's that?"

"Would I take you back if you tried to go in that direction."

"No, she didn't!"

Imani was not exactly sure whether he wanted to know the answer to that question. "I told her how much I loved you back then, and I always will love you. But love evolves and what it feels like— what it *is*—when two people meet and begin to develop as a couple is a different love from the love those same two people feel years later. Sometimes it's mature and special, and sometimes it's reliant and taken for granted. What I know for sure is that I can now meet someone new and be open with that person. Available— emotionally and psychologically—to that person. For quite some time, I chose to go on a date with someone strictly because I knew I wasn't interested in them. They were safe. Letting go entirely with a man—it just didn't seem possible. Some part of me didn't know *how*. I didn't trust myself."

They shared a grace-filled moment.

"I mean this, Imani. That man—whoever he is—will be blessed to have you."

Her voice was gentle. "Thank you."

In silence, they watched ice-skaters in their wool scarves, gloves, caps with fuzzy balls dangling on either side, which sheltered them from the bitter cold air.

"So when do you plan to go back to Seattle?"

"My business manager and my office manager—they've been taking care of everything for me right now. I feel bad leaving Jean-Pierre in a bind at Café Neuf. But I need to see this through first. I *need* to know who would kill my father in cold blood and walked out of that bodega like he's some damn Al Pacino in *The Godfather* or something."

"Oh, that scene was the bomb, though. I mean, one of the best scenes ever in motion picture history. Seriously."

She loved Blaine deeply; Imani understood that clearly now. She sipped her drink before she said, "Yeah, but whoever that lowlife was, he was no Al Pacino. Michael Corleone was smart, but this guy...he's stupid! I wish I knew why he did this. Anyway, he's lucky the video camera didn't work at the bodega."

Blaine was somber when he told her, "Dante was like a father to me. I want to see that lowlife's... Clearly he didn't know who it was that he shot."

"Good morning," Sicily said, reaching for her mail in the Academy mailroom..

Rawn looked up from a letter he had opened seconds before and flashed a deceptive grin. "Good morning."

"So, don't keep me in suspense. Tell me."

"Tell you?" He felt awkward, and hesitated before he replied. "Tell you what?"

"What you think of Tamara."

All weekend Tamara's voice kept coming back to him: *It's between you and me.* "She's cool people," he managed to say persuasively.

"So you approve?" she asked.

"What do you mean by *approve?*"

"You agree?"

"With what?"

"Okay. I guess I'm not using the correct language. But you think she's good for me?"

It was not Sicily's style to seek, let alone need, someone's approval. In Rawn's mind, he played with the theory that she was too intoxicated by Tamara. Janelle said to him when he broke off their engagement and she walked away from him for good: "I should have listened to my intuition."

"Enjoy this, Sicily. Whatever it is you and Tamara have, just go with it."

She held his eyes for a beat, and if Sicily did not know him better, she would think Rawn was guarding a secret. "Tamara's authentic and I like that. Hey, by the way, did D'Becca tell you? We had lunch Friday." Sicily stuffed her mail in her briefcase. "She's in love with you. So what's going on with you two?"

Rawn pretended to be distracted by the letter, and continued to keep his eyes on the page to avoid looking into Sicily's trusting eyes. "She mentioned you two hooked up. By the way, how much of my life did you share with D'Becca?"

"What do you mean?" Sicily acknowledged a passing teacher and extended her a friendly, "Good morning."

Rawn, polite, nodded to the colleague. He looked into Sicily's hazel eyes and they were gentle, kind. She spent time with D'Becca out of respect she had for him. Moreover, it was obvious Tamara mentioned nothing about their running into each other at Pacific Place. Depending on how he chose to look at it, it could be a good thing or it could be a really bad thing.

"It's nice that you and D'Becca are friendly. Now you can get off my case about the fact that I'm seeing someone who isn't Negro."

Amused, she said, "Oh, and Tamara liked you. Want to go to Café Neuf for lunch?"

He mulled over the idea, hesitating before he finally said in a passive voice, "Sure."

Once she left him standing alone at the mail slots, Rawn's mind raced. He was not confident that he could maintain such a despicable deception. The veil it cast over his life made him uncomfortable. He was brought out of his train of thought when he heard two colleagues entering the mailroom in the midst of an animated conversation. He turned to see who they were and offered his thoughtful "good morning," and their replies followed him out of the mailroom.

"Khalil Underwood!"

"Khalil, hey, it's me."

"Whatup?"

"Take me off speaker, man."

The tone alone made Khalil place his bottled water on his cluttered desk filled with paperwork. His office, which overlooked the entire West Hollywood community, was equipped with a basketball hoop, and posters of the athletic elite—from Michael Jordan to Tiger Woods. There were framed photographs of him and a few female public figures taken at Hollywood parties and various social events. He looked up to his assistant. "Give me ten."

Standing, the assistant said, "You have a conference call in five."

"Find a way to make it in ten."

"It took weeks to make this happen."

"Ten minutes. Make that happen."

When his assistant closed the door behind her, Khalil took Rawn off speaker. "Why do I *know* this ain't about Vail?"

"Would you have kicked your assistant out of your office if you thought this was about Vail?"

Khalil exhaled a deep breath. "What? No, wait up! Uh-huh, no way!" Rawn butted in on his best friend presuming to know exactly why he called, and attentively, Khalil listened while Rawn gave him the blow-by-blow. Oblivious to the fact that he came to his feet, Khalil put his earpiece on and returned the receiver to the carriage. It took roughly four minutes for Rawn to set up the scene—from Pacific Place to Tamara's—and when he finished, Khalil said, "Damn! Are you?...Man, what. the. fuck! You know you can't even tell Sicily about this. Listen up, Rawn. *Do not* tell Sicily. I know you'll feel compelled. This thing'll start messing with your head...Man, don't—*don't*—tell Sicily!"

"Look," Rawn began. "Sicily is whipped. She's crazy about this woman."

"I told you to stay away from her. You are way smarter than me, so what about the word *trouble* are you not ascertaining, man?"

"It's not like I knocked on her door."

"But did you have to go hanging out with the bitch, man? That idea went looking for trouble. You just couldn't resist it."

"I'm lying to Sicily..."

"Now, not bringing it up isn't what I call lying. Omission, granted. But I believe a lie isn't officially a lie until you start making stuff up. Long as you don't go there, bro, you cool. Trust me, Tamara won't tell Sicily. She likes the whole idea that the two of you have this secret. See, that's how she plays it." Khalil heard a tap, then a pause, then another tap, then another pause, then a knock. He spoke up, "In a minute."

"I better let you..."

"Listen to me, Rawn. You have to understand, this woman is not wrapped tight. You remember when I got arrested because that actress I dated put that restraining order out on me?"

It was for the first time Rawn took notice that Khalil always referred to his ex as "the actress." "Who could forget."

"You know and I definitely know, I am no stalker. Okay, I lost my head for a minute. But I didn't *stalk* her. Getting that restraining order—she made her point! But man, this lady—Tamara, she'll stalk you...She stalked Daphne."

"You never mentioned that."

"Dude, you gotta...Put this to bed!"

The assistant barged into the office with a hand pressed against her lean hip. "Khalil!" Her coiled hairdo added to her dramatic, stylish look.

He lifted a finger and nodded. For a few seconds, he listened to Rawn while the assistant walked into the office and came directly in front of his desk, attempting to intimidate him with her look— eyes rolling, neck popping.

"I'm not sure what to do..."

"*Khalil?*" The assistant raised her voice.

"Whatever you do," Khalil advised his friend, *"don't* tell Sicily!"

CHAPTER NINETEEN

When she answered the door, D'Becca rushed into him, and there was a look of anguish in her eyes. "Rawn, I'm sorry. I'm sorry…"

When he let her go, Rawn noticed traces of recent tears that she tried to camouflage by not meeting his eyes. "What's going on?"

"I…" She took his hand, guiding him. "Let's go in here."

The living room was candlelit, and buoyantly the voice of Andrea Bocelli played. D'Becca stood awkwardly in the room. Dressed in a pair of Rawn's 501s—flesh tight against her trim hips, and there was a rip right near the crotch—she looked quite vulnerable. With a faint smile, he gave a passing glance at her nipples vaguely visible through the Old Navy Tee she was wearing.

"You have reason to be confused." His words verged on an apology.

He turned his back to D'Becca, slipping his hands into his black trousers pockets. He tried to decide if he was going to stay or leave. He walked deeper into the room and slipped off his bomber jacket and placed it over the arm of the chair nearest to him. He sat in the plush cushioned loveseat and looked to the fading fire in the fireplace. Rawn crossed his legs.

D'Becca moved quickly to the sofa and sat on the edge, not taking her eyes off Rawn. She leaned forward, her elbows pressed against her knees. "What is it, Rawn? What?" Her voice was laced with acute worry.

"I'm—I'm not sure." He looked at her, but then averted his eyes.

"What do you mean?" D'Becca knew the way he had been acting lately was not solely her imagination.

They made love.

But whatever pulled them together in the preceding months—whatever kept them coming back again and again—that was over. In silence, Rawn lay on his back, his arms behind his head. She turned to her side and watched Rawn's distinct profile. She said it so softly he could barely hear the words: "I love you, Rawn." It was a risk, but before Rawn, D'Becca had never felt whole with a man; she never let go, or allowed herself to get terribly close. Her innate wisdom led her to believe she should not put everything on the line for this man. Letting Rawn in could have had something to do with his unique masculine manners. He was a profoundly intriguing personality.

Rawn climbed out of the canopy bed and went to the window. The rain had abated and a full moon was peeking out from behind passing pelican-colored clouds. He caught sight of a Beamer parked directly behind his Jeep. Certainly that was no coincidence. It was difficult to establish in his mind whether someone was in the car because of the shaded windows, but it was unquestionably the exact same BMW—always polished, well-cared for. With a look of puzzlement, Rawn stepped away from the window. While he dressed, D'Becca could see him in her room as clear as the moon against the brilliant evening sky; and she understood that his mind, his very core, was no longer accessible to her.

"Rawn, stay."

Rawn never heard D'Becca so fraught, which made her especially vulnerable.

She lifted herself up, letting the weight of her upper body rest on her elbows. "Stay with me tonight. Don't go."

For a moment he studied her curled up in the bed, one breast exposed from the silky tailored bedding. The evening's theatrical sky seeping into the room made her face look so childlike. D'Becca was complex. On the one hand, she was instinctively smart and naturally clever, and on the other, she was insecure because of the nature of her childhood. She was an only child, and her parents were so damaged by their own childhoods they did not know how to demonstrate their love for her. He was initially drawn to that deep complexity. "I have papers to grade."

"Rawn…" She stopped herself because something told her anything she said would not matter—there was no need to expose herself any further. He went to the bed and bent down to kiss her cheek. She moved her mouth under his and slipped her tongue in his mouth. His body reacted without his mind's consent; the sensuousness of her kiss made him weak for her. Some part of him—the part of Rawn that *cared* for D'Becca—wanted to stay.

"Good-night."

Even when she called out his name, he did not turn around or come back. She could hear the front door close behind him and the rejection cut so deep. If she did not know it days ago, it was now so brazen—D'Becca had backed herself into a bad emotional corner.

"Ingrid?"

Tamara's client rushed into the boutique in a poncho-style wrap that sheltered her from the chilled night air. Ingrid's shoulder-length, dirty-blond hair streaked with gray was covered by a trendy cap. Tamara would never have recognized Ingrid on the street in that get-up. She knew when last Ingrid had sex with her husband, but she did not know how the woman looked when she was not making herself appear so together—her Washington State public image. When she pulled off the chic wrap and tossed it to the nearby chaise, Tamara nearly gasped. In a pair of denim, which she paid six-hundred dollars for in Geneva, Ingrid was so thin Tamara could blow at her and she would stumble. *Jeans. God knows they told the whole truth and nothing but—flat butt, hipless, chubby thighs, high waist, thick middle...*

With her palms pressed together in prayer-style, Ingrid said in a calm but strikingly confident voice, "I have a favor to ask of you. I can't trust anyone else. You..." Her green eyes meeting Tamara's... "Are the only one I trust. Because I know you would understand." Once she made it to *trust*, Ingrid began to weaken, but she suppressed the tears in her throat and pulled the cute hat off her head and, without looking, tossed it to the chaise where it landed on top of the poncho-wrap.

Slowly, Tamara removed her chic reading glasses and slipped them into the collar of her sleeveless tee, which exposed slender, toned arms.

Each woman saw the other in a new light that evening. Ingrid had not once seen Tamara so casual. On previous occasions, when she came to Threads, Tamara purposely selected outfits to wear so as to promote her line of unique, although overpriced, dresses. Ingrid never saw a model wear a pencil skirt the way Tamara did. Often she would have on a skintight skirt with deep black hosiery and something as simple as a sleeveless sweater cut very low in the back; or a suede jacket designed to be worn deliberately close to the curve of a woman's physique. Standing tall and effortlessly sensual, she was in a pair of nicely cut winter-white corduroys and red suede stilettos that made her look even taller, and glamorous. Tamara had such an eye; only she could wear that outfit and it came across quite smart, creative. Another woman would come across like she was trying too hard.

"Ingrid..." Tamara took two steps. The words—the woman's *tone*—was disturbing. "What's wrong? What's happened?"

"Sebastian!"

Allah. She's killed the S-O-B!

"He's obsessed, Tamara. I've never seen him like this." Ingrid crossed her arms. "Once, about ten years ago, he met someone. And while it didn't get serious enough to consider divorce, he couldn't stop thinking about her. He would not…let her go. I never thought…" She shouted: "He's making a fool of not just *me*, but himself…with this back-street floozy!"

"Ingrid…"

"Can you believe when I asked him who this—this woman was… he told me she'd met someone. He thought she was in love with… another man. He was hurt. Not that he felt betrayed. Sebastian was absolutely *hurt*."

"What?" Tamara chuckled.

Ingrid looked up to Tamara, who stood several feet away, and said, "What do you find amusing about this?"

Tamara's shoulders slumped and she replied sarcastically, "Well, listen. Truth be told, I thought you finally got up the courage to cut off his balls." It was apparent Ingrid was upset and she was not in the mood for Tamara's ridicule. "So what does all this"—and she spread out her hands—"have to do with me?"

"I don't…"

"Who is this woman anyway? Where does she live?"

"Tamara, I need a *friend*. I can't handle this…This, it's different. I don't trust myself. I put everything on the line—I sacrificed a career. I have to be subjected to some bitch having more access to my husband than me?…. She's ruining everything I've sacrificed for!"

CHAPTER TWENTY

D'Becca could hear someone outside the front door. Sprinting to the stairway, D'Becca nearly tripped down the spiral landing. She called out "Rawn!" with the hopes he changed his mind about staying the night. But instead, when she opened her front door, she collided with Sebastian Michaels standing in front of her. "Sebastian!" D'Becca's wet eyes nearly popped out of their sockets. The shock was acute; her pulse quickened. "Sebastian?…Hi." She spoke just above a whisper.

Sebastian slipped his keys in his pocket and walked around her in the doorway, through the foyer and to the spiral stairs. He stopped at the third stair and turned to look at her. He knew her better than anyone. She was confused and sad. "We need to talk."

D'Becca met Sebastian Michaels in Rome three years ago. She had finished a show in Milan the previous day, and it would be her last show in Italy, although at the time, D'Becca did not know it. Her body was not reacting too well to her having switched three different time zones over the past week, and she was lonely. Saying *ciao* to a model friend at Trastevere train station who was headed for Gstaad to go skiing with her boyfriend made her feel abandoned, like when she was a child. For long moments, she sat alone at the table. Not necessarily lonely, but she contemplated whether she should fly to Deauville and drop in on a friend she had not seen since Fashion Week in New York over a year ago. D'Becca often felt isolated when she was in Europe; she could use the company. And Deauville was so quiet, so calm. Or better yet, she could go to Vienna; it was an ideal place to hibernate until her next assignment.

She was not in the mood to be with a man. D'Becca was increasingly becoming apathetic toward men. She spent way too much time accommodating men that she now found herself emotionally distant whenever she spent time alone with them. The physical closeness meant far more to her than the sex itself. Sex, however, was most often what men wanted from her. Like a number of models she had met over the years, she too had an uncanny way of choosing men who could not show up emotionally; who could not commit. They showed up in the flesh. When she left her small town in North Dakota and headed for Seattle on a whim, she was convinced she had nothing going for her but her looks. Even at the time, she was not aware her looks would support her financially. The men she met helped her get her feet on the ground; they showed her things she would need to know; they gave her money and taught her how to please them which only taught her how to please other men. And they gave her attitude. D'Becca was a quick study, rapacious for knowledge. For such a long time, she spent so much time trying to create an emotional bond, and D'Becca used sex to try and attain it. But now she realized that sex was not about love, which in essence was what she had been seeking. With all the mixed messages, from childhood, society, and men, shuffling around inside her head, she came to trust that life was solely about suffering—the First of the Noble Truths. In her lifetime, it never made sense—life. At times, when she felt so terribly alone, D'Becca would pray because she had grown tired of lifting up every brick herself. It was awkward and unnatural when she would try to meet God halfway. One day she decided her prayers were never taken seriously; yet it never occurred to her that her appeals to God were not sincere.

So, that cold and lonely night when she went to a small, quiet restaurant in Piazza Navona to have dinner, she was bored. She was fed up with male company and *ciao bellas* and accents that were not

American. She wanted only to be home. Perhaps that was why, when Sebastian Michaels addressed her at the table, she was pleased. Not naturally good-looking, but he was an imposing figure, and his presence in the restaurant demanded attention. He was *someone* or he was rich. Even while the detailed suit and his look in and of themselves were impressive, it was his hands that revealed the truth. Hands that belonged to a man whose money worked for him, not vice versa.

"*Scusa. Buona sera, signorina. Sei da solo?*"

D'Becca looked up to the man and directly into his aqua-blue eyes. Straightaway she knew he was American. Oh, his Italian was persuasive, but he was American. Despite his European style, she had been living and working between Milan and Paris for quite some time; she was fully aware of the difference by now.

"*Non capisco,*" she said, lying.

"*Parla inglese?*"

"Yes," she replied, pretending to be demure. "I speak English."

"You are American?"

D'Becca's full mouth spread from ear-to-ear. "Yes, I'm American. Aren't you?" A parenthesis-shaped brow elevated subtly.

Inside a minute he joined her at her table and ordered Mezzaluna for himself, and an aperitivo for D'Becca. The American said, "I am Sebastian. And you are?"

"D'Becca."

"D'Becca?" he asked, his slender lips producing a faint smile. "That is such an unusual name."

"My mother's a big dreamer, and she used to fantasize about being in Hollywood movies. Actually, when I was seven, she did a commercial for a cleaning product, like Mr. Clean, only it wasn't Mr. Clean. And she thought someday I'd go to Hollywood and be famous like Raquel Welch or something. Mama thought Raquel was so gorgeous, and she was this amazing sex symbol. Like Raquel, she decided D'Becca was a stage name."

"And you? Are you an actress?"

"Oh, me?" D'Becca chuckled. "No. One day, who knows? But I'm not sure I'd like acting. I'm a model. You might have seen me back in the States." She paused to see what influence this would have on him.

"What are you... What is it the Italians call it, *supermodelo?*"

He couldn't care less what she did; Sebastian just wanted to get her in his bed. She knew this, but D'Becca pressed further, dropping her résumé with this ad she had done and that product she had endorsed, and the lingerie she had posed seductively for in mass market lingerie catalogues. "I also starred in a pop music video once." But the American took a drink from his glass; nonchalant, he glanced at his Rolex. Despite his indifference, D'Becca went on. "You don't look like the type to even set foot in a Métro, but I was working in London last year and I saw myself in a few tube stations...the Underground?"

They left the restaurant and wandered through Piazza Navona for half an hour. They talked about D'Becca mainly, and her life as a little girl in her small hometown, her life as a model, and somewhere in between, she avoided telling him about her real life. Unknowingly, she cared what this man thought of her.

D'Becca wanted to stroll along Piazza di Spagna, even while the shops were long since closed. She suspected a man like Sebastian Michaels would have a spacious suite at the Hotel Hassler with its incredible panoramic views from oversized terraces, set just above the Spanish Steps; and he would invite her to his room, eventually. She had always wanted to stay in one of the rooms at the Hotel Hassler, and to see the spectacular, romantic view of Rome.

"I like the cobblestone streets; how they twist and turn and you never know where the hell you'll find yourself, even with a really good map. Do you mind?"

Amused, Sebastian shook his head.

His driver whizzed speedily through the sometimes congested, sometimes deserted streets of Rome nearly colliding with Vespas and taxis, and through a narrow street, he barely missed two pedestrians. Because he said nothing, she assumed Sebastian Michaels was indifferent to the way the driver riskily drove him through the enchanting city. Before D'Becca knew it, they were at the foot of the Spanish Steps.

"In spring, the Steps are so beautiful. The azaleas, you know? In the summer the Steps are swarming with tourists and Gypsies, and local con artists. It's sad because the loitering and riffraff cheapens the Fountain of the Barcaccia." D'Becca lowered her eyes. "I want to walk. Do you mind?" she asked Sebastian.

In limited Italian words, he spoke to his driver with deliberate authority, and Sebastian and D'Becca were walking through the maze of streets beyond Piazza di Spagna within minutes. Along via del Babuino, where antique shops lined the constricted street, D'Becca said, "I want to have my own place. My very own, someday. I lease a large flat which isn't so bad, but when I have my own place it will have space and I will decorate it all myself. Every single square foot."

"So you like antiques?" Sebastian assumed.

Solemnly, she nodded, staring in the window of one of several antique stores along the *strada*. "No, not antiques. I like contemporary, and French country. And I like Art Deco, but I wouldn't want my home to be decorated that way. Someday it would get boring because Art Deco can be cold. I want my home"—she looked over to him morosely—"when I get it, to reflect who I am. What I like. Light colors, and lots of windows."

Sebastian thought she was lonely, and a foolish over-sentimentalist with extravagant ideas. She had dreams, he got that, and she would make them come true, come what may.

They walked along the constricted streets lined with famous boutiques housing upscale fashions, and passed a man standing just outside a vinerie talking fervently in Italian on his cellular. He had a faint resemblance to James Dean, and smoked a cigarette a few feet away from a black Ferrari.

"Do you come to Italy often?" D'Becca asked.

"Usually when I need to get fitted."

"Fitted?" She laughed. "You mean you come all the way to Italy to get your wardrobe?"

His eyes suggested approval. His very silence said a mouthful.

"Do you like Italy?" she asked Sebastian.

"Yes, I like it well enough. The food, the culture. And you?"

When she looked over to him, she saw something new, something she had taken for granted previously. In the essence of a full moon, he seemed more of one thing and less of something else, but D'Becca was not sure what changed. She realized she was becoming attracted to him, or who she thought he might be.

"Yes. I wish I could stay forever. But whenever I go to Paris to work I feel the same way about France. And then I get homesick and I start wanting things you can only get in America. Is that ridiculous?"

"Not at all. Come, I want to show you a to-die-for view. It's difficult to find anywhere else in Rome. Come along," he said, taking her hand and linking her fingers possessively into his.

The Villa Aventine, in the heart of a desirable, lushy residential district, was a low-key, word-of-mouth hotel once known as the Federici Villa. For many years, it was rumored that the villa was owned by the daughter of a Greek slave, who inherited the baroque villa through an Italian prince. Since the early 1800s, the real history of the Federici Villa remained a feeble tale; it was impossible to relay the authentic story anymore because the history of its inheritance was handed down for nearly two centuries in slanted detail. The Villa stood atop Aventino, rising above the Tiber just southwest of the Palatine. Secluded convents and churches scattered below the villa, and the church bells could be heard on the hour.

Sebastian's suite—with chamois painted walls, wide-planked flooring the color of espresso mostly concealed by massive rugs— was twice the size of D'Becca's one-bedroom apartment, a charming place overlooking Lake Union and the Space Needle. She loved the room's antiquity, and the smell of burning wood. Presumably a night chambermaid was instructed on when to burn the logs each evening when she came to turn down the bed. The view— probably the most captivating in the City Centre—was unmistakably one of the best she had ever seen in Rome. The serenity of the Tiber from one window, and beyond the river was the Vatican City and an enchanting view of Ponte Sant'Angelo, and within its setting, San Pietro Basilica. From a window on the opposite side of the suite a vista and a sector of the Colosseum posed inside stillness. Sebastian knew how to touch every sensitive place D'Becca possessed, even when he had not known her. She liked this man. She really liked this man. And she wanted what he had to offer: his fabulous world, because his world could not be anything but.

It was not until the following morning, when she crawled out of the classic Victorian cast iron bed and walked over to the window and opened the shutters to get a feel for the day did D'Becca learn Sebastian Michaels lived in Seattle. It was a startling coincidence. Not that she was being snoopy; she happened to notice his passport amid other papers lying near a briefcase on the table. She reached over to pick it up, and his address was listed in the Madison

Park neighborhood of Seattle. D'Becca felt light and happy. Sebastian stunned her and asked, "What are you looking for?" She caught her breath, dropped the passport back on the table and put her finger in her mouth, feeling dreadfully embarrassed.

"Are you married?"

Sebastian did not wear a wedding band, yet D'Becca had learned that meant nothing. A lot of married men did not wear wedding bands. But married or not, D'Becca had her own agenda.

"Yes. I am married."

What was left of Sebastian's trip they spent together. They stood in espresso bars amid well-dressed Italians consuming espresso in the ubiquitous demitasse, and ate gelato cones for the thrill of it. They roamed piazza after piazza: from Campo dei Fiori to Piazza del Popolo; to St. Peter's Basilica to study the newly restored Sistine Chapel for hours. D'Becca was struck at how casually artistic lingo such as "frescoes" and "veils of color" dripped from Sebastian's tongue. She even wondered if he studied classical architecture. In fine detail, he explained to D'Becca the ceiling's visual metaphor: Humankind's desperation for salvation which is obtainable by God through Jesus Christ. *The Creation* moved Sebastian so, and D'Becca had never been intimately involved with a man so deeply touched by art. At one point she thought a tear would slip involuntarily from his deep blue eye. She was so happy to be in the company of this man. Sharing her day—her body—with *this* man. Mysterious and strong, he would teach her many things. Take her places. And for once she would feel the raw essence of love.

They traversed many squares and streets throughout Rome in the late hours of the night, and since the city was all but deserted during siesta, they shared the city with tourists and random Italians along the vacant streets. Sebastian was fascinating and real to D'Becca. No other man she had known had been so incredibly captivating and genuine. By the weekend, she thought she was in love with him.

When age began to gradually threaten her livelihood and D'Becca wanted to get away from the startling invasion of Seattle, Sebastian bought a townhouse which came with one sole restriction: it was hers to live in as long as there were no other men in her life but him. Then one day, following her work in a commercial played during the Super Bowl, jobs became available once more. D'Becca was in demand and invites started pouring in out of nowhere and she liked being around different types of people and having fun. She was the person she wanted to be in the presence of company she wanted to keep. D'Becca traveled frequently again, to Rio, South Beach, and Dubai. Sebastian had family obligations and a sophisticated business that demanded a great deal of his time; he was not always available to be with her. Being with him was a sacrifice she told herself she could handle, but there were times when she was so lonely, she ached. Once, her desperately unhappy mother said to her daughter: "The other woman is never first, Becca."

Sebastian became increasingly demanding, wanting D'Becca to be around when he wanted to see her. At times he got jealous, even of Troy, her dearest friend who was gay. He became needy and neurotic. Sebastian wanted her completely to himself, for himself, and available when he wanted her, like his many possessions, and more importantly, because Sebastian Michaels *could*. Before she was able to catch herself, she looked up and Sebastian had rearranged her life to fit inside his. Next thing she knew, she was pushed into a life against her will. It was not until she met Rawn that D'Becca wanted to control her own life—how she spent her time. It was Thanksgiving and spending the day with Rawn and Sicily and Tamara that made her see for the first time how being with Sebastian isolated her from the outside world. D'Becca liked knowing people her age; being with colorful, creative, intelligent and likeable people, who did not try to control her.

"You have to decide, D'Becca. I won't pressure you to stay with me, but you must also remember that we had an agreement."

Tears of disappointment and tears of broken dreams filled her eyes.

Sebastian reached down and kissed her cheek. "You need some time, I see."

He went for his overcoat and draped it over his arm with his inherent finesse. Casually, he walked to the bedroom door. Framed inside of the arched doorway, Sebastian turned to look at D'Becca in the bed curled up, her back to him.

"You're in love with him. How did you let this happen?"

When a reply was not forthcoming, Sebastian turned to walk away.

The moment she heard the front door shut, D'Becca leapt from the bed and hurried to the window and looked down at Sebastian. From her bedroom window, she watched him step into his BMW, turn over the engine and drive away. She wiped the tear leading in a solid line down her cheek.

Yes, Sebastian. We had an agreement.

Only three months after they had met in Rome, D'Becca had returned to Seattle from working a show in Toronto. Sebastian had said he would be at Sea-Tac to pick her up, and after being away from him for four days, she was excited to be in his company again. It had been a slow travel evening. He had pulled up to arrivals, and when she jumped into his car, he blindfolded D'Becca.

"What game are we playing, Sebastian?"

"I have something to show you?"

"How will I see it with this thing over my eyes?"

"Have you ever been on Crescent Island? It's a pearl along Lake Washington. They have this secluded restaurant, Rochelle's. It serves the best pan-roasted salmon I've ever tasted. But there's something else."

Sebastian got a kick out of surprising D'Becca.

She knew this was a big one.

When he had unlocked the door and ushered D'Becca into the empty townhouse, he had removed the blindfold. Initially, D'Becca was confused, but when she began to walk through it, she knew that it was for her. In the full-sized, high-ceiling living room, her eyes met a huge crystal vase complete with two-dozen long-stemmed jade roses, which sat on the striking parquet floor. Sebastian had told her, "Be happy, my love."

Her heart filled with utter joy, D'Becca had laughed. "Sebastian, I love it."

Nervously she dialed a number. When Troy answered, she sniffed her runny nose and said, "I'm in trouble. I need to come to Miami."

CHAPTER TWENTY-ONE

The first thought that ran through Rawn's mind when he opened his door was how she had managed to find out where he lived. There was no way Tamara would have asked Sicily because that would have come across suspicious. Or was she so undeterred she would inquire knowing it would lead Sicily to wonder why she even asked. While the island was small, it was not that small. Somehow Rawn found his voice. "What's going on?"

"So you aren't going to invite me in?"

He stepped aside.

With a judgmental eye, Tamara checked out the place. Faint lighting came from the direction of the kitchen. Rawn stood by the piano, awkward, unprepared. He had walked in the door not more than three minutes ago. *Khalil said she stalked.*

"What are you doing here?" His words were abnormally blunt and his pitch impatient.

She slipped off her long wool coat, suitable for the especially cold winter night. Rawn, literally, could not believe his eyes. She stood across the room wearing quite revealing lingerie. "Listen, don't be ludicrous, Tamara."

"Come on. It's what you want. Don't pretend you didn't like... us."

He hurried across the room. Rawn reached for her coat on the floor where she dropped it. When he draped the coat over her, she slapped him.

"What the hell is wrong with you, woman?"

"Don't mistreat me!"

"You need to leave!"

She flung the coat off her shoulders and came within an inch of him. "What are you going to do, huh?"

Rawn covered his face, heaving. *Dammit!* A sobering reality set in, and he was in a quagmire. Rawn saw it so clearly now: he would indelibly intertwine with Tamara for an ill-defined period of time, and behind one reckless moment. Nothing between him and Sicily would ever be the same, whether he came clean—or Tamara came clean—or not. If he said nothing, he would always know what Sicily did not know, and that knowledge played with him in a disturbing way.

"Listen to me, Tamara…"

"Come on, Rawn. Don't be so uptight. Lighten up, relax." She reached for his hands and he snatched them away. "I promise, I won't tell Sicily. You have my word."

"Do you get it? You need to grasp the concept: Sicily is my *friend*. Do you have any idea how much she's into you?"

"She thinks I'm her soul mate. Please." Tamara smirked. "Sicily—she was a moment."

"Obviously you don't give a damn about her."

Furiously, Rawn snatched her coat from the floor and draped it over her shoulders once again. This time he buttoned the top button and walked away from her. Words Khalil said about her began to play over and over in his mind, like a song he could not get out of his head: *That woman isn't wrapped tight*. He turned when he heard Tamara say ever so casually…

"I care about Sicily, too."

Care. That word stalked Rawn. It was not until she said it did Rawn have appreciation for how a seemingly small term to describe human emotion should come across as inconsequential

"Tamara, this misbegotten idea…There's nothing here for you."

"I remember something D'Becca said to me on Thanksgiving." Tamara closed the gap between her and Rawn. "She said, 'Rawn can put a spell on a girl, so watch out.' At the time it meant nothing to me. But there hasn't been a man I wanted to be with more than Henderson. Not until you... When you came to my place and we spent the evening together. It's...Let's just say you're attainable."

With a grimace, Rawn said, "Did you say attainable?"

"You think that Sicily won't approve, right? She might be disappointed..."

"Disappointed? You definitely don't know Sicily."

She moved into him, gingerly resting her hands against his chest. "She's a big girl."

"You have to leave. I've made up my mind. I need to tell Sicily..."

"How immature! *I need to tell Sicily...* You sound like some teenage boy afraid his mommy is going to catch him in a lie. It's rather interesting...amazing, actually. Because when you were in my mouth, you were very...receptive."

"I take credit for my part in what went down. But you have to leave. I mean you have to *leave*."

She reached for his crotch. "Oh, boy. You want me, don't you?" She stroked him, and with her lips barely touching his, said, "This doesn't *lie*."

He grabbed her wrist tightly and said, "Leave!"

She laughed sarcastically. "Are you *sure?*"

Rawn walked around Tamara. Annoyed and disgusted, he reached for the knob to the front door. "Leave."

Without prolonging the inevitable, finally she left. For a good ten minutes, Rawn sat on the ottoman, amazingly frustrated. The telephone rang several times while he sat there. Probably his mother; could be D'Becca; one of the guys in the band checking to see if he was planning to be at the Alley. It did not matter. He reached for his keys, and before he knew it he was going eighty across the floating bridge, headed for Seattle.

The night was dry but bitter cold.

When he pulled onto First Avenue, there were no parking spaces. He drove around for a good ten minutes before he came upon a space on James Street. He walked four blocks, and his mind had been spinning, spinning so erratically he failed to notice that he was underdressed and Occidental Square was quiet, empty. His bomber jacket was not enough for the raw air coming off Puget Sound, and Rawn had not worn gloves since he left Denver, but his fingertips felt numb.

Khalil urged him not to utter a word to Sicily about what went down with Tamara, but Tamara's idea of it being between the two of them was not reliable and he had to take it with a grain of salt. Besides, he wanted to come clean with Sicily almost immediately after he left Tamara's, but she was so caught up in this thing with Tamara that Rawn genuinely believed the kindest choice was to say nothing. Although he feared how things would go if he was fully honest with her, it would be insensitive on Rawn's part if he did not warn Sicily of the type of person she placed such faith in. Even if it meant losing her as a friend, he needed to catch Sicily before she ended up in a place she would spend years regretting.

His pace brisk, he turned onto Occidental. He bumped into a young woman, and beer splattered over her faux leather coat and Rawn's hand and bomber jacket sleeve.

"Oh, oh, I'm so…" The young woman's words ceased when she looked into his familiar bedroom eyes. Her grin shaped from ear-to-ear.

Rawn thought she looked ridiculously goofy. "It's okay." He walked around her and threw her a perfunctory, "Stay warm," over his shoulder.

The young woman called out, "You don't remember me?"

He spun halfway around to look at her standing there with her warm bottle of beer and silly grin. There was something vaguely familiar about her, but Rawn could not recall where they might have met, or if they ever had.

"Jazz Alley. I ask you if you got a girlfriend. You ask me what made a girl a man's girlfriend. Remember?"

Rawn slipped his hands in his jacket pockets to warm them up. The frost coming from the young woman's nose reminded him just how cold it was. "Yes," he said. "Right."

She took a few steps and said, "You okay? I mean you look... kinda sad."

Rawn was too distracted to fully take in her words.

"Is it your girlfriend? She ain't doin' you right?"

"There's no issue with my girlfriend. I'm not sad." His tone was borderline defensive.

She took a few more steps and tilted her head. "Well, you look it."

"What's your name?"

"Stefanie." She felt very attractive just by the idea that Rawn wanted to know her name.

"Stefanie, what are you doing out here in this cold?"

"My car won't start. I was over at the Latin Quarter. Left there, planning to go home. Don't got triple A, so I'm headed for the bus. But that's how fate work."

"Fate?"

"Yeah. If my car started, I wouldna' run into you."

"Where do you live?"

"The Beach."

"*Rainier* Beach, you mean." He did a surveillance of the square. When he was walking toward Sicily's, he was distracted and did not see that the streets were mysteriously deserted.

"You wanna give me a lif'? I got gas money."

For a suspended moment, he studied her young face. He remembered her now. What made it difficult for Rawn to place her at first was how different she was from when she attempted to pick him up at the Alley. Back then she tried too hard to look older, and her clothes and behavior made her look desperate. "I have something I need to do."

"You thank?"

"What do you mean, *you think?*"

"My mama always told me when you come up against a situation that ain't feelin' right, deal with it with a clear head. Rawn, you don't *look* clear, baby."

"How did you get so wise?"

Her laugh was happy and genuine. "I guess it be genes. See, if you give me a lif', that might give you some time to thank about whatever it is you *thank* you need to do. 'Cause I betcha, if you had some more time to thank it through, you might just change yo mind."

Whatever you do, don't *tell Sicily.*

"Okay, look. If you leave your car, you'll get a ticket. I have roadside service. I'll hook you up."

"Baby, you so fine."

While Troy went to his recently opened South Beach gym to show his face around the place for a few hours, D'Becca chose to stay at the condo. For quite some time, she stared at the brilliant morning sunshine and the bay that looked like glossy indigo-blue paint; the water was so blue it looked fake. The waves would come but so far, and suddenly, the water would become tranquil. How long did she stare at the mysterious, exotic beauty beyond Troy's extended living room window?

Without telling Rawn she was leaving town, D'Becca caught a red-eye to Miami two nights ago. Since Troy left for the gym, she had been gazing hopefully at her cellular for nearly two hours, wishing Rawn would call her and at the same time dying to call him. Every time she got up the nerve, something she could not name pulled her back. D'Becca imagined that it was a god's whisper, or just her own lack of courage.

When Troy picked her up at Miami International—his arms stretched out like wings to hold her—he looked amazingly at peace and there was life in his eyes like she had not seen before. He was so dark; the sun had tanned him three shades since she last saw him. Thinking back on it now, D'Becca realized how presumptuous she sounded when she asked, "Who are you sleeping with?" At that moment, where her mind was, she trusted that happiness was linked to intimacy, love, and another. Troy laughed and came back with, "Myself!"

When they first met, D'Becca needed a personal trainer to stay in shape. At the time she was getting a lot of work to model swim-wear and it was crucial that she kept her body toned. Airbrushing took care of small imperfections—cellulite and stretch marks—but she needed to be *in* shape. Troy taught her how to eat better. A nutritionist by trade, he introduced her to organic foods and gave her the inside scoop on how to cheat and still stay in shape *and* eat healthy. He was desperately in love at the time and she had just met Sebastian. In time they realized while they genuinely liked each other, the attraction came from their dysfunction when it came to falling for the wrong man. It took no time whatsoever for them to become hanging buddies, going to dinner and taking day and weekend trips to Victoria where Troy had friends. The first couple of years they held each other when they needed some-one to lean on. So it came as a complete shock to D'Becca that he looked not just physically healthy, because Troy had a great body

even at forty-one years old, but he was, as he said the evening before, *in the best place I've been in my life.* Because she had not heard
him say anything like that before, she took him at his word.

But within hours of being in Miami, perhaps it was envy that
made her say, "It's only been four months. What saved you in such
a short time?"

"I stopped going out with people because I was very attracted
to them. I spent days—even weeks—alone and got in touch with
in here." He pointed at his chest. "I can't keep falling apart just
because someone breaks up with me, Becca."

"But…"

"I didn't want to tell you. I knew it sounded desperate and
wretched. I know that if things worked between Jim and me, I'd
never have left Seattle. Before we got serious, I spent two years
working on opening a place in South Beach. I kept putting it off
because I was in love with someone who lived thousands of miles
away and had a business there so he couldn't tail behind me. Anyway, I moved to that gloomy town just to be *with* Jim."

The sound of D'Becca's cellular, which she held in her hands,
shifted her thinking. The familiar number displayed across the
screen was her agent's. Their conversation lasted ten minutes.
D'Becca needed to pack and be in New York the following morning—early. She would only have to work for two days, three at the
most, but work would do her good. While she was packing, her
cellular rang. She looked over at the mobile across the room set
on the nightstand and knew it must be Sebastian, who had been
calling her several times a day without leaving messages.

When she reached for the mobile, it was the call she had prayed
for all morning. "Rawn?"

But he had hung up before she could answer. Her first impulse
was to call him back, but not aware of why, she halted. D'Becca's

heart was racing; she was so confused and at a loss. She flopped on the bed and stared at the cellular for several minutes, her mind going back and forth to the conversation she had with Troy the previous morning.

"I'm pregnant, Troy."

Troy had been making a smoothie and talking about having a small get-together so D'Becca could meet some of his friends. He dropped the banana he was about to peel. "Did you say you're pregnant?"

D'Becca had been washing blueberries in the sink. Her voice was detached from her emotions, and "Yes" had sounded like it came from someone else in the room.

"Pregnant?" Troy repeated. "By…Who's the father? Do you even *know?*"

It was then D'Becca broke down. For fifteen minutes, while she sobbed uncontrollably, Troy held her. Eventually, when she pulled herself together, she said, "What am I going to do?"

"Do you want this baby?"

"Troy…" She had sniffed her runny nose. "I'm not particularly mother material. I'm selfish; I don't like cleaning Chai's litter box. Do you really think I'm up for changing diapers?"

"Do you have any idea who the father is? No, wait! Becca, why weren't you using protection? Aren't you on the Pill?"

"A month ago I was working in Montréal—it was a last-minute thing and I was rushing…and I left my birth control at home. I don't understand…There's a doctor in every city—models have access to them, and they'll give you a pill for anything. He refilled my prescription. I *was* using birth control, Troy. The only time I slipped up ever was in Montréal. Two days, that's all."

"Okay, let's figure this out. How many weeks?" When Troy had looked over to D'Becca, she seemed to be multiplying in her head the number of days she was late. Troy had said, "It has to be only weeks because you don't look pregnant." With wet eyes, D'Becca had added, "I think I'm about four weeks. I haven't had any morning sickness. Is that unusual?"

"Thank God, because I need to work." With wet eyes, D'Becca had added, "I think I'm about four weeks. I haven't had any morning sickness. Is that unusual?"

With a *how-should-I-know* look, Troy had asked, "What if this baby's Rawn's?"

D'Becca bowed her head and had let out a heavy sigh. "I don't know. If I had a choice, I'd want Rawn to be the father. It wasn't until I began to spend time with Rawn that I realized I didn't love Sebastian. I was in love with…something, but not Sebastian."

"So would he—would Rawn be okay with having a biracial kid?"

"I'm not sure, but Rawn's not…By nature he's not the hypocritical type. I just don't know if this is something he would want." Unconsciously, D'Becca had brushed away tears that stained her cheek.

"Would he?…"

"I know what you might be thinking. Trust me, Rawn is accountable. He would never turn his back on *his* child. But I don't know that it would be fair to do this to him."

"Fair?"

"This wasn't planned. We never talked about having children. I know he loves teaching young people, but is he ready for that level of responsibility right now?…"

"If you don't want children, do what needs to be done to make sure that doesn't happen. Yes, condoms aren't foolproof—nothing is. But I don't leave home without one. Any man who doesn't want to leave something behind that might in any way implicate him…especially having babies he doesn't want or isn't ready to have… Come on! Both people need to take responsibility. There's an epidemic out there, and it doesn't discriminate. You've been sleeping with two men. You should've protected both of them, and you should've used a condom every time."

"Rawn did... Except...three times he didn't."

"And what if it's Sebastian's?"

D'Becca had swallowed hard. "He said he didn't want more children. Three was his limit. I promised him I would never do that to him."

"You're a lot of things, Becca. Risqué and reckless as hell. But you do keep your word."

She rushed to her feet and covered her face. She had turned to Troy and said in a distressed voice, "What do I *do?*"

"Ask yourself: What choice do you have?"

The cellular chimed, and it broke D'Becca's musing over a past she could not change, and her nomadic thoughts. She looked at the number flashing. Reluctantly, she answered, "Hello, Sebastian."

CHAPTER TWENTY-TWO

Khalil was on a Virgin Atlantic Airways flight to London when he called Rawn, and in particular to finalize the plans for Vail. "I got my father's timeshare and I need to know what to do about lift tickets," he said. "So is D'Becca coming or what?" He tried to juggle the in-flight phone while he simultaneously perused *Black Enterprise* and talked to Rawn.

"Do you want to know what's gone down in the past two days or should this wait until we hook up in Vail?"

He was about to down the remainder of a gin and tonic from the plastic cup, but replaced the beverage on the airplane table. "If you tell me you told Sicily, man, I swear!"

"This thing—it's sideways. I can't even figure out *how*."

"Hold up! How can it be sideways? The only way this thing can go completely wrong is if you run your mouth off to Sicily." As an afterthought, Khalil asked, "You didn't?"

Rawn sighed and sat on the edge of the bed in the semi-dark. "Tamara came by here."

"Came...How'd she find out where?..." Khalil lowered his voice—"Bitch is stalking." His mouth turned upside down.

"I can't keep this charade up. How do you do it time after time, and like it's nothing?"

Khalil bypassed the remark because the surface of things was never exactly what was beneath its façade. He preferred to let his best boy go out believing he was always on top of his game. "Don't tell Sicily. Let it go," he urged.

"She's my...I report to her. Yesterday we had lunch and man she couldn't stop talking about Tamara. Her head...it's—she's got a serious jones for this woman."

Khalil poured the last droplet of liquor in the cup. He had his own issues, but would not put those before Rawn's pressing circumstance. It was not the time to be selfish. But it was flying that always freaked Khalil out. Without stopping, he gulped the gin and tonic down with the hopes of unwinding. "If you haven't made reservations, make them, but don't even tell Sicily. It could all be innocent and everything, but she might drop your itinerary—and it may not be intentional—on Tamara. I sho' nuff don't want her showing up uninvited. There's no love lost between us, man. Tamara freaks me out."

"I haven't seen or talked to D'Becca in days."

"What's up with that?"

"Clueless. Don't know."

"Have you gotten what you wanted out of this or what? No, even better: Has the Tamara episode made you rethink D'Becca?"

Exhausted, frustrated, Rawn said, "Hell if I know."

"Listen, come to Vail. Getting off CI can help you gain some perspective. Moon thinks I'm making you up. She wants to meet this Rawn dude for herself."

"Yeah," Rawn said in a subdued voice. "Sure."

Rawn purchased a roundtrip ticket to Denver on Priceline.com. When he was under the sheets with the hopes of shutting his mind completely off, his telephone rang. Blindly, he reached for the receiver. "Hello."

"Hi, Rawn. It's me."

"D'Becca? Where are you?"

Once Sicily finally managed to straighten out ongoing complex issues with a student and her single parent—an owner of a small but lucrative personnel agency—and they agreed to meet again in two weeks, she flopped in her chair and took a deep breath. She opened her calendar to check and see what kind of time she had before her next meeting, but within seconds, began to reflect on how much she loved her position as the first headmistress and the first African American to head Gumble-Wesley. One wall in her office signified that pride; her accomplishments were framed proudly, along with her degrees. Sicily had hoped her time would be better managed. Strategically, she scheduled every meeting in fifteen-minute intervals, and yet it never quite worked out, so her executive assistant suggested she not do parent/student conferences back-to-back. She had to meet with faculty in ten minutes; that gave her enough time to drop by the ladies and detour to the pantry and grab a bottle of mineral water.

She reached for the receiver and dialed Tamara's home number—digits she learned by heart the evening they met. While they had sat in the Alexis Hotel's Library Bistro having drinks while Pricilla Miles finished up an interview, they had exchanged numbers. Tamara leaned over and said, "We need to get together." Beforehand, Sicily wrestled with what approach would be appropriate; Tamara had a rather nebulous nature and it was hard to read exactly what her sexual orientation was.

"Hey! I'm worried about you. Did you go out of town and forget to tell me? I thought you were coming by last night. Listen, remember my professor from Seattle U? You know, the one I told you used to hit on me?" In good spirits, Sicily laughed into the receiver. "Well," she blushed, "he's having this dinner party tomorrow night at his home in Leschi and I thought we could go. It'll be a good time to schmooze. I'll go ahead and RSVP, but let me know your schedule, okay? I miss you. It's been a couple of days. Call me. 'Bye-bye. *Call me!*"

Sicily stared at the receiver in the carriage momentarily before looking up, startled by her assistant standing in the doorway. She wondered how long had she been standing there. "Hi."

The two women were friendly and shared one thing in common: they enjoyed gossiping about celebrities and would set their VCRs so not to miss an episode of *The West Wing*, which they liked talking about. And for that reason, their relationship was relaxed and not so formal from day-one.

"Did I spook you?" the assistant asked, her lips shaped into a wide and toothpaste-commercial smile.

"Daydreaming." She pretended to be adjusting her earring. "What's up?"

"Mrs. Bishop…"

"Tell me no! Not again."

With laughter, the assistant said, "Do you want me to handle it?"

"Would you?"

"Absolutely! Oh, and John Davies called about the events committee meeting for next week. He needs to talk to you before end of school…"

"Yes, I know what he wants to talk about. I've gotten a few e-mails. There's brouhaha on who actually invented e-mail, but whoever the real inventor is deserves a Pulitzer."

"I hear you. Sometimes…it's good to *not* have to deal with some people in person or by phone. Click send, and hello! I'll take care of Mrs. Bishop."

Sicily pulled her laptop closer toward her. She checked Rawn's calendar. She sent an e-mail checking to see if they could hook up around six o'clock.

The bell chimed. Tamara looked toward the door. D'Becca entered Threads. She nearly gasped, but managed to suppress the sound. *What is she doing here?*

"Hi," D'Becca said, walking toward Tamara, taking a fleeting glance at dresses hanging chicly from satin hangers, and the smoke-gray and topaz-colored hangers hung strategically from wire. *I love the colors she works with. An olive-green and tomato-red pencil skirt. Bold.*

"Hi," Tamara replied. "What a surprise."

An Everything Dayna shopping bag dangling from D'Becca's fingers. Tamara flinched at the very idea of Everything Dayna. The chic boutique was her competitor. On any given day in downtown Seattle, one was bound to see at least one Everything Dayna shopping bag draped on the wrist of a young woman who spent her lunch-hour browsing and hard-pressed to walk out without a purchase. At least a trinket.

"I was passing by and thought I'd drop in. I know you are by appointment only, but…"

"I wouldn't dare turn a customer away. And certainly not a friend of a friend. You're welcome to drop by anytime." Tamara looked at her wristwatch. "Although I do have a client coming in in a few. Did you want to look around or?…"

"No," D'Becca said. "Dropping by. Wanted to say *ciao.*"

She doesn't know. She can't possibly know. Not that I give a damn.

"Well…" Tamara spread her long arms, and a striking bracelet that suspended from her wrist caught D'Becca's eye. "Looking for anything in particular?"

D'Becca was about to take a step when she felt the room spiraling. With the back of her hand, she touched her forehead. She grabbed at air like she expected it to suspend her.

"D'Becca?" Tamara took a step and D'Becca gripped her wrist

in order to hang on to her equilibrium. "D'Becca? Are…do you need some water? Are you all right?"

Swiftly, D'Becca pulled herself together. "Wow!"

"Have you eaten? You look a little…You're not binging again, are you?"

"No, no. I was working in New York. I ate very little. Spent two days on the supermodel diet, save for the cigarettes. Gave those up a few years ago. I guess I should eat something…"

"I have World Wrapps. It's chicken. Haven't even had a chance to take a bite yet."

The charming bell sounded, alerting D'Becca and Tamara that someone had entered the boutique. In unison, each turned to find Ingrid Michaels standing in the doorway, her cellular to her ear and stylish sunglasses masking her green eyes.

"I should go. Your client's here."

"Are you okay? You can go in the back and rest for a bit if you'd like."

"No, really. I'll grab some soup. I'll be okay."

"Hello!" Ingrid said.

"Finishing with a client. Ingrid, D'Becca; D'Becca, Ingrid."

"You look familiar," D'Becca said. "Have we met?"

"I cannot tell you how often I hear that," Ingrid said, in a strangely good mood. "We probably have met…somewhere. You look… We've met, yes?" She removed the large-framed sunglasses from her face.

"It takes five minutes to circle downtown Seattle, so we've probably crossed paths in Starbucks. You can always find a Starbucks in this town," she said facetiously. "Anyway, Tamara. I'll make an appointment."

"Promise?"

"Promise. And Ingrid. Pleasure."

When she left the boutique, Ingrid, unconsciously intrigued, walked deliberately to the front of the store and watched D'Becca cross Second. When she could no longer see her, Ingrid walked back to greet Tamara who was bringing material out to show Ingrid, which was the reason her client made the trip downtown to begin with. When Tamara phoned her to tell her about the fabric, Ingrid was leaving Bellevue. "I can stop by on the way home. Thanks so much, Tamara." Even then, Tamara sensed Ingrid was in one of her better moods.

"When I saw this fabric, I knew... What's wrong?" Tamara asked.

"I think that's her."

"What do you mean?"

"That's the woman my husband has made it perfectly clear he is willing to toss twenty-seven years of marriage to be with. She doesn't come across as the slutty type. She's not only prettier in person, she's prettier than the last one. I think I'd like her if she weren't screwing my husband!"

Very few things took Tamara by surprise anymore, but she was nearly floored. "Are you sure?" Her face was shaped into a curious frown.

"That's her. I found a photograph of her in Sebastian's briefcase. She's a model, isn't she?"

"D'Becca models, yes."

Ingrid crossed her narrow arms. "You didn't tell me you knew the woman Sebastian was involved with...that she was a client."

"I didn't realize it was D'Becca. You mentioned she modeled, but she wasn't in your children's generation. That could be plenty of women, Ingrid."

"I want to know everything you know, Tamara. Everything!"

"Go on Yahoo! There's probably enough of her business on the Web."

"Where does she live?"

"You can probably find that out on the Web, too."

"Sebastian; he'd have her tucked away somewhere neat and tidy. Some back-street paramour cottage. Something rustic. Bainbridge? One of the islands. He's so bloody quixotic."

"Like I told you weeks ago, break down and hire a private investigator. Really, Ingrid."

"You know something. I can feel it."

Tamara sighed. Other than the fact that she was sleeping with Rawn—and Ingrid knew her husband's lover was sleeping with another man because Sebastian Michaels so much as admitted it to his wife that she was in love with another man—there was nothing to tell. Fluffing out the fabric, it struck Tamara at that moment. The fainting spell, the askance look D'Becca gave her when she offered her her World Wrapps. *Well*, thought Tamara. *Could D'Becca be pregnant?*

Surely that knowledge—provided it's accurate—would earn me a few good karma points!

CHAPTER TWENTY-THREE

It did not feel like the first weeks of their relationship, back when they could barely peel themselves away from each other; yet it was clear that Rawn and D'Becca had a connection. Rawn was not necessarily back on track, but his mind was less on Sicily and Tamara and more on skiing in Vail. He was present enough to relax and take pleasure in fleeting moments with D'Becca. When last did he think everyday thoughts? He reached over and touched her tenderly; he began to rub her lean tummy with his hand. While Rawn made small kisses against her abdomen, D'Becca's mind drifted from moments long past to moments not yet lived. Finally, she was getting a real taste of conventional love and yet she felt quite melancholy, lost inside a deep loneliness. *God, how can I tell him about this baby? How can I explain Sebastian? How would he react? What, oh my, will he think of me?*

Rawn stopped at her soft pubic hair; he was not getting a reaction. For a few seconds he watched her staring into the air. "Hey! Where are you? You okay?" He laid his head on the pillow, resting his forearm against his forehead.

She mumbled something about being tired. D'Becca fibbed, "I think I'm coming down with something."

"Like a cold?"

"Yeah." Her voice was hollow, sad. She turned to her side and made an attempt to lift the corners of her mouth. With affection, she caressed his rich Hershey's chocolate skin. "I went by Tamara's today. Her boutique, Threads."

Rawn was reticent. He finally spoke, "Oh, really?"

"She's talented. I'm not sure I liked her designs as much as I claimed to have liked them on Thanksgiving. But she really does have a good eye. The dresses I saw today look ahead of their time. She could probably do well as a costume designer."

Rawn stared up at the ceiling. It was not guilt he was feeling; it was purely regret. Similarly, he was rueful that he left Pacific Place and went to Tamara's and did not take his best friend's warning earnestly.

"Rawn?"

D'Becca lifted him back in to the present moment.

"Yeah?"

"I'm afraid."

"Of what?"

"I haven't…I've never been here before. I don't know what to do."

"Been where?"

She dared not reveal the side of herself he had not been acquainted with. D'Becca could not bring herself to admit to Rawn that she was one step short of a kept woman. He knew her as this rebellious kid who got on a bus and came to Seattle when she was only sixteen, defying the odds. And from there she built a life— yes, perhaps by using her looks and unconsciously using her sexuality—and she was independent, her own person. She was not at a place yet to let him think any less of her. She could reach the precipice—giving birth to the words, *the truth*. But she was not there quite yet—in the place to admit that she spent years with a married man. D'Becca knew what Rawn would think of her choices. Besides, she was ashamed that she did not have enough faith in herself and thus allowed a man to influence her and to take advantage of her vulnerability. Not once, over the three years since her relationship with Sebastian Michaels began, had she felt kept.

But of course she was; like her mother said when D'Becca had called and told her that a rich and very successful man was crazy about her. "Is he leaving his wife?" her mother had wanted to know. Rawn took for granted she sustained her comfortable lifestyle strictly from the money she *earned*. He had no idea that she was losing more and more work to girls twelve, fifteen years younger than she with breast jobs and thin as a blade of grass.

While she lay beside Rawn, thinking and organizing her thoughts, she tried to calculate whether she had enough in her various accounts to no longer need Sebastian and still hold on to what she had—the Z3, townhouse, the lifestyle she had adapted to years ago. Although D'Becca had a diverse portfolio, she invested in a few dot-com startups primarily because she was advised to do so. But there was a buzz—and economists were predicting it so— that NASDAQ had reached its peak and the bubble, essentially due to the dot-com mania, was not sustainable. Would such a burst create a Wall Street crash like in 1987? Should she take the risk and sell her dot-com shares? The idea started to take hold of her imagination.

Dear God, what if I lost Rawn and *Sebastian? Troy was right: what choice* do *I have?*

D'Becca was not the type of girl to pray. She needed to learn how to pray. Rawn once said to her, "You can always find God in the details." *Fix this; please make it right, God.* Deep down, D'Becca had no real individual understanding of God, not even a mere image. She could never forget, when she met Sebastian in Rome, how moved he was when he stared solemnly at Michelangelo's depiction of God painted on the Sistine Chapel: The elderly man with a beard—intimidating, aloof. D'Becca did not relate. The idea of Rawn—his thoughts, his laughter and humor—not flowing through her days, her life…She had fallen in love with him. It was

Rawn she truly wanted to spend her life with. Now, on that night, she understood it so fully. *I want* Rawn's *child.*

"Remember that night…not long after we met? When I bought all those candles at Pier 1 and we soaked in your tub…"

"Oh, yeah. I said that was my first. Firsts, no matter what, will always stick with you."

It had been days since she laughed freely, genuinely. "Right. You did say that was your first time."

"Thank you for that, by the way. Soaking in a tub with a fine woman by candlelight…Every man should have that experience."

"You said…"

They spoke in unison: "I thought this only happened in the movies…" A spark ignited, and they were making their way back to the deeper meaning behind their relationship. They were close again.

"What made you bring that up?" Rawn asked.

"You told me that night that you wanted children someday. You never did tell me how many you would like to have."

Rawn's mind wandered momentarily. He then looked over to her and said sincerely, "As many as we both agree to. That is, the woman that I end up having children with. I refuse to be one of those men who has one kid by this woman and one kid by that woman…I want *one* woman to be the mother of all my children. And when I do marry, it will be once. If I mess it up, I'll never make that mistake again."

All of a sudden her heart began to race. *I can't do it. I don't know how to do this.*

Something—instinct, desperation—made her blurt out, "Would your parents approve of you having biracial children?"

"I don't think they would take issue with who I marry. I'm confident my father would prefer that I keep the bloodline thick, but…

Hey, he's warm and fuzzy on the inside. Half the time Tera and I feared him growing up, but he'd probably be okay with it. Eventually. My mother's as open-minded as they come. Her parents used to travel all over the world. They were artists. Truthfully, I have no idea how my mom and dad ended up together. She sees the world—she sees life—differently than he does, in nearly every way." Rawn was talking more to himself than to D'Becca when he said, "That's really what Sicily's play was all about: how we go for the thing we are most attracted to and yet it's the least appropriate thing for us."

"I love how you speak of your parents. I envy you."

An hour later he left her apartment. When Rawn met the sidewalk, a stranger startled him. They exchanged fleeting gazes, and Rawn said, "Excuse me," and moved around him and continued in a brisk pace. Over his shoulder, he took another—a better look—at the man once more, because he looked familiar. Dressed in a sophisticated overcoat cut in sheer detail, the man's salt-and-pepper hair blended evenly with his strong face. Rawn knew he had seen him before. He jumped into his Jeep and headed home. At the stop sign, from the corner of his eye, he caught a Beamer parked along the curb. Had the parking lights not been on he would have missed the BMW altogether. The night was misty, a deep dark. Turning onto Lesley Avenue, a white SUV came dangerously close to side-swiping him. The luxury vehicle continued at a high rate of speed along the residential street. Rawn was certain that the driver was completely unaware that they even shared the road. He observed the fast-moving vehicle in his rearview mirror. For a split-second he was flustered, but once the vehicle was out of eyesight, Rawn continued toward his apartment, being mindful while he drove through the thick fog. A hushed mystery fell over the empty streets.

Not two minutes after Rawn left, Sebastian dropped by. They talked briefly before he told D'Becca he had something he needed to take care of and said he would be back in roughly fifteen minutes. D'Becca stared dreamily into the quietness of her room. Her eyes wandered to the walls she had had painted the color professionally known as Winter's Silence, a calming avocado-green. It felt as though she stared robotically for a very long while, but it had only been minutes. *I should change the color of this room. It would look good in apricot.* She decided to take a warm bath, and she would add one of those aromatherapy bath bombs she bought at Lush when she was last in Victoria. The thought of it was making her feel somewhat better by the idea itself. While the steaming water ran, she sat on top of the basin and reflected on her conversation with Rawn earlier. Should she tell him about her pregnancy first, or tell Sebastian when he returned from taking care of something? She was not 100 percent sure who the father was. Unless the baby looked indisputably biracial, D'Becca could not know without a paternity test. Never could she have imagined her life coming to this strange place, this unforeseen moment. Plenty of scenarios played out in her head over the years how things would work out for her, but nothing could have prepared her for being pregnant, and at the same time, not knowing who the father was. Under such twisted conditions, how could she tell Rawn she was pregnant? She got lost in her sadness for quite some time.

The bath water was nearly full when the doorbell rang.

CHAPTER TWENTY-FOUR

D'Becca lay bleeding, shivering, and her head throbbed. She felt disengaged from her body, and everything in the room was spinning. In the back of her mind, she thought she heard whispering. Every muscle in her body seemed to ache. Her mind flickered in and out of consciousness. Snippets of detail in her mind's eye came and went: a female voice asking if she was okay; Sebastian standing over her; the urgent sound of Sebastian's voice talking to someone; a hard blow against the side of her face. The sequence of events did not make sense to her fractured mind. *Is this how it feels when you have a lobotomy?* Darkness, and then light again. She could not decipher between what was happening and what had already occurred. In the back of her mind D'Becca heard two voices, but she could not trust herself to make sense of what her mind was telling her. Flashes. Darkness. And glimmers of light again. She felt the pain press against her brain. "Sebastian," she whispered. "Sebaaaastian…" her voice slurred. She made out Sebastian's voice; it was his words she could not discern. Blood flowed evenly from her nose, stopped at her upper lip, and then proceeded to trickle to the edge of her chin. "Seba…"

She attempted to move, to crawl for help. A black boot came into view. Then pain, piercing and jagged, shot through her face and the sting ricocheted against her skull. She could hear sounds, like a band, echoing loudly in her right ear. The horns grew louder and louder in each ear. In and out of consciousness, D'Becca pushed back a similar scene when she was a little girl. Her eyelids felt heavy and her vision kept slipping away. Her mind was failing, yet the memory was terribly real, so exceedingly clear in her reverie. Her mother lay on the kitchen floor, blood dripping from her mouth, landing onto the linoleum floor in tiny droplets. It had been D'Becca who washed up the blood; her mother went to the sofa and had a drink, the glass wobbling in her blood-stained hand.

Suddenly, everything went gray. Flashes of white. Before long, it all faded to black.

CHAPTER TWENTY-FIVE

"Hey, lady. Got your message. It's been such a chaotic week, and I'm so—I apologize profusely for not returning any of your calls. I wasn't blowing you off... Listen, I'm out of town and when I get back, I'll call you. I think I'll have to miss meeting your flirtatious professor. *Ciao*, luv!"

Tamara ended the call and pressed ten digits to make another call. "Pricilla? Hey, friend. Where are you?" She turned into the underground garage of her condominium high-rise. "It's Tamara," she continued, leaving Pricilla a message. "Call me." She pulled into her parking space, and without turning off the engine, dialed yet another number.

"Henderson!"

"Hey, baby."

"Hello. And where have you been? You must be all up in some man's arms...you haven't returned my calls since...it had to be before Thanksgiving."

Turning off the engine, Tamara laughed, although it was contrived. "What's up?"

"Are you in L.A.?"

"Nope, Miami."

Tamara tried to suppress the sound of frustration, which began to build the moment she received Pricilla's voicemail and did not get a live voice. Where was that parasite when Tamara needed her? *Still traveling around the country promoting that damn book!* She attempted to sound nonchalant. "When will you be back in L.A.?"

"Why?"

"Okay, now. Henderson, am I on the wrong side of you today?"

"No," he said flatly. "The question was simple. Why?"

Tamara walked toward the door that led to the building elevator. With a sigh, she began, "Hen…"

"What do you *need*, Tamara?"

"Why do I have to need something, *friend?*" She pressed the elevator button.

"I know this ain't good."

"I thought you didn't use words like *ain't*." She stepped into the elevator. "As I recall, something about it sounding ghetto. So when did you say you'd be back in L.A.?"

Imani and Kenya sat at a table, everyone around them speaking in Spanish. Imani and Kenya pretended to be comfortable with the decision to meet with a young woman in a Washington Heights café, and who spoke no English. When Kenya told Imani, she said, annoyed, "So tell me, how exactly will be able to talk to her?" With a shrug, Kenya said, "We'll manage." Neither was at ease. Even while they could easily blend in with the bronze-skinned South American clientele, they looked out of place. Not because the patrons looked foreign; it was more so because Imani and Kenya looked sophisticated—well dressed and polished. Hardly speaking to each other, the sisters put on a front; it was something they did most of their lives. They were good at *faking it*. Make-believing they held no resentment; make-believing they were close; make-believing their love was deeper than their differences; make-believing Dante loved them equally. But was it possible to love two children *equally?*

"She's late," Imani said, leaning into her older sister.

"She'll be here. She wanted to meet *us*, remember?"

"We should order something. Everyone's staring at us."

"They aren't staring. You're so paranoid, Im," Kenya whispered.

Taking in a deep breath, Imani reached for the plastic glass of room-temperature water. After she took several sips, she said, "What are we going to say to her? After all, she can't speak a word of English."

"Don't be so judgmental."

"Judgmental? All I said was she didn't speak a word of English."

"Yes, that's what you said. It's your tone that was speaking louder than your words."

Two women entered the establishment, allowing cold air to re-arrange the perceptible force suspended over the tightly situated room. They were appropriately bundled up in wool clothing. Both had long brunette hair flowing beyond their waists. One was in possession of a baby stroller. They stood at the door and it looked like they were seeking out a free table. The young waitress who waited on Imani and Kenya earlier greeted the two young women with enthusiasm, speaking in Spanish. Their voices were eager; their laughter happy. Within moments, the little one in the stroller became the main attraction. The woman who worked for the café pointed toward Imani and Kenya, and the sisters sat erect. Curious, and their heartbeats starting to elevate, they reached for each other's hands. Wordless, they sat there, not sure if the woman they had been waiting for for twenty minutes was the woman at the door. Their independent thoughts were confirmed when the three women walked toward their table. Instinctively, Imani looked at tables nearby and there would be nowhere to put the baby stroller.

"Jello," one woman said. "Imeeni jan Keyna?"

"I-ma-ni and Ken-ya," said Kenya. "Magdalena?"

"*Sí.*"

"Can someone speak English?" Imani asked of the three women.

"Jes," said the woman who was with Magdalena. "I speak English. Magdalena hees my sister. She…"

"I speak English. I am American," the woman, working at the café, butted in.

Imani and Kenya looked to each other; they were most likely thinking the same thoughts.

"Magdalena…she could not wait to meet you. She got out of hospital but the baby…" The waitress turned to the baby in the stroller. "It was tiny. So small. But she never can forget about the man who save her life and her precious little angel, Dante."

In unison, Imani and Kenya caught their breath.

"She named the baby after my—our father?"

Magdalena's sister said, "Jes. Oh, jes. Dante wisk his life…for our angel."

"Can we…see?" Kenya said, leaning forward.

"Por favor, jes."

When Magdalena pulled the baby from inside the stroller and into her loving arms, Imani and Kenya came to their feet, rapt by the moment. Before they knew it, the entire café was on their feet, coming to see the tiny blessing, Dante. The infant blinked open his small black eyes, coming out of a gentle sleep, and then gently shut them again.

"Oh, my goodness. He's gorgeous," said Kenya.

"Jew hold heem?" Magdalena offered. Kenya assumed the young woman rehearsed the words all morning.

Kenya reached for the baby, and Imani smoothed his fine hair, the color of coal, with her fingertips. "Hi, Dante. Hi." Kenya smiled into his small, tan-colored face.

"Hola, Dante," Imani said.

In Spanish, a group of people began to sing a song. The room warmed to the quiet love that engulfed the small café. Finally, after several minutes of communal spirit, the waitress of the café explained that everyone in the café was in some way related to Magdalena and her sister. They were so happy to finally meet people who were close to, and loved, Dante; the man who saved their Magdalena's life, and that of her unborn child.

The five women sat at two small tables pushed together near the back of the café. Magdalena explained in Spanish, while the waitress translated the tale in English, what happened that fateful day at the bodega.

The waitress began, listening with care to Magdalena's words and interpreting word-for-word: "I was standing near the back of the bodega. I heard loud voices. People was shouting." The waitress stopped translating and said, "Magdalena understands English better than she can speak it." As Magdalena spoke in Spanish, the waitress continued: "The owner told someone he won't give up his cash. That the young boy had two options: to shoot him, or leave. There was shouting and there was the sound of a gunshot." The waitress's voice grew passionate. "I was so scared. Scared for my baby. Scared I would never see my baby...I want to leave the bodega. I want...want to get out of here—there. I didn't care...I care about my baby...I ran for the aisle and I stop because there is a man lying on the floor...he bleeds, but his eyes was open. I walk over him...I am a shame that.... not stop to help him, but I was scared for my baby...unborn baby."

Magdalena looked down at the sleeping infant in the stroller. Her eyes were filled with bittersweet tears. She continued, while the waitress explained in English: "When I got to front of bodega, your papa, Señor Dante, he try to tell the man...the boy with the gun not to kill the owner. He reach for his wallet and say, 'Take it. There, three-hundred dollar...more than the man have in cash register. Take it, take it,' he yell at the boy. He was…he was no more than sixteen or seventeen. I no see his face. He wears the hoodie. His back to me. Señor Dante, he threw hees wallet at the boy and tell him to go! 'Go!' he yell. Then I knock something and it fall… I want to try to run for the door, but I was carrying the angel Dante—almost eight months, I carry the little angel Dante…and… the boy look over at me, and Señor Dante, he try to, to…"

"Distract?" Kenya butted in.

"Sí, *deestract*…" Magdalena said, and then she resumed.

The waitress related the tale with verve, using her hands to add to the urgency of what she was communicating to the beautiful sisters sitting before her.

"The boy he…he point the gun at me…Señor Dante run to the front of the gun and he say to the boy, 'You shot one man…' He say, 'You so f-word in the head that you shoot pregnant woman? What is the wrong with you, *mon*'? *Mon*, he say. And I all of a sudden hear shot…The Señor Dante fall to the floor…"

Magdalena covered her face, weeping. In a whisper she said to herself in Spanish, "God, forgive me." She made the cross.

Kenya reached over and took her hand. "It's not your fault, Magdalena."

She began speaking once more in Spanish while the waitress translated: "I try to help Señor Dante. I try…there's blood every-where. The man at bodega call nine-one-one. But your papa lose the consciousness in my arms."

In the taxi, driving through the crowded streets of New York, from uptown to downtown, Imani and Kenya were silent, somber. A senseless act of violence took their father away from them. For Kenya, she was able to begin her healing process after meeting Magdalena. It was the opening of her closure. Imani still grieved. The following day, when Blaine came to New York, he and Imani went to visit Dante's grave. They stood silently for a while. Imani looked over to Blaine and said, "He's a beautiful boy. Dante would have laughed knowing there's this kid taking on his name. Dante... this is what I know for sure...would not have changed that moment. He lived such a full life, Blaine. He told me once, after my mom passed away, that we spend a lot of time while we're living being careless with our lives. When we stare death in the face...when death snatches us up, we know death has arrived at that moment, and what flashes in our mind in that brief moment of realization is that we squandered so much time. But Dante believed that when death takes us, it's because God's purpose for our lives has been served. Every breathing thing, he believed, is connected." Her throat clogged, she said further, "Dante was so sure of that."

"I never asked, when was the last time you saw him?"

"My birthday. He surprised me and came to Seattle. I took him to this club on Crescent Island, where I have my Pilates studio, this place called Moody's Jazz Alley. Next thing I know, he's up there playing with the band that plays there regularly. I think he was killing two birds with one stone."

"How so?" Blaine asked.

"He had heard a lot about the Alley. A lot of his friends and colleagues have played there. Like Dante, they dropped in unannounced." Imani stared out at the day for a little while. "It was amazing. My best birthday yet. I had no idea..."

"When was the last time you heard his voice?"

"Two days before he died."

"He called me about a month before...he was in Boston." Shaking his head, Blaine said, "I was too busy....."

"Blaine...don't go there. Dante understood, trust me."

He reached for her hand. They stood quietly while a soft snow fell.

CHAPTER TWENTY-SIX

"Sorry to bother you. There's…an issue."

Sicily looked up from a mound of paperwork. Puzzled, she asked, "What's the issue?"

"Two detectives are here. They want to see Rawn Poussaint."

"About?"

"They wouldn't tell me."

When she came to her feet, Sicily adjusted her tailored jacket that cut just below her slender hips. "Rawn…he's teaching French?"

Sicily knew her faculty's schedule better than she knew her own, and without having to consult her Palm Pilot. It was a personal rule she established early on at Gumble-Wesley: be very accessible to faculty, staff, students and parents.

"Yes, I checked."

Taking in a deep breath, Sicily walked around her desk. "Would you put them in the Lake Washington conference room. Is it available?"

"Until two-thirty."

They stood a few feet apart.

"I'll get Rawn. See that Samantha Rivers covers the remainder of his class while he's in conference with the detectives."

With a nod, the assistant said, "Understood."

Sicily stood outside Rawn's classroom door, her hand on the knob. She tried not to rush to any conclusions. Memories—and in particular the ones that shaped perception—could contain a unique range of influences, albeit unconsciously. The fact that two detectives, and not uniformed officers, came to the Academy made Sicily feel ill at ease. It was the middle of a school day. Was he an eyewitness to a crime? Sicily was more concerned with what staff would think. When the board of trustees got wind of this, what conclusions would they draw? Gossip was a strange thing, and people were nosy and predictable. Even if it was innocent, two detectives arriving in this way would certainly initiate rumors.

When she was in eighth grade, one cold winter's day ten uniformed police officers had arrived with sirens blaring—some of the students became quite frightened. The authorities had come to arrest the janitor of her school. A black man, who had been accused of raping a white girl, caused quite a scandal at her boarding school in 1977. The black man was convicted and sent to prison. Many years later—while Sicily lived in New York—her mother called to tell her that the girl from her boarding school, who now resided in Tucson, had recanted her story. But the black man's journey had already been taken and, while the retraction eventually set him free, his character would be forever marred by her deception.

Rawn looked over to the door when it opened. Most of the eighth-graders reacted to the headmistress entering the classroom; their demeanor changed, or they grew attentive. A student was standing when Sicily entered the room. She had just finished an exchange with Rawn in French. He said to the student in French that her accent had improved. When the student's gaze met Sicily's, on impulse she took her seat.

Sicily dreaded interrupting. "Good afternoon, Mr. Poussaint."

"Good afternoon." Her look freaked Rawn out. She was too solemn, *too* professional.

"Can I speak with you outside, please?"

He said to the classroom, *"Excusez-moi, s'il vous plait."* When he approached her, he greeted Sicily with, "Hey, what's up?"

"I need you to come with me. Sam's on her way; she'll take over your class."

Rawn was not sure what to think. "Why?" he asked.

"We'll talk outside."

"Mr. Poussaint, good evening. I'm Winston Sanders, Gumble-Wesley's general counsel. Sicily requested that I come."

Both men produced firm hands and shook.

Calm, steady, Rawn slipped on his bomber jacket. He looked tired, but Winston Sanders noted he was not particularly shaken, which made it difficult to size him up. They started walking down the small hallway of the Crescent Island police station when Rawn said, "Where's Sicily?"

"Oh, Mr. Pou..."

"You can call me Rawn."

"Sicily must remain partial. She can't...I have advised her to keep her distance from the situation, you must understand." Sanders stopped walking, as did Rawn. The two men eyed each other, and the general counsel was confident Rawn appreciated his words, but he concluded, "I understand that the two of you are friends, so you must realize her position."

With a vague nod, Rawn said, "Sure." He resumed walking, but Sanders reached for his arm.

With a curious brow, Rawn met the general counsel's eyes.

"There's something I should make you aware of."

"What's that?"

"The media."

Exhibiting no particular emotion, Rawn said, "What are you talking about?" Nonchalantly, he straightened his collar.

"It's...This story is all over the news. The coverage has been—it's breaking news."

Only vaguely taking it in, Rawn said, "Breaking news? I only learned about D'Becca a couple of hours ago."

The general counsel's expression stated everything Rawn needed to know.

"My car's right outside. Let's get you home." He placed his palm on Rawn's back, guiding him. When Sanders opened the door, long-lens 35mms and video cameras were pointed in their faces; a small crowd of reporters and videographers blocked their exit. Before Rawn grasped what was happening, several uniformed officers thrust through the madness to assist them to Sanders's car parked a short distance from the station exit.

A series of questions were yelled out by reporters:

"Rawn! Rawn! Can you tell me, what exactly was your relationship to D'Becca?"

"Sanders, is Rawn a suspect?"

"Rawn, how serious was your relationship with D'Becca?"

"Do you know Sebastian Michaels?"

"Rawn!"

"Rawn!"

"Rawn!…"

Rawn, Sanders, and a gang of uniformed officers pressed their way through the small crowd of reporters and photographers that blocked their passage. In time, several officers came from another direction, and with force, maneuvered their way through the pack. Sitting in Sanders's car, Rawn stared out at the chaos, stunned.

"What the hell!"

Sanders started the car and cautiously backed out of the space, attempting to avoid hitting any one of those in the media. He said, "Do you have a lawyer?"

"Lawyer? Why would I have—need—a lawyer?"

"They won't say it, but you've become…let's say, a person of interest. This thing is about to be national. Henceforward, life as you know is all but over."

The loft was quiet now that Kenya went back to Toronto. Her cellular rang constantly; she blow-dried her hair every morning and left heaps of towels on the bathroom floor; she snored and Imani could hear her clear across the loft; and she and her husband argued over the smallest of things every time they spoke by phone, which was at least four times each day. Imani felt alone but not lonely. She made a fire, grabbed a bottle from Dante's wine cellar and decided to watch television, a luxury she never had in Seattle. Blaine teased her when she told him she did not have cable. She reached for the remote control, and from the corner of her eye, she caught sight of falling snow. Melancholy swept over her, but it was a short-lived feeling. She was not where Kenya was—"I'm over it"—but then Imani's emotional investment in her father was more intense than Kenya's. Their connection was preserved because she lived with Dante when he was not on the road. But Imani dared not utter those words to her big sister. In reality, though, her Jamaican blood was no thicker than Kenya's.

Since they learned the day before that there was a break in the case, Kenya felt she did not need to keep trekking back and forth to Manhattan. Besides, she needed to get back to her work. But Imani needed to see the young man's face. She channel-surfed until she reached a cable news network. She poured herself a glass of wine and for a while stared at the warm fire burning in the fireplace. Occasionally, even though she tried really hard not to, she glanced over at Dante's beautiful piano. The sound of a female voice saying, "Crescent Island," made Imani look away from the piano and to the television screen. Even in Seattle, she never heard much about Crescent Island. Imani's torso became military erect. Her face went from casually interested to nonplus. "That's. That's Rawn! What's?"...Imani placed her wineglass on the table and reached for the remote control to elevate the volume. Unaware, she stood. The reporter on the screen was speaking, "Rawn Poussaint, a local schoolteacher, was questioned for several hours in connection to the death of supermodel D'Becca Ross..." Imani gasped. "D'Becca? She's dead? How?" She hurried to the television and stood directly in front of it, like that would relay enough information and fill in any details she was not privy to. She covered her mouth, "She was *murdered*? Oh, D'Becca!" Sadness rested in Imani's throat; her eyes turned watery.

She looked at her wrist but was not wearing her watch. In the corner of the television screen was the cable network's logo along with the time. "It's...Okay, it's not that late on the West Coast." Imani rushed to the receiver supported in the carriage and when Jean-Pierre answered, she said, "It's me, Imani."

For fifteen minutes she and Jean-Pierre talked, and when they said their goodbye Imani sat stunned at how long she had been away from home. It was not until Jean-Pierre asked when she would be returning did she realize how long it had been. She did miss Trouble. She longed for her personal belongings that were at her fingertips in her cozy houseboat, and she even missed the drab Seattle weather. She missed teaching Pilates; she missed her life.

Imani had moved to Seattle when she broke things off with Blaine. She had gone to visit Carmen, Jean-Pierre's wife, whom she danced with when Imani was in a dance company and traveled all over Western and Eastern Europe. Imani was enticed by Seattle on the spot. Shortly after Imani relocated, Carmen discovered that she had ovarian cancer. Less than a year later, she died. That's when Imani and Jean-Pierre grew closer. While she supported him through Carmen's cancer and subsequent death, Jean-Pierre listened kindly, closely, while Imani tried to move through the hurt inflicted on her by Blaine's deception. Because Jean-Pierre's English was *comme ci, comme ça*, he wanted a worker who could speak French and English, like his wife, Carmen. It was she who decorated the café and created its unique ambience. Jean-Pierre was trained as a pastry chef at École de Cuisine in Paris, but it was his wife, Carmen, who had the ingenuity to create Café Neuf and made it a five-star attraction on the island. Working for Jean-Pierre was meant to be temporary, but Imani actually looked forward to working at the bakery-café for a few hours each morning. Jean-Pierre's café was reminiscent of the life she had when she lived and danced in France for a year; when she was so, so happy.

The following morning, when she finished talking to her business manager and ran errands, Imani returned to Dante's loft and was greeted with a ringing telephone no sooner than she opened the door. Catching her breath, she answered, "Hello!" When she removed her hoodie, her hair was disheveled.

"Ms. Godreau?"

"This is she."

"Detective Rodriguez."

"Oh, hello, Detective."

"We caught him. You won't believe it, but he's been hiding out in the Bronx, living among the rodents in an abandoned building. Eventually, he started talking too much, telling squatters living in the building why he was hiding. Word got around. Someone ratted him out. He was skin and bones. When we put the cuffs on his wrists, they slipped right off!"

Imani gasped.

"What the hell, man." Khalil was tired. His flight was long and he could not sleep through all twelve hours. He was never able to sleep on flights. Once, his girlfriend Moon gave him sleeping pills, but they were ineffective.

Rawn walked around his best friend. He was a few inches taller than Khalil. They had similar body types, but Rawn was leaner. It was drizzling; city lights grew farther and farther into the dark horizon. The ferry was practically empty with the exception of a handful of late commuters working on laptops, reading newspapers and catching a few Zs. Rawn and Khalil stood out on the deck, sharing a joint.

"Rawn! Man, what! the! hell?"

"D'Becca's...dead." The way Rawn sounded was not necessarily the way he felt.

"That much I know. But wha—damn!"

Khalil passed Rawn the joint, and he inhaled one long hit.

"I mean, murder? That's...deep."

"The coroner ruled it a murder."

"Not an accident?" Khalil stood in disbelief.

Fatigued, Rawn was not in a good mood.

Gazing at the homes dangling from slopes off hills across Lake Washington, Khalil whistled. "I don't know what you're gonna do. A black man accused of killing a white woman. And, man, it's national, too. This is too close to the O.J. thing."

"Khalil, come on. You're comparing me to O.J.?"

"Not comparing you *to* O.J. Just saying it's O.J.-like. Keep in mind, cross-burning ain't passé. Damn, homeboy. Two realities have collided: you are black and she's—*was* white. That's always a bad recipe when dealing with the Man. Trust me, they are gonna tie you to this thing. They won't find a bloody glove, right? But they will find *something*."

Rawn extended the tiny butt of the joint and Khalil waved it away. Rawn flicked the roach out into Lake Washington.

"Man, don't let this D'Becca thing break you down to nothing. You're my boy. We need to play Starsky and Hutch and find out what really went down. What about…this old dude who found her?"

"He's someone she was seeing."

"She was doing you and some other dude?" It was quiet for a while. Khalil said, "Did you know?"

Khalil went on the right side of his best friend. They stood profile-to-profile. Speechless, Rawn leaned against the railing. It was not like he was asleep to the truth. *Yes, I had to know.* He knew, but he was unaware that he really, really *knew.* He suspected. He entertained the idea. Because Rawn never trusted coincidences. He saw that Beamer one too many times in close proximity to D'Becca.

Khalil leaned against the railing next to Rawn. Khalil's back faced the fading city across Lake Washington while Rawn faced the residential homes of Seattle with imposing waterfront views.

"This whole episode, it's like out of a flick. It's deep. But the dots don't connect. It's like there are scenes missing from the plotline. So, tell me, man. What's the plan?"

The night was like a blotch of ink. The ebony sky reflected against the deep, dark Puget Sound. With the exception of the chilled body of water beating against the ferry, it was an eerie kind of quiet.

Khalil brushed his brow with the tip of his forefinger. "I gotta head back tomorrow. So, I guess Vail's out, huh?"

They laughed and it shifted the somber mood.

"Thank you for stopping by before you went back to L.A."

"I always gotcha back, bro. Look, for real. I think you should call this attorney. Remember when Henderson Payne was on trial? His attorney, he's who you should talk to."

"Do you think they'll arrest me? They don't have anything, man. I didn't *kill* D'Becca. Besides, Sebastian Michaels is the one who found D'Becca and when he was arriving, I was leaving. He even told the P.D. that."

"Well, from what that *USA Today* article said, he left and he was gone some twenty minutes and came back, so that means you had time to backtrack…"

"Are you deliberately trying to make me feel worse?"

"Look, I'm—I'm speaking some truth here, man. You got to look at the facts."

"Your idea of truth is some help."

With a chuckle, Khalil said, "Look, all I'm saying…This Sebastian Michaels dude ain't no alibi. I see his ducks are all lined up. He's no suspect. What, is he like connected?"

"Truth will prevail."

"There you go, man. *Truth will prevail.* You always do that. There are a lot of people, man, in jail, in prisons waiting for truth to *prevail.* And this thing, it's huge, bro!"

"It's all bogus. I had nothing to do with D'Becca's death."

"I know that. You know that. D'Becca, God let her soul rest in peace, knows that. But some woman—a neighbor, right? She told the Man you and D'Becca had some really heated arguments, up to the night she was killed."

"We didn't have *arguments.* That article blew it out of proportion or the neighbor lied. We argued once. One time, and…The night she died, it was—we were good that night."

"This neighbor—she must be nosy and all up in other people's business… She's claiming y'all were physical. So, did she lie about the slap and yelling at you to leave her crib?"

Rawn felt awkward and tired and totally insecure.

"Whew! Y'all were…Was it worth it?"

Rawn lowered his head and swallowed hard.

Rawn was good at holding it together, but Khalil could see the strain D'Becca's death—and the attention he was receiving—placed on him. It was in his eyes. Not once could he recall his best friend ever needing a life preserver. Rawn had a power that he himself lacked. It was that invisible, nameless quality, along with the Poussaint armor, that could sustain him. While Rawn always believed Khalil had it good, Khalil failed to ever admit it: Rawn had it better. He did not care that he had a quiet personal power that could affect people. And even now, when his life had the potential to explode, he still held it together. Rawn was naturally urbane. Khalil reached for his friend's right hand and took it in both of his own large hands. In one solid motion, he grabbed his friend's frame and embraced him. Rawn returned the embrace while a lump rose to the back of his throat.

When the shuttle ferry approached Crescent Island pier, Khalil said in his best friend's ear, "Aphoristically speaking, of all the people I know…This whole thing, it ain't right, know that. And I wish I could pull a David Copperfield and make it all disappear."

CHAPTER TWENTY-SEVEN

Two days ago, Sicily, struck by sadness and perpetual struggle, called Tamara and got her voicemail. She left a message. When she did not get an immediate response from her, she made one last-ditch effort, despite every muscle in her body, every feeling in her toes and fingers, and everything her recently celebrated thirty-six year-old life taught her—*this woman has left my life*. No matter what her still small voice urged her to hear, or the forces pressing against her soul, she said into the telephone wire, eyes blinking back tears, "I know you had to hear about D'Becca. It must be a slow news cycle because it's all the media seems to be covering. I don't recall even Columbine getting this much coverage earlier in the year. Did you hear about Rawn? How he's this…what do they call it…'person of interest' in her death?" Sicily brushed away the tear that slipped down her cheek. "Lady, I could use a friend. *Please* call me."

Yet Tamara never responded to her appeal.

Sicily was crossing the floating bridge heading to Crescent Island, holding her coffee tumbler in her trembling hand when she heard her cellular ringing. She attempted to change lanes. Because her Everything Dayna-endorsed bag was on the passenger's floor, she could not grab it. She reached for the dial and lowered the volume of Maxwell playing on her CD player. His voice—his lyrics—kept her from thinking about what she most wanted to think about. *What might have been.*

Once she exited the freeway leading to Crescent Island, she

placed her coffee tumbler in the beverage holder and pulled over to the side of the isolated, two-lane road. She parked feet away from a sign in large letters, "Welcome to Crescent Island," that greeted each visitor or local upon entering the islet. When she reached for her cellular, she spoke, "Three messages?" Her heart began to pulsate, but Sicily was not even aware of her racing heartbeat. *Tamara?* Anxious, she listened to the first message, but was instantly crestfallen. While the second message played, she began to sit upright. "Oh, Lord!" Sicily listened to the third message. "What?" Hurriedly, she dialed her office and her EA answered on the first ring. "It's Sicily."

With a sigh of relief, the assistant said, "You *are* coming in today?"

"Why would I not?"

"I wouldn't blame you if you didn't. It's pandemonium!"

"I've received three calls, all about the media—the satellite vans, everything. Homeowners adjacent to the campus, they are complaining. All I need to hear next is that there are helicopters flying overhead. Please tell me it's not so!"

"Not helicopters. But the press…what do I tell them? They are so pushy."

"No comment! That's what you say. No matter what they say to you, you tell them flat-out, *no comment!*"

"Okay, sure."

"Did Rawn Poussaint come in today?"

"He's here, yes."

Sicily was hardly surprised. "Look, I'm fifteen minutes away. The board president has called an executive meeting. Start sending e-mails. Find out each trustees' availability and make it work."

"Will do."

Sitting in her car, the sound of quiet consuming her, her heart and mind rushed much faster than her emotional state could handle.

Sicily was confused, not about how to handle Rawn, but about Tamara. *This was the one.* In every conceivable way, Tamara was the one—talkative and charming and educated, and she was complex, which for Sicily meant that there would always be some level of passion. And she knew how and where to touch. Tamara had almost all of what Sicily wanted and needed. They coalesced beautifully; they clicked—and from the start. In a blink of an eye, she went from attached to alone. Disappointment, most often, was a profoundly deep thing.

I forget to Om.

Two nights ago, Dr. Poussaint was about to leave for the airport and taking the last flight out of DIA into Seattle when Khalil called him.

"Dr. P., I think you should hire Ezra Hirsch."

"Hire him, why? Who is he?"

"He's an attorney, and Rawn needs one. I can't talk sense into his head, but you can reach him."

"He didn't kill the woman. What does he need with an attorney?"

"We both know that. But, Dr. P., we live in voyeuristic times. The media is controlling this. That puts pressure on authorities...I think you should at least contact Hirsch."

Impatient, Dr. Poussaint reached for a pen and pad nearby and asked, "What's his number?"

Now, days later, he sat with his son in Café Neuf. They attempted to discuss anything and everything except the obvious— D'Becca. Ezra Hirsch was late, and Dr. Poussaint loathed how some people did not place more value on time, especially his.

Rawn felt his father's exasperation. "Daddy, it's probably traffic. Plus, it's raining."

Dr. Poussaint did not want to take out his frustration on his son. He sensed that he was not himself. He wanted to diminish any lingering tension, so he said, "The ferry might have saved him some time."

With weary eyes, Rawn looked over to his father seated across the table, and quietly, he smiled because he knew it was what his father needed to see.

Jean-Pierre greeted their table. "Anything more, Dr. P?"

"*C'est tout*, Jean-Pierre. *Merci*."

"Rawn?"

With his eyes pressed shut, he nodded, sliding an Orangina to the side.

"Anything, *d'accord?*"

"Definitely."

Ezra Hirsch entered Café Neuf. Rawn looked up to the tall man standing at the entrance, raindrops dripping from his gray overcoat, his dirty-blond hair flat against his skull, and not holding an umbrella it made Rawn reminisce the day he first set eyes on D'Becca. She had rushed into Café Neuf out of the cool summer rain, her outfit soaked, her expensive shoes ruined, her hair she spent hours waiting to have done at Gene Juarez was— and the phrase Sicily jokingly used on Thanksgiving—a hot mess. Soaking wet, Ezra Hirsch was a mildly good-looking man in his early-forties. A polished and highly visible Seattle attorney, he won a high-profile case last year for the famous running back, Lou Baker Washington, on rape charges. Rawn, and everyone he discussed the case with, believed Washington raped the young woman, but the pundits who went on television talk shows to discuss the case said Hirsch chose the right jury and the chances of Washington being acquitted were pretty damn good. Hirsch appreciated something the prosecutor did not: both men and women would give Washington the benefit of the doubt, in particular, because he had a solid reputation and he was, at least publicly anyway, happily married; whereas the young groupie, who had pursued the ballplayer for months, was less credible. When he had invited her to his room following a game in Seattle, Hirsch had persuasively argued to the jury that things did not turn out as the accuser had hoped. Because she had felt dissed after their sexual encounter, the following afternoon she had walked into a Seattle police station and said to an officer seated at the desk, "Lou Baker Washington raped me last night."

"Ça va!" Jean-Pierre greeted the attorney.

At first puzzled, Hirsch eventually cracked a grin which revealed a visible diastema. He said, "Ça va."

"Can I?..."

"Ezra Hirsch?" Dr. Poussaint called out.

"Oh, the solicitor. Welcome!" said Jean-Pierre.

"I'll go..."

"*Oui-oui*. Anything you want? Café au lait?"

"You don't serve beer, do you?"

"No, not the *bière*."

"Fine, I'll...Sure, a café au lait."

Rawn and his father were on their feet when the distinguished attorney approached their table. In a formal manner, they shook hands and introduced themselves.

"We appreciate that you would see us on such short notice."

"Well, I follow CNN like a lot of Americans. And Khalil tells me the two of you grew up together. He thinks—and I likewise think—you need a lawyer. At the very least, you need legal counsel."

"We need to find out what's going on. There has been no new information. This woman that was killed...D'Becca—her death remains a mystery. There are no suspects; not even this Sebastian

Michaels, whom the authorities have cleared. Only my son. They don't say he's a suspect…"

"Yes," said the attorney. "He's become a person of interest."

"His name…his reputation is being tossed around like a Frisbee. When this kind of thing gets started…Once information gets put out there, you can't control it. It's like the mathematical theory of chaos. The whole idea that a powerful storm in New England may be caused by a butterfly flapping its wings in China…" Dr. Poussaint looked over to his son and back to the attorney. "Mr. Hirsch…"

"High-profile events can have a butterfly effect, yes. And it's Ezra, please."

"Ezra…as we speak, the private school where my son teaches, the trustees are having a meeting."

Jean-Pierre said, "*Pardon!*" He placed the café au lait on the table. "I make café au lait like Rawn like." He grinned.

Out of politeness, Rawn's lips curved faintly.

"Okay! *Merci!*" said the attorney.

"You very welcome." A non-intrusive man, Jean-Pierre excused himself from their table.

Hirsch took a sip from the bowl, and with an approving expression, said, "Now that's the real deal!"

They laughed, which eased any anxiety that might have existed since he arrived.

Hirsch leaned into the birch and polar wood table, his hands wrapped around the bowl of café au lait. His tone and body language solemn, he said, "I won't discuss my fee until I hear what Rawn has to say. What you tell me here at this table doesn't leave this table." He looked to Dr. Poussaint, the person who had reached out to him and most likely the person who would be paying his retainer. "What Rawn says here at this table gives me an idea of exactly what I need to do. Or what I *can* do for him." He turned to Rawn and looked straight into his somber eyes.

Rawn nodded, leaning closer into the table.

"I'm familiar with the board of trustees of Gumble-Wesley. I play golf—and yes, Dr. Poussaint, I understand that you are quite the golfer, but that's a subject to follow up on at a later time...I play golf with one of the trustees. Insofar as there being a conflict, there's no conflict. But I would trust that, as you say, Dr. Poussaint, the board *is* discussing your son as we speak, and they're probably deciding on whether Rawn should take a leave..."

"A *leave?*"

"Let him finish, Rawn."

"The coverage at the Academy has been on nearly every news outlet. Yesterday, footage of you leaving the school and getting into your Jeep was looped over and over—the media tailing you like you're a celebrity. It's unfortunate or fortunate, depending on how you choose to look at it, that you're photogenic and educated and come from a background that—how shall I put it?—is not typical in potentially high-profile cases when the accused is not a public figure. All the cable talk shows are still talking about you. It's become a cause célèbre. *Politically Incorrect* and Leno, probably even Letterman, commented about it last night. It's...Rawn is a distraction."

"I see your point," Dr. Poussaint said.

But Rawn did not.

"What do you feel comfortable sharing with me?"

With a shrug, Rawn asked, "What do you want to know?"

"Why don't you start at the beginning?"

CHAPTER TWENTY-EIGHT

S icily had been pacing back and forth and chomping at the bit for ten minutes. Of all the times her cellular was turned off! With the mobile in her hand, she recited a simple, barren prayer: *Please call back, Tamara.* Something innate told her this one would not be answered in her favor. Still, her heart did the believing, not her spirit. Not her logic. Not her God-given good sense. Good sense did not *feel*.

Her telephone rang, and she looked over her shoulder, startled by the sound. "Oh, great! She's calling on my landline." Sicily could not reach the telephone fast enough, and once it was in her hand, she punched the receive call button. Anxious, she greeted the caller with a rushed, "Hello!" Her shoulders slumped. "Oh, Rawn. Hi."

"Can I come up?"

Instinctively, Sicily turned to look beyond the stunning paned windows that took up a full wall and offered her a gloomy Elliott Bay view. "Where are you?"

"I'm at the payphone on the corner."

"Rawn…" Hearing his voice confiscated the stone that rested in her heavy heart. "First, I'm getting you a cell phone, and two, it's pouring! You could've pushed the buzzer." She walked to the window and looked out at the cold rain painting the city a fusion of charcoal gray and silver. Sicily thought, rain always rearranged the energy in the universe.

"I wasn't sure whether you were alone. And…someone might see me, and I don't want it to get back to the board, or end up on one of those gossip TV programs."

"Aren't you a little paranoid?"

"Situationally…Hey, this thing has been surreal."

When she opened the door to her loft, Rawn stood before her drenched, coolly and rationally as usual. He did not look like a man the authorities were eyeballing for the death of D'Becca, and investigating whether he was the one who could murder someone and behave as though he were innocent. Sicily could not help but wonder what her life—their lives—would be like in that very moment had he never met D'Becca, and she and Tamara never exchanged phone numbers at the Library Bistro the night of Pricilla's reading and book signing at Elliott Bay Books. Who would they be if she were straight? If she had the slightest urge to be with men—like Tamara—Rawn would be at the top of her list. She knew when they first met—and before she trusted him enough to tell him she was lesbian—that Rawn had a thing for her.

"Come in!"

"Oh, great!" he greeted her, the room smelling of sandalwood. "A fire. You aren't expecting?…"

"No." She cut him off, closing the door.

"I needed…You're the only person I can really talk to. Khalil might as well move to London. Tera…she's so busy. You won't believe it. She called Janelle for advice."

"Janelle? Your *ex*, Janelle?"

"That Janelle." Rawn peeled his bomber jacket off; it was soaking wet.

"Did you talk to her?"

"Janelle? Yeah."

"Let me get something so you can dry yourself off. Place your jacket on the back of the stool."

When Sicily left the spacious room, Rawn stood in the middle of the loft. He caught a glimpse, although barely, of Queen Anne

Hill. *D'Becca used to live there. If she never moved away, she might still be alive.* The northern end of the downtown Seattle skyline, with the tip of the Space Needle in the background, looked like headlights through a windshield along a crowded freeway. Rawn placed his jacket on the stool. He blew his hands with his warm breath and walked to the fireplace. He held his hands close to the flames. Sicily returned to the front of the loft.

"Here you go!"

They met each other in the center of the floor, and before he took the towel, Sicily watched him retreat into a daydream.

"Rawn? The towel."

"Oh!" He reached for it.

"What were you thinking?"

He shook his head side-to-side. "When someone you know dies... someone you were very intimate with dies...it's strange how you keep experiencing flashes and snippets of that person everywhere. The simplest of details. Someone might stand next to you and wear the same perfume. A laugh from someone you can't make out—the laugh is similar to hers. All the idiosyncrasies crowd your mind with chaos."

"What did I conjure up?"

"The first time D'Becca came to my apartment, she ended up there because we were walking, and typical of Washington weather, it started to pour down rain. When we were at my place I gave her a towel, like you did now, and it seemed—back then, Sicily, I couldn't imagine being in this mind-set, in this...situation: someone you were intimate with dies a violent death; the constant not knowing."

Sicily took a breath and replied, "I know."

When Rawn looked up, because of Sicily's demeanor and the pitch of her voice, he sensed that she was down about something.

Over the course of several years, they had grown quite close. Rawn could not determine if she was uncomfortable with his being there, or something else was going on in her life. He did not feel particularly at ease in seeking details, even when he knew she might want his ear. They were in an awkward place, and not solely because of his temporary leave of absence. Rawn was a very visible man at the moment; especially locally. The ongoing publicity his situation placed on the Academy was something that could only die down if he stopped teaching at Gumble-Wesley; at least until the spectacle eased up. Even though there was no direct evidence and Rawn had not been arrested, the Crescent Island police department's investigation focused strictly on his relationship with D'Becca. They looked into her relationship with Sebastian Michaels, but he was swiftly cleared.

And then there was, for Rawn anyway, the issue of Tamara.

He decided to ask because she was sulking. "What's wrong?" He was not sure which he preferred: that she claim nothing was wrong, or that she pour out her heart to him.

"I don't have beer, but would you care for wine?"

"Sure. Whatever."

Minutes later they sat on Sicily's aubergine velour sofa and she said, "Tamara left!"

Rawn looked away from the burning fire and turned to Sicily, his face implying bewilderment. "What do you mean by *left?*"

"I broke down. It goes against the values I live by, but I did it; like a desperate woman, I went to her boutique because she wasn't returning my calls. Some young girl—probably not a day over twenty-one—was, as she said, 'boutique sitting.' She claims Tamara went to Europe on business and she wasn't sure if she would be back before the New Year."

"Why do you say *claims?*"

Her eyes glossy, Sicily sipped her wine, and Rawn noticed that her hand was trembling. No longer in his comfort zone, he was not sure who to be or what to do. All of a sudden, his life was demanding that he be someone he was not sure how to be—emotionally, spiritually. He would have to navigate through all of it blindly. He would have to pick up survival instincts along the way.

"Rawn…" Sicily pursed her lips. "I fell for her. And harder than I thought."

Rawn looked down into the deep magenta wine.

"I know you need a friend right now. And Lord, poor D'Becca. I prayed for her, Rawn. I actually *liked* her. I gave you a hard time, I know. But I got to know her a little and realized she is—was good people." Sicily lowered her eyes. "But…" She reached over and rubbed his arm that rested against the back of the sofa. "I guess I've been too selfish."

Rawn swallowed hard.

"Tamara shared some things with me, but…." She paused, trying to decide whether she wanted to reveal the information. Sicily gazed into the burning fire.

Although Rawn was not sure he wanted to know, he asked, "What, Sicily?"

"She gave me several hints. I look back now…And I know we didn't know each other long, but… Not as long as you knew D'Becca."

"You said hints?"

"Let me say this: she talked about Henderson constantly. That was not even a *hint*. That was like waving a red flag at a bull. I have a Ph.D. in psychology, Rawn. If a gay person came to me and told me that someone they were falling for or talked nonstop about another person—especially a person of the opposite sex—I'd advise them to run and don't, *don't!*, look back. She was—no, *is* obsessed with Henderson Payne. She told me that she connected with women from the soul, but that men made her feel *whole*. What the hell does that mean? She's definitely not gay. I'm not even sure she's bi. She plays with your mind. I believe we're getting really obnoxious when it comes to labels, but what would you call someone like her? She uses...she manipulates people. The psych in me knows that very well. But..." She reached for her wineglass and took a long gulp of the liquor, like she was drinking water. "Experience has taught me all too well not to get tangled up with a woman who has an obsession with a *man!* How can I reconcile my own weakness with?..." Sicily finished off the wine.

Rawn had to push the memory of Tamara's face in his lap into the back of his mind. The sound of Sicily's self-pitying voice kept him focused.

"One night we were at her boutique. In fact, the last time I saw her. She needed to stop and get some sketches. I was walking around looking at the dresses while she checked her website for orders. I saw this journal amid paperwork. It was a beautiful leather journal which is why it probably caught my eye. I couldn't stop myself from picking it up. I knew it was private, although Tamara's the type to hand it over and say enjoy! But I digress." Sicily pushed her hair away from her face in that quite feminine way she often did. "I looked inside. I wanted to know what, if anything, did she say about me—us. What we shared, what it meant to her. I didn't want her catching me, so I flipped through it clumsily and I'm not even sure how I ended up on the last page. It was dated the Saturday following Thanksgiving." Sicily's voice was borderline sarcastic. She was verging on contempt. "That entry," she went on, "was all about someone new she met. A *man*. What the?...I couldn't believe it. She wrote *He's my new Henderson*. Those were her exact words. And still..." She started to take a drink of her wine but realized her glass was empty. "Stupid, stupid me! I wracked my brain…Who is this man? Tamara is insane when it comes to Henderson. This other man…I mean, Henderson is… She's sooooo obsessed with Henderson. Henderson this, Henderson that…"

"You were vulnerable…"

"How?" she raised her voice. "*How* could I be such a fool? I feel like all that internal work I've done…for what?"

Sicily began to cry and Rawn did not know what to do. One part of him wanted to hold her and another part of him wanted to rush to his feet and run. Run fast and never look back. How many men—cowards—did this? Got caught up in what Khalil referred to it as a ménage à trois and could not handle the consequences. It was less complicated, without all the name-calling and in-your-face confrontation, to disappear.

"Sicily…"

She wiped the tears from her eyes. "What?"

"Look at me."

Ashamed, it took a moment for her to turn her head slightly. Feeling short of humiliated, she met Rawn's somber look. In a quiet voice, she said, "What?" sniffing her runny nose.

"There's something I need—something I should tell you."

CHAPTER TWENTY-NINE

The week leading up to Christmas was a lonely time for Rawn. One week ago, while he sat in Sicily's warm and cozy loft, he knew what he was about to say meant that he could not go back, and the touchstone of their relationship would never be the same. While he sat listening to her lost in a deep melancholy, he kept battling between full disclosure and enough of the truth so it would set him free. In doing that, it could cost him a friendship.

He sat in his apartment alone, pecking with the keys to the piano. He tried not to think about his life over the past month or whether he should go home for the holiday. Rawn slowly began to grasp the idea that life was not merely mysterious; there were ambiguous nuances. Still young, yet a mature soul, he never paid close attention to his experiences, and nor did he take them too seriously. When something happened in his life, he acknowledged it in a rather oblique way. He did not stand that close to the moment. When it became apparent that a shift took place, Rawn could not determine exactly what; he adjusted his thinking without analyzing it. Now, however, he paid attention to each moment to the point of distraction. He took notice of the changes in the day, its rise and fall; its color scheme. How long had he taken things—his life—for granted? "You can be so basic, Rawn," Khalil had once said to him in a conversation. Had it never occurred to him to be on the lookout for an occasional surprise? No, it was not the way Rawn thought; he did not approach life in that way. And yet as his mother said to him not twenty-four hours ago, "It's time to grow up, Rawn." Her words stunned him. She concluded, "It's time to be your own man. Your father can pull out his checkbook, but he cannot save you from *you*." Rawn admired his mother's honesty; her directness. But what he failed to say to her was that he was only human. Perhaps because it was what he had said to Sicily that rainy evening at her loft, and her response to those words made him feel as though they were much too hollow.

Rawn never had to work very hard at anything. He was naturally smart, naturally good-looking, and effortlessly perceptive. It was the glorious nature of his life's blessing and the solid foundation upon which his life had rested. Growing up, he took advantage of his father's season seats to the Broncos and the Nuggets; without knowing it, he took for granted being able to ski in Vail and take hikes in Aspen. Growing up, it never occurred to Rawn that his experiences were not everyone's experience. Right after high school graduation, he and Khalil took a six-week trip to Europe, getting high off hashish, and sleeping in hostels long enough to get some shut-eye. He had quality resources at his disposal. His life had been a profound blessing. Rawn now understood, though, that even when life was limited to having things generally go your way, the extraordinary nature of living similarly came with a downside.

While he wanted to contact D'Becca's parents—at least her mother—he was advised not to do so. But nothing felt right. Nothing made sense. The one person he could let go with, other than Khalil, was Sicily. That trust had been damaged, which was a byproduct of deception. Rawn, nevertheless, held out hope that the mistrust would not be eternal.

He stopped pecking at the keys, and because he thought he heard someone at the door, he turned. He listened. He waited. It was probably a squirrel, he told himself. Every now and then he would stop what he was doing and turn around, expecting D'Becca to be there. Would that turn out to be the case with Sicily? For days after the evening at her loft, Rawn tried very hard to bury the feelings. The look on her face when he had told her, "I think Tamara might have been referring to me"—it had reduced him to an empty shell. The information was not offered because he was so full of himself, as Sicily had accused him of being. It was presented in view of the fact that he had knowledge Sicily was not privy to.

"And what exactly does that mean?" she had said. By the look on her face, it was like she had known all along.

"The day after Thanksgiving," he had started. "I was supposed to hook up with D'Becca. I wasn't in the mood and as... Later I decided we could catch a film. We had planned to go shopping at Pacific Place. She left a message on my machine that she was going to go without me. Something in her voice...I picked up on her disappointment so I came to Seattle. When I got inside the mall, it was crowded and I couldn't find her." Rawn did not look directly into her face, but from the corner of his eye, he observed Sicily crossing her arms stiffly. "I ran into Tamara. She invited me to her place for..."

"She invited *you* over to her place?"

His look told her to let him finish. She exhaled a deep breath; her body language gradually became colder and stiffer. He had sat in her loft wondering, would that decisive moment—on Black Friday—eventually recede from his mind?

"We talked for a while and I looked up and she was...she was there..."

"I don't want to hear anymore!" Sicily had rushed to her feet. Her back to Rawn, she then said, "I...D'Becca—we both picked up on you two. I knew it wasn't only me, but I didn't give it that

much thought." She had then turned and looked Rawn dead in
the eyes that were truly the windows to his soul. "I knew that you
would never betray me. Even though I got lost inside Tamara, I
admit I didn't trust her completely. But you, Rawn? I would trust
you with my debit card and the PIN number because I know
you'd never steal from me. How could?…"

The pain in her face was palpable. Rawn was not altogether
certain what the pain was from—his complex betrayal or Tamara's
wicked deception, or the sum total of both. He had swallowed
thickly and tried to avoid finishing his story by putting the half-
filled wineglass on the table and rubbing his hands back and forth
against his closely cut hair. With his elbows resting at his knees,
he had said, "I'm sorry, Sicily. I tried to find ways to tell you about
her. You were so"—*obsessed* was at the tip of his tongue—"happy…"

"Oh, you were trying to tell me the type of woman Tamara was,
but you weren't going to…if D'Becca hadn't been…you would
never have told me this: what you and Tamara…"

"What *me* and Tamara…I admit I—I'm human, Sicily. But there
was never a Tamara and *me*."

She had shaken her head side-to-side while tears hung inside
her hazel eyes. "Please leave."

Christmas came and went, the New Year was set in motion,
winter was wet and cold and bitter, and Rawn felt a new low. It
was an intense human angst. He had reached a low the moment
he was able to fully ascertain what his actions put into motion.
When exactly was his defining moment? To what degree was he
accountable for D'Becca's death? He tried to make sense of the
enigma of his experience. He grew up with the understanding
that divine purpose was behind anything merciless that happened.

In every fiber of his being, he sustained the belief that the universe acted in good faith and what any particular human being faced, long before it touched their life, they were given the resources—insight, fortitude—to see it through. Irrespective of how events unfurled for him lately, Rawn trusted his theory even more.

The following afternoon—it was sunny but brisk—Rawn was arrested.

icily stared at her image in the sprawling mirror that hung above the bathroom basin. Moments ago she washed off the day's makeup and exfoliated her skin with a mild cleansing bar. *I look lost.* She must have stared at her reflection for countless minutes before tears silently began to trickle from her hazel eyes. She would not know, even years from that moment, what possessed her to remove the colored contacts from her eyes and flush them down the toilet. Her tender, deep brown eyes changed the entire contour of her face. Softly, she cried, but within seconds snapped out of it as if some voice in her head warned her: heal, evolve, move on. The only way she could stop thinking about everything that happened over the past two months was to do something that would distract her. Not work; that would not do the trick. Yoga? It was too late to get to a class. Food? Sicily was not the type to go to food to fill up a void or to pacify her loneliness. She walked through the loft hoping something would come. An idea; a revelation. *Something!*

Despite the fact that she hired a cleaning company to come in and clean the loft once a week, she knew that cleaning would help her to relax and *be here now.* "I need to get through this time, right here. I know the anxiety will pass if I stay in this moment." She grabbed cleaning supplies and went to the bathroom and began scrubbing the floor on bended knees. Before long, she had worked up a sweat and her heart was racing like she had trotted up twenty flights of stairs. She scrubbed the corners, mumbling to herself that the cleaning lady missed a spot and she would reprimand the company "first thing!" When she cracked a nail, she pulled off the rubber glove, inspected the uneven nail and said beneath her breath, "Damn!" Ultimately, her arms ached and she needed to take a break. She leaned against the bathroom wall and her eyes rested on a corner of the ceiling. "I know that's not a spider web!" Sicily ran through the hallway into the front of the loft and to the granite-adorned kitchen. She reached for the broom and practically stomped her way back to the bathroom and used the broom to sweep away the spider web. "I'm not taking this! I'm going to cancel that cleaning service *first thing!*"

With one hand resting against her hip, she tried to slow her heartbeat. Emotionally, she was overwrought and she had trouble catching her breath. She needed to calm down before she had an anxiety attack. She sat on the commode. With her left hand gripping the broomstick, she reminded herself that no matter what, *every moment is perfect exactly as it is.* Sicily really tried to honor that, but she knew deep down like all sentient beings that while it sounded so poetic and brave, it was nothing more than Zen-ish mumbo jumbo. Before she was aware of what she was doing, and when the dust settled, she would still not know what on earth came over her. She dashed for the nearest telephone, which was in her bedroom, and with force punched digits. She knew she would receive voicemail and that was fine by Sicily.

"Listen to me, you bitch! I never ever want to hear from you again. If you see me out in public, don't even think about stopping me. Not even a smile or a hello. Don't think of saying one word to me. Do you get that? If you should happen to see me dying on the street, keep stepping—don't stop. Let me die, bitch! You get that? I never want to see your two-faced...You pathetic human being. I never want to hear your voice again. *Do you get that?*"

When Sicily released the call, she gasped. "Oh, my God. I can't believe I did that. What's wrong with me? *What is wrong with me?*" Afraid she would risk another out-of-body moment, Sicily tried to collect herself. She sat on her bed staring at a painting on the wall, her mind completely blank. When she looked down at her hands, they trembled.

Every moment is perfect exactly as it is. She repeated the mantra over and over; she convinced herself she felt better. Not because of the message she left Tamara, but because she wanted to genuinely trust that perfection rested in every moment, and no matter the lack of control one had over the trajectory of their life, or for that matter heartbreaking experiences, life remained beautiful and a blessing. If she did not hold on to that, she knew she had nothing. Nothing at all. When she went back to the bathroom to put away the cleaning supplies, Sicily happened to catch her reflection in the mirror, and the image looking back at her made her weep. For several minutes she sobbed, and in between her sobs she tried to recite the mantra, *every moment is perfect exactly as it is.* Sicily had not felt this bad—this low—since the *Post* outed her nearly eleven years ago. All the internal crap she spent years working through. *We are a work in progress.*

"No, no, no, no, no!" Sicily screamed. For a long time she sat on top of the toilet stool trembling; she rocked back and forth. Finally she cried out, "Why did this happen to me? I'm so humiliated." When she dropped to the floor, she began kicking the walls like a child having a temper tantrum. Sicily pulled at her hair and banged her fist against the spotless, tiled flooring. She reached for the toilet paper and yanked it until the entire roll was in a heap on the oval-shaped bath rug. She attempted to get to her feet; saliva dripped from her mouth and dissolved into the pile of toilet paper. She slipped on a lone square of toilet paper and landed on one knee. Sicily pressed herself halfway up with her hands, but collapsed to her knees. She then begged a god—any god—to set her free.

Exhausted, she curled into a knot on the floor until she fell into a light and dream-free sleep.

Since his arrest, Rawn's days left him tired and troubled, and it felt like the chaotic nature of his feelings would never recede. Everything about who he used to be was like dried leaves a cool autumn breeze swiftly blew away. He was repeatedly haunted by strange, incrementally persuasive dreams and visions of D'Becca. And while he tried not to get totally lost in the cacophony of his circumstance, the still nights, too often damp and frigid, made him come to look directly—and not circuitously—at his life. His connection to events that led him to this lonely place was too intense; he needed more distance in order to gain a fresh and open-minded perspective. It was Martin Luther King Day when he heard a gentle knock at his door. He had fallen asleep on the sofa while reading *Sports Illustrated*. It had snowed the evening before, and while it did not stick, the leafless limbs on the trees were a reminder of the beauty and mystery of Mother Nature. Disoriented, his eyes darted to the clock on the VCR. The second knock was louder, though not demanding.

Rawn came to his feet, wiping his face. He walked to the door, quite curious who could be on the other side. He stood at the door with his hand on the knob for several seconds. The media disappeared a week or so following his arrest. There was nothing to cover since the story went cold. Rawn was warned by Hirsch to expect various mediums to return a few days leading up to the trial. Although a date had not been set, Hirsch requested a speedy trial and the judge appointed over the case had approved cameras in the courtroom. Guardedly, Rawn looked through the peephole.

When he opened the door, the sight of her touched him in places he knew only seconds ago were closed to her, and anyone else, forever.

"Janelle?"

Rawn had not seen her since her wedding day and could not recall her looking so astonishing and marvelous. Against the winter-white peacoat, her dark skin was flawless. Average height, she stood before him with her wide smile and inspiring eyes. It amazed him that it felt like time—*their* time—stood still.

For a while, they sat close on the leather sofa in the stillness of the living room, and to Rawn the feeling was so strangely familiar. Janelle had changed so much since they were together; or had he come to look at her on new terms? It was not the way she looked, but the way she spoke and the animation in her voice when she talked. Everything about her was recreated; she morphed into acute beauty. Every dream she dreamed came true, but for the life she planned with him. She might not have the courage to tell him how much his setting her free put everything good about her life in motion. Only several years ago, she was confident that she could never forgive him, but he loved her enough to know that the boundless good on its way to her did not include him. There was someone more fitting for her and for the life that was designed solely for her and it could not come to fruition *with* him.

"How did you know what I couldn't understand three years ago?" she asked.

"Honestly, I didn't know. It could've been something inherent, who knows? I'd like to believe back then, ending things between us, I was doing you a favor. But my reasons were nothing more than selfish."

"Your goodness is inbred, Rawn. Doing what you thought was right doesn't make it selfish."

"If there's anything I've learned in the last month, it's that we aren't aware that each day we take so much of our life for granted. Daily life can be…an illusion."

"Rawn…"

"No, listen, Janelle. I'm good. You didn't need to do this—come all the way here to check on me."

"I'm not sure about that."

"I'm not angry, really."

She matched his gaze, and neither blinked. Before speaking, Janelle rehearsed in her mind exactly what to say. "No, not angry. But you're a new you; in a new place. This is unfamiliar territory. That Rawn Poussaint optimism and confidence, it's been side-lined. I was crazy about that side of you, by the way."

His eyes unconsciously lingered on her plump lips painted in a plum-colored lipstick. Quietly, he said, "Thank you."

"For what?"

"Surprising me. You have gumption, girl, knocking on my door." Rawn chuckled. "You didn't know who was going to answer. I'm not even sure who I'm going to be on any given day." He reached for her hand and could not help noticing the diamond on her ring finger. "I know Tera put you up to this."

"Your baby sister is strong-willed—a Poussaint to the core—that's for sure. But I knew you needed a *friend*. And I can't imagine not supporting a friend when he's in trouble."

"You have no idea. Your friendship has been sorely missed."

"We'll need to change that."

His lips moved, but Rawn did not make a sound: "I hope so."

He still had some influence over Janelle, which was precisely why she retrieved her hand. "Well…" She stood. "Since I've come all this way—a plane, a taxi, a ferry and yet another taxi—the least you could do is whip up your crawfish étouffée, because I'd love some. I tried to make it once. It tasted nothing like yours."

"I don't have the incredi—"

"Markets don't close this early on Crescent Island, do they?" she butted in, a hand planted on her swelling hip.

"No, but…"

"Okay, Rawn. Look, while you cook, I can give you all my ideas about your case. And I want to meet your attorney."

He stood in front of her. "What are you talking about?"

"I'm a lawyer, remember?"

"Yeah, but I have a lawyer."

"Hirsch is a damn good attorney. I know his reputation, and even before the Lou Baker Washington case. I watched snippets of the Henderson Payne trial on Court TV and fell head over for Hirsch. He's a fine Jew, but it was his courtroom charisma that hooked me. The opportunity to work with him…Do you know what this would do for my career? Being second chair in a high-profile case…I have a shot at partner."

Rawn looked closely at Janelle. He knew she was ambitious, but it never occurred to him how much. "But you do civil not criminal law, right?"

"Minor distinction."

"I trust you completely. You know that. But…"

"Who is this Rawn I rearranged my calendar to see? Uh-huh, no! I don't want to hear another but!" She walked around him and to the coat rack near the front door. She reached for his overcoat and said, "Stop it! Here." She held the dark heather-gray coat by the collar with her forefinger. "Come on!"

When he walked over to her, he yanked the coat from Janelle, somewhat facetiously. "Does your husband know you're here?"

"Of course! We—well, *I* don't have secrets. Men, you guys are hoarders when it comes to information." She helped him with his coat. "You always did have style, Rawn. I like this cut. You wear it well. Still have that bomber jacket you wore all during grad school? It could be ten below and you'd be walking across campus with that bomber jacket. It became your trademark, did you know that?"

With a wink, he said, "You know I still have it."

"Should have known."

When their eyes locked, with affection, he took her curvy body into his arms. Rawn embraced her long and hard. "I love you," he said into her ear, and then rested his chin against her shoulder.

With her eyes pressed shut, Janelle knew that he loved her and waited three years to say those words without the burden of commitment. She was completely unaware of when it happened, but she forgave him some time ago. In a sincere voice, she whispered in his ear, "I know."

CHAPTER THIRTY-ONE

I mani was standing on line at Grand Central post office when, in her head, she talked herself into getting a cellular. With a grin on her face, she reflected on what Kenya said to her the day after they went to the bail hearing for the seventeen-year-old boy who, allegedly, shot their father in cold blood and another man who would spend the rest of his life paralyzed from the waist down: "Would you please, you stubborn cow, get a mobile!" When she slid the key into the lock of Dante's loft, she could hear the telephone ringing. Imani rushed inside and to the nearest land-line, reaching eagerly for the receiver before the ringing abated. She did not know Dante's code to his answering machine, which currently held the maximum messages—fifty. Imani had no way of retrieving them.

"Hello!" Imani walked back to the loft door and closed it. "This is she. I'm sorry, your name again?" She listened momentarily. "Sure, okay. Now's a good time. And where?"

An hour later, Imani stepped inside Le Bateau Ivre on East Fifty-first. She did not spot a mature woman sitting alone which meant she arrived before Pearl St. John, a friend of Dante's, whom she agreed to meet at the café. When a woman who worked at Le Bateau Ivre approached her, Imani said, "I'm waiting for someone." The café worker gave her a not-so-friendly look and without saying a word, walked away.

Imani looked around when she heard a soft voice: "Are you…"

When their eyes met, the woman's face rang no bells. Imani never met this woman in her life. A long mahogany fur draped over the petite woman. *You'd better hope that no one remotely connected to PETA is in this café or its adjacent hotel!*

The stranger practically stared into Imani's wide eyes. "Oh, yes. You are definitely Dante Godreau's daughter."

"You said you were a friend of Dante's and that you needed to meet me in person?"

"Yes. Yes, we were dear friends. Your father and me. Can we take a table?"

"Oh, sure."

They sat at a table by the window. "We met years ago in Montréal. Before Kenya's mother, and before your mother."

They ordered when the not-so-friendly café worker came to their table.

Imani said, "I can't tell you how many cards and letters and notes my sister and I have gone through. I've started answering them. Did you write us?"

"Yes, in fact I did. And I left several messages…"

"What exactly…I mean, what is your connection to Dante?"

"I loved your father. He was a gentle man."

I know.

Their glasses of Beaujolais were brought to their table. The not-so-friendly waitress left not having uttered a single word.

Their conversation swiftly became informal, and Imani liked Pearl. She guessed her to be a tad bit younger than her father because Dante always dated younger women. Imani's mother was shy of twenty when she met Dante, and he was in his mid-thirties. With a soothing mien, Pearl grew up in Southern California during a turbulent time in American history, and as a result of the Watts Riots in 1965, she became quite political. The straight and long blond hair—with subtle strands of gray and a permanent part in the middle—was archetypal Southern California. She starred on a soap opera for six years, but when she met and married a real estate investor, she did not renew her contract and the soap opera decision-makers killed her off. When her husband died four years ago, Pearl St. John was set for life. Although she did not say, Imani guessed she was one of Dante's numerous flings. "See, while I was a bit of a scoundrel," Dante had once told Imani, "back in those days there was no AIDS, no HIV."

"I wanted to meet with you because in my note to you and your sister, I asked that you contact me before you left New York. I kept calling Dante's home number, leaving messages. But got no response. I last saw Dante about six years ago. He was very proud of you and Kenya. She a CPA, and you a professional dancer."

"Why exactly did you want us—me—to contact you?"

"I own a production company in Santa Monica."

"How fascinating!"

"I know that your career as a dancer ended after a skiing accident four years ago."

"Actually, I was on a Vespa and it crashed into a brick wall. Five years ago. I broke my leg and arm. But how did you know I danced?" And before she let Pearl answer, Imani said, "Dante!"

They laughed, and it was clear to them both a friendship was inevitable.

"The last time I spoke with Dante…it was about two years ago. He said you'd traveled all over the world." Although Pearl came across kind, and there was a hint that she was pleased with her life, there was a look of sorrow in her eyes nonetheless. "But!" She took a small sip of her Beaujolais. "I read that you own a Pilates studio in Seattle."

"Actually, on Crescent Island. And it's a Pilates studio and smoothies bar."

"Clever! You know, I've been to Crescent Island. Once. An old college friend lives there. It's lovely. It's doing well, your studio. I checked."

"Oh, really! How?"

"The World Wide Web is a game-changer. But I was hoping to interest you in doing a series of Pilates DVDs."

"DVDs?" Imani frowned. She was not certain what she expected Pearl to say, but making DVDs was nowhere close to her line of thinking.

"My production company produces exercise tapes, among other things. But you are very beautiful, one. You are fit and lithe, two, which would be very marketable. And three: Pilates is becoming quite the new way to stay in shape. Obviously you're savvy. Your studio is the only one on the island, and while I haven't done the research, I'd be surprised if there were even three in the state of Washington. Even in L.A., there aren't more than a handful. Probably in the entire state of California! It's always good to get ahead of the demand. And Imani, your DVDs would sell out! I can make you the Jane Fonda of the 2000s. I know it because I've been doing this for years, and I've been quite successful. Your videos and DVDs would be best sellers. Oh, yes. We could make a killing."

"But how would that all work?"

"We'd make, let's say, three videos and DVDs, and get them on the market *tout de suite* and test your marketability. We'll see how they sell and take it from there. Would you be interested?" Pearl's penciled-in eyebrow lifted.

For a short time Imani was hesitant, but the idea itself was compelling. She was not one to *think*. Every choice—the good and the bad ones—was based on her feelings. Rarely had her inkling led her astray. Even Blaine was a good feeling. That feeling, while it cost her, taught her some things—about men; about herself.

"Can I think it over? I can say here at the table, it sounds…different. And I'm like Dante in that way. I love to do everything I can that isn't already tried and true. At least not in the typically commercial way."

From across the table, Pearl studied Imani. Her dark hair cut in the fashionable style her age was wearing at the moment; her softly made up face—gentle browns and creams—was oval shaped; her stunning skin color—she was radiant! *I was a lot like her in my day. I know exactly why she's single and has yet to marry.*

"Let's toast!" Pearl said, raising her flute.

When she walked into Dante's loft, Imani felt woozy. *Off two glasses of Beaujolais?* She flopped in the sofa and rested against it. "Wow! Is the room spinning?" Moments later, she lifted herself up from the sofa and reached for the remote. Kenya told her that she was addicted to CNN, but it was more like a strange guilty pleasure. Since Rawn's arrest, Imani listened for updates at least once a day. Since *TalkBack Live* was on, she headed for the telephone. Blaine's voicemail greeted her and Imani giggled. "Hi, it's me. When you come to New York this weekend, I need you to help me get a cell phone. And I have something wonderful to tell you. I want to hear your opinion. It's exciting…"

Rawn walked into his apartment frustrated, yanking the dark blue tie from his neck. When he entered the kitchen, he caught sight of the bright red light blinking on his answering machine. It indicated he had eight unheard messages, and this aggravated him even more. On a weekly basis he received several calls from producers of television talk shows, or a journalist from a newspaper or magazine. Hirsch informed him the day before that a publisher had offered him a publishing contract; he was very interested in Rawn's story. Whether Rawn entertained the idea or not, in all likelihood, he could be challenged from profiting from the crime he was being accused of committing. It was difficult to evaluate his days. He was not working and the isolation was taking its toll.

Rawn left his father a message: "Hey, Daddy. A date's been set."

While leftovers heated up in the microwave, Rawn listened to a Godreau album released in the early 1980s. He could not say how long he stared into dusk. The sky was dreary, and an odd thing occurred: a slice of sun, which had been absent all day, began to fade into the horizon. Rawn was startled when the telephone rang. He and his father talked roughly thirty minutes, and after they said their goodbye, Rawn ate his meal at the kitchen table. Not once, since moving into the apartment less than three years ago, had he ever sat at the table, not even to have a meal. While he was cleaning the dishes, the telephone rang. The urge to answer sat with him, but he did not want to get into some kind of tête-à-tête with a journalist who was not really interested in him or the case, but in the fictitious portrayal of the relationship he had with D'Becca which the media exploited. He—they had become a voyeuristic frisson and Rawn resented it. When he saw Troy, D'Becca's trainer and friend, on one of the evening entertainment news shows, he was aghast and infuriated. He had made a startling comment: "D'Becca spent her life fighting for every breath." Eventually, he came to understand why Troy might have made that choice, since no one else was speaking positively on her behalf, but for unemployed models who claimed to have worked with D'Becca at some point or other. Of course they likewise had an opportunity to be in the spotlight and claim their fifteen minutes.

Rawn thought it better to let the answering machine pick up.

But then it occurred to him it could be Sicily. At least that was his hope. "Hello."

"Poussaint, hey man, it's Chap."

"Chap, what's going on?" Some part of Rawn was relieved. Grateful that not only was it not a journalist, but that it was not Sicily after all. Rawn was torn, because he deeply wanted to talk to her, and yet he was not sure what to say. Besides, she had not returned any of his calls.

"How'd it go today?" his musician friend asked.

"I have a trial date." Janelle had suggested to Hirsch that he request a change of venue, which he had considered himself. The judge granted that request, which the prosecutor vehemently opposed. Rawn said, "The trial will be tried in Seattle."

"That's good. Not that in Seattle this thing isn't water cooler talk, what my dad used to always say about Watergate. Everything about this, man…it's freakin' insane!"

With his head down, Rawn sat against the back of his sofa. "Yeah," he agreed solemnly.

"I mean, how did this thing get so sideways? I thought it was all some mix-up. That millionaire, Sebastian Michaels, the one that found D'Becca; he said he saw you leave when he arrived, and she was still alive. When he went into her place…nothing was wrong with her."

"The truth will prevail."

"Damn. You're a better brother than me. I'd be on Tavis Smiley making it clear that I was an innocent black man. In-no-cent, you dig?"

Rawn chuckled to himself. "You would, too!"

"You up to coming to the Alley?"

"I don't think that's such a good idea."

"Trust me…"

Crossing his arms, Rawn used his shoulder to hold the receiver. "Really, it would be such...."

"Everyone at the Alley knows you. They know this is all B.S. 'Sides, everyone's always asking about you. We're like family. Re-think this, Poussaint."

Marvin Gaye's "Wholly Holy" was ending when Rawn sat at the bar. He and his musician friends played a set before a full room. Weeknights at Jazz Alley were slow; every now and then, and out of the blue, a crowd showed up. It was not something that could be predicted since it was so random. All the musicians, including Rawn, played their souls out.

While sitting at the bar daydreaming into his drink, two women at one end kept giggling, whispering to each other, and looking his way. Rawn had become accustomed to being looked at. Often when he entered a room or walked through the aisles of QFC, people would do double-takes or speak in undertones. However, he had not gotten—and nor would ever get—used to *why*.

"It must be the moon," Stefanie said.

From head-to-toe, Stefanie was overkill. She wore too much makeup; her artificial nails were thick which made them look all the more fake; and she wore gaudy rings on most of her fingers and one thumb. Her face had a glow, and she was easy to be around. Rawn learned the evening he let her use his roadside service card that she did not get real worked up. With a good attitude, she approached life with the intent to *live* it however it came at her.

"What do you mean?"

"Excuse me," Stefanie said to a woman about to take the empty stool next to Rawn. "I was here first," she said to the thin young woman holding a drink in her hand. When she slid onto the stool,

Stefanie yelled out, "Bartender!" While she waited for him to attend to her, she turned to Rawn and said, "This place was on it tonight!" She slammed her hand against the bar. "Something told me to come. It's gotta be the moon!"

Derric, the bartender, said, "What can I get you?"

"Another rum and Coke for my friend. And I'll have a California Cooler."

When Derric walked off, Rawn said, "I have to drive. I don't need another rum and Coke. And Stefanie, aren't you too young to be drinking?"

She rested her elbows on the bar. "Oh, and like you didn't drink at twenty!"

"Touché!"

Delicately, she rubbed his hand. "How you doin', baby? I pray for you every single night. I tried to call you. Did you change yo number?"

With a shake of his head, Rawn said, "No."

"I must've transposed the numbers when you gave me a lif'. I got dyslexia. So tell me something?" Rawn looked directly into Stefanie's eyes, but her eye-shadow was so over-the-top it distracted Rawn. "You remember that night when you help me wif my car?"

Derric returned with Stefanie's cooler and Rawn's rum and Coke. "Thanks, Derric. Put it on my bill."

"So, guess what?" Stephanie said.

"What?" Rawn asked, amused.

"Remember you tol' me I should think 'bout goin' to college?"

"I still think you . . ."

"Let me finish, Mr. Poussaint! So, guess what?"

Rawn looked up to Stefanie, and it was her tone that ignited his curiosity.

"I got into Central. They actually accepted me."

"Stefanie, that's awesome!"

"Ain't it?" She grinned. "I gotta tell ya, I was shocked, though!"

"Congratulations! I'm proud of you."

"I would'na done it if it what'n for you, Rawn." She reached over and kissed his cheek, leaving a dark rouge-lipped impression against his skin.

Touched, Rawn reached for her hand and squeezed it. "Call me if you ever need any help. Will you do that?"

"You know I will!" She laughed. "I'll probably drive you crazy and you'll change yo number fo' sho'. But nothing for nothing, you ain't change it and all these nosy reporters know it."

From the corner of his eye, Rawn caught a woman at the end of the bar who looked like she might be waiting for someone. Amid a crow, her presence stood out in the room. She caught Rawn looking at her, and Stefanie took a glimpse across the bar to see what or who got Rawn's attention. Before she could distract him away from the noticeably pretty woman, Rawn cut his eyes away. He reached for his rum and Coke and emptied what was left in the glass.

"By the way," Stefanie said. "I was about to ask you something before Derric butted in on us."

"What's that?" Rawn's eyes drifted back to the very attractive woman at the other end of the bar. She was no longer there. He tried to stay focused on Stefanie instead of seeking the young woman out in the club.

"That night when you help me wif my car? Remember you was...you needed to do somethin'. And I toldju that if you gave me a ride, maybe what you thought you needed to do..."

"I remember."

"Did you ever do it?"

Rawn replied with, "It's all good."

Stefanie reached for her cooler. "See, I toldju!"

An hour later, Rawn stood in the shower, letting the water purify his skin. His mind was unnaturally blank. His thoughts were always several steps ahead of him. He was not sure that he heard his telephone ringing, and it was very late—nearly two in the morning. It had to be his imagination. Once he was out of the shower, he roamed through the shadowy apartment in his robe. He knew he would not be able to sleep. He ended up in the kitchen. With the full moon pouring into the room and giving him sufficient illumination, he did not bother turning on the light switch. He reached for a red pear in the fruit bowl. He leaned against the counter and took a bite. The sound of a tree branch scraping against his window alerted Rawn, and he turned to look out. Raindrops glistened against the nude branches of the tree on the other side of his large naked window. He would remind himself to call the apartment manager to have the branches trimmed. He tossed the half-finished pear in the trash. Rawn caught sight of the red light blinking on his answering machine. He pushed the button to hear the message, and he assumed it was Stefanie making sure she did not transpose his telephone number again.

"Hi, Rawn. Baby, I'm sorry."

The electronic voice on the machine said, "No more messages."

"Tamara?"

CHAPTER THIRTY-TWO

"The trial of *Washington State v. Rawn Poussaint* gets underway one week from today. We will bring you live updates on the hour. Ezra Hirsch, the high-profile attorney who defended Lou Baker Washington one year ago, and Henderson Payne in 1993, has managed to not only get the trial moved to Seattle where the jury pool is more diverse, he has also managed to…"

Khalil clicked the remote control to silence the audio. "Blah, blah, blah. I never did like her. How'd she get that job?"

"Bad mood?" Moon said, flipping through a day-old *International Herald Tribune* in bed. Clad in a silk spaghetti-strapped nightie, she picked up her black tea and reminded Khalil, "My flight leaves at six."

He slipped his slacks on and turned to admire her waist-long jet-black hair spread out over the pillow. She looked like she was posing for a shampoo advertisement. "You'll be back during the trial?"

She looked up to him, skeptical. "Would this be the best time to meet Rawn for the first time?"

"It's support, Moon. Black folks have a different way of doing things…you being at the trial won't in any way offend his sensibilities."

"Yes, then of course I'll come back to be a support for him. I heard the trial was going to be at least a month long. This whole thing is so…Even in London, it's popular conversation. D'Becca Ross was a beautiful woman. It's tragic."

"Why does it take a beautiful woman…No, a beautiful *white* woman to be murdered or abducted or whatever to make the media notice and for it to be *tragic*."

Moon was fully aware that it was a statement, not an inquiry.

Slipping on his shirt, Khalil studied Moon closely. While she read the paper, she occasionally sipped her tea. Moon was very feminine, and graceful. "That's the right black tea, right?"

When their eyes met, she winked flirtatiously. "It's perfect, baby."

Khalil said to himself, "I know that's right."

"I'm sorry?"

With a grin he said, "Nothing."

His cellular rang, and Moon retrieved it from the nightstand. She handed it out to him, saying, "Here's your accomplice."

Reaching for it, he laughed. "Khalil Underwood!"

"Hey!"

"Henderson, my man. You in Boston?"

"Yeah, man. And it's cold as hell."

"Wait! Anything wrong?"

"Why something got to be wrong, dude?"

"I'm checking. You don't usually call me on the road unless it's important."

"Can we hook up?"

"When do you guys get back to L.A.?"

"Tomorrow. But let's make it day after."

"I can come to you or we can hook up in the Marina."

"Come by the crib. Say four o'clock."

"See you then."

Khalil tossed the cellular onto the bed and sat at the edge of it. When he bent over to slip on his shoes, he felt a weird, unconscious panic.

The following morning, he cancelled two appointments in order to meet with his most high-profile client. Henderson Payne lived in the Hancock Park section of Los Angeles; a ride that was approximately fifteen minutes from Khalil's cottage above Sunset Plaza. His office, not far from the cottage, was ten minutes from Henderson's. At that hour, and with traffic, it took fifteen minutes, give or take. The street Henderson lived in was enchanting with Old World charm; it was wide and antediluvian tree-lined. Each time Khalil pulled into the long drive, he saw something new about Henderson's home. Set away from the street, the Italianate had a washed sienna façade with extra-tall palm trees amid beautifully cared-for foliage with meticulously manicured lawns. Henderson purchased it when he signed his new deal, and it was grand, opulent. Following his acquittal in 1993, Henderson spent a year in Italy playing ball, and was seduced by the culture's charm and immortality. While residing there, he bought a villa. When he returned to Los Angeles, whenever he passed a beautiful woman, he would say *ciao bella*, the way the Italians did it, and his wardrobe was strictly Italian, right down to his shoes. While in Italy, he managed to sign several lucrative endorsements. The Italianate was on the market for a week, and Henderson bought it sight unseen. The purchase made the front page of *The Wall Street Journal*.

Henderson's black convertible Porsche was halfway between the front of the home and the four-car garage in the rear. Daphne generally kept her Range Rover parked in the rear by the garages until she was in for the remainder of the evening. Khalil did not see her SUV, and this made him superficially edgy. When he turned off his engine, two stunning Dalmatians rushed up barking. Henderson stood inside the frame of his black double doors in faded Levi's with a slit in the left knee, a white designer T-shirt and flip-flops.

"It's love, man. Don't freak—they know you," Henderson called out, laughing. "Pepper! Seville! Come back here!" Henderson commanded the Dalmatians. "Come on, girls! Come back in the house."

When he stepped out of his car, Khalil received a call. He elected to disregard it in case it required time or privacy. When he reached the door, he and Henderson shook hands and shoulder-bumped.

The house loomed quiet. Henderson walked Khalil through the entrance gallery that led to an airy living room highlighted in soft watermelon-hued walls. The artwork that hung in the room was purchased while he lived in Italy: vivid and exceptional pieces that made no sense to Khalil. A fire was burning which added a serene ambiance to the ornate room. Several plush sofas and chairs sprawled the wide, rectangular area. The living room's arched French doors enhanced the indoor-outdoor spaces, as each led to a different angle of the west loggia outlined in aged brick that spilled out onto the limestone-paved courtyard and pool.

They left the rambling living room and entered a sitting room richly decorated in chocolate and amber, with suede sofas and velvet overstuffed chairs. A striking photograph of Daphne on the cover of *Vogue* Paris hung in an oversized frame on one wall, and the opposite wall was adorned with black-and-white and copper-colored photographs of Henderson's children—in the park, at his games, one of the children's sleepover, having a bubble bath, at a birthday party, asleep in their father's arms while he read a newspaper. Those photographs—unbelievably breathtaking—relayed an ambiguous tale.

"I thought we could have beers…or naught. It's a nice day. One of the reasons I worked my ass off to get here. Or would you rather stay inside?"

"Either way. I've always been pulled to this room."

"Cool." Henderson sat in one of the exquisite ivory-black chairs.

Khalil took a seat at the edge of the suede loveseat.

"Should I have Lucinda bring us something?"

Khalil crossed his legs. This was, to all intents and purposes, his employer. Since taking him on as a client, they went to a few Dodger games together, and last year Henderson took him to see Kathleen Battle for his birthday. He spent one weekend with his family on Catalina Island during the off-season; and they drove to Palm Springs for a golfing tournament and to Vegas for a boxing match. They were not friends per se; Khalil made every effort to draw the line between business and personal matters because it had the potential to cloud his judgment if he became too close to a client. Yet when Henderson called and invited him to do this or go there, he was often irresolute. He was among several of his most visible clients, and getting personal came with the job; thus, one showed up! Generally, he knew why he was meeting with Henderson. All day the day before he could not imagine why he summoned him to his home.

"I'm cool. But Lucinda does make one good margarita."

"Should I?..."

He threw his hand out. "No, really." Khalil uncrossed his leg.

While the room did not feel stuffy in the least, Khalil was not exactly relaxed and at ease with his client's intrigue. He crossed his leg again while Henderson, casual, rested comfortably in the seat. His long legs stretched out, he placed his finger to his temple while his thumb rested under his chin. "You know I have two, possibly three good years left, right?"

"Of course."

"Jabbar is my hero, but I don't want to be forty-two when I retire my number."

"Sure; fine."

"How's your friend?" Henderson asked.

Khalil realized he was inside his head and was not exactly sure what Henderson said to him, although he knew it was a question. "Excuse me?"

"Your friend. Rawn?"

"Oh, Rawn!" Khalil leaned forward. "As good as he could be under the circumstance. He's magnificent in the way he's stepped bravely into new territory. I know I'd handle it differently for sure."

Henderson extended a polite nod.

Khalil wanted to ask him why he inquired about Rawn, but then Henderson knew that Rawn was his friend, and anyone who was not in a coma knew about the case and D'Becca's murder. Henderson's wife, Daphne, knew D'Becca. They worked together in Europe, although it was some years ago—early on in their respective careers. Khalil still could not wrap his head around this thing being classified as a murder and Rawn's alleged involvement.

Henderson broke his agent's roving mind. "I remember that commercial she did. Remember, for the Super Bowl? Half the time I never even pay attention to all those ads, man. But I stopped for that one. She was advertising beer?" Henderson chuckled. "Reminds me of music videos. Babes are practically naked, grinding the floor, the walls, each other…And what exactly does that have to do with the lyrics, know what I'm saying?"

"But you don't mind?…"

"Oh, no! No, I don't mind." Henderson's famous grin rearranged the contour of his face. He reached out and he and Khalil fist-bumped. "Yeah, that was a few years ago. But I remember that commercial like it was this morning."

"It was memorable. You won't believe it, man. But Rawn didn't even remember that commercial. She's a—was a beautiful woman; it's tragic." Khalil found himself repeating what Moon said a few days prior.

"He must've missed it."

"No, we went skiing in Tahoe the weekend of that Super Bowl. We saw the commercial. Rawn didn't make the connection."

"Well…how's it looking for him?"

"There's no direct evidence. Their so-called eyewitness is D'Becca's next-door neighbor. But Hirsch, you know him. He'll poke holes in her questionable timeline. Other than her saying she saw him leaving *after* Sebastian Michaels, that's all they have; and that's not accurate. What's the motive? There's no weapon. As I understand it, they aren't even able to determine whether she was killed as a result of her head hitting the bathtub or some blunt object she was hit with. Man, it's so circumstantial, if that. Wrong place at the wrong time. A brother on Crescent Island." Khalil shook his head.

Is this why I'm here?

"Man, that's a beautiful place. I thought about buying property there. Daphne loves it."

"Why don't you have a place in Washington? It's home."

"When I went over to Italy, I let my sister take over my place in Madrona. Anyway, I like staying downtown whenever I go home. The place has changed so much. Starbucks on every corner, parking's tight…It's so different…"

The dogs started barking and Henderson looked over his shoulder anticipating them to run into the room. Khalil could hear Lucinda, the woman that managed the Paynes' home, telling the dogs to calm down. Each man sat quietly in the room for several minutes until Henderson said, "I want to ask you something."

Khalil made note of the seriousness in his tone. Henderson was not an easy man to interpret. "What's that?"

"When I was on trial—and this was before we met—did you think I was guilty?"

Khalil met Henderson's earnest gaze. He understood it fully: he needed to be forthright. The question was not random or casual. Henderson asked because he wanted to *know*.

He did not hesitate when he replied. "I never once thought you were guilty."

Before he said anything, Henderson looked Khalil straight in the eyes. "Man to man…"

"Man to man—no. When I heard that you were arrested for drug possession…four *kilos* of cocaine and weapons possession, naw." Khalil grimaced. "Uh-huh, man. Listen, anybody who followed sports during that time knew you had a habit, okay? It was no secret. Come on, man. You can't have a damn near four-hundred-dollar-a-day coke habit and not expect that to be leaked. You can't go hanging out in the hood doing crack with homeboys and not expect *that* to be leaked by somebody," Khalil said, shrugging sarcastically.

"Okay." Henderson nodded. "You're right. And I appreciate your honesty."

"But you do recognize that when your agent suggested you go to Italy, it was the smoothest transition for you? God rest his soul, but Saul had your back, Henderson. And I don't say that because he was my mentor. I know how much you resented having to play in another country."

"Oh, well, I'm over that. Going to Italy, it changed my life. But you have to know what it's like to be accused of something you didn't do and then go through the so-called justice system. Man, that…" Henderson looked to be in thought, his head bowed. His eyes pressed shut, he lifted his head. When he looked straight at Khalil, it was something Khalil understood for the first time: how much the trial—and the criminal accusation—affected his client. "Your friend Rawn. Is he standup? Brother-to-brother, I mean *standup?*"

"Hell, yeah. I trust Rawn with my *life!* They don't come standup better than Rawn."

"Yeah, right. See, it's wrong that a man who's innocent should go through what he's going through. I was lucky. Twelve Angelenos were not exactly confident that I—me, Henderson Payne, a celebrated ballplayer, would leave the scene of...a drive-by? Why would I even be involved in a *drive-by?* I don't carry my gun *on* me. And leave kilos of cocaine in the backseat of *my* ride and several Uzis in the trunk? Seriously. To this *day* I feel what that trial did to my reputation. And that's why when Saul advised me to do it, I went to Italy. But man, I still think about it. Not every day, but I've gone to parties where a bowl—and I mean a *bowl*—of cocaine is sitting there...and I remember"—he tapped his temple three times—"that night, and I get up and leave the room. So it won't even be linked to me, I leave the house!"

Khalil nodded with understanding. But there was simply no way for him to comprehend the scope and magnitude of Henderson's experience.

"So if you tell me your friend would never be involved with something like what he's being accused of, he shouldn't have to go through this, man. It's—it's not right."

"They never did catch the dude that stole your ride, did they?"

"No," Henderson said, shaking his head. "Man, I was high that night. I'd done some serious blow; I'd hit the pipe a few times, too, and I could have given the devil the keys to my ride. All I remember is getting a phone call real early the next morning. It was all over the news that there was this drive-by and some cat was shot three times, and my ride was involved. Two hours later, I get a knock-knock at my hotel door. That brother who took my ride? He was a thug, but he wasn't stupid. He had the good sense to wipe my ride clean of his fingerprints. DNA wasn't reliable back then. All the fingerprints on the weapons and kilos of cocaine belonged to some Latino dude who probably sold him the stuff. Hell, he was in the wind; probably crossed the border before the news even broke in the media.

"You tell me. How—why…" Henderson spread his hands. "Would *I* have that kind of paraphernalia in my Benz? See, the drive-by was two blocks from where I scored my cocaine. So-called eye-witnesses claimed they saw me get in my car, leaving. I was with my 'entourage.' Because I couldn't find my ride, I assumed it was stolen. One of my homies took me back to the hotel, man. Despite what the prosecution claimed: that my so-called entourage was living off my celebrity and they'd say whatever I tell them to say; so even their testimony didn't help me. But as I sit here, it's God's blessing"—Henderson kissed his fingertips and looked up like he was sending God a private message—"the jury took something I said on the witness stand to heart. *They* trusted me."

Khalil let Henderson work through the memories. He knew, if he was being tested, he passed. But he was unable to ascertain through their conversation why he was there. While every past had its mystery, that time in his life was over; besides, Khalil was not his agent back then. He could not make the connection. And what he feared was that something happened and Henderson was afraid his past was going to come back and haunt him. He was not *involved* necessarily; like he had no involvement in the drive-by or in possession of kilos of cocaine and illegal weapons. Khalil rested his back against the love seat and mused on his own past. Was there something back there that might come back and revisit him? He was halted from getting too caught up in his history when he heard Henderson say something.

"What did you say, Henderson?"

"I have a story I want to share with you…"

"It's me," Khalil said, making a sharp turn off Rimpau onto Third Street. "I need you to book me a flight."

"What about the Antoine deal?" his assistant said on the other end of the line.

"Fax it to my e-mail. I'll print it out at the airport. And I need you to book me a room."

"I thought…"

"I need you to book me a room! Hire me a car." Khalil dismissed whatever it was his assistant was saying; he disconnected the call, turning right onto Hauser with the hopes of avoiding the height of late-afternoon traffic that congested the city streets at commute time—between four and seven. He speed-dialed a name and a woman answered in a very professional manner. At the red light at Beverly and Martel, he said, "Hello, this is Khalil Underwood…"

CHAPTER THIRTY-THREE

"What's this meeting about, Ezra? Why did we all need to be here?"

"There's a break in the case."

"What?" Rawn said.

"Did the neighbor admit she was lying about…?"

Mrs. Poussaint interrupted her husband and said, "Let him speak."

"When Janelle gets in from the airport…"

"Janelle? I spoke to her last night." Crossing her arms, Tera continued: "She told me she would arrive on Sunday afternoon."

"We confirmed these details late into the evening. Janelle got on the first available flight out of Denver. Her plane landed an hour ago; she should be here momentarily."

"We're all in suspense, but we've put our faith in Ezra up to this point. Let's wait until Janelle gets here," Rawn's mother suggested.

"We're waiting for Janelle?" Rawn asked.

Mrs. Poussaint, with a gentle touch of her son's forearm, said, "Rawn."

The conference room faced Puget Sound from one angle and Smith Tower from another. The sun was sharp against the sky; it was an unusually warm late morning. Everyone sat upright in armchairs while their faces revealed curiosity about the hush-hush turn of events. They all made an effort to remain unmoved by suppressing any inquisition that rested at the tips of their tongue. Tera reached for a bottle of Talking Rain spring water. A woman entered the conference room in a sharp pinstripe suit and said, "Ezra, you're needed. I'm brewing up Tully's. Anyone care for a coffee?"

Dr. Poussaint looked up from his BlackBerry and said, "I'd like a cup. Black, please."

Everyone else declined.

"Where did Ezra go?" Mrs. Poussaint asked anyone who cared to answer.

Rawn shrugged while Tera looked over her shoulder and watched people through the spotless glass, walking around while taking care of their individual tasks. "I don't see him." She moved into her brother. "Have you talked to Janelle?"

"Not since she was last here."

"What does she know that you don't know?"

"Hell if I know," said Rawn.

Shortly after the assistant returned with Dr. Poussaint's coffee, Ezra and Janelle arrived holding Tully's coffee cups. Janelle, speaking familiarly to the Poussaint family, was in a nicely fitted pantsuit and a soft leather briefcase hung from her shoulder. With a cellular in one hand, Ezra pulled out a chair for Janelle with the other. Rawn was suspicious because it was unmistakable that Janelle avoided eye contact with him. He sat upright in the chair and looked from Ezra to Janelle, trying to get a read on what they were up to—what they knew that he did not know. This was his *life*.

"What's going on?" Dr. Poussaint asked.

"We're waiting."

"For?"

Janelle looked over to Ezra and finally her eyes met Rawn's. She winked, and the corners of her full mouth lifted ever so subtly.

"We...I got a call two days ago. I was told in this private conversation that..."

"Sorry we're late," Peter Abrams butted in, entering the conference room balancing his briefcase, coffee tumbler, a stack of paperwork and cellular. Another man, younger, followed behind him. "This had better be good, Ezra." He looked over his eyeglasses resting at the edge of his nose. "Opening arguments are in two days."

Ezra stood and said, "Gentlemen, thank you for coming to the city on such short notice. Take a seat."

The Poussaints were visibly confused. Why was the District Attorney's Office involved in this meeting? Surely Hirsch would not have arranged a plea without consulting Rawn. Before Dr. Poussaint could open his mouth, his wife touched his hand. He reached for his coffee and took several sips, but it was a challenge to hold back what was on his mind.

"As I was about to tell my client, I received a call several days ago with some new information."

"And you chose to share this with us *now?*" said the boyish-looking assistant D.A.

"I agree I should have come to the D.A. with this information the moment it was brought to my attention, but there were some legal issues that needed to be considered."

"Good morning!" Khalil said with enthusiasm, entering the conference room.

Mrs. Poussaint turned to her son and said, "Why is Khalil here?"

Rawn was clueless.

Ezra was on his feet. "Khalil, please join us. Grab a seat."

When Khalil sat in the chair, he glanced over to his best friend. And because he knew him so well, he recognized the indignation that outlined his wearisome face. To settle any anxiety he might have been having, Khalil whispered, "David Copperfield."

"What does David Copperfield mean?" Tera asked her brother.

Rawn recoiled when he caught sight of Henderson Payne standing in the doorway very well dressed and looking cooler than a cucumber.

"Henderson Payne?" Tera said beneath her breath.

It had been a while since she felt sanguine and greeted the first breath of morning without a stone resting against her already weakened heart. Once again, she saw life—her life—with a mélange of possibilities. For weeks Sicily felt like she had been pushed to the edge of life. Spring break saved her. She went home for a week and rested. Her parents sensed that she needed enough space to breathe and thus allowed her to spend hours in her old room in the attic hibernating, even when they had not seen her in a year. Since she relocated to Seattle, their face-to-face talks were infrequent. Sicily came home to mourn; to let go and to not look back. Her last day in Philadelphia, she took the train to Manhattan and went shopping with an old friend. The traces of a new spring brought color to the otherwise prosaic steel-colored landscape during the early months in New York City. The air was breezy, but the spring wind was calm. It not once crossed her mind how much she missed Manhattan until she began to walk along a crowded sidewalk. The aggressive cabbies blowing their horns, and she blending effortlessly within the frenetic energy of the city, was a reminder that her soul would forever be linked to the Big Apple.

While they waited for their lunch, she shocked herself when she revealed to her longtime friend, "I'm going to have a baby." Sicily made the decision to tell no one until she was ready. Rawn would have been the first person she shared this type of information with.

Her friend was about to take a drink of her Pellegrino. With curious eyes, she asked, "Are you pregnant?"

"No! No, not yet. But I'm going to…"

"A sperm bank? Dear, God! Sicily, are you sure?"

Their lunch arrived and once the waitress left, Sicily concluded, "I've thought it through. I spent days up in my old room, and the weeks leading up to this moment, all I could do is see through a glass darkly. I was so ashamed."

"Ashamed of what?"

"Rushing blindly into something out of desperation. The need for a physical connection."

"Have we all not done that at least once? Come on, Sicily, emotions have no conscience."

"Well, in answer to your original question. Yes, I'm sure. This is the right time for me to do this. I'm ready."

By the time she had to head back to Seattle, Sicily was cleansed. There were moments still when she would stare out into the open air. Painstakingly, she tried to assess every moment she spent with Tamara to determine what part of this woman was so captivating, so alluring; and Sicily wondered what part of her was so weak or needy?

The day she had what she later described to her mother as a mini-breakdown, that same evening Sicily called a hotline. Years before, she had volunteered there the first months of her new beginning in the Pacific Northwest. She witnessed how having someone to talk to that did not know your personal story made the *listener* more attentive. Housed in a small office on Capitol Hill, the hotline was set up for the gay community; particularly for the clinically depressed with suicidal thoughts. Without holding back, Sicily described herself as untrustworthy to the counselor who answered her call.

"Why do you say this about yourself?" the counselor had asked.

"I don't know what to expect from myself."

They had talked for twenty minutes before Sicily, in an abridged monologue, described her mini-breakdown and why she had concluded it happened on that day. Once she finished, the counselor had asked, "Why are you placing all the blame on yourself?"

"Because between the two of us, I was the strongest, at least emotionally. I know the warning signs of a manic."

"Has this friend been diagnosed as bipolar?"

"She never told me, but her pathology…I know the signs—euphoric one minute, down the next. Erratic behavior despite whether the patient is up or down. Perhaps she's not manic in the clinical sense, I don't know, but…"

"Friend," the counselor interjected. "Let me say this: you need to assess the situation rationally. And furthermore, you cannot allow yourself to be hoodwinked by society's pressure to be all things. It's a sham. It's impossible. That standard is simply too high and costs so much. You fell in love and it felt wonderful. The last thing the heart knows how to do is to turn itself off because someone bamboozled you with their looks, personality, human and social capital. On the surface she had it all. The heart doesn't recognize those qualities belonging to someone out of balance. My friend, you are *human*."

I'm human. Those were some of the last words Sicily ever heard Rawn speak.

"Unfortunately, even with your upper middle-class upbringing and degrees, you will always be vulnerable. Even the most unlikely person who cannot be swayed by very much is vulnerable to something. I know that if you were on my end of the line, you'd ask the person at the other end to start slowly by finding each day a way to forgive—you, her, and your male friend whom you believe betrayed you."

Within a week of returning from the East Coast, Sicily was feeling stronger. She was starting to like herself again.

"Good morning!" Sicily was in a benevolent mood.

"Oh, good morning! You take it to-go, right?"

With her head tilted to one side, Sicily said, "You have a good memory."

"Double shot latte?"

She laughed. "Am I that predictable?"

Cordially, she laughed, too. "It'll be right up."

Within minutes, Imani placed the to-go cup on the counter.

"You know, I thought you quit or something. It's been a minute."

"Yes, and it's good to be back. I was on the East Coast."

Sicily placed a five-dollar bill on the counter. "Welcome back. Oh…although we've seen each other a dozen of times, we've never actually met. I'm Sicily."

"Imani."

"Pleasure." She took a small sip of her espresso and turned on her heels. "See you soon! I mean, *bientôt!*"

Imani called out, "Hey, don't forget your umbrella!"

"I take it," Jean-Pierre said, reaching for the black classic umbrella on the counter.

Sicily and Jean-Pierre met halfway. *"Merci!"*

"Bonjour, ça va!"

When Sicily left the café, she walked calmly toward the Academy, and quite pleased with the double shot latte Jean-Pierre prepared. After a block, she paused. She turned around and it looked like she forgot something, but then resumed her walk to the Academy. Slowly, her mouth raised into a crafty smile. *French sperm?*

CHAPTER THIRTY-FOUR

Tera stopped reading the magazine that lay in her lap. She whispered, "You haven't said a word since we took off. You okay?"

With his head resting against the airplane seat, Rawn turned away from the window that offered a breathtaking view of the burnt-orange-colored sun that tainted the bank of clouds stretching for miles like an endless quilt above the earth.

"Yeah, I'm good."

"You sure? I mean, I'm not Mama. Or Daddy. You can be real with me."

Good-naturedly, he elbowed his sister's forearm off the armrest and said, "I wouldn't lie to you. But I do appreciate you coming with me. I didn't feel comfortable facing D'Becca's mother alone."

"And that's why I volunteered. You could have asked. Why do you feel you have to go this alone is a mystery to me. Anyway, I was coming with or without your invite." Only vaguely interested in advertisements that graced the pages of *Talk* magazine, Tera continued to flip through the publication. "We'll check into the hotel and have dinner. We can meet with Mrs. Ross first thing tomorrow. Does that work?"

He nodded, thoughtful. Rawn turned back to gaze out the window. He stared at the evaporating daylight. He tried to remember his life a year ago: how he felt, what he thought; the things that mattered then in comparison to what he felt and thought, and what mattered now. By the time he trusted that he had a handle on who he was, Rawn was no longer the self that he knew. He kept changing and noticed the nuances of those vivid alterations; not his physicality, but his psyche. It was a strange thing.

He was not sure when, but at some point he looked forward to his trial. Perhaps it was because he wanted the truth to be out there, especially since there was so much about him available to read about on the Web, like the *Starr Report*, which comprised of critical, painstaking details on President Clinton. In the end he hoped the trial would clear his name. The morning Khalil and Henderson arrived at Ezra Hirsch's office, everything changed and yet everything felt like it stayed precisely the same.

When Henderson had arrived in the large conference room, his presence stunned everyone except Khalil, Hirsch and Janelle. His swagger suggested he was not just used to, but likewise welcomed, the attention his presence stirred. He was a man of style, and he stood in the room in an expertly tailored black suit and pale-taupe shirt. Rawn, open-mouthed, was plain mystified. A man that came to Henderson's upper chest entered the conference room and stood directly beside him. Hirsch rushed to his feet and greeted both men with businesslike handshakes and formal but friendly welcomes.

Henderson had walked casually, confidently to a chair when his eyes met Rawn's. His nod had been subtle and courteous. Henderson's attorney sat next to him. Khalil wanted a neutral spot, and the best view was at the head of the table opposite Hirsch at the other end.

The district attorney, Abrams, had sat erect, deeply curious. "What exactly is going on here, Ezra?"

Hirsch had made introductions. When he had sensed that everyone was at ease, he turned to a stenographer and nodded.

"We all know why we're here. Rawn Poussaint is going on trial first thing Monday morning here in Seattle. He's been accused of manslaughter for the death of D'Becca Ross. Should the district attorney prevail in this case, he could spend up to twenty-five behind bars."

The prosecutor had projected a level of confidence, swinging side-to-side in the chair, his left elbow against the edge of the severely polished maple wood table.

"Several days ago, Khalil Underwood met with Henderson Payne at his home in Los Angeles. At that time, he revealed information that is pertinent to this case."

The younger prosecutor for the state had sat upright in the chair and interrupted his adversary. "Should we be before Judge Whitehouse?"

Abrams had replied in a stern voice, "No, I want to hear this. We're covered; it's on the record."

Hirsch had been taken aback by his being remarkably reasonable. He began to consider whether Abrams was not particularly sure he could win the case. He resumed. "The reason for not bringing this information to the attention of the district attorney, and to my client, sooner is because Henderson Payne needed to consult with his attorneys. A lot's at stake. But after a host of conference calls, he was counseled to come forward with the information that he has. There's a provision, however. He will not be charged under any circumstances. That is the deal."

With a dark brow, Abrams had asked, "Mr. Payne, what exactly can you add to this case? We've been preparing for trial for months. With all due respect, this case is more high-profile than…your case a few years back. I respect that you have a demanding schedule… Where the hell have you *been?*"

Before Henderson had been able to open his mouth, his attorney had said, "I prefer that you direct any questions to me, Counselor.

Mr. Payne is not here to be interrogated, but to offer some important facts about the case. Ezra, perhaps there needs to be some parameters before we proceed."

Hirsch had said, "I don't think that's necessary. All we need from Henderson is what he *knows*, if anything, about this case. And that he will not be charged on any counts."

Abrams had required time to think it over. His assistant had whispered something in his ear. Abrams looked over to Henderson, nodding. With a pointed finger, he had said, "There's a condition."

"What's that?" Hirsch asked.

"If Mr. Payne is directly involved in Ms. Ross's death in any way—and let me make myself clear…"

"My client was in Miami the night of Ms. Ross's death. The game was broadcast live. He scored thirty-three points, with five assists and five rebounds."

"Are you suggesting these facts, as you refer to them, can exculpate Rawn Poussaint?"

"You need to hear what Mr. Payne knows."

Abrams's tone had suggested he did not care what Henderson knew or where he was the night of D'Becca's death. "Again, and I caution you, Counselor; if Mr. Payne is directly involved—legally speaking, and you know what that means—we can bring charges. Including hindering prosecution."

"In order for my client to tell you what he knows, he will not be charged on anything related to this case. That's the deal. And I'll make myself clear: my client was not in any way involved with Ms. Ross's death. Before we proceed, I need assurances that he will not be charged on any counts, including hindering prosecution."

"If he has anything at all to do with…"

"Mr. Payne is—had absolutely nothing to do with Ms. Ross's death. He never met the woman," said his attorney.

Khalil's upper body had stiffened. *What does* involved *mean exactly?* had been at the tip of his tongue. And hindering prosecution? Why didn't Henderson's attorney ask him to do this thing off the record? "Legally speaking" was so broad.

Without his knowing it, Rawn was then no longer confused. He knew by Khalil saying "David Copperfield," something had gone down—a twist of fate—which conspired in his favor. Even while he had no clue as to what was unfolding, he was no longer in the dark.

"Shall we proceed?" Hirsch had asked, his eyes darting from the attorneys for the state, and Henderson's very high-priced attorney.

The Poussaints were more confused than ever, and the fact that Henderson, who was in the middle of playoffs, was there made no sense whatsoever. Meanwhile, Rawn had a flash. An image had rushed through his mind, but he could not make out what it was. He had blinked, and the flash—large and white, moving fast—whisked past his eyes. Slowly, he had turned to look at Henderson, whose hands were clasped beneath his chin. He had stared directly at Rawn, and Rawn was confident the popular athlete could read his thoughts.

Abrams, who had studied his watch, said, "Okay, if Mr. Payne has information that can lead to a conviction, he has a deal." He leaned into the table. "Let's hear it."

Henderson's attorney had said with a thoughtful nod, "You can proceed."

In a calm, assured voice, Henderson began.

It was his day off. Generally, Henderson tried to remember to turn off his cellular so he would not get needless disruptions and could spend quality time with Daphne and the children. It worked only half the time, if that. At roughly eight-fifteen, the cellular rang. The children were safe in their beds and asleep. Daphne, at the opposite end of the sofa, was having one of her marathon conversations with her sister in Providence. Henderson looked away from ESPN and decided to answer his mobile.

"Henderson!"

He raised his torso and his dark eyes bounced to his wife laughing with her sister on the telephone. She looked over to him and he frowned and rolled his eyes, which suggested it was someone they both knew, and Henderson would prefer to have avoided.

Daphne's lips shaped into *Richard?*

Henderson nodded and came to his bare feet. He walked to the other end of the quietly lit room. "What's up?" he said into the mobile. "Huh?" He sneaked a peek at Daphne, preoccupied with her conversation with her sister. "Uh-huh," Henderson mumbled. "Yeah. Yeah. Why?" He turned his back to Daphne while listening to the urgent voice of his caller. Over his shoulder, he could see Daphne was not paying him any attention. Normally when his cellular rang, she was suspicious. She reached for a pillow and hugged it, laughing more than she was talking. She and her sister had spirited conversations, often lasting hours at a time. Her laughter grew louder and more animated, and Henderson knew she was not the least bit interested in him. He pushed a fist into the back pocket of his Levi's, oblivious to the fact that he was tense. "Okay." He moved toward the window, but was too apprehensive to even peep out. "*Okay!*" He did not intend to raise his voice, and could not bring himself to look Daphne's way to see if she was alerted by his tone. He released the call. Daphne looked over to her husband, and the look on her face suggested, *What?*

"I'm going to hook up with him for a minute. He's tripping. I should be back in an hour." He slipped on his sneakers at the foot of the sofa.

Covering the cordless, Daphne asked, "Is it about Sheila?"

Henderson did the best he could about not lying to his wife. He shrugged, since that would be noncommittal. He reached for his keys and wallet in a bowl.

Henderson interpreted her expression to mean *poor, baby*. With a wink, he left the room, hearing her receding, "It's really windy, baby!"

He called out: "I'll leave my cell on in case you need anything."

The Santa Anas made the Los Angeles air feel sultry. The sky was sinister, deep indigo blue, and the cool wind that pressed against the air was strong enough to shed palmate leaves from the palm trees, littering the empty streets. Henderson entered the Windsor Village community, and pulled into a space on Lucerne. He spotted the cream-colored Lexus parked a few cars away. On the seven-minute drive to the park, he tried to decide how he was going to handle the situation. Instead, when he turned off the engine and jumped out of his Porsche, slowly, he began to release some pent-up frustration that most likely had nothing to do with the moment. When he approached the haphazardly parked vehicle, he tapped his wedding band against the window three times before it rolled down.

Tamara stepped out of the vehicle with the slyness of a cat—her long and slender legs lifted her out of the taupe interior.

Angry, Henderson started with, "What the hell is wrong with you? You are one crazy!"—he managed to stop himself. "Don't you *ever*—I need you to *hear* me, Tamara—don't *ever* sit outside my house again. I am *married*. You are an educated, intelligent woman, so what about keeping it *light* do you fail to comprehend?" Henderson did not let Tamara respond. He continued: "Don't ever threaten me again. Don't try to work me. Who the hell do you think you're dealing with? Huh? And one more thing!" Henderson tried to calm himself. It had been some time since he felt this worked up. Tamara pushed every wrong button he had, yet he had a spot reserved for her in his heart which he did not understand, for the life of him. She knew it and played it to the hilt, and that messed with Henderson. Despite the fact that their relationship was platonic, he understood how unhealthy she was for him when he played in Portland and she drove down so they could hang out together.

Tamara needed to cut him off. He was unnaturally incensed with her, and his anger was visibly visceral. "Henderson…"

But Henderson hardly cared why she was there. He was too irritated with her to even listen. "Were you stalking, Tamara?"

Abnormally defensive, Tamara said, "No! I don't *stalk!*"

"Why did you call me outside my home?"

"I…I guess…I don't…"

"What the hell! What are you doing *here?*"

"I need your help."

"With?"

"Something happened."

"Like?"

"An accident."

Henderson contemplated with the idea of getting back inside his Porsche and leaving her there. But even on his worst day, he was not so vicious as to leave a true friend tossing about in the wind. He looked around the dark night, the park quiet and lifeless. The massive trees that dotted the area swayed like hula dancers against the wind speed. Tamara was a naturally provocative woman, which was any man's fatal flaw should he acquiesce to her—what Henderson once referred to it as—weapon of mass destruction. She used it like Daphne used her American Express card—pulling it out at will, confident it would secure her every need or want.

Tamara's sexy cleavage was quite revealing from a low-cut angora sweater. Henderson would like to think the choice to wear it was deliberate, but Tamara did not think that way. He darted his eyes away from her momentarily, checking out the immediate area for anyone walking their dog, or taking a late-evening run. When his eyes roamed back to Tamara, she looked sad, lost.

"What are you talking about? What accident?"

"Henderson," she said in a breathless whisper, "I messed up."

Henderson met Tamara at the House of Blues during a period when he and Daphne were not in synch, disconnected, sleeping in different rooms, and they were like ships out at sea passing through a remote night. Had it been another woman, Henderson might have been a stronger man—he knew, however, that was no excuse. Still, Tamara came on strong and he was weak. Over the years, he must have been subjected to every hot and cold emotion she could feel. There was a time when he even felt sorry for her.

There was never an occasion when Henderson saw Tamara vulnerable. Her father and mother were highly regarded politicians but no more than functional as parents. Writing out checks was their expression of love; therefore Tamara was used to being on her own. When she left home to go to college in New York, and only shy of eighteen, she was astonishingly shy and self-conscious. Perhaps that was the only time in her life when she was innocent, gullible, and naïve. Something happened to her back then; Henderson had tried a few times to find out what. But to no avail. He never could get it out of her. Yet while standing in front of her— this seductive woman who managed to take a halfway decent talent and risky concept and went on to become a successful fashion expert by any standard—he did not need to look too hard to observe that she was indeed powerless. It was not because she came to him; she had come to him a few times when she panicked. Instead, it was because she stood in front of him trembling. Henderson knew she would never allow herself to ever *need* someone. Occasionally, she craved companionship; there were times when she wanted intimacy. But to actually *need* someone—that was not Tamara. Her voice, the look on her face, told him to cut her some slack.

"What happened, Tamara?"

"I don't want you involved."

"So why am I *here?*"

"It's not good, Henderson."

"So what is it you need from *me?*"

"I need to get away."

He looked at her closely. "How much do you need?"

"It's not money."

"Then what?" He shrugged.

"I want to use your villa."

"My *villa?* In Portofino?"

"Yes." Tamara took one step, and her voice sounded desperate. *"Please."*

"Get in the car." Henderson started walking around the SUV to the passenger's side, but Tamara stood there, rooted to the spot. The street light spilled over her which revealed this childlike innocence he would never see again.

Once they were both in the vehicle, Henderson said, "What's what?"

"Tamara!" She was the last person on planet earth D'Becca expected to see at her front door.

"Hey, girl!" she said. Standing beneath the delicate lighting which glowed above the front door, Tamara looked not only chic, but alluring in her black velour pant and a cropped leather jacket with a faux fur collar and suede gloves. "Are you inviting me in?"

D'Becca stopped reeling from her astonishing presence and moved aside to let Tamara enter the foyer. Tamara did a swift assessment of the exotic flowers in immense vases and artsy paintings on the soothing violet walls. *Hmmm, she has good taste.*

Tamara turned to D'Becca who was shutting the door. "Are you alone?"

With clumsy fingers, D'Becca combed her hair away from her face. "Uhhh, yes. Why?"

Nonchalantly, Tamara shrugged, and wore a cocky smile on her face.

"Well, come on up. I'm running a bath. I don't want it to flood the place." She attempted to make a joke.

Tamara tailed behind D'Becca trotting up the spiral staircase. When they reached the top, Tamara said, "You have quite a setup here. It's like romantic meets feng shui."

"Yeah, I love it."

"Did you decorate it yourself or did you hire someone?"

"I did."

"You have a good eye." Tamara scanned the full hallway with attractive photographs bordered in maple-colored frames. When she looked around, D'Becca was not there, but she could hear her in the bathroom, a few feet away. When Tamara entered the full room, D'Becca had turned off the running water and was drying her hands with a hand towel.

"Candles?" Tamara lifted a brow, teasing D'Becca. "You sure you're alone?"

With her hands on her hips, D'Becca replied, "Yes." She crossed her arms and looked into Tamara's conniving-laced eyes. "How did you know where I lived?" The pitch in her voice suggested she was more than curious.

"You're on my mailing list," she said, fast on her feet.

Although skeptical, D'Becca went along with it. "Oh!"

Tamara looked fleetingly around the bathroom—flowers, photographs, books, fluffy bright-colored towels in an oversized rich brown wicker basket—and she said, "This place must have cost you some change. I guess it's why you still need to model, huh?"

"Let's say I made a wise investment."

"I'm sure," Tamara said in a sardonic tone.

"So, Tamara, what brings you here?"

"I was in the hood," she joked. "Dropped by to see Rawn on the other side of Crescent Boulevard." She waited to determine what, if anything, her comment would provoke from D'Becca.

"Rawn? You mean...R-A-W-N? That Rawn?"

"Oh." Tamara chuckled. "I didn't realize he spelled his name that way."

"And yet you two are friends," D'Becca stated sarcastically.

"Did I see Sebastian Michaels leaving your place as I pulled up?"

Distracted, D'Becca forgot that Sebastian had left only minutes ago. "What do you want?" she asked, needing Tamara to get to the point.

"I told you..."

"Yeah, that you were in the hood." She walked around Tamara, but she blocked D'Becca from leaving the bathroom. Tamara was slightly taller and at least ten pounds heavier than D'Becca. "Excuse me, but what exactly is your problem?"

Tamara moved so close to D'Becca that she could hear Tamara breathing through her nostrils. "You're pregnant, aren't you?"

D'Becca dared not reveal any explicit emotion. "You need to leave!"

"I could be pregnant, too. And it could be Rawn's."

D'Becca chuckled, but Tamara's look was somber. Contemptuously, she remarked, "In your dreams!"

"Whose is it? Rawn's or Michaels's? Did you know that the woman you met at my boutique today is Ingrid Michaels, Sebastian Michaels's wife? That's why she looked familiar to you."

D'Becca flinched.

"She hates you with a passion. The very idea that some uneducated bitch that got by because of her looks…That he would fall for someone like that. *Love* someone like that? Humiliate her like that! That he would buy a place—what did she call it? 'A back-street paramour cottage,' so he could sneak off and be with her. Yes. You had better pack your bags, luv. When Ingrid discovers that you're pregnant and that Sebastian has the potential to be the father… When a woman wants revenge, she can be so cold. You know what they say? You'll never do lunch in this town again. Ingrid, you must realize, knows *people*. And if she learns about the"—she whispered sarcastically—"baby, wow! She can be one evil bitch, trust me!"

Her scorn and her ridiculous smirk made D'Becca very angry. "Get out!" she screamed.

"I'm going to tell Rawn. We've become quite close, the two of us. And I think he'd like to know about Sebastian Michaels. And I'm going to tell him you're pregnant with Sebastian Michaels's baby!"

Not aware of what she was capable of, D'Becca slapped Tamara hard enough for her to stumble. Tamara managed to sustain her equilibrium by gripping the doorknob. When she turned to look at D'Becca, she looked so proud of herself, standing there with her hands on her hips.

Tamara grabbed a vase on a glass stand overstuffed with lilies and slammed it against D'Becca's face with all her will. Blood flung across the bathroom and landed on a wall in a splattered line like an artist took a paint brush and splashed a canvas with deep red paint.

She heard it so clearly: D'Becca's skull hitting the edge of the claw-footed bathtub; Tamara watched it happen in slow motion. D'Becca's sleek body dropped to the floor with a discernible thud. Blood spread quickly, and a solid line trailed methodically toward Tamara. She stepped away so it would not ruin her suede bootie. She was not sure how long she stood there holding the cracked vase in her amazingly balanced hand. The flowers were still intact, except for one crushed lily resting limply against the thick hairline-fractured glass. With her mouth agape, Tamara stared at her reflection in the mirror. How long had she been standing there? Her eyes darted to D'Becca trying to get up, her body losing strength every moment that slipped by. Tamara snapped; all of a sudden she was back in the present and she was calm. She stepped over the trail of blood, and bent over and reached out but did not touch her. "D'Becca? D'Becca? Are you okay?" She made a strange gurgling sound. She tried to reach out to Tamara, but Tamara stepped back, witnessing in her mind's eye her entire life flash before her.

Tamara looked around, studying every detail—small or overt—of the bathroom. She stepped over D'Becca's leg and headed for the door. With the vase still in her hand, she took one last look at D'Becca trying desperately to crawl toward her, but her life was giving up.

Chai tagged behind Tamara through the long hallway that led to the airy, dark kitchen, and along the way leaving bloody paw prints on the spotless floor. Much too calm, she looked around for the back door, which led to D'Becca's garage. Chai sat on her hind legs for a brief moment, making a depressing meow sound, but then turned and dashed away. Tamara closed the door and moved swiftly around the Z3 and to a side door which led out into a small patio. Luckily, she would not need to raise the garage door to alert a neighbor. To her chagrin the side door required a security code. Despite the darkness, Tamara managed to find a button and the garage door lifted. When the door opened, she pressed the same button so that it would close behind her.

She tossed the lilies in the trunk of her car, and while pouring out the water from the vase along the curb, she caught sight of headlights coming her way. She jumped in her car and ducked. The car pulled to the curb, feet away from Tamara. There was the sound of a car door being shut and immediately after the noise a remote control key made when a car door was being locked. Footsteps began to recede. Tamara slowly pressed herself up with her hands. She saw a man—it looked like Sebastian Michaels because of the distinguished coat she had seen him in earlier—enter D'Becca's with a key. *Why did he come back?*

Her first instinct was to call Ingrid Michaels. At the stop sign, she pressed Ingrid's name and immediately there was a ring. "Answer, you bitch!" But Ingrid's voicemail answered instead, and Tamara was too impatient to leave a message. Sicily? No, she liked Sicily enough not to involve her.

It took an hour to get home because only one lane was opened on the westbound floating bridge due to a minor accident involving several cars. When Tamara made it back to Seattle, at a stoplight she prayed that D'Becca was dead.

CHAPTER THIRTY-FIVE

When he returned from North Dakota, Rawn had exactly eighteen messages on his machine. To go through them would take time, and he was not in the mood to hear anything related to the death of D'Becca. He grabbed his mail and began going through it methodically. Hirsch's assistant had sent him a box, and inside was mail from all over the country. He chose to deal with it later. He relaxed in the sofa. Rawn took a long gulp of his beer. Perusing each piece of personal mail, he started placing them in piles of three. They included bills, junk, and letters from students at the Academy. Getting letters from students was something Rawn had not anticipated. Unconsciously, his frame lifted when he caught sight of a letter formally addressed to him, which was from the Academy. There had been half a dozen meetings, both with Hirsch and without him, in regards to Rawn being able to return to Gumble-Wesley to teach. Some part of him feared opening the letter, primarily because no matter what it entailed, it would unquestionably have Sicily's signature.

His heart racing, he slit it open and unfolded it in haste. Rawn's eyes fell to the bottom of the letter to identify Sicily's signature, but the trustee's president's name was typed out, which struck him immediately. The letter went on to say how pleased the board was that the charges against him were dropped. They were excited for his future. His students were steadfast on his behalf, singing his praises. He was, without question, an asset to the Academy. The final paragraph was polite, well thought out and yet quite formal.

They regretted to inform Rawn that it was best that he seek a teaching position at another school. He would, however, be generously
compensated.

Rawn was not the type of person who looked, or ever prepared
himself, for surprises. This revelation blindsided him. Not solely
because he lost his position; in some tiny way he understood that
his presence would place unsolicited interest toward the Academy.
While he could fight to get his position back, Rawn knew that
would only cause more problems for Sicily, and he already felt
awkward that this whole thing put her in such a compromised
position. Besides, Hirsch counseled him that there was the strong
possibility this would be the outcome. And because Sicily failed
to speak with him, he saw nothing good coming out of returning
to the Academy. Rawn trusted, even when he understood that Sicily
felt brutally betrayed, that the friendship they had built over the
years would withstand any test. He was confident that in time they
would rise above Tamara's—and more importantly his own—
duplicity. When he hugged Tera goodbye at Sea-Tac, she whispered in his ear, "Give Sicily *time*."

Rawn folded the letter and leaned back into the sofa. He gripped
the bottle of beer in one hand and took the remote control with
the other. He flipped through channels until he came upon CNN.
A female reporter was talking, but Rawn could not hear her. He
turned up the volume. "Portofino is the pearl of the Italian Riviera,"
the reporter was saying. "It's a uniquely exquisite fishing village
with unspoiled charm and romantic seascapes, and one of the most
picturesque inlets along the coast. Surrounded by hilltop villas and
a castle hanging on its summit, the breathtaking Mediterranean
ambience was the place where award-winning fashion designer
Tamara had been in hiding…" And in the corner of the screen
they were showing footage of Tamara being escorted to a police
car, handcuffed. "…Staying here at a villa owned by Henderson

Payne since the murder of D'Becca Ross and her unborn child—"
Rawn switched the television off.

Later in the day, he began listening to his messages. The very last message was from Sicily. "Hi, Rawn. First I want you to know that I championed for you to return to the Academy. But I didn't prevail. I can't even begin to tell you how sorry I am that I brought Tamara into our lives. I'm still working through what happened last year. One day we should talk. You know, when someone deceives you, whether it's conscious or unconscious, forgiveness seems so difficult. It feels like your forgiveness in some way absolves the person of what they did to you. I won't lie: I wanted you out of my life forever. I even had the nerve to think it was easier than forgiving you. If this had happened to you, I'd tell you that holding on to bitterness and withholding forgiveness would only make you the victim. When it's not happening to us, we see it so impartially. Intellectually, we understand human flaws. But when there's emotional investment, it's like we lose sight of everything." There was a brief silence, and Rawn was about to delete the message until he heard Sicily resume. "There's a colleague of mine I think you should reach out to. I know you won't see this as a great opportunity... at least not yet. But I really think this is something you should consider. And I urge you to make the call, Rawn." After she gave him the name and number, the sound of her tender voice when she said *"bientôt"* made him strain to even hear it. He replayed the message twice and then saved it for reasons that were not clear to him at the time. And it was not until he needed a teaching job did Rawn revisit the message.

Several months later, in the midst of Rawn attempting to recreate his routine, he found that he could not go back to the things he did before. He was not that person anymore and thus had developed different interests, different desires. Not aware of what those interests and desires were yet, he had always been naturally curious. He knew, even if he was not in touch with whatever it was yet, he would welcome the challenge and be open to whatever was coming his way.

He was at the door, keys in hand, when his telephone rang. Although he did not receive as many calls regarding interviews and book deals and hate calls, Rawn still hesitated before answering his phone.

"Hello!"

A familiar, long-awaited voice said, "Hello, Rawn."

T he intense fog, combined with steady drizzle, made it nearly impossible for Rawn to go any faster. He could hardly see a foot in front of him; and although he could chance it, was it really worth it? Especially after everything he had been through over the past year. Moving beyond all the emotional wear and tear on his spirit had not been swift. Perhaps another man would have moved through it with finesse, or pride.

Not going quite 50 miles per hour, he was confident he would make his flight to Los Angeles. It was Khalil's thirty-fifth, and his girlfriend Moon was going all out and throwing him an extravagant party, which was his best friend's style. Of course Rawn would not miss it for anything; absolutely no way would he miss this celebration!

The exit came into view; he would make it, no doubt!

Once he parked in short-term and made it to the airport entrance, Rawn was taken aback at the crowd. Sea-Tac was swarming with airline passengers, and he had never seen such masses of people in the airport, even during the height of tourist season. With his e-ticket, he bypassed the chaos of frustrated travelers seeking assistance, amid tired and testy children. He was lucky not to be in the middle of all that stress. He headed straight for his gate.

No sooner than Rawn arrived, he was greeted with an announcement that all flights were delayed due to heavy fog and there were no inbound or outbound flights until further notification. The level of anxiety within the gate went way up upon the broadcast

of that message, and people were dangerously close to being out-
raged by the inconvenience. Rawn contemplated whether he
should go back to Crescent Island or hang out for a while. Since
the party was not until the following evening, he could take an
early-morning flight into LAX.

Another announcement was made, informing the passengers to
stand by for updated instructions. Rawn decided to hold off leaving.
He took a seat nearest to the window, and it was so dark he could
not see anything—not the evening sky, certainly not a twinkling
star, the crescent moon, and not one tiny drop of rain. His eyes
met with a woman coming directly toward him; her strides were
optimistic and determined. "Hi, excuse me," she said. On the spot,
her face rang a bell; Rawn, however, would not have been able to
place her even if he put in the effort to try.

"Yes?" he said.

"You are Rawn Poussaint, right?"

He pondered over whether he should lie, but then it was
apparent she knew who he was. "Yes," he did not hesitate.

"My name's Siobhan Frasier." She extended her arm.

Courteous, Rawn shook hands with Siobhan Frasier.

"I'm not going to play this thing down, okay? I saw you over
here and I swear I couldn't believe my luck. First of all, I saw you
this morning, at Café Neuf on the island? You probably don't
remember. Anyway, I wanted to say something this morning, but
I really, really didn't want to intrude. But here you are. It has to
be fate. It *has* to be. I've contacted you at least a dozen times and
your attorney at least half that. His assistant tells me you aren't
doing interviews and I get that, I swear, I do. But..."

"I really don't do interviews."

"Don't I know," and her mouth shaped into a delicate frown.
With her palms pressed against her cheeks, she continued. "But I

also know this has to be fate. I've tried to give you some time and I've tried to be compassionate and I tried to respect your wishes and…I really would like to do this interview. I'm a freelance journalist and it's really competitive, you know? Things are changing. With the World Wide Web…journalism is on an entirely different level. Even the canons of journalism—at least in my book—need to be revised. Where's the truth and accuracy and objectivity? The fairness, the integrity? The world, it's changing, and so fast."

"Maybe you need to find another career."

"Don't go there. Besides, I digressed. Look, I can do this really nice. I will do what you ask and not betray you…you can trust me. I really…"

"I really do not do interviews."

"Okay, let me try it another way. I swear!" Siobhan held up her palm as if to be sworn in at a trial and to profess she would tell the truth and nothing but…"I will be fair and most assuredly accurate. Please, please, Rawn, hear me out." The journalist could sense that he was losing his patience. "Hear me out, okay?" Siobhan assumed because Rawn did not protest he was giving her some wiggle room. "I was on Vashon Island for a wedding last weekend. I decided to go up to Vancouver to see an old friend. I drove back yesterday to make a red-eye but such is my luck the rental got a flat. I had to wait for nearly two hours for tow service and so I missed my flight. The next flight out was tonight, ten-thirty. Now I have to wait until who knows when to get back to New York. If I hadn't had a flat tire, I would have made my flight and I'd be back in my cozy Williamsburg walk-up and eating something unhealthy to feel better about myself. Since my flight wasn't leaving until tonight, and I had all day to search the Web and… Early this morning, when I got up and read through my e-mails, I got this clever idea to take a chance and get on the ferry and go to Crescent Island to meet you. It's common knowledge that you stop in Café Neuf from time to time, so I went there. When I saw you—first, I didn't realize how tall you are, and…well, I-I felt like I should leave you alone and I did. Right? I did!

"So you see this whole thing that's happening right now… it's…the good spirit of the universe is at work. I don't believe in randomness. I don't think the world operates by chance. I could have been rude and pushy this morning at Café Neuf, but my colleagues have tried that, but you still haven't relented and that's highly unusual. Even Richard Jewel did an interview or two. Anyway, if I'd have approached you this morning, you would have been even more nonresponsive than you are right now. Before I even came over here and introduced myself, I attempted to talk myself down. I said, 'Siobhan, let it go.' But then…"

"You don't believe in randomness?" He was purposely sarcastic.

"And neither do you. I know that you don't!"

"But I don't do…"

"…Interviews, fine!" The journalist took her past-the-shoulders brunette hair and clipped it with a barrette. "Okay, how about this? I go through Ezra Hirsch? We set some parameters and you—or he—can tell me what we can or can't talk about. For example, whether you were the father of D'Becca's baby. How's that? I know this story will be syndicated. Every magazine…the list—Rawn, oh, gee whiz, it's endless. Finally, I will be respected and…I've worked my ass off and look! Do you know I can wait for hours outside doors and through hallways to get a quote? Where is it written that that is fair?"

"But the answer is still no!" Rawn did a fine job of suppressing his amusement.

"Your protest—I can tell—it's not as strong, and I feel—you and me—we've bonded. I don't think you want to talk, I really trust that. But you cared for D'Becca; everyone believes that, which is why you've stayed silent. And I know that you'd like to clear up some of the stories that are on the Web about your relationship and about her life. I know it! You have to give me some credit, Rawn. Come on!"

"Okay, look. Do you have a business card?"

"Yes!" Fast on her feet, the journalist reached in her designer backpack and produced a business card that listed a cellular number, a fax number, and an e-mail address.

Rawn looked over the information. "Okay," he said.

"Are we at maybe yet?"

"We're at let-me-think-it-over-and-I'll-get-back-to-you-even-if-I-don't-do-it. How's that?"

The corners of her slender lips elevated. "I can live with that."

"You have my word. I'll call."

"I know you will. This bond, it's not superficial. I can feel it."

He watched her walking away. She turned to wave, and Rawn stood.

He called Khalil but received his voicemail. Rawn left him a message that his flight was delayed. He failed to bring reading material and sensed it was going to be a long night. He decided to check out the bookstore on the other end of the gate. Instinctively, he looked for Siobhan, making sure she was out of sight; he did not want her following him. Apparently a lot of people had the same idea. Upon entering the bookstore, Rawn had to squeeze his way through. He made his way to hardbacks. He picked up a title, and before opening the book, he was urged by an invisible force to look to his right. *No f'in' way!*

What about her had he not noticed over the years? It seemed every angle had been carefully scrutinized. He even knew her gentle feminine scent, which the air always welcomed. But in watching her, he saw something was different. Not her hair or the clothes she wore—it was subtle, too indescribable.

Should he take the gamble? Was he even ready to take such a chance on something that was—as the callous complexity of D'Becca's fate taught him—so amazingly spontaneous? If he allowed himself to think it through—to analyze it—too much, he most certainly would turn on his heels, and because two moments were never identical, he might never—*never*—have this moment again. Typically, Rawn was not weak-willed, but he wanted to sense that internal quiet which would lead him to *know* for sure he would be fine. The decision to, or not to, was of significant magnitude in his mind. Before he could turn and get lost in the crowd of stranded travelers—they all were hoping to find something to blur time while being forced to wait—she turned to him and her soft mouth, concealed by a delicate rust-red hue that highlighted the kind shape of her lips, spread sweetly. At once, Rawn noticed her holding Pricilla Miles's much-talked-about new book.

Trying to pretend she was not off guard, she said, "Hello." She managed a measured monotone.

"You're going, right?"

"Yeah, you too?"

"Yep. L.A."

"Me, too. I thought I'd grab something to hold my attention since I might be here a while." Their brown eyes traveled to the controversial best seller. "I needed something juicy." No sooner than those words left her did she wish she could snatch each one of them back. "I mean, I wanted to read it because I understand her facts can't be disputed because her publisher's legal team went over it with a fine-tooth comb, or so I hear."

Rawn was not sure what to say to her. He couldn't care less about Miles's book, even when he knew details about him were in it. Not that he had read it, but Hirsch's paralegal team deciphered it cover-to-cover to verify the book's authenticity as far as Rawn was concerned, and if it was not completely factual, whether a libel suit could be filed on his behalf.

To make her feel at ease, Rawn said, "I've heard it's a page-turner."

"But you haven't read it?"

He confirmed with a slight shake of his head.

Her eyes rested on the cover. Pricilla's name larger and bolder than the single title, *Vulnerable*, made her unconsciously back away from the idea of reading it. "I probably shouldn't, really. I mean… it's all so salacious and…D'Becca's not here to defend any of this, even if every word is true. And I know what that's like. My father had plenty of horrible things said about him over the years. Some were not true, but even when things were true, they were often taken out of context."

Who is your father? was at the tip of his tongue, but her contemplative "Yeah…" made Rawn lose his train of thought. She replaced the book on the shelf. No sooner than her hand left it, another customer retrieved the book like a seat at a hot slot machine in Vegas. "Whatever Tamara did, it's unfair that someone would take things she said in confidence and then betray her and use it to take their career to another level. It's so wrong." She chuckled. "I'm so glad I ran into you. I was getting caught up like everyone else. Isn't that amazing how that happens? Like a car accident. My mother used to call people like that looky-loos. Suddenly one person stops, then another, then another. Why do people choose to be an eyewitness to the pain and suffering of others? It's so strange."

All Rawn could think about was her mouth; how visually soft and luscious it appeared to him. It was like when he was a child and they sliced open the first watermelon of the summer. Rawn could not wait to take his first bite.

"Can I buy you a drink?"

"I-I'm..."

"Let me. To make up for this morning at Café Neuf."

"What do you mean?" Imani said, tilting her head to one side.

"You know what I mean. I noticed a bar around the corner. It's probably crowded so we might not get to sit. Come on."

"Okay, sure." She was stunned at how eager she was, for she did not waver, not for one split-second.

The bar was packed and there were groups of loud and excited people trying to forget about how their precious time was being compromised. She watched Rawn graciously waiting at the crammed bar, and a few lingering glances came his way. It had been nearly six months since the charges against him had been dropped. Still, Rawn garnered such curiosity. Imani knew it was based upon multifaceted reasons, including his elusive nature and his good looks; but perhaps more so, his deafening silence. Just by the success of talk shows, these days everyone wanted to get on television and be a part of the popular narrative.

By his presence at Café Neuf that morning, she knew more than anything else he wanted to be ordinary. Strangely, ordinary was not something many people chose to be. The whole experience he suffered through had to be raw. Yet it was remarkable because it was the quintessence of a journey that required him to have hope, faith, and to forgive. A poignant life lesson required strength and courage. The contradiction of his circumstance—it was all so complicated, and she understood that more than she cared to. A friend, a lover, was killed. He had been accused of causing her death. Still, he had to move on; to live his own life. What motivated Imani to reach for Pricilla Miles's best seller was due almost entirely on the information that was printed on the bond pages. She, like so many, was curious about the details that sound bites could not fully convey, of course.

When she first saw Rawn, probably shortly after they both moved to Washington, the comparison she made of him to that of Blaine was swift. He had the same naturally good looks and polished manners. No doubt, it was why she could not dare be interested. The risk was simply too great for her to fall for the same type yet again. But gradually, when they had polite but small chats at Café Neuf, and on an occasion or two in public places like PCC and Street Two Books and Café, she knew it was unfair to compare him to her ex. Yet Imani did not trust her judgment. Once, she mentioned Rawn to Dante and she told him that Rawn was so elusive and unreachable and those traits were much too dangerous. Dante told Imani to stop using him as an example. It surprised her, because Imani never realized that she was using her father as an *example*.

Unconsciously, she stood erect off the wall when a man, seemingly aggressive, approached Rawn at the bar. He had ordered but still had not gotten their drinks from one of the two overworked bartenders. The man who approached laughed, as did Rawn, and they shook hands. Before she could go and rescue him or understood what was happening, the man walked off and disappeared in the crowd by the bar. Did he know the man, or was he a stranger? Closely, curiously, she studied Rawn while he tried to seek her out amongst the many people stranded at the airport. With a generous, happy face, Imani waved. Rawn's handsome face lifted into an open, carefree look, and he waved back with a casual hunch of his shoulders and rolled his eyes about everything that was happening: delayed flight, crowded bar, fifteen minutes spent trying to get a drink, and the curious nature of *fate!* She made out that he was chuckling as he reached for his wallet in his jeans pocket. In that moment, he touched something inside her unexpectedly. Imani pantomimed, "I know!" And Imani mimicked him by facetiously hunching her shoulders and rolling her eyes.

Content, and so present time was elusive, she laughed back at him. *I like him, Dante. What do you think?*

Her cellular broke the imaginary conversation she had with her father. She dug into her tote and felt for the cellular antenna. "Imani!" she answered. "Oh, Pearl." She grinned. "You got my message? Yes, it looks like we'll be here a bit longer. I would guess we won't leave for at least another hour. The fog's lifted a bit. They announced that a runway is opened for flights to land, but nothing about when we can fly out. Yes, I'm excited too. Change my life; how so?" Imani, not aware of her action, looked over to Rawn at the bar. At last, he got their orders and was paying the bartender. "Yes, maybe." Imani was glowing; her body even trembled. "I'll call you prior to us boarding so you can know when my flight leaves. A driver? No, please, Pearl. That's embarrassing. It's not necessary. I can rent a car." With an unconscious blush, she gave in, "Okay, okay!" Happily, she laughed. "I promise. See you soon."

"Here you go," Rawn said, holding out her drink. "A champagne split."

"Thank you. I love champagne."

"What's the story behind that?"

"My father. He was born on New Year's Eve. We always had champagne to celebrate. I think I was...I might have been about ten when I had my first glass of champagne."

"So what's—or is it who's—in L.A.?"

"You first."

"Why should I go first?"

"Because, that's why!"

"All right, okay. My friend Khalil celebrates thirty-five tomorrow. His girlfriend is a corporate planner in London, and she's throwing this extravagant party." Rawn took a long gulp of his imported beer. "Hey, you should come." He nudged her playfully.

"I should?"

"And bring your friend ..."

"Wait, there's no *friend*. I'm going to L.A. on business."

He met her eyes and stayed with them long enough for her to pick up on what he was feeling. But her expression alone suggested to Rawn she had no clue. "Good. So you'll come."

Yeah, I'll come. "We shall see." She tasted her drink for the first time. "Mmmm, this is great! Oh, wait! We should toast."

"Toast to what?"

"Uhhhh..." Imani attempted to come up with something. "I know!"

Rawn's forehead creased, accentuating his curiosity.

"Timing! To timing!"

No sooner than they clicked their beverages to make a toast, an announcement was made that runways were reopening.

"Timing!" they said in chorus, laughing.

His look turned somber. "I was actually going to leave and take the first flight out tomorrow morning. I'm glad I changed my mind."

"I was going to do the same thing. Heck, this temperamental weather—who knows!" With an expression solemn but tender, she said, "My father would really have liked you."

"Why do you say *would have?*"

"He's not with us anymore." Imani noticed it right away: the first real sign of letting go. Since his death, she always spoke of Dante in the present tense. "In spirit, I feel him every single day. But in the physical sense, I will never get a chance to feel his loving embrace. Or smell the cigarette smoke on him. But wherever he is, he's happy. I—I know it!"

"You sound pretty confident."

"He's with my mom."

Rawn could not help but see her eyes tear up, but he was not going to mess this thing up by insulting her with an attentive gesture or soft-spoken words that she was too strong to accept. Instead, he spoke what he wanted to say. "You're parentless. That must be tough. I mean, you're still young."

In a faint voice, she said, "Yes." She bowed her head briefly. "But I'm good because I'm blessed."

"Of course you are. It's a good thing that you're aware of that." He reached over to touch her shoulder gingerly. When her hand caressed his, he sensed an internal moment of reckoning: where there had been a void, he now felt the boldness return in his heart.

In a quiet voice, she said, "Thank you."

"I understand…"

"Yes, I know you do." When her lips spread, her soulful eyes softened, and subtle lines which gently touched the corners gave her face depth.

"You were very close to him."

"Very."

"Then we should make another toast."

"For, to?…"

"Your father."

Cheerful, Imani exclaimed, "Oh, how apropos!" She lifted her glass. "He would love that. He was a wonderful man, my father, but I must confess, he was very conceited. So, to Dante!"

Rawn was about to click his beer bottle against Imani's toasting flute and it occurred to him what she said. "Dante?"

"Yes, Dante. Dante Godreau? He was my father."

The End

ABOUT THE AUTHOR

Bonita Thompson is the author of *The New Middle*. She currently resides in Los Angeles. Visit her blog at http://www.bonitathompson.wordpress.com